UP STRAWBERRY VINE

Alberto Bonilla

Yigüirro Books

This is a work of fiction. All names, characters, and incidents portrayed in this story are either the product of the author's imagination or used fictitiously. No identification with actual persons (living or deceased), places, buildings, and products is intended or should be inferred.

Copyright © 2024 by Alberto Bonilla

All rights reserved. Published in the United States by Yigüirro Books. No part of this publication may be reproduced, distributed, or transmitted in any form or by any means, including photocopying, recording, or other electronic or mechanical methods, without the express written permission of the publisher, except as permitted by U.S. copyright law.

Hardcover ISBN 979-8-9872835-4-7

Ebook ISBN 979-8-9872835-5-4

For my Father

Chapter 1

A Baptism of Shadows

Redeem this token for your designated class. The purple bold sentence lights up in a Coptic font at the top of my holographic ticket.

I hold onto it with my left hand. My arms dangle as I wait in line, only stopping when I raise my right hand to my lips to bite my thumbnail. My nasty habit of coping with anxiousness. Too scared to put the ticket in my pocket for fear of the plastic folding, I grip onto it like a lifeline. I glance down at it, moving it at an angle so the outside ominous white lights in the prison yard bounce off it.

I turn the ticket from side to side and its projected image of a black jaguar is put in motion. It leaps forward and jaws open, unearthing its menacing canines. Incontestably used for killing. Its visually hypnotizing fangs pierce the imagination with thoughts of gnawing and ripping apart its prey. It then makes a retrograde fall into the backdrop, partially obscured by a billowing grassy plain. Its glowing citrine eyes stare back at me through the tall grass. Its jaws catch some Z's as I stop moving the ticket. I'll wager ten bucks it awaits the turn of my wrist to pounce into focus once more.

I bite off the tip of my thumbnail and spit it onto the dirt. The mark on the ventral side of my right forearm, as I lower it from biting my thumbnail, conveys the real sprightly me back in the day. I got the long scar in the north shore of Oahu, Hawaii. It extends vertically from my palm up to the start of my bicep.

The Pipeline wave I rode that day, when I was sixteen, crashed into a jagged coral reef just mere yards from the shore. I proudly wear the permanent scar as it goes extremely well with the tough guy image I try to exude. Even when I don't feel so tough. That's often the case in this fraternity.

There're monkey hoots contesting the eased rain clattering off leaves beyond the chain link fences at my sides with razor barbed wire on top. The fences congest all one man and one hundred plus boys into a tight space. Every one of us trooping in an orderly single file between them. The much-needed relaxation I garner from these ambient rainforest sounds, and the fragile scent of this sweet, crisp rain is getting interrupted by a constant ping.

I hear a pest behind me sliding a stick across one of the fences as the line moves forward. It slips into the spaces in the fence and taps a steel link with each step. A flimsy wood bashed on a rich metal. A clash of swords when a penniless serf picks a quarrel with a noble knight.

"You know the fence is meant to keep out unwelcome visitors. Ergo, the electric detail. Now I'm not your dad but we're about to be brothers so I caution. The voltage of the shock you'll draw in from playing with the fence will cause you more than discomfort. It'll paralyze you."

Like clockwork, another ping sounds behind my right ear. *Not scared of being shocked is he.*

"Those sounds with your toy stick might elicit a response from those we try and keep out. And it's a bit galling," I notify him politely of my annoyance.

The line stops. I'm mellow as I turn around to look at him behind me. He's improvised clothes for himself by wearing an upside-down jute burlap potato sack with holes in it for his arms and head. The sack is tattered with claw tears over his chest and stomach.

The outfit is adorned with a wide headband made of a highly reflective and bendable metal around his forehead. Flaxen lowlight streaks in his hair ground his bright cropped do' that stays risen despite the weather trying to weigh it down. A few pear-shaped droplets rest on the ends of his hairs. His tousled head appears as though he stuck his head out of a car window for several miles. Yet only one clump sum of his mussed-up corn-yellow hair marks a line over the headband onto his right brow.

He emanates an air of boredom. His face lacking wakefulness with deep bags under his ebony eyes and plum circles around them; close-set with the daintiest turned-up nose between them. So young and overworked in preparation for this moment. If it weren't for my understanding of what he's been through, I'd think he doesn't care much about the outcome of tonight. So long as he gets some sleep.

Must've barely made it past the last round.

I see a seventeen-year-old me in the mirror encompassing his forehead. The mirror's curves generate a squeezed panorama of the environment with me at its center. I wake from the trance remembering I'm a Nihil now. I'm no longer a teenager, let alone a child of vanity. The movement of the line carries on and I walk backwards as he remains oblivious to my presence.

"We're here trying to stimulate ourselves by obsoleting the past us. Stop allowing others the flattery of their reflection and put that headgear away. It makes anyone who looks into it vain." This time I'm indirect with my impatience, nitpicking what else to place blame on for my growing annoyance with his toy stick.

The line stops once more and I with it. He takes a break from moving the thin tree branch on the fence and snaps it in half with one hand. He finally got the point. There's a long pause.

"I don't take orders from a Nihil. You're one of us old man." The abrasive attitude in his response is weak.

The stacked undertones in his voice are telling me he's frightened but all too ready. He's got spunk. I don't intimidate him, but I do know what frightens him. The same thing that frightens all of us waiting in line. It's that sturdy plastic ticket tucked under his headband by the left ear. Just a corner sticking out that'll fossilize his position in this fraternity of man. Forever a part of this all-capitalist brotherhood. My annoyance is his coping mechanism for what's to come, finding a way to distract himself as I did in biting my nails.

He stretches his arms out, capable of touching both fences to his sides in unison. With his now broken stick, he uses one half in each hand to make double the noise of wood beating on metal.

"For fucks sake," I grunt, stepping backwards a few spots as the line moves forward. I bore into his eyes. "You know what's out there, right?" I make a quick glance and nod towards the fence.

"Monkeys." The boy tries to outstare me.

There's something raising a slight furor amongst the monkeys swinging in trees. Their noise is steadily rising and gaining coherence.

"Apart from what we can hear, there're silent pigs stalking us. The size of buffalo with their pet cronies; sly, man-eating lizard monsters. I've seen the lizards with my own eyes, and they've seen me. Ever-present in the sight of golden flakes whisking in the air." I try to ward him from his insolence in disturbing the peace.

He lacks in knowledge what he'll bring upon us if he pursues his childish diversion. The prison yard is based in a covert arena so the brothers can gather in peace. Lately, we've withstood attacks from members that dissented from the majority. Rumors developed about why they left and somehow, it led to their recognition as giant pigs. They're watching us. Reason one of two on why this baptism is being held in silence alongside this restful rain.

You can't just wait in line quietly like the rest of us, can you?

I bump my back into the back of the boy behind me as the line abruptly stops. "Sorry," I voice with not a care in the world reflected in my phlegmatic apology.

"Giant pigs? Keep daydreaming. While I deny your welcome to dreamland, I do have a hankering for probing a mad man's muse. Where fantasy penetrates reality. Tell me mad man, at what point does your fantasy penetrate this reality?"

"I'm not insane. Funny and sad you think my warning of great fiction," I reply, my lip curling.

"The final round must've taken a serious toll on you if you expect me to believe in colossal swine and reptilian monsters. I don't believe in campfire stories," he says softly, staring up at the blurred night sky. Muted raindrops timidly tap his forehead and then circle their way past the soft edges of his face to meet at his receding chin. "Now go back to sleep," he continues with the same subdued tone in his voice as his sight lowers back on me.

"You're the sheep," I express in an almost childish tone. I resume walking backwards, beginning to take great delight in something so puny. The pest advances, reminding me of his ability to multiply one stick by two as he taps each on both fences to his sides. He's insistent on getting under my skin.

The fences shield us from what lies in the outer darkness surrounding this sunken court. I truly have seen what nightmares are made of in the eyes of the lizard. God sent the lizards, with their respective omens, to command man back into submission. The pigs are more of a myth I'd heard through the grapevine from the brotherhood. But I believe they're out there, circling us as the baptism ritual progresses. Hiding away behind the abundance of wild plants and trees that border these fences.

The pigs and their lizards crave Immortal Jaguar blood, they told us. Soon to be our blood they crave.

Tonight, we'll be placed in a class system. To join the rest of the brothers who've already been initiated into their discrete classes. In becoming a part of something bigger than oneself there's opposition. Why the brothers label the opposition as pigs with pet lizards and fictionalize the pigs as elephantine in stature is unbeknownst to me. Maybe it's just pushing their agenda, teaching us to let go of reality. But their accuracy on the lizards when emphasizing the aspect of their monstrosity was spot on.

There's a frequent wave of insects buzzing that keeps bouncing on and off my exposed lower legs. I'm surprised this rain hasn't washed them away.

Why're bugs such imbeciles?

The ones that interrupt my workout when I'm in the prison yard benching and plague me by flying directly into my mouth. My face contorts into the mask of a sour, irked Shar-Pei. I kick the flying insects on my legs wishing I'd worn jeans. I hear my name above the trees creaking and wind howling.

"Koata Califf to platform three!"

The call is an indistinguishable robotic voice from one of the in-made voice amplifiers of the stylized gas masks the Prefects are wearing. Not enough robot to veil the sex of he who spoke out but enough of a twist on his diction to take me out of this world. This is the first major break in silence of the night. My name getting called aloud wasn't a planned event on the baptism itinerary.

Prefects use the gas masks as their first line of defense against the odorless mercury vapors rising from two levels below. There exists an underground industrial factory where workers use liquid mercury to extract gold from alien computer parts. Workers are restricted from using gas masks down there.

The gas masks are an item reserved for two classes. The Aedile, better known as the groundskeepers' class, and the Praefectus—a class of eleven men who control the prison. They also make the game a Nihil is to play to determine their class. The results of a Nihil's gameplay are coded in the tickets we're carrying on us now. We're given these tickets after we've undergone a saga of four rounds spanning the course of fifteen years. Ultimately, leading to this baptism today where we take on a new, major part of our identity in the Immortal Jaguars' class system.

I face forward toward the movement of the line. There're eleven cone-shaped tents glamorized in harlequin black opal enamel. The tents work as booths on a stage. Their color inspiration comes from the rarest black opal gemstone pattern of them all—the harlequin opal. I've only seen the stone as one modest oval on a metallic strand. It clasped the neck of a past lover. The piece, worth a little over 15,000 US dollars, came as a gift from her brother on New Year's Eve. A romantic gesture that made their relationship seem virtually incestuous.

The artists who crafted the tents at the end of this line managed to replicate the harlequin opal's colors. Colors reminiscent of the great southern lights. On display now with rain sheening the tents' nylon fabric. An eye-popping light, equivalent to a firefly's bioluminescence, appears to glow a layer beneath the fabric, though the effect is part of the same nylon sheet.

I focus on a new color with every look I aim at the tents. My eyes route colors I'd not charted in previous glances. Violet welts blue and yellow lacerates green into pieces. The entire color spectrum is exhibited on every tent with scarlet filling the position of the most prominent color in each. That scarlet multicolor is intensified by an underlying Prussian blue. A blue reminder to me that while I'm stuck here for now, I yearn to be back in the ocean surfing. Even when I'm old and ailing, I'll ignore the doctors, surfing my days away.

To the left of the stage, a raised wine purple flag has the insignia of a white top hat positioned at its center with a ring around it. The wine purple flag droops on a towering black spiral lamp post, curving the image of the white top hat with its wavelike folds. That lamp post has a sculpted jaguar head at both ends. The bottom head is inverted. A bundle of dim, red fairy lights clog their open mouths. Appearing dim because the white prison lights overshadow the red.

I can't see the facial expressions of the Prefects inside the tents from my spot in line for their gas masks cover but their eyes. Though I doubt they're as tired as the boys here or as uncomfortable as us. As Nihils, we get antsy one week prior to our baptism while the Prefects have been off in Cozumel, Mexico, this past week celebrating the success of their game. They returned this morning. Now we're getting wet and they're in their cozy tents sheltering them from the rain. I'm not complaining. Rain alleviates the sweating my body's generating from this humid night air.

Each tent is occupied by one coral pink desk and posh chair for a Prefect to sit on. From there they can activate the machines that'll give the boys ahead of the tents their class. Each class has its own job. Prefects are the only ones permitted by the Caesar to run the machines that'll reveal an individual's class. It makes sense since they created the game that determines which class we belong to.

Moving forward, I step on the back end of the boy's shoes in front of me. A seven-foot gothic-dressed brown boy with long, flat-ironed toxic green hair and black eyeliner looks over his shoulder to see me unblinking. I stand there, buttoned halfway up in my lousily tucked in white dress shirt with the sleeves rolled up to my elbows and navy blue cargo shorts. This is my second time agitating this kid. He scowls at me. I'm not looking to entertain his anger, wanting me to show pity for his black platform shoes. He's not the shah of Iran for me to care. I jog from my spot in line toward the booth I'd been called to, unintentionally brushing some shoulders with mine along the way.

I skip the single file line of twenty boys ahead of me, skipping briskly to the stage. I avoid the boys who glower at me suspiciously. Their ages range from fourteen to eighteen. I'm the only man here. The only man with a real beard. None of that stubble kids get in high school. My beard is thick, dirty, and black like my existing grubby hat hair. I've kept it untrimmed because it took months to grow. Never thought I'd grow this scraggly beard in my teens, but I guess some guys are genetically set to grow a beard in their thirties. As is the case with me now at thirty-two.

I began my journey into the Immortal Jaguars when I was seventeen. Late when compared to the boys in line who at the earliest must've begun the Prefect's drawn-out game a year before they were born. A concept that defies biology and reality as we know it. My experience here has challenged the very fabric of time and existence therefore, while this concept is evidently absurd, I know all to be possible, even if it defies the fundamental laws of our known reality. Perhaps they studied subjects like cosmic calculus or prenatal poetry in their mom's belly. Nevertheless, my age has gained me more infamy than friends throughout the years. I'm the old guy no one looks up to and people despise. I don't fit in with my own. I admit that.

At the end of the day, yesterday, I was a Nihil and not fitting in would've rattled me but by the end of the day today, I'll have a place among a class that'll hopefully welcome me as one of their own.

I exit the narrow pathway to the stage as the fences come to an end. Where the fences end is a protective force field that encloses the stage and some of the surrounding forest land within it. Thousands of sensors are hidden by shrub palms on a circular path around the stage. The only sign of their existence comes from the deep, pink glow they cast inconsistently through breaks in the palms. Their shape echoes a referee's whistle. I got a close look at one when they were setting up the stage.

How the force field works is these sensors, when triggered by say an explosion, a bullet, or even a bird flying by, will signal a laser closer to the stage to heat up that section of air, producing a plasma guard. The plasma has the adequate temperature and density to deflect and absorb any impact from the sensed threat. One monkey made the mistake of knuckle-walking too close to the stage when the tents were erected, and the defense system activated. Its slip has taught the rest of local wildlife a lesson. A reason to exercise extreme caution near mankind.

I make a left and belt to the side of the stage, splashing through two puddles along the way. The staircase to the stage is uncommonly steep. It could be exchanged for a ladder perpendicular to the ground and that'd offer up the same challenge in climbing this staircase. I walk up the metal steps and slip on the second to last, catching myself on the stair railing. I increase my grip on the plastic ticket with my free hand as one sandal slides from my foot. I grouchily pick it back up with my big toe and let it ease itself back into its job.

Prevailing over the short interruption, I follow the stair path up to my destiny. From metal steps to an ash timber stage plucked from a construction site, I pass two boys standing by their tents with apathetic reactions to their results. I arrive at the third booth and look to both ends in the line of cone tents.

The eleven tents are lofty traditional teepees held up with a single black pole inside them at their center. There's a burgundy sitting jaguar statue on my far right occupying the space in between tent ten and tent eleven. Internally it's composed of cast iron and stainless steel. Its height and width mirror the tents'. Between all the other tents there's nothing but a space. I put myself mentally in between all those tents.

I am nothing. I'm a Nihil.

It's common practice to rid oneself of their identity and of the memory of their physical form before accepting their new lives within the Immortal Jaguars. We're forbidden from seeing ourselves in a mirror till after the baptism as a result.

The tents' sturdy nylon framework splits at its front, bottom up from the stage to make an entrance. When unopened this morning they looked like exquisite curtains before a fortune teller's parlor but have now had their bottom ends pulled apart making their triangular opening present. From the wide opening comes a clear savor of cinnamon and pine. Vertical fabric folds mold themselves onto the tents resulting from the pressure of the two silver nails holding each tent open. The silver nails are punctured into the thick tents themselves and go through the stage.

There're cubed dark green crates a few inches outside the entrance to the tents. Their coloration comes from the moss that's devoured the crates whole. A light green in the sun, the moss takes on a dark hue at night; made darker tonight as it's dampened by rain. The cubes are meant to be used as platforms for the Nihils to stand on so we're at eye level with the Prefects. Their chairs and desks have been so highly raised as if to underscore their prominence over us.

Around the floor of platform three lie scattered silver nails. I take one big step onto my platform, two feet off the stage, and immediately sense it's hollow. Looking to my feet, I see the dark green moss and wood surface caked in the same five-inch nails. Some are twisted from being hammered into the wood the wrong way, from their sides. Others lay flat, yet to be hammered in, waiting to afflict pain onto any who might be barefoot.

I've white rubber sandals on that slide in with two straps in the middle. They come without a back strap, but their deep heel cups keep my feet in place. I relate their comfort to the likeness of being barefoot, so I feel uncomfortable with the silver nails around me itching to strike my feet.

I hear the cry of winding water above the serene rain. Between my feet there's a break in the crate. Below the fracture, I see a crescent hole in the stage. The nails that once pierced the stage were probably meant to keep the floorboards intact but failed. I catch a glimpse of circular capillary waves inside the hole. Waves flow below me. I, a notable elevation above them, calm myself with their sound. I take a deep breath and am soothed by its smooth release. I lift my head to face the Prefect sitting in front of me.

"When ready," the masked man speaks with his robotic voice generator volume lowered to a more intimate level.

I've been allowed to cut the line of my fellow Nihils for a reason. The two eyes behind this Prefect's gas mask appear to be that of David—my chosen herald. He stares me down through the clear dual eye-openings of his gas mask. He's the only person I've ever met to have heterochromia. His left eye is a deep blue, and his right eye is a light green. He let me skip the line. Late, as I only had twenty boys ahead of me when my name was called but he's kept his word. Now he just has to keep true to the second part of our bargain in placing me in the Quaestor class. My cheeks suffuse with color once I'm sure it's him.

My face shows promise in how I'll repay him by tracking down Tommy, but we've been instructed not to speak throughout the duration of our baptism. Mainly to avoid or to at least limit the excess inhaling of mercury fumes from the underground factory. Reason two of two for the silence of tonight with an exemption for the occasional howling monkey and this mild rain resonating across the prison yard.

David's in a Prefect's chair despite a Prefect baptizing the role of his life Mercury. Not the element that I'm momentarily breathing in but like the patron messenger god of Ancient Rome, David's job is to deliver messages. He's disguised himself as a Prefect, in a Prefect's seat according to an agreement we discussed during round three of my gameplay. The agreement was, I get my desired class in this fraternity in exchange for bringing him an escaped prisoner.

Prisoner 1313. The boy named Tommy. A supposed commander in chief of the opposition or pigs as they've notoriously come to be called. Tommy's the biggest pig of them all and the first name that'd come to mind if the Immortal Jaguars had a list for most wanted.

Skipping the line and getting this process over with means I'll soon be able to avenge a dear friend who was left on the outside. The friend in question is Ramze. In the Quaestor class I'll have the financial oversight in a mission to find Ramze and clear his name. I lost that friend to the pigs in the cloud forest long ago. He was kidnapped by them. The Governor class record shows he's one of them, but I can't believe that. Their evidence is tainted. Becoming a Quaestor is my only chance of getting my friend back.

David's gas mask is made of faux leather, hand-painted black with the brass and copper fittings consisting of valves, straps, hoses, and a bronze zipper straight down the front of his gas mask. The zipper ends at the mouth, firmly locked to a copper hose that twirls down to an air filter. The metal canister holding the activated charcoal that filters air is a broad tin cylinder, about seven inches tall, sitting on the right side of the high desk within the tent.

David's behind the coral pink desk on a royal blue chair with an exaggerated tall back. He has black rubber gloves on each hand and is wearing a cardinal red hazmat suit. The black pole holding the tent up stands erect from behind his chair.

"Ready," I voice quietly.

His left hand makes tapping sounds from his fingers bouncing on the surface of the desk. The tapping breaks out into the furious gallop of a horse. His right hand slowly makes its way to the golden call bell at the center of his desk. My heartbeat imitates his left hand and then slows itself with the unnecessary suspense of his right hand.

With a single finger, he dings the bell and my heart calms. This is my signal to enter my ticket into the machine inside his desk. He then props his chin on the palm of his right hand, waiting. The desk has a slim rectangular opening for the ticket to slide into, leveled at my waist. I push the ticket midway into the slot and the rest of it's swallowed into the machine.

The grating noise of the machine within David's desk is like the distant echo of metal on metal, faintly audible unless you're within arm's reach of the source. Thankfully it ends in three seconds with a click. A hidden compartment opens out from the front right side of the desk releasing an odd aroma of a rustic old cabin and cheaply scented deodorant soap. It's an empty drawer with a matte silver interior that burst forward. The machine extrudes a round white gold gear with square teeth along its side and the image of a top hat imprinted on the face of it. The size of a silver dollar, I take it quickly from the drawer longing to see the word on its tail end.

The drawer retreats inside its cubby and I notice the square outline of it on the desk. I'd previously thought the gear, which is meant to be part of a larger apparatus, would be handed over to us personally by the Caesar. The highest class and the only class with one position. The chair of this organization. Had it been the case the chair handed us our result, this agreement between David and I would've never worked.

Moment of recognition for all my assumed hard work these past fifteen years. My results are in. I'm a... I pause in suspicion holding the gear between my thumb and index finger.

"Plebeian?"

Chapter 2

No.

I want to express my doubts concerning the veracity of this result.

It's a mistake.

"There's to be a mistake."

"Are there cockroaches in heaven?" David asks behind his black and copper gas mask in a static droid voice.

I look around in confusion, unsure of what he's suggesting. I confront him on our deal raising the gear to him above my head.

"What's this? We made a vow. You put me in the Quaestor class, I bring him to you," I mutter heatedly glancing about the other tents, assuring no one else overhears.

"Tommy is no longer called for," he says violently standing up over the desk. He slams his hands flat on it and looks down on me. I become paranoid, looking around once more, believing others might've heard.

I shush him and ask what's wrong with him.

Before I can get a valid answer, a surge in the wind current hits me from behind and jolts me forward, off my platform. I fall onto the front of the desk. David leaps from his place in the tent onto the surface of the desk. He squats on top of the desk and stretches his left arm down to me, offering up his hand with his palm face up.

"Do you fancy a challenge Plebeian?" David asks, tilting his head.

The humid night temperature drops, and I look to the sky at the sound of a falling old fighter airplane. Meanwhile, David stays watching me unreceptive to the sound. A fiery translucent egg descends from the night sky off in the distance. A meteoritic fall into the darkness of the cloud forest. It blasts an icy gale into the prison yard while in transit from the air miles east. The sudden gust of wind lifted the wine purple flag on the black spiral lamp post in a grandiose sweep and hardened the textile so it froze in place. It's as if time stopped as the flag was waving. The boys on stage freeze standing followed by the boys in line.

There're screams. The freeze goes from a hypnotist preventing movement to a surrealist artist sculpting freakish ice sculptures. The first to turn in line was to be the next Nihil to come up on stage. A blond boy in an extra-large magenta dress shirt, no pants, and a white lab coat. An homage to Salvador Dali's 'Crucifixion' oil on canvas painting; this boy is frozen with his arms reaching out to the ends of the earth. Blocks of ice materialize on his wardrobe and it's unknown whether he himself is levitating or there's ice amassing under him that's lifting him. Due to the height of the stage, I've an obstructed vision and cannot see all that happens below as above.

Monkeys outside the force field crank up their volume to make a terrifying unanimous howl. The tumult of shouting melds in my head and I can't tell apart the monkeys' howl from the boys' screams.

Nihils' exposed skin transforms into patches of chalky white and clear, lightly tinted blue crystals start to form on their clothing. From their blotted bodies rise lengthy spikes of ice. A number of Prefects collapse from their chairs and onto the stage floor, trembling.

The first Prefect to come tumbling out of his tent and onto the stage has a voluminous yellow cape with the hallmark of a golden tree on it. Its roots and branches with triangular leaves make up a strange geometric pattern on the cape that extends to his individual earth yellow gas mask. The finest taffeta fabric of the cape is as lustrous as the polished metal of his gas mask. He rolls himself into a cocoon using the appreciable cape. Rows of spikes that resemble thorns tear through layers he's made over his skin, only managing to stick out an inch from the top cloth.

One Prefect rips off the jacket portion of his solid black slim-fit suit as his legs swipe the stage floor. He manages to stand up on stage and a spike of ice rises at an elevated angle from his chest, through his white dress shirt, popping out three of its buttons. With it, the single spike of ice takes the red ascot silk tie around his neck and as it extends the tie begins to choke him.

Within the clear glass that showcases his eyes inside of a platinum gas mask whiter than snow, he turns to face me steps ahead of the burgundy sitting jaguar statue and a step behind the boundary of the stage. The blood vessels in his eyes burst and scarlet lightning lances down his face. The beige in his irises succumbs to a thick coat of milky white frost. His lifeless body falls on stage once more. The ice spike, withholding the tie that choked him, busts as a glass vase would if dropped on concrete. He lies face down with an arm and leg dangling over the edge of the stage.

Survive this and tomorrow will come.

A Nihil next to me on platform four grows becoming abnormally round. His head sinks into his shoulders and his limbs disappear into his torso. He possesses the same spikes of ice as the boys in line, taking after a blown-up pufferfish as he continues to grow more globular. The dark green cube splinters under his weight. As a ball he keels over, shattering the ice spikes protruding from his skin on the stage as he rolls. His feet face me as an emboss of what once was.

Off the stage and onto the dirt below he goes. By the time his mutated body contacts the ground, ten to one he's an obliterated statue. His body demolished with the swift pop of a dozen balloons bursting all together at once. I can't see the aftermath left over the stage and on the ground below. Though rising is his body's only remnant—a cloud of fine, powdery ice resembling snow.

Chaos is smothered. The whisper of my heavy breathing is the last scrap of sound.

Every white light within the prison yard goes out instantaneously. Only the red lights within the jaguars' mouths on the ends of the black spiral lamp post remain lit. No longer dim. They illuminate the stage up to my platform with the threatening warmth of a fire-heated branding iron millimeters off the skin. At the end of the red lights' reach is Dante's Ninth Circle of Hell incarnate. Prefects on stage and Nihils in line lie in darkness, encased in ice. Each brother progressively coated in greater spikes.

The stage cracks under my feet. In the mixture of the red fairy lights and starry night, I only see his big glossy eyes. The sound of hail smashing on the metal stage rises above my breathing. Not a drip of that benign rain that came before the shock wave. I'm able to see a faint ring just outside the line of his right eye's deep-blue iris.

"David?" I get on my tip toes and reach out to grab his offered hand.

"You're a cheat Mr. Califf. Squeal as they die and you fall," he alludes to me being a pig.

A trap door swings loose, and I fall, taking his black rubber glove with me. I drop down into a wide gulf. I scream, feeling the ultimate betrayal.

"David!" I bellow, my voice fleeting.

I descend along with a cascade of nails hoping the waves I'd witnessed below me are water. If not water, then it be liquid mercury from the underground factory. Shall it cause my skin to fall off? A snake sheds its skin to make room for a new resplendent coat. Nature hasn't equipped me with the chance to.

The dark green wooden platform I'd stood on tilts into the open gap in the stage. It falls following my descent from over my head. I try and position myself for a dive into a whirlpool of churning fluid. Instead, I quickly hit the fluid flat on my front side and with a mighty splash. I hold my breath as I roll over on my back. I'm whipped afloat by a geyser of this free-flowing substance. Admittedly, there's no immediate burn. This is water.

I vacuum seal one last breath, pumping my cheeks. The dark green moss concealed cube drops straight on my face, and I suffer from an inescapable blackout.

Now I can sleep.

Chapter 3

May 29, 2012 CE

    The universe is as our oceans in its ever-flowing nature. You stand at the edge of a beach and look out into a never ending blue or you stand with an eye at the tip of a telescope and look out into a never ending black.

    Among an indefinite end as far as the eyes can see, there too from the Atlantic Ocean outside the monotonous corridors of my father's apartment building I see limitless darkness. The heavy swell, blustery winds, and showers from the clouds this past week have forced light to vacate the shoreline. The once still ambiance on the edge of this beachfront property has become an eerie force cheapening the getaway experience for its inhabitants.

    I draw my surfboard underneath me, pulling it forward through my legs. I smoothly sit up on my board as mellow waves roll past me. A white building sways in my line of sight. This, the only building on Sebastian Inlet—Tunglo Tower.

    Each movement of the water rocks my body back and forth from side to side with the tower following my gaze upon the hills of sand. It's the shape of a buffalo's horn. A curved cone fourteen stories high where the bottom end narrows to a point and the top end broadens to a disc. The very top supplies its resident with an entire story full of glass walls marred by frost deposition—the opulent penthouse.

There's not a body I can point to on the beach. What's better is I've all these waves to myself as no one seems to be out in the ocean either. If there's something I can look to for entertainment, it's the shadowy figure up in the penthouse currently skipping out onto the balcony. The hedonistic existence of embracing a female's nude body comes to mind.

A peach-colored, small-waisted woman with long, shaggy warm brown hair skips to the brink of the balcony unclothed. She stands over the glass rail with glazed eyes lost in the perfect blue of the ocean. Her hands reach out in front of her, suspended for a moment as she amusingly overlooks what I presume to be a pretty manicure, then drop like a feather onto the rim.

Her substantial breasts are impossibly perky with the peach pink areolae as delightful to look at as cherry blossoms. Her nipples, softly flushed and pert, are erect from exposure to the cold and misty salted air. She does a quick twirl with a quiet look of euphoria. I see a hippie in her, placing that first paper tab of LSD on the tip of their tongue, embraced by sunlight in an open field of daffodils.

The weather has failed to thwart my activities. I'm out in the ocean during daytime, surfing through an irremovable fog or lying on the beach at night, staring out into space with the blear eyes of a bat. Both sites are covered by the grayness that this months-long category 3 hurricane has brought. Defying meteorological norms, it started in April and is said to keep going strong till the fourth week of May, roving to and fro between the equator and the Caribbean. This past Sunday it surged into Florida for the first time. Today it travels back.

It shrouds my favorite sites in gelid, inky mystery.

Can anyone hear a silent scream? About every forty seconds there's one. The fall of an unknown personality. Another one of mother earth's living creatures is lost. I watch unfazed as the naked woman jumps from the balcony and plunges into her most disturbing death. Her head twists to the back of her neck once the body breaks motion with contact to some hard-packed sand. Her skull cracks open like a coconut but instead of the clear, slightly sweet, and refreshing liquid of young green coconuts, a retail business owner's display of burgundy liquid eyeliners topples from its top shelf and shatters, soaking the sand.

This is what I witnessed as a kid and recurrently see when I surf this beach's waters in a gathering gloom. Ten years ago, was it? The penthouse is now ours. Father bought it after that sad episode of a suicide. I'm past bearing the sorrow of another unknown life.

I've seen women get beaten. I didn't do anything. Children getting abused. I didn't do anything. Rioters pummeling a man to the point of no return—a death sentence brought down upon a simple bystander. And I didn't do anything. I'm just afraid that when I'm the one in need of saving, no one else will do anything.

I'm haunted by regret, but I couldn't save her, and I haven't been able to save anyone since I saw her after the fall. A mangled body on Sebastian Inlet. Once gorgeous head to toe. The damage irreparable though god knows how long she was broken. Poor shattered beauty and lost soul. I'd like to believe she's in a better place now. As am I.

UP STRAWBERRY VINE

I ride a wave back to shore on my six-foot black onyx quad fin surfboard. I only bring this baby out when there's no sun. It would attract too much heat in any other weather condition. The wave dies out before I can make it back onto land. I'm dropped off at a sand bar and roll off my board, sinking below it.

I take a moment to feel the lack of air constrain my throat and water muffle my hearing. My surfboard lightly floats above me, eclipsing the sky. I dig my feet into the sand momentarily before the ocean current unveils them. The mineral salt scatters between my toes as the water tugs on me, signaling me to follow it into the deep. Guiltlessly, as does every child to get their guardian to follow them into the toy aisle.

I rise, squinting at a red bulldog tearing into the hills. A firecracker red Jeep Wrangler zooms through the beach without its hybrid soft top, sending up clouds of dust in the air. I take my raspberry surf leash from my ankle, pulling back on the strap attached to it via Velcro. The bulk of the surf leash is the cord. I begin to coil it up around one of the surfboard's rainbow-colored honeycomb patterned fins. I carry the surfboard on my side as I walk the rest of the way through the shallow ocean water onto the beach. Moments later I'm home.

Chapter 4

"Ok I caved. I admit it! I said I wouldn't go surfing on my sister's wedding day, but they broke me down. I just needed to catch a good one!" I say cupping a hand over my mouth to hold in this modest laughter.

I'm envisioning how releasing it might make things worse. I bind my laugh to my throat; in a quarrel with myself to forbear this grin its rightful place upon my face.

Staring to the left at the standing graduation photo of my best friend, Lucas Farnham, and I framed on a desk, next to a neatly arranged stack of my favorite manga, I notice how good I look when I simper. I do covet every moment I get to show the world my pearly white teeth.

Taking my hand away from my face and arresting this laughter, I reveal the greatest attribute to expression—a smile.

"Koa I'm going to kill you as soon as this wedding is done. Now hurry up and get your ass in your tux before you gets yourself into even more trouble."

I shrug. "Well, where is it?"

"You're impossible," Malia voices, turning from me and fidgeting towards my closet. She proceeds into the walk-in closet to scour through all my formal apparel. Grousing to herself as she slides clothes on hangers with the word 'trouble' repeatedly making an appearance.

"What trouble? I'm here, aren't I?"

Malia's look daggers at me. She tries to mollify her stress as the maid of honor by circling her hands up to her chest, taking a deep breath, and then lowering them down slowly. She empathizes with her pressured self, telling herself, "I'm a good friend. I is maikaì."

I find it comedic to see her so riled up. Calmly, I grab my black onyx surfboard that lay tilted on my bed frame and place it on the bottom shelf of a high rack. It's subsumed into a colloquy of sixteen other boards; each with a story to tell.

Seventeen. Can't complain.

Every year on my birthday I receive another. They've been coming ever since I was born. With so many compiled over the years, my sister Jade decided to straighten up the clutter by gifting me a surf rack. Each board is separated by about a foot of empty space. This organizer has an automatic platform located to the left of the rack that lifts me up to get to the ones at the top. I solely step on the stage, and it rises till I press a red button on the platform's stage with my foot. If I want it to descend, I purely keep my foot sustained on the red button.

The delay in between the time I step on the red button and hold it is a long enough stall for me to retrieve the surfboard I crave. My room is an oval and has a high ceiling, so the concept of a vertical rack was wiser than a horizontal one. Two engineers from She Core are the fitted makers for any amenities in this house, including the surf rack.

All the stacked boards were a gift from my father; adored immensely by my brother, sister, and I. She's been highly obnoxious lately. I struggle to envision how stressed she's been over this wedding of hers. The spun-out process and futile efforts to make this day perfect, espoused under her wedding planner, exasperates all of us. The wedding planner even misplaced an item my father gave Jade.

My father left behind an aged blue hair pin for Jade that she swore she'd wear on this big day as his mother had on her big day. It's an heirloom graced with three white pearls. The wedding planner was supposed to get it polished, and we later found it in our dog's food bowl.

I walk back to my bed and sit at the end of its black wood frame to wait for Malia. Thunder roars outside. At once, the surf rack to the left of my closet quivers slightly.

His present to me annually is everything that remains on that rack. It's a well put together set. He solemnly handcrafted and painted all of them up until board number ten. That one and the rest, apart from my black onyx surfboard, are either simply white or a plain color. They're untouched by his artistic hands.

I picked up the eight untouched boards from my father's company storage unit in Germany. A group of surfboards lie there that've never been sold due to minor defects. I've done this every year since the tenth anniversary of my marriage to life.

Modification of boards by him in his business was rare. Only for his sons and daughter would Daniel carve and paint the boards. The more personal the meaning of his gift became as it was directed towards family. The ones produced directly for the consumer are manufactured by surfboard shaping machines in Germany. The stamped designs are also done by machines in Germany. Nobody single-handedly paints those. It'd be inefficient for mass production.

Each of the others my dad gave me are unique. The surfboards were custom made to fit my character and size throughout the years. I ordered them based on the years in which I got them. The latest is the one I just placed at the bottom of the rack. They get older the higher I tilt my noggin, till my eyes reach my very first surfboard at the top.

The first surfboard I ever got was a deep carrot orange. It stands four feet two inches small with an eccentric lemon yellow octopus sketched onto the board. Sunglow paint shrouds the borders of its figure giving the octopus an ill-defined shape. Daniel's intention was for the public to notice an unfixed shape in the artwork, then discern the motion of the octopus from its natural habitat. He saw all marine life as misshapen by water.

A clear, glossy acrylic sealant with hints of gold throughout the body of the board gave way to all the rich, sunny colors it has now from years of exposure to the ocean water and sun. I thought the colors would fade because of how cheap I'd been told the sealant was in later years. Instead, they mixed in time. An unintentional but ultimately positive effect.

The variety of deep carrot and bright lemon shades expand from the inside out as a result. It gives the illusion that a fiery entity is blazing through it as this eerily awoken octopus painted in a countercultural manner holds onto the board. The animal wraps its eight arms symmetrically around the front of the golden board and reaches out beyond it where the backside reveals the asymmetry of its extending tentacles. Now it's just a work to admire as I'm too big to ride it.

My dad was an artist. Not professionally. Apart from painting my first nine boards, he'd portray his art on large five-by-five-foot linen canvases. His paintings never did get the recognition they deserve. My sister has them hung all over the house with most of them depicting different sceneries amid one of the ocean's many faces.

Daniel had a strange affinity for the peaceful and the violent.

Some of his art I regard more as a bit of an experiment. A rough draft to a painting that never came having an erratic approach to the use of a paint brush. Like the one exhibited downstairs in the kitchen. It's of a sailboat caught up in a tsunami with many swirls from his wrist movements that held the paint brush. The way his hand moved created eddies over the sailboat, in the windy skies.

The lower half of the painting features a secluded community of neon fish with a queer anatomy. They've taken refuge in the skeletal body of a similar sailboat to the one pictured above. Giant air bubbles prevail in an underwater cave with high ceilings where there too lie the remains of yet another sailboat akin to the other two. If I were to sketch a line with pencil from one sailboat to the next, an equilateral triangle would appear at the center of the painting connecting the three.

The one hung up in my room is my favorite. It fronts a ballerina performing an arabesque with a whirlpool at her pointed foot that touches the ground. It's dark. The water pastels carry an awful lot of blood red with oxford blue. The living, splashing water drowns her as she emits all her energy to the splendor of one last ballet performance.

It's her form and facial expression that makes me feel strong but scared when I look at her. An unsettling, dicey sensation creeps over me when observing the painting for too long.

The art itself speaks for breaking free, titled 'Bailarina Liberada.' It also suits the banded colors on my walls. If I'm standing at the entrance of my room, facing the painting or the end of my king bed, the left half of my room is adorned in a bright red wallpaper boasting a charming pattern of silver strawberries, delicately scattered across its surface like a constellation of celestial fruits. Their intricate details, from tiny seeds to delicate leaves, are meticulously captured in the metallic sheen. They continue onto the right half of my room, captured about a dark blue wallpaper. The silver strawberries seem to cascade in a whimsical arrangement, as if frozen in a moment of gentle descent about the two colors. I couldn't decide between my two favorite colors. His painting hangs above my bed within a hollow in the wall, pressed into the center of my room. From behind it, a vertical line splits my room in the two colors.

The idea for my first board's design was in relation to what I hooked onto after birth. I'd been fascinated by a gold chain with a golden octopus pendant Daniel wore the day I was born. To this day, my brother, Kosta Califf, adorns himself with the gleaming necklace. He avers his ownership over it vehemently, maintaining it was given to him by father.

That first board now lies at the top of the rack, on the right blue side of my room. Probably amassed with dust over the years, however still bright enough so that I can see it from my bed where I happen to be sitting now.

There're three wide rectangular windows that run vertically from the ceiling to the floor in my room. One in the bathroom, one on the red side of my room, and one on the blue side of my room. Sunshine regularly tickles the boards, streaming through the blue side window, to the left of the surf rack, like gentle fingers. On a sunny day, the orange-yellow octopus surfboard will reflect on the ceiling a shimmering gold shade. The windows are currently in view of the ashen clouds that're starting to run short of this previously harsh rain.

The sound of thunder tiptoes away.

Within minutes of being in my room, I notice one board is missing.

"Now you wouldn't happen to know where my brown carbon fiber Ubermotion board is would you?" I ask bewildered, glancing at the surf rack as my left hand glides across my messy black hair.

Malia looks at me with a disrupt look in her powder-blue eyes. I can't tell if she's nervous I'll be mad. As she stands at the edge of the closet doorway, the shadow cast from the surf rack cunningly contorts her features into a delicate, mousy visage.

"I kind of borrowed it for this upcoming weekend," she says in a worrisome tone with her lower lip protruding in a humorous pout. "Please don't be mad. Your precious shortboard is safe at my loft. I promise," she says in earnest as she flits from the closet to hand over my gray tux.

I stare at her suspiciously, myself standing up. Hesitantly I grab the tux on a hanger from her extended hands. It's packaged in a clear plastic bag that the hook of the hanger goes through. "If you say so. Watch yourself though. Some people might interpret taking things without permission, oh I don't know, as stealing," I jokingly tell her raising both eyebrows and staring her down.

"I know. I'm sorry Koa."

"I'm just playing with you Fish. I really don't care as long as you're ripping it on these hurricane waves." Telling her this, I recognize just how nicely she's gotten ready for the wedding. I must admit, I've never seen this girl dressed so proper. She's always in sandals, tiny jean shorts, and rainbow tie-dye tank tops with her straight dirty blonde hair let down just below the shoulders.

Malia Bixby is a native Hawaiian with olive skin and a dab of freckles over her nose and cheeks. She's twenty-three and has a killer grip on her board when it comes to doing some gnarly surf tricks. Her feet never leave her surfboard when she's riding a wave. Performance wise I'd give her a nine out of ten and any other day I would deny that she's a better surfer than me but today I'm feeling positive, excited for my spring travels to continue in Malaysia. I'm in a good mood since I'll be going there to surf next week. The adventure kicked off in Costa Rica last week. I was there for four days.

I'm sure if Malia had the time to travel, she would and I'm sure she would've knocked this pretentiously dangerous hurricane out of the ballpark if she'd come out and surfed this morning with Jake, Lucas, and I.

Malia is wearing a bateau neck, cocktail length taupe dress that complements her eyes. It reaches right above her knees with a full pleated skirt and is set in a shirred midriff. She's all dolled up with dewy skin makeup, a kiss of rose blush over her sculpted cheekbones, and a smokey bronze eyeshadow illuminating those morning glory eyes of a heavenly blue, papery pastel bloom.

She has her hair in a twisted side ponytail and is wearing the same fossilized shark tooth necklace her boyfriend presented her with for their anniversary. It's one giant shark tooth. About four inches long and three inches wide at the base. It's said to be around a million years old. The carbon black fossil dangles on an elegant fourteen karat, white gold two string chain roped twice around her neck.

Apart from when we surf, I don't believe she ever takes it off. Though she'll place it under the neckline of her dress to match the other bridesmaids once we arrive at the event.

Malia Bixby is my friend's girlfriend and my sister's good friend. She's always looking out for me and on this day, the day of my sister's wedding, she was sent out to go look for me by who other than my sister herself.

"Jade must be so pissed," I murmur to myself.

"Damn right she is!" Malia yells back at me.

She comes up next to me at the front of the bed and gets down on her knees to reach for my black dress shoes that she'd stowed under the bed, still blabbering.

"You're lucky I know you well enough to know that you would be the type of brother to go surfing on your sister's wedding day. I mean seriously Koa, what the hell were you thinking? What if you hadn't been at Sebastian Inlet? What would I've done to explain all of this to your sister?" She stands back up. Swinging the pair of black dress shoes in one hand with two fingers, one in each heel cup, and the other hand on her hip.

"Come on now Fish, when are the waves in Florida ever going to be this big again? Hurricane season came early this year. Besides your boyfriend was out there with me too," I laugh, giving her a small nudge with my shoulder.

"Jake left the beach over an hour ago because unlike you he has his priorities straight and he's well on his way to the wedding as we speak so don't bring him into this. She is your sister, not his. You're fortunate your sister asked me to come find you because otherwise you wouldn't be a part of her special day."

"Alright, alright calm down Fish. I'll go take a shower and get dressed, ok?"

"No time!" Malia shouts fuming. The front sole of her right foot is tapping on the carpet floor quite frantically. She's currently barefoot.

"But I'm wet." I shiver as I shake myself trying to get dry from the cold ocean water.

"Here, use that towel." She puts down the shoes next to me and walks toward the desk with a graduation photo of Lucas and I, kneels slightly, and grabs a towel from off the floor. She hurls it at me in low range and I duck to catch it on my head.

I then lay the tux carefully on my bedside stool while taking off my black long-sleeve rash guard. I only lift the rash guard up to my neck and not over my head.

"Koa you're helpless. What're you possibly going to do with your life now that you've graduated? I mean come on! You couldn't spare one day of being surf free for your sister?"

I don't see how my high school graduation and my sister's wedding are relevant to what my plans are for my future but I'm not trying to get her even more agitated than she already is. I take the mint green towel off my head and finish taking off the rash guard, dropping it on the light-gray carpet floor. I speedily rub the towel all over my seminude body.

"Chill, I'm already dry. Now look away so I can get dressed. You wouldn't want Jake to get jealous." I wink at her and smile.

"Oh, shut up Koa. Your commercial smile isn't sweeping anyone. I'll be waiting for you in the car. You've got two minutes. Chip-chop!" Her voice echoed as she shouted out and left my room, slamming the door behind her back.

I take my hands and wiggle my pinkies inside each of my ears. Assertive women like Malia can be loud and so can their antics. She has the tendency to slam my ear-splitting bedroom door.

I slip out of my lime green board shorts feeling the cool air conditioning on my bare white butt. I then run to my drawers inside of my closet to scavenger for some clean underwear. I scramble into the black tight-knit boxer briefs I pulled out while I reach for a wristwatch aloft the dresser.

Among a horde of men's jewelry, I seize my favorite timepiece. I buckle its red rubber strap to my left wrist. A Gulixua watch from Galicia, Spain. It has a round stainless-steel case with a black chronograph dial, white gold-tone stick indices, two hands, three sub-dials, and a detachable compass on the strap. The case itself is bulbous and curved like a water droplet resting atop a leaf.

I return to my bed to rip the clear plastic bag my tuxedo is in. I quickly put on the rest of my outfit and then make my way into the bathroom located on the left red side of my room. Checking myself in the bathroom mirror, I spray some earthy sandalwood and tobacco scented cologne on the sides of my neck, directly under my ears, and tux shielded forearms. After which I brush my teeth, soak my head in the sink to get out the last of the beach's sand from my hair, and comb it wet to the side.

Taking one final glance at the man in the mirror, I note the slight darkening of my normally satiny black hair, dampened by the sink shower. I wish my soft facial features would better complement the intensity of my deep brown eyes. My straight nose, slightly pointed at the tip, feels sore, and I observe that my lips appear darker than usual.

I crack my nose with my right hand and then grab some spearmint lip balm lying next to my toothpaste, thinking that gliding it over my lips will make them lighter. I turn my lips inward and then pucker them, licking over the top lip to get another taste of the spearmint. It does make them shiny. I lean in closer to my reflection, putting my hands over the sink on the counter and turning a cheek to the mirror.

"If only you'd grow some facial hair you wouldn't look like such a wuss. Someday. A smile is all I need. You handsome devil." I back away from the mirror and give an overemphasized smile with my eyelids pinched shut.

Looking fresh as always, I run out the bathroom and out the bedroom door. I hit my foot on the seven-foot Norfolk Island pine tree in the hall. One of Kosta's recent undertakings was purchasing and caring for these trees. They range in size from six to ten feet and are potted around any part of the house accommodated by a vertically oriented long rectangular window. They don't give my home a particularly strong or distinctive scent. Jade took it upon herself to envelop our home with a zesty aura by infusing every corner with citrus flowers.

I hop from there, out of the house plant's way, passing my three-year-old Japanese Akita, who pops his head out from behind the tree with the position of his neck expressing power. I'd say he's the king of the house but Kosta's cat, Caligula, would beg to differ.

My dog has thick triangular ears, slightly rounded at the tips, and a well-curled fluffy tail. He sports a white and tan coat with a deep rich reddish tint and tone. He likes playing hide-and-seek so I'm not startled whenever he appears out of nowhere.

"Bye Toothache!"

He barks at me. Then he pushes his butt into the air and places his broad black nose onto the ground, eagerly wagging his curled tail.

An elevator for my surfboards but none for the house.

Sprinting down the hall with natural lighting and whipping around a corner, I flash down a flight of white limestone steps. Each step's interluded by black marble tile risers. I trace the black metal railing with my palm the whole way down till the only surface below it is a dead forest rebirthed as copper red walnut planks.

I make a swift landing on the front doorknob. Before I go, I backtrack in the opposite direction of the light buttercream French country style double doors with aero blue accents past the foyer, towards the kitchen. Opening the stainless-steel fridge, I glance about to see where I'd stashed them. Right next to my brother's protein shakes where I left them.

"Ahh," I exhale, finishing a pineapple peach energy shot.

"Sei Whale throws it right up to the rim. Fin Whale comes flying from the right corner." I pretend to dribble the bright yellow plastic bottle with a tipped powder blue cap and toss it towards the trash can from ten feet away.

Caligula is resting on the kitchen countertop above the trash can. The plain open roundness of her lemon-shaped sky blue eyes fool people into thinking she's approachable. As a Sphynx breed, she has no visible fur. Her skin's predominantly a dim gray with a black patch across the center of her face and around the edges of her wide open and upright ears. Before the small plastic container can hover over the trash can, Caligula knocks it down with her left paw.

"Fin Whale dunks it. Score!" I jump up throwing one fist in the air and then jolting it back to my side pocket. Shifting inside my pocket I make sure to have my cellphone. I grab my brown textured-leather wallet off one of the butterfly green granite countertops in the island kitchen. Now two more of these shots and I should be set from dying of boredom at this event since I'm typically not used to acting all proper and what not. I grab two of the small Kombucha energy shots from the fridge and drop one in each pant pocket in case I nod off during the wedding. The fridge door closes on its own.

    I make my way back to the vintage wood double doors when Toothache bites an inch of my dress pants. These pants weren't tailored and pressed so my dog could rip them. I lift the baby of the house and he licks my face in three strokes before I put him back down.

    "My you've gotten strong. I'll see you later buddy," I assure him, tapping him on the head. The rain rendered his hounding me outside the house impossible. He doesn't appreciate wetness.

    I exit through the main doors, closing them behind me. I run into the grass and jump over the short hedges instead of following the avenue of Versailles travertine that's the set path to enter my home.

    Wedding here I come.

Chapter 5

Waiting at an end of the U-shaped spruce blue natural stone driveway in front of my half Tuscan, half modern home sits the red bulldog revving its engine. I hop in. Fenced in a summery bloom, in the center region of the driveway, poses a white marble sculpture of my grandfather on top of a mustang horse, embracing the drumming of rain for it works to polish. Remarkably, the sculpture remains white unlike the others of tortoises in the front yard which have transitioned to more of a light gray marble dulled by years of pitiless weather.

The light rain patters upon the marble statue, hitting it at an angle so that a congestion of raindrops at the horse's right lower lid effuses the blue snapshot of a crying stallion. Malia steers the car leisurely around the dark salmon and peach pink yarrows encircling the crackerjack statue. Together, the flowers and the perennial spitting image of a jockey, who'd once espoused cavalry mores in his youth, are positively baroque.

The car eases into the presence of the ten-foot dual swing, aluminum contrived, and burly gate. At once the automatic gate opens from the car sensor. Malia stomps on the pedal before I can ask, "Where's Carrera?"

At first, seeing it was her who drove the Jeep on the beach took me by surprise. I now know. Jake only uses his Jeep when he goes to the beach. His great ardor for sports cars took a front seat when he met Malia, whose Porsche he loves more than apple pie, a sweetness no one can deny. It's his adopted kid now.

He'd been driving the Jeep when he got me earlier in the day, around civil twilight to go surf. He and Lucas ditched me at the beach to go get ready for the wedding. She must've stopped by his house on her way to the beach to switch cars since a two-seater Porsche has no vacancy for a surfboard, unless that surfboard's attached to a keychain.

The hurricane weather hinders into a simple drizzle. The streets are still flooded with vast black puddles.

We're going 90 in a 45-mph zone—in a Jeep! I love living life like there's a world where there's no speed limit, but this isn't the autobahn and we're in a freaking Jeep! It in no way rivals her Porsche Carrera. These cars are not built for speed. At best, this car could go 115.

At least the top is on now.

Malia's changing lanes without using her blinkers.

"At the intersection ahead of us we have to make a left," I inform her without vigor.

The car slid across the coming turn having its rubber wheels screech and another car almost collide with us. The silver vehicle was making a U-turn from the parallel road onto the same lane. They sound their horn coming to a complete stop as we drive off. Hearing cursing from behind, I turn my body to her.

Whoa Fish, you wouldn't want to get ourselves killed now, would you? I try and verbalize, stunned by her driving. Out comes a gaggle fuck of words. "Wow-ish, would not us killed right?"

"We had the right of way," Malia sings as if to mock my shock.

The Kombucha energy shot kicks into full gear hyping up my awareness. "We nearly died."

She's mad. I can tell by the way she's gripping onto the steering wheel that she wants to tear my head off. The news correspondent on the radio reports that Hurricane Raziel will diminish by tonight. I'm unsure of her own certainty as the wind howls loudly from out on the streets where small houses are left roofless and palm trees have been ripped right off the grounds of our neighboring towns. It's mainly the impoverished folk who get the greatest portion in property damages.

The news correspondent begins stating some new Guinness World Records. Her flamboyant voice makes the weather report sound like an intro to a game show. This hurricane has stolen the lifespan record from Hurricane John which lasted thirty-one days in 1994. It also takes the record from Hurricane John for farthest distance traveled. Today would make Raziel fifty-two days old and a traveler of 10,000 miles compared to John's 8,000 miles. This news is trivial to me. By the looks of it we're going to make it.

Suddenly, the whole world comes together and there's that brief tightening in my stomach where I realize that my sister's getting married. I never thought this day would come. At least not this early. Not insinuating she's ugly but she's still young. Even if being an adult starts at eighteen in some cultures, marriage at twenty-three, the decision of that lifelong commitment being made at twenty-three is puzzling. Her fiancé holds a four-year seniority over her, which may not constitute a significant age gap. His perspective on what the appropriate age is to get married certainly differs.

I love my sister and I'm more than happy to welcome her fiancé, Erik Manta, into the picture. Being a Marine, he ain't as stiff as I'd expected the man to be, and boy does he know how to party. That bachelor party was totally rad. I could write a novel on that night alone. If I start to think about it too much, I'll get pumped and say something about last night better left unsaid at a wedding ceremony. All I know is that he's a respectable guy and I trust him with someone as special as Jade.

"We're here," Malia informs me as she unstraps her seatbelt and gets out of the car, lending the valet her keys.

I was beginning to think she'd swallowed her own tongue. The thoroughly kempt blue-black-haired, dimpled young man in his black dress shirt and supplemental bright blue dress pants, opens up a transparent umbrella for her but is cruelly ignored. Malia shoves him out of her way. He then comes to my door and knocks on it while I sit there buttoned up in my tux. I hadn't even noticed the car stop.

That was quick.

I know he's knocking but from the corner of my eye, his wide eyes and nervous smile are priceless. I can see clearly from his worried pushing to get my attention that he's been informed of us two being late. I finally open the door in a hurry and Malia is already jogging in high heels to the common area where all guests are to be seated. I don't know how she managed to drive with those on.

I step out of the car and then it hits me just how fast that Jeep was moving. The dizziness takes its toll on me as I too ignore the valet attendant's offered umbrella and continue walking.

"W-wait up!" I croak as I sway from side to side looking like a complete drunk. Great, now the aftermath of the bachelor party is flooding back to me. I press my hand to my stomach and bend forward.

Malia stops jogging and starts walking when she gets up to the main entrance where a curvy, crushed stone walkway awaits leading the path towards the temporary great hall of Califf Manor, giving me some time to catch up. The actual great hall is undergoing construction in another part of the manor, away from the wedding. A widespread white tent is over the area where the wedding is to take place. An alluring view from my position as it seems I'm about to enter a fine circus.

"We're almost there idiot! I'm in high heels and I'm ahead of you," she shouts out with her head turned drastically over her shoulder as if she were an owl and this were a race.

She seems to enjoy the pain of my headache caused by her lunatic driving. I stand up straight and gently grasp the inside of my tux jacket from each side as it's slipping off my shoulders from trying to reach Malia. I realize I'm sweating. It could be some leftover ocean water on my tux. I sniff it just to make sure.

Nope, that's definitely man stink.

Should've put on more cologne. Oh gosh, if I wasn't already in a panic from Malia's driving this sure did the trick. It reeks of onions. Almost got a tear out of me. Malia turns once again to look back at me as I go through the silver arch that's the main entrance.

"Are you crying?"

"No, it's just my man stink!" I exclaim in thought that I may be duplicating a homeless puppy's appearance in her eyes.

I don't cry. Men don't cry and that debate's over—finito.

Preoccupied with my scent, I don't notice the crowd fast approaching. A host of redness. The world comes back into perspective as the smell sweet flowers...I take a long sniff of the air.

No. Not just any flowers—

Roses. Lemon, apple, clove. Their capricious fragrance fills the air. Often, I find there's no smell to a rose, but an old rose emanates a musk, loamy scent.

Califf Manor—a western country club possessing an enormous garden lined with miles of red roses, only available to us because of the company my sister works for. Availability to rent out this place is slim to none. Only to elite members of the company is this area open for events such as this. I'm uncertain of what her position in that company requires of her. She Core is the company name. I normally tend not to ask questions and go with the flow. So, if I receive an invitation to a lavish garden party that happens to double as a wedding affair, complete with delectable food, you can count me in.

Besides this place having my last name in its title and being an associated She Core partnering events holder; I can't make any other connections as to why the wedding is here. Figures point to it being owned by someone in the family. Perchance a distant cousin.

I follow Malia up the walkway as all I can think of as I look her down is, *That's a perfect ass.*

I can't believe Jake won over such a bombshell but then again, this Adonis of a surfer, Jake Gauthier, isn't so bad looking himself. He, like Malia, is five years my senior. He's a few inches taller than me with long sunny blond dreadlocks that fall below his shoulders, lazily humorous light-green eyes, and a slim but toned body. Still, Malia's modelesque figure is out of his league by a long shot.

I don't try to give off the wrong impression when people ask me about her. She attracts much attention. Malia is a beautiful gal, but Jake Gauthier is one of my best friends and I'd never do him wrong. Plus, he and Malia are bonded like gum to a shoe. Those two love birds are inseparable. They're such cutie pies, I think to myself as we reach another silver arch. This time into the tent.

We walk into the temporary great hall where the wedding is about to start. People are seated on jumbo, bean-shaped lavender pillows laid out haphazardly across massive sky blue blankets. The mix of people on blankets remind me of an early afternoon picnic at the park, beside a lake. Families are gathered in groups on the floor and pillows instead of your regular lined bench seating in church weddings. They sit in various formations with some lying with their legs flat out in front of them on the blanket and others sitting Indian style, knees to chest, and mermaid style. The last position is used principally by the women of the crowd. All these men and women are in vogue wear including the children who look about ready for a fashion photoshoot.

The tent has a retractable roof that's motorized by some control room in the range of the gardens. It opens, I assume, by a lever as the ceiling divides above us in a diagonal line. It raises up two right triangles that form a rectangular roof when together but panel out by separating to show the skies. Each triangle bends outward, curling over the longer walls of the rectangular compound and attach themselves to the outside gardens. Upon touching the grass outside of this temporary great hall, the cessation of motion from the flexible, sturdy poles upholding the structure induces subtle ground vibrations.

Promptly the skies rid themselves of any weather that'd inconvenience guests. The drifting hurricane was a glint in the eye of the skies as we drove here, with the sun gradually managing to come out the closer we got to Califf Manor.

The unique wedding altar between the bridesmaids and groomsmen is a fireproof and soundproof glass sphere that can hold a group of five adults inside. It has a rectangular opening that Erik stands in front of, waiting to take Jade's hand so that together they can enter the sphere. It'll close to contain the bride and groom at the time of their vows, offering them some unconventional privacy in what's commonly a shared moment with guests.

On top of the sphere sits a bald Buddhist monk in the Indian lotus position. He wears a mustard yellow robe that's been wrapped to cover his left shoulder but leaves the right shoulder and arm bare. He'll be the wedding officiant today. There's a flammable gel coat over the sphere spread thin enough so that it's unnoticeable to the human eye. Using a match, the sphere will be lit on fire by the monk after the ending ceremony kiss. In a manic magic trick, he, Jade, and Erik will disappear in the flames to be seen again at the reception.

The Buddhist monk's simulated self-immolation is his art piece as asked to be performed by Jade in remembrance of Quảng Đức—a Vietnamese Mahayana Buddhist monk who stood up for religious equality. Something Jade as an activist, past journalist, and caring human being feels strongly about.

Two professional photographers at the front of the hall will be ready to take the perfect snapshots as this and other memorable moments occur throughout the wedding and reception. One photographer was hired by Erik for their personal use in collecting memories while the other was invited by Jade to post the photos on some political media forum. Hoping it'll attract attention for a cause she believes has long been forgotten. Mainly in countries that've dwindling religious diversity due to an overreaching regime.

I quickly run to the groomsmen side where my spot is last in line. Malia has to go on the opposite side with the girls but not before she gives Jake a big smooch right on the lips, getting beige nude lipstick all over him. Jake jokes that her kissing quota has been filled for the day. I overhear another groomsman mutter under his breath, "Lucky bastard."

I look to Jake, only two groomsmen to my right now that I'm facing the pool of two hundred guests. He crisply utters, "I know."

He's only wearing the vest portion of his tuxedo above the waist, with gray dress pants and black surf leather sandals under the belt. The gray vest has trim white lines that run vertically down the fabric and is at the very least buttoned.

"Dude seriously? To a formal event?"

"Yea bro, you know me. Always on that beach bum status on and off the beach." He sticks his tongue out and does the surfer hand gesture called the shaka. The right hand's three center fingers curled into the palm and the thumb and pinky sticking out in opposite directions like a pretend cellphone. Jake owns the surfer stereotype.

I should've worn a tank top. Then I wouldn't be sweating right now. All other eight groomsmen match my outfit. I stop staring in Jake's direction and avert my gaze down to my black dress shoes after I see Erik being the resolute groom in his Marine's navy blue uniform, giving me the evil eye.

Erik's a tall, blond crew-cut, trim man with a square jawline and chiseled nose. His piercing dark brown, velvety eyes condemn me for tardiness. Doubtless I'm late but better I got the surfing out of my system this morning or I wouldn't be at the reception.

With a subtle flicker of nervousness, I direct my sight to the long white carpet at the smack center of the temporary great hall. Two flower girls emerge, wearing pink spaghetti strap organza gowns, bearing hefty baskets akin to big bird nests, brimming with pink ballerina rose petals. They're Erik's nieces. As they glide forward, each step a dance of grace, the weight of their burden seems but a whisper in the breeze, delicately offloading the petals and coating the white carpet. It's as if nature herself had laid down a pathway of solemn benediction for the bride's sacred passage.

There I stand waiting for my sister to walk down the aisle when she comes out ever so majestically. A princess so buoyant she could float in the scene of these warm blue skies emulated by the floor blankets guests are seated. Dressed in a sparkling white dress that's long sleeved at the top and bloated with ruffles of shantung fabric at the bottom. The bouquet itself is an arrangement of eight-inch hot pink peonies with teal turquoise jewels, wrapped in a wide sheet of taupe silk.

Flamenco music progresses with sounds of rhythmic hand clapping and finger snapping. A petite woman in a brown floral lace dress with a white hat that resembles an orthopedic pillow, sits on a small, raised strawberry garden bed at the far right of the guests. The strawberries are in tune with her ruddy lipstick.

She begins to play her acoustic guitar producing a romantic Latin rhythm. More music follows with the band to her side coming together to add an ornamentation of festive elements from drums to trumpets and maracas. The whole crowd turns to look at the bride as she dances and twirls her way down the aisle smiling as if she's in an ad for whitening toothpaste.

The top half of the gown is practically all lacing. At her waist is a teal skinny belt which matches us groomsmen's teal ties. Being strapless at the top, her neck holds no jewelry, but her ears carry large teardrop diamond earrings. The blue hair pin with three white pearls that my father had given her, glistens so softly as it pinches her hair, one might miss it.

One of the most beautiful and glorious sights I've seen since the waves from last summer's surf session in Peru. She brightens up the entire outdoors with her beauty. Her dazzling big brown eyes give life to anime animators. Her long brown hair is rolled up in a high-rise bun with her favorite flower, a light pink dahlia, sitting frail above her right ear. There're blue-black viburnum berries on a slim delicate branch next to that flower, matching her dark chocolate hair color. If her hair wasn't styled up it'd fall ending at her hips.

The music playing is cheerful and heartwarming. A tear runs down my cheek. The man stink, I think. Wait...no-no-no-nope. Can it be that I'm actually getting emotional? I haven't cried in eight years since my dad died when I was nine. Now I'm tearing up a bit for the first time in so long. It was contradicting of me to think that men don't cry.

All men are supposed to be emotionally ostracized from showing any sort of emotional passion towards anything in this world. A man draws a tear and he's not a real man. Can't believe I gave in to that illogical thinking walking into this wedding. I wipe the low-key tears from my face and smile as she dances down the aisle escorted by my older brother Kosta. He's to her right, letting her take center stage as he walks two steps behind her clapping along with the sound of music.

Only two years my elder, Kosta looks exactly like me. Same black hair, shrewd dark brown eyes, five-foot-nine, big strong hands, and a perfect white smile achieved from braces and good hygiene. Although I'm slightly better looking despite the small difference in muscle tone. He has muscle mass and definition over me through his extra doses of protein powder and creatine in the pantry. His distracting tall mohawk though is what truly sets us apart. However, it isn't as distracting today for my eyes are solely set on the bride.

She's so happy. Ah, the illimitable human capacity for joy when in love. And the infectious nature of one happy soul to put the squeeze of not thinking too hard about being happy on all others.

The carefree atmosphere leads me to recall memories of us when we were kids. I flash back to a time in which all three of us would fight over the toy in the cereal box. The times we'd play hide-and-seek and she'd lock me in the closet making me sob. The time where she and Kosta taught me how to swim and then scared me into thinking crocodiles rest in the deepest part of our pool. Living in Florida, a backyard pool coming with a side of crocs or gators is not far off from reality. It certainly got tedious having to inspect every nook and cranny of our pool each time we went out for a swim, just in case some primitive reptile decided to set up camp.

Then there's the moment in which Jade whooped my ass after I popped the heads off all her plastic dolls and hot glued them together to make a soccer ball. Cutting off her favorite unicorn plush toy's mane was the last straw. I can still sense the faint impressions of scratches over the sides of my neck from when she choked me. Kosta managed to pull her off, slackening her grip by hitting her across the side of the head with a wooden rolling pin.

And then the moment she received that call. That dreadful sorrow of a call explaining that dad was gone—forever. She attempted to relay the message to my brother and I, but she was reasonably shaken and thus unintelligible. The terror on her face said it all. That day all the fighting stopped. We grew up, having to navigate the crucible of childhood amidst the shadow cast by his absence. How much she's always cared for me comes to mind.

It's amazing what the human mind can remember. I remember when I was a baby she'd sneak into my room and lift me up from the crib to hold me and play with me. Little did I know from that moment she'd be there for every surfing competition, every birthday, and all my graduations from elementary through high school. Always cooking for Kosta and me.

She cleaned up after our messes. Not just the physical ones in one of our homes. From our brother antics like breaking a window in the penthouse by playing catch to getting us out of trouble at school and helping us ward off crazy ex-girlfriends. The mother I never had. The woman I admire most in my life and aspire to be as courageous as is Jade.

How she could raise two young boys at the age of fifteen I'll never cease to wonder. I wish our dad could see her today. He would be as immensely proud as I am to see her in all the success she's accomplished from working. The lifestyle she's managed to maintain for us after my dad's passing could only be something of a dream come true.

Money isn't anything but a current medium of exchange; no longer backed by gold but by debt. Once I was part of that world where materialistic things mattered but no more. I'm grateful for Jade's success but I'm only happy if she is. And I always take to heart the lessons she and my father bestowed upon Kosta and me. This thought has sustained me throughout the years: to be compassionate and not thrive off stupidity in life is the road to eternal peace within.

As Daniel used to say, 'Up strawberry vine, then adagio till sunrise.' The phrase alludes to the natural process that is one's maturation in life not unlike the ripening of strawberries. 'Up strawberry vine' refers to the growth phase which may require an initial climb, while 'adagio till sunrise' signifies a period of rest or dormancy until the next phase of growth. The way I see the path to marriage, Jade has earned this period of rest in which she can savor the melody of wedding bells, finding peace in knowing she's found the one. Soaking up life's slower moments and patiently immersing herself in a new beginning.

I miss my dad but right there and then, when Kosta handed Jade over to her husband and I saw that aged blue hair pin settled in her hair, I smiled knowing he watches from above.

Chapter 6

The ceremony took all of what was about ten minutes in my head. After we left the manor's open tent, the crowd walked the formal gardens to arrive at the French provincial housing an after-party. The walls here on the first floor are a sheeny dark brown, toeing the line with a licorice black in some of the faintly lighted corners of the ballroom. The room itself is split between those dining at the round tables decked with white linen and those partying on the Calacatta gold dance floor.

Two children, a small boy and a slightly taller girl, are chasing one another on the dance floor, dodging the swinging dancers whilst holding Day of the Dead figurines in both of their hands. They exit the dance floor and egress the area by heading into another room. Fluted pilasters aside carved overdoors lead way into these other rooms spread about the mansion. Their extended leisure is for those who've another taste in music than the present upbeat country song being played.

Off-white sofas are at random edges of the ballroom and scattered with gold and brown tapestry pillows. The interior windows above the sofas offer a glimpse into neighboring rooms where guests might be lounging or drinking away from the main festivity. Some in solitude. Though all I see through the window I'm staring at is those two unsupervised kids, untethered and free, lost in the innocence of youth's sweet reverie.

I fix the cuffs of my jacket and dress shirt to look down at my red wristwatch, realizing it's been a solid three hours since the commencement of the wedding. The expression time flies is an understatement. The time reads 9:00 P.M. The season finale of my favorite show 'Zombie Surfer Utami' is on in two hours. A time restriction should be placed on television after this show because nothing good is ever on after midnight. Just infomercials of US made products in which they say, 'Don't spend another nickel on the sub-par of yesteryear. Today and today only, we have a special offer on a stupendous, unpretentious, most tremendous innovation—the light bulb of our time. It's America's most popular vegetable shredder for nineteen dollars and ninety-nine cents!' I'd rather use the money I pay for shipping and handling to wipe my ass.

Society should stop the excessive spending on products they don't need and put their money to good use. Start a business, save up money, and use it in the case of a special event such as a wedding; making memories. Even though a wedding is an overly lavish extravaganza to spend a crazed amount of money on if it's only a day. However, people like me who've got the money because of the hard work of others and seize the privileges are sadly naive which is why having wealth should come with its own restrictions for heirs.

I remember when I got my wisdom teeth pulled earlier this year. I was so high off the numbing prescription drugs that as I lay in bed recovering, I called in and bought a treadmill and ab machine from one of those late-night infomercials. I didn't recall ordering them when Kosta confronted my chipmunk self on why'd they'd been delivered under his name at the gate. Apparently, I used his credit card. I've hated infomercials ever since. Too persuasive to those too indolent to do any thinking after supper.

Jade didn't become vice president of She Core by buying her way in. She wasn't accorded certain favors because the privileges of the rich were a kind spokesperson. Rather, because she's rich and young, many did and will underestimate her. She was accredited with being one of the world's most daring journalists. Something that earned her the attention of her current boss. She wasn't persuaded by what others told her the smarter path in her career was. She hustled her way up the corporate ladder and has been fortunate in keeping our family at the top of the social ladder. She's a worker bee of outstanding merit.

People have criticized her means of moving up in the world. A small payoff to being a powerful socialite. Some characterize her as stubborn but if being stubborn works for her, it works. Through it all she's spent her money right so that we may never have to worry about the financial troubles that curse many.

I suppose there're not many people who realize the hardships of not having anything. I've heard stories from Erik of when he was deployed to Iraq and the things he saw. What he went through was a horror taken right out of an action-packed slasher film. The people he witnessed die from missile strikes, a wave of suicide bombings, and white phosphorus. All that can make a person go insane or flip the script, appreciate what they have.

When I asked Erik at his bachelor party what he was most grateful for coming out of Iraq he'd said, "That's easy. Jade." He looked me straight in the eye, baffled I'd even ask. Overcome with emotion, he amicably placed a hand on my shoulder. "Your sister is the best thing that's ever happened to me. Losing her would be the end of my world and my reason for living. I love her."

I believed him because he was crying simultaneously as he told me this and if ever I thought a man could cry to another man it is because they're brothers. Or perhaps in Erik's case because he was drunk.

Erik is now a huge part of my family and I trust him. He's a rich man who lacked any financial incentive to commission as an officer in the military but he did because he was giving back to the country he loves. Now he's found someone he can love. He understands me when I say money isn't a direct means to happiness. Too bad after all we only have one good person in a pack of a thousand to see that wealth is best when sharing it with the rest of the world. His world is now her.

I look around the ballroom searching for Malia but she's nowhere in sight. The great mass of people dining like pigs and topped with diamonds head to toe is ridiculous. Even more so is the grand chandelier. Hanging in the white dome ceiling of the ballroom, it has enough crystals in its tiers to end world hunger. One kid in a mini black tux lays vast asleep on the floor in front of an ornamented marble bust with a turquoise flower crown.

Where're all these kids' parents?

There're two other marble busts at the entrance of the ballroom. They're placed facing each other at opposite ends of the supreme scarlet double doors with ornate black iron hinges, currently open to a hush night and a 2000-acre paradise. Strange decorative choice to place the marble busts on the floor. Kosta has one of Aristotle on the fireplace mantel in our home's study.

Lucas Farnham comes up to my side while holding a napkin with a soft-colored yellow macaroon. He's dressed in an impeccably sharp blue hue suit and wears a navy tie that has a pattern of white and gray zigzags on it. His chestnut brown hair with natural butter highlights is combed to the right with a skin fade that tapers from the length of the hair all the way down to the fair skin on his neck. He takes a bite of the macaroon and stares at me with a touch of sable in his keen and hard medium-brown eyes.

"How're you enjoying the festivities of tonight? Aren't you the tiniest bit tired from surfing this morning and the bachelor party last night?" Lucas' macaroon beckons me as he asks.

"I think we can all acknowledge that scheduling the bachelor party the day before the wedding was an unconventional and imprudent decision. Haven't got much sleep cause of it but tonight's event has been quite a comedy. I laugh at people who feel the need to have everything when the truth is reality isn't real. The life of luxury many of these people operate or have been dealt is a wall hiding a denial of sadness and neediness for the fulfillment to be somebody. Some even hiding their lack of self-worth with overt debauchery."

He nods his head listening as he munches on the light, airy dessert. I place both my hands in the pant pockets of my dress pants and assess the guests.

I'd forgotten the energy shots were still in here.

"Look at that girl over there in that short pink dress. She doesn't appear to be of legal age and she's sitting on a man's lap that could be her grandfather. Not sure how comfortable the people around them feel as he's sucking on her neck. Now look over to the three o'clock couple by the photo booth. They look to be around their thirties, both with wedding bands on their fingers, and the husband can't keep his eyes off the lonely playboy model bending over the floor to find her lost earring. The woman's taunting him. She found the earring four minutes ago. It's in her left hand." I nudge Lucas with my shoulder. "And that old woman over there with a black and white chinchilla fur coat. Seriously, who does she think she is with a diamond tiara on her head?"

"That's actually the matriarch of House Mora whose struggles to repair the tarnished image of her family name persist to this day. Having found a foxhole here in the city of Sebastian to become a virtual recluse."

I'm completely flummoxed he knows that. We both crack a smile and take humor in the ludicrousness.

Lucas gives a word of advice, "Look pal, only God can judge em. Who am I or you to pass judgment eh? You're no saint either." He places a hand on my back. "Seems like you've got quite the knack for people-watching. Ease up on the creeping, will ya?"

"I'm just saying man, reality in what you show off is worth a miniscule amount to the type of person you know you are. Let me reiterate that. Few of the people here are people I'd say I trust. Most of them aren't pacifist workers and have fought their way to the so-called riches of life by back-stabbing their partners. Seemingly kind socialites that're tactical in where they project their money and to whom they commit an act of selfishness to earn more money."

"They call it business." A man with a deeply defined English accent hovers over me.

I turn around to see the tall figure standing from behind me wearing a white top hat. I hadn't even noticed Lucas remove his hand from my back. When I turn to my side, I see him back at the dessert table gathering more macaroons.

Ravishing, it's my sister's fifty-year-old boss. A top of the line, mock-straight-edge English man with red hair combed to the side, available for all to see when he takes off his white top hat to bend forward as if honoring me. His swift hair falling over his hazel eyes and the cocky twist of his head letting his hair fall back into place as he straightens out.

"Pardon me, good lad. I couldn't help but overhear your little tirade on my people."

"How'd you even hear me?" I respond.

He coughs twice punching at his chest, gathering his voice, and then putting his white top hat back on. "Well, you were rather inadvertently broadcasting your thoughts for all to hear, don't you think?" he says looking down on me with his right brow raised.

I look him up and down, seeing him taller than usual with a dark purple suede tuxedo that's most certainly more expensive than the groom's yet it looks cheesy at the same time. A man not known for his subtle taste in evening wear. It broadens his shoulders and slims out his waist. When at the office he normally dresses casual showing off his baby gut from excessive wine drinking and hard liquor followed by his favorite meal of Asian-spiced pork or lamb chops with frizzled herbs. I can smell the smoked pig with intense strawberries awake in his breath now.

"Hello Rick. Mmm...nice traditional rioja you must've had today," I say taking a big whiff and then turning my back to him to walk the other way.

"Well hold on there ye old chap. Why in such a hurry to go? If I wasn't mistaken, I'd say you're avoiding me and that'd be an awfully rude gesture to direct at someone who controls the source of your family's primary income."

"Goodbye Rick," I pointedly disdain his invitation to chat. I left his sight before that small talk became an argument with my fists.

I hate it when my sister forgets something at home that she needs at work. She calls me and I have to take time out of my day to go to the company. That's when I'll be let in and must wait outside Rick Harford's office on a bench till my sister comes out to pick up what it is she asked of me. His door is always open. From his crimson sculpted leather executive chair, behind his curved aluminum desk crafted off an airplane's wing, he tries to make small talk and sometimes he'll even call me into his office for a drink.

Usually, I won't budge but my sister and he commenced a project aside from the workplace that's set to launch a sparkling wine with the working title 'Gorgon One Champagne.' A substitute for wine with all the hallmarks of wine and the symptoms that come from drinking it. The wine is designed to emulate fine vintages without the long, tedious years that come in storing and aging the best wines. Anytime I see the precursor sitting on his desk I'll accompany him. One thing I've learned from our chats in his office is that all champagne is sparkling wine but not all sparkling wine is champagne just as every jungle is a forest but not every forest's a jungle.

The bottle Rick and Jade co-created is of garnet-colored glass designed with simplicity. There's a matte black papal cross on the body and base of the bottle. The cork is shaped like a wentletrap seashell. I don't get the background story, nor do I care as it's the best alcohol I've ever had the pleasure of tasting. The release date for the drink is an unknown but wine enthusiasts will have a field day when it comes out exclusively in England and Chile.

I don't mind taking my orange Yamaha raider out for cruising. I take pleasure in it but the problem with delivering packages to my sister at work is that after getting there people still don't know me. Too many times have I had security at the door stop me and ask the same front desk receptionist for the past two years if she recognizes me. A middle-aged brunette that dazzles in her pantsuit while fixing her azure, fat edge frame eyeglasses to search out the computer database for any reference to an appointment. I even know her first name by now. It's Mocha like the coffee. I wonder where she is now or if she even got an invitation.

Either way if my small family would make an outreach to our relatives from Costa Rica then maybe most of the invited guests here wouldn't be from the company but rather family.

Thank god for Erik's wonderful family. They too know a thing about old money, owning one of the world's preeminent oil refineries and trading some of the biggest stocks on Wall Street. They've two charities I know of all in support of the less fortunate, keeping up with their goodwill. They've a vacation house here in Sebastian, Florida, but their permanent residence is in New York's Upper East Side. I walk over to greet them at their table.

Lucas startles me, grabbing me by the hip from behind. "Hey buddy, don't forget to start packing. Get ready for surfing in Malaysia next week."

I turn to look at him still eating dessert. Now with a piece of buttercream cake on a round plate lying flat on his hand with a fork on the side. "Yeah, I'll bore you with my lack of conversation skills there too."

He winks and smiles at me. "Take it easy stud, I'm done for tonight."

"More like you're full for tonight." I lean in to hug him, and we tap each other on the back.

"Aren't you going to say bye to the newlyweds?" I ask.

"Nah, they won't even notice I'm gone. Besides, they look pretty cozy on the dance floor."

"Ok. Want to go surfing again tomorrow if Hurricane Raziel is still making waves at Sebastian Inlet?" I ask while he picks the fork up from his plate and digs into his cake.

"For sure. Doubt it'll be the hurricane making waves though. News says it's done in these parts." He takes one bite of the cake and leaves the rest on an occupied table next to us, on top of a lady's unfinished dinner platter.

The lady was in the midst of berating my sister's wedding before Lucas cut her meal short. "All I'm saying is if you're going to break tradition, why have a wedding at all?" She comes to a halt, sneers down her nose, and whacks the cake off her plate.

Jeez lady. It's only salad.

Lucas pulls his lips inward, widens his eyes, and walks off in a hurry. Guess he heard the news correspondent woman on the radio too. Wonder what's got him in such a rush.

I approach the packed dining table where the Mantas are seated. It's a full house but all the brothers' wives are missing. "Hello Mr. and Mrs. Manta. Mind if I care to join you this fine night?"

Mr. Manta gets up. "Please do Mr. Califf."

I, giving him a firm handshake, sit down next to him and his wife.

Mr. Manta is in his prime. Though nearing seventy, he's built like an ox, richer than he's ever been, and his grizzled white hair adds not age but wisdom in my eyes. His right hand, Mrs. Manta, is a robust platinum blonde with neck-length hair coiled in a half-up, half-down top knot.

You can tell on the dot her radiance, exuding an unmistakable charm and elegance, much like a trumpeter swan navigating the serene waters of a picturesque lake with poise and beauty, owes much to the skilled hands of a talented surgeon. She has heavenly deep cloud gray eyes that strike as olive green at first glance with bolts of blue lightning flaring at every turn of her long, slender neck. Her high cheekbones and plump lips are a derivative of Aphrodite. Ipso facto, she's a Burmese ruby to the skin-deep male.

"How's it feel to have your son married, huh Mrs. Manta?"

"Please, call me Debby," she says chewing on some steak.

"Ok Debby, so you expecting grandkids anytime soon?" I ask her with a tittering laugh.

I make her blush with the small sign of a forthcoming expression.

"My gosh," she responds swallowing a piece of steak, then putting her fork and knife down to widen her eyes at me. "If heaven bids it, I'll be more than happy to welcome more grandkids, but I'd give it some time." Her eyes lower to her meal as she picks her fork and knife back up. The Botox keeps her face frozen. I had assumed I'd be able to discern her expression, but I was mistaken.

I don't know why she's hesitant on welcoming grandkids. She's not getting any younger. Even in the face of how much plastic surgery she undergoes. Deborah is unmindful of the people who recognize her beauty's been enhanced artificially. All her sons are married. Erik's two nieces are her only grandkids. They're his oldest brother's daughters. They're adopted. One from India and the other girl from Vietnam.

Only one year apart, the oldest is six and she's the Vietnamese one, sitting with her pink dress next to the only black person at the table—Abeni Manta. Haven't seen the younger one since we walked into this after-party.

Deborah goes on to boast about how her boys have made her so proud in all their accomplishments. Each from a branch in the military. I'm introduced to Erik's three older brothers around the table and his younger sister, Abeni, across from me. Even though I've already been introduced to them countless times before. "I know the family Mrs. Manta," I try speaking but fail and whisper with my words a passerby to her hearing.

The eldest is Robert Jr. named after his dad and then there're the twins, Kyle and Beckford. You can tell them apart by a flaw in one of the brother's faces. The right side of Kyle's face has a cut up ear with bandage wrappings over it and a winged scar alike a washed-out wishbone reflective on his cheek. Beckford's the twin without disfigurement. Robert Jr. is a part of the Air Force and works as an intelligence officer while the twins are in the Navy.

The three of them are all blond, tall, heavily built, and dressed in their issued military dress uniforms. Robert Jr. is in a single-breasted dark blue mess jacket with two columns of three silver 'winged star' buttons. His broad black shoulder boards reveal his rank, of which I'm unlettered. The blue satin bowtie on his white tuxedo shirt is a snazzy requisite for formal events and while the white gloves are sharp too, they're scarcely ever seen at weddings for a requisite here they're not. Or at least, that's what I believe to be so. Not entirely certain it's a standard component of the uniform.

The twins are in the Navy's classic dress blues. The uniforms consist of a nearly black navy blue double-breasted sport coat with six gold-colored buttons, a white dress shirt, and a black silk necktie. On the table are the twins' white military peaked caps with a black visor, gold strap, and the Navy Officer insignia—two fouled gold anchors crossed on the underside of a silver shield capped off with a silver eagle. Its wings spread grandly and head facing right. Sublime in conception.

The brothers' short, tidy, and waxy hair is the marrow of what sets them apart in a queue facing right. Others might point to their ranks and branches to mark them off as unique. Had they not been uniformly uniformed today, no option but mine would fare well for distinguishing from brother to brother. Robert Jr.'s hair is brushed up, Kyle's is combed over right, and Beckford's is slicked back.

Robert Jr. has the most awards in the form of ribbons over his left chest pocket followed by Beckford and then Kyle. They've earned the right to wear their uniforms even if this event isn't about them. The decision by all three of Erik's brothers to wear their uniforms may have sibling rivalry overtones. A gentleman wouldn't dare try to steal the limelight from the bride and groom yet here the brothers sit with their medals and colors on another's big day. A classic suit that subtly exhibits their masculine physique would've done just fine.

Abeni, I believe was taken by Robert Jr. out of a distraught village in Eritrea as his own but in the midst of always having to work, could not care for her. So, in stepped his parents to support and provide for her. Legally, Robert Jr. remains her adoptive father along with his two other adopted daughters. Those flowers girls were adopted three years ago. Years after Abeni began living under Jr.'s parents. The way life worked out, Abeni refers to Robert Jr. as brother and Robert as dad.

Abeni's four years my elder and has adapted well to the simple life though her tribe's symbolism still shows in the form of a black panther on the side of her right shoulder. Erik told me his parents offered to have it lasered off, but she refused to go through the pain of removing a tattoo that's instilled righteousness within her and will forever remind her of her roots.

Abeni Manta is a dark-skinned African American beauty that looks more like a woman than any of the surgically enhanced females in this ballroom. That is, she's physically defined at the waist as an athlete, carries some extra weight at the hips and thighs as do the natural beauties of Barbados, and has a bust that'd make any man take a second look; not on the ball to their probing eyes. She has a cascade of enchanting braids over her left shoulder tonight but the last time we saw each other she had a gorgeous extra-short mohawk. Unquestionably, it's her signature look. It goes well with her beautiful oval face and edgy style.

She's wearing a red sleeveless, low-cut dress that ends right above her knees with a colorful but predominantly blue stone amulet pressed tightly against her neck on a thin metallic chain. I believe it a rare harlequin opal. The oval is fitted amid five rounded petals of sapphire, exhibited in the mouth of a white gold doe. Her skin is glowing. She takes a mini travel size perfume bottle from her silver clutch and sprays it once on her chest, taking the tips of her fingers and rubbing it in across her collarbone.

The perfume shimmers on her skin as sunbeams do on my body when drenched in ocean water. I can smell the fresh scent of strawberries coming from across the table on her body. I move the center piece of cup-shaped summer white clematis and apricot roses. They're stuffed in a bubble glass vase that's filled with ice water and light up mauve bulbs in the shape of cubes.

"Are you studying at a university up in New York or do you even plan on continuing school at all?" I ask her, now with a full view of her cleavage. She stays silent and seated, poised in form. I wonder if she can hear me as the brothers are all carrying out conversations of their own at the table. "I asked for an answer," I continue, raising my voice.

"Excuse me?" she replies peeved, taking off the white cloth napkin from her lap and chucking it on the table. She heatedly gets up, tugs down on her dress, and leaves without excusing herself.

That escalated quickly in the wrong direction.

"Sorry Mr. and Mrs. Manta," I say getting up to chase her, almost pulling the white tablecloth with me.

"It's Debby," Mrs. Manta replies with a wink. She drags the tip of her tongue across her upper lip and moistens it. Then she bites her bottom lip, leering at me.

Did I just imagine that?

Did Mrs., I mean Debby, really wink at me? Perhaps Erik's family is too nice. His mom anyways. She grips the side of my tux jacket before I can go. "Don't be too long. Robert and I have a special toast. We'll be making it in a few minutes." She smirks at me and then flaunts her fake eyelashes.

"Ok Debby," I reply nervously, worried that she's practically flirting with me right in front of her husband. That's not a guy I'd want to piss of. A strong resemblance to all his sons, he's a brawny, stern fella with what I'm sure is an iron fist. I throw the peace sign as I head out.

I've met some awkward turtles but she's a rare species.

Chapter 7

I walk onto the dance floor where the bride and groom are all the rage. The bride's let her hair down and changed into a white bustier crop top with spaghetti straps, a knee-length flamingo pink tutu, and glossy hot pink stilettos for the reception. The main attraction. The lion of the zoo. Can but one guest stand aside to let me through? I make my way, little toeing. Inwards, this knavery succeeds at last. One in which I whisper as I pass,

"Is it not the simplest delight? The Sapporo white sweetheart chocolate biscuits, light as powdered clay, honeyed as the yellow moonlight, awaiting there, in the inner courts, wanting to charge all gourmets with rapture?"

They're clueless for I only want to see the fox. I shove people making my way towards Abeni when Kosta appears from the rest of the crowd. Before me he stands six-foot-two because of his hair. The rooster of the family. His spiked up mohawk with buzzed sides begs no more attention than a street rat from a king. His jet black hair's as dark as a cursed goblet. If it wasn't for that stupid haircut of his people would think we're twins. He's two years my senior. Still, he's kept a baby face.

"Step out of my way Kosta. I need to find Abeni. Wait—" I stop myself. "Have you seen Malia?"

"She's left with Jake. About half an hour ago just as the dinner course was being served."

Super, I muse, letting the news sink in. Malia was my ride home and I left my cellphone and wallet in her boyfriend's car. Wasn't going to risk my phone going off during the wedding ceremony. I move past Kosta, rolling my eyes, pushing him out of my way nettled, not at him but at Malia. No matter though. I'll go home with someone else here. There's to be someone around that'd be so generous as to provide me with a ride home. I think of my options.

Kosta can't take me for his plans after the wedding involve his girlfriend and a nearby hotel. Quite sincerely I don't think I could endure another car ride with him. I'm tired of listening about his intern position as a broker's shadow. Don't know if he's taking the internship seriously. He seems to be more adept at clandestine services than stocks.

The broker he works for, Cadu, has some abundantly rich clientele that require Kosta to analyze the market and continuously research stocks. Sometimes Kosta is his own telemarketing center, on duty and making calls twenty-four seven. Cadu, when hiring for this position Kosta has filled, was heedless of the person he was hiring. Cadu is Erik Manta's broker and it seems by hiring his client's new bride's brother, he's made his job vulnerable to watchful eyes. He hasn't bought any bad stocks or sold any inordinately profitable ones so I'm unsure what information Kosta's trying to extract from Erik's investments.

I could go talk to my sister's boss, Rick Harford, about giving me a ride home. Forget it. That guy's a clown. My sister's unavailable. Obviously. She's going on some romantic getaway right after this with her lovebird, Erik. They're traveling to Bora Bora. I went to surf near there when I was a kid with my dad and the waves were tiny and the water was immoderately light blue.

Come to think of it, the chlorine-based pool look of beach water is actually kind of nice. The color is natural, and they'll be staying in one of those huts overwater. Their lush bungalow is on a private island surrounded by the crystal lagoon of Bora Bora. My side of it is that if and when I get married, I'll ask the honeymoon not be situated in an alluring, touristy go-to spot because no matter what my new wife and I will be spending the whole time in the hotel room. It'll most certainly be more pleasurable than any of the features a site may possess.

The problem I find in most girls is their unpredictability. One of the reasons I might never find a girl to be betrothed to. Malia never struck me as a great surfer yet she's terrific. She's so uptight you'd think she spent her leisure time practicing ashtanga and power yoga to demarcate stress. Debby never seemed like a woman who was unhappy with her marriage but acting like a coquette cougar got me to think twice on where her loyalty lies. Then there's Jade who's made a great replacement mom for Kosta and me, and Mocha who's smart enough to run the front desk of a high-end company but who can't remember a guy's name to save her life. I'm the company's vice president's brother and I'm nearly there twice a week. She can at the very least remember my face.

As for Abeni, she's mysterious about herself but says plenty about others. Her gossip crew is a woman-only club. She's a quiet gal with the boys. The first time I met her was in Hawaii with my family and hers bonding over the engaged couple. It was a short trip, but I got Erik to surf on that trip while his brothers were busy with wives of their own to attend to.

Abeni's lived a great portion of life under conservative rule. She might not remember when she was taken out of Eritrea by Robert Jr. but he sure remembers the dangers that faced her. She was abandoned in a mudbrick house as her whole village was attacked by rebels, leaving her to fend for herself at the age of nine. When Robert Jr. took her under his wing, he raised her like another one of his military comrades but as the struggle of raising a child that was approaching teenage years and having to always be out of the country got to him, he had no other choice but to find her a new home.

At the time Robert Jr. wasn't married so Abeni couldn't keep getting raised under different nannies. It wasn't a healthy living. It'd seem that this type of tutelage was more foster care, less basic social unit. Lucky for him, his parents always wanted a daughter, viewing their son's burdensome balancing act with work and fatherhood as a gift from above.

The lessons taught to her by Robert Jr. impelled her to guard herself from the outside world. That restraint from the outside has made her as gentle as a daffodil. Those lessons continued under Robert and Debby's household as they've raised four military bound sons who know the world's not so pretty. For every daffodil in the world there's a rodent. Her guardians have put forth this idea of adding a fifth soldier to their legacy. Abeni's cordially declined—twice. And while she's negated interest, the option remains on the table.

I'm not surprised she hasn't considered a role in the military given her isolated upbringing. Maybe that's why she's quiet, cloistering herself from the family regime and becoming a doughty champion of individuality. Forevermore on the outside of honor.

Outside. That's just where she heads as I notice her red dress drift through the wind made by a closing backroom door at the far end of the ballroom. The dress catches itself on the closed door and only a piece of it is left for the eye to see. The door then reopens to let that part in. I make my path, walking casually to the door and staring back at the guests to check if anyone's watching. I don't believe I'm allowed in here, but I do let myself in only to enter an inner roofless courtyard.

There's a sizeable garden full of genetically engineered blue rose bushes and imported date-plum trees with a bountiful of miniature orange dates on their branches. They're illuminated by blue wind chimes with a powerful inner light source. For a second, I even thought those dates were blueberries. The light-up brilliant blue tubes are lined up in a row suspended from a high ledge above me. At first blush, an endless row of Atlantean performance mufflers.

There's one false balcony on the second floor behind Abeni; ideal for growing a Mediterranean herb garden. The balcony's black iron double doors have a scrolling and floral window grill design; incongruous with the Plain Jane design of its contracted belly railing.

A bobble-headed brown cat with incandescent jasper red eyes casts a long and furtive look down past the bowed rails.

It moves sinuously across the balcony, balancing itself within what limited space it has, flirting with the curves of shadows. Through the camera lens of its freakish eyes, it appears to be staring right at a ballooning flame. Howbeit, from where I'm standing there's only blue.

Abeni sits with her long thick legs crossed on a durable fiberstone replica of an Ancient Greek garden bench.

Thought this place was designed strictly off French influence.

The elongated, somewhat curved bench carries with it the carved images of Theseus and Pirithous. I can tell it's them, finding no need for words. Several panels depict their narrative on each side of the squared-off pillars holding the bench. Such meticulously rendered scenes, speaking volumes of mythic tales and timeless camaraderie.

Best friends from an Ancient Greek myth. The two thought themselves worthy of marrying the daughters of Zeus, Helen of Troy and Persephone, and thus attempted to kidnap them. Zeus' brother Hades, wise to their plan, invited them to feast with him. The friends sat on chairs to dine with Hades. These chairs were cursed, erasing their memories of an identity and of their mission. Hercules took on the role of hero, as he often does in these myths, and saved Theseus but failed in freeing Pirithous. Pirithous stayed, forever trapped in the underworld.

Abeni's head is leveled down with her eyes closed. Her beige, chunky-heeled ankle boots rest next to her on the bench. She's roused from a phony nap, noticing me staring. She lifts her arms up and then extends them to separate sides of the bench with a long yawn. She begins to size me up head to toe. "You followed me out here for a reason."

"I–I wanted to check up on you." My speech falters awkwardly as I approach her.

"Get comfortable sweetie," she says rising from her seat and then shaking her head like a wet dog as she's preparing for what's to come. She communicates to me her lust. I stop in front of her, slip out of my black dress shoes, and kick them off to the side. She snarls like a cat, and I pick up what she's throwing down.

"My pleasure," I reply tugging on my teal tie as she leaps and cavorts toward me, winding up ensnared in my arms.

She leans in tight against me, grabs me by the hair on the back of my head, and pulls me into her lips—moist like succulent cherries. We start making out and it's like second nature. She sticks her tongue down my throat, and I don't know what else to do but to go with it and caress it with mine. I follow her lead, grabbing her by the waist, picking her up off her feet, and carrying her with me as I walk backwards. I then spin her to the wall with blue lights. I push her onto the wall with my body firm against hers and her legs wrapped around my waist. She places her soft hands on both of my cheeks, stopping me for a second to look playfully into my eyes.

"A bachelor so in demand. I never took you to be a man so in charge." She smiles, biting her lip and stealing a glance at my belt.

"I had some awareness of you wanting me in Hawaii. Always sizing me up when I was shirtless on the beach, but I never thought much of pursuing it with you seeming the shy type."

"Shy? Honey I've been playing hard to get," she giggles.

I continue to kiss her vigorously and then she begins to kiss me on the neck while her hand slowly finds its way down to my belt buckle. Before she can loosen my belt, I take her off the wall and let her ground herself with her feet hard on the grass. She bustlingly undoes the buttons on my gray vest, white dress shirt, and pulls down my pant zipper. She gets lower, coolly tugging on my gray dress pants till they're completely off. I tenderly push her away when her fingers slide in behind the elastic waistband on my black boxer briefs. I disrobe my tux jacket followed by the vest and shirt she'd unbuttoned.

I'm not acting like my regular self, but I can't stop myself from going further so I bring her up to her feet, both my hands lifting her up from under her armpits. I put one hand behind her back to unclip her bra. With her dress still on, I place my hands under it, lifting it up to her stomach and then fondling inside. I squeeze her breasts with stiff hands. The liberation comes to me as I rip the rest of her gown right off.

"That was easy."

"Cheap. I made the dress out of some sexy stripper gowns."

"Oh yea?" I look at her pleadingly.

I'm able to let some ease back into my hands once I see the red lingerie. I make a short sinking whistle. "A girl can never go wrong with red or black," I tell her, the anticipation for sex growing.

As her bra falls to the grass, I begin nibbling away at her nipples and then circling my tongue around the edges of the entire breasts, finding my way back to her lips. My fingertips dance along her luscious skin and voluptuous curves. Her soft brushing on my groin eradicated any guilt I had before doing this. I take off her panties using my bite and then get back up and sternly turn her on her back, seeing those precious dimples I love at the end of a woman's back. I remove my black boxer briefs and my erection springs out into the open air, pointed like an arrow to her.

With one hand grabbing onto her waist and the other holding her wrist against her back, I put my throbbing thulian pink mushroom head inside her vagina. I slowly enter inside her allowing her vaginal fluids to ease my cock in. I fuck her and begin humping her at an intensely fast pace. She's in for it. Small drops of sweat start to run down my forehead. I push deep inside her heart-shaped lips with cushion from her plush and round derriere banging on my pelvis. She slides her free hand on the wall in front of her.

"You're mine," I grunt.

She takes her hand off the wall and successively, I feel some minor pushback from her. Out of the blue she's yelling stop. At first the cries are hesitant but then they come to me as exacting. Still, I don't lull. I'm locked in by my sex drive. It's clear she wants me.

I slam her head forth on the wall, demanding of her—silence. Her wrist jerks under my grip but I only tighten it further, causing her gross pain. Stark is her discomfort for she lets out a harrowing wail.

She twists her body sideways and an elbow plunks into me on my side. The blow to my stomach's trifling. I yank her wrist, turning her full body towards me. Her face centimeters from mine, I glom onto her neck with terrible strength. Her body's trembling and her breath's short, languishing with every passing second.

"You fucking slut! Who do you think you are?" I ask spitefully; her face specked with my spit.

Abeni averts her eyes and strikes me passionately in the gut with her knee. She slithers from me. My vision's blurring. I turn, managing to wrench her by the braids before she flees and violently shove her naked body onto the grass. She makes a piddling effort to get away, crawling towards the exit leading into the ballroom. I lunge at her body, seizing her mouth and continue inserting myself inside her. Tears roll down my knuckles as I tenaciously thrust harder, buried deep inside her.

Taking a break from looking at her prepossessing swanlike neck, I allow myself one sideways glim and see the unmistakable face of a soldier. There's Kyle. His mouth wide open and eyes absolutely incensed, unforgiving of the scenario that's unfolded. He backs away and descends further into the garden dropping his lit cigarette onto the grass.

I bust and Abeni moans without holding back. I slap her ass and it jiggles. I tell her to shut up, gathering my drawers and then picking up my pants to zip them back up. I start to buckle my belt that was left on my dress pants and realize I must hide this boner of mine to diverge unwarranted attention from my crotch region. I pin down my boner against my waist by tightening my belt.

"Damn it," I whisper panting. I'm shocked. I raise my arms over my head and drag my hands from the back of my head over my face. She backs away from me and sits down on the bench jaded.

"What did you just get me into?" I say, looking away, rushing to gather my clothes off the grass. I position my white dress shirt on me, as neatly as I can, and throw my tux jacket over my shoulder.

"This was your idea! You said you wanted more fun in our sex life," Abeni yells, her forehead creased.

"Can you keep it down? My god, do you want the whole world to know we're fucking?" I tell her, my muscles tensing up.

"Is that what you think five months of my time is? Fucking! I've flown down here from New York more times in the last month than you've visited me throughout the entire time we've been dating. I don't need this. You agreed you could do long distance. I try this carnal fantasy of yours of violating a stranger at a wedding and you get mad when we get caught."

"Ugh," I look away pained. She's so reckless in her way of shoving off the fact that her brother caught us in the act. She seems indifferent to that aspect, but there's a part of me that's strangely drawn to that side of her.

I don't even have time to button my dress shirt or tuck it into my dress pants before I leave, leaving Abeni there naked on the bench with a ripped dress and all the rest of her undergarments plus my vest and tie lying on the ground. The fluorescent blue lights make her look like an avatar of Lord Vishnu, sitting there with downcast eyes like the goddess she is who seduces her prey.

I run back into the ballroom and the first thing I see is the left side of Beckford's face. He's standing outside the door holding a round glass amber beer bottle, giving insight to the short gasp I make when I think it's his twin, Kyle. He asks if I'm ok and I assure him I'm alright.

"You sure? You're more naked than Jake in his vest," he snickers.

I start buttoning up my dress shirt rapidly.

"You might want to tighten your belt there too buddy before your pants fall. What's up with you?"

Crap. He's seen my boner.

"I was going out for a swim," I say the first thing that comes to me.

"Uh-huh, sure. Stay out of trouble kid. I was young too once. Your pants are fine by the way, but I did make you look."

He asks if I know where the bathrooms are and I point him in the right direction. I glance back at the door I just closed and having neglected Abeni, a girl who was only helping my search for some release, I take the tux jacket off my shoulder, open the door, and lance the jacket at her face without taking a second look.

"You forgot your shoes by the way." Beckford sneaks up on me.

"Jeez!" I slam the door shut.

"Thanks!" I say irritated.

He walks off joyously and raises his hand—perfectly rigid—to shoulder level. "No problem."

For that split second, I think I saw her naked, curled into a ball on the grass and that it was crying I heard but it wasn't because I left. I'm confident she was tearing up before that when I promoted ruff sex. I hope she uses that tux jacket as some form of coverage and not take it as a sign that I'm mad because I threw it. I talk to myself aloud. "Alright, pull yourself together. What're you going to do?"

First thing, shoes. I open the door again and walk to my shoes where I left them. Abeni's nowhere in sight but I hear Kyle, a few of his derogatory slut-shaming terms, and a female weeping.

I suppose I don't have time to stay for the cheers.

I put my dress shoes back on. I need to go before things get out of hand. There's that little voice in my head telling me to speak but I choose to grapple with it instead of blindly following it.

You're a coward Koata. Stand up for her already! Is she not the one who makes your heart skip a beat? Go on, listen to your heart and be a man. Pffft, that mushy stuff? What do I know about matters of the heart? Should I intervene in family matters? God, you're being a total chicken.

I ignore the voice. It wasn't loud enough this time around. I walk back inside and to the main dancehall. I run up the lateral steps of the ballroom where the rooms used by the bride and bridesmaids to get ready are located. Rustic Greek blue doors mark both sides of the upstairs hallway. Anyone would recognize these blue doors as distinct to the Cyclades.

They mark the white stucco towns overlooking the Aegean Sea. At once I open the first blue doors to my right revealing a large balcony with an exquisite view of the large red rose gardens—an adjunct to Califf Manor since the roses are only seasonal.

I scope out the area. The temporary great hall's straightforward with its roof now closed, about half a quarter mile away. Dark clouds float above it. I notice Malia's white Porsche Carrera parked by the tent with the inside fogged out. The car's bouncing up and down sporadically. They haven't left then. Still, the brief jaunt to get there isn't worth discovering her and Jake in the nude, thrusting in a tight space.

The balcony is set up with blue cushioned teak lounge chairs, cream outdoor sofas, and silver-plated round tables. I need to rest my head before I go on looking for a phone. I feel nauseous but if I don't call someone to pick me up right now, I may be exposed in front of Erik's family. I owe it to Jade not to ruin anything else from her wedding day. I was already late. I walk to a curved, cream sofa with navy accent pillows when hastily I look up in response to the sound of fireworks.

It's only thunder. I stare up at the myriad of clouds unfolding like rolled cookie dough in the sky and see lightning jutting through their curves. I sense a rainstorm heading down the path of the empty road from which this wind approaches. Thumb tacks poke at me with a dainty touch as mist gets into position from right above me. It blows onto me, washing away the hint of cologne coupled with skin on my neck and the glimmer from my black dress shoes.

I look at the time on my timepiece. It's swapped its earlier red rubber strap for an orange one. Gulixua watches have a proclivity for changing colors. It's 10:00 P.M. sharp. One more hour till 'Zombie Surfer Utami' is on channel fifty-two.

Red rose pedals flow onto the balcony floor from out in the gardens and swirl around my feet. I close my eyes and listen to the sound of my heart beating. A cap is twisted on a shaken-up bottle of soda. There's a slight pop. A bullet explodes out of a gun and into my back. Pain dawns on me. As I open my eyes, the pain pilfers my sense of time and seconds begin to drag.

Not a bottle of soda.

Whose gun was triggered that broke the clock? The roses beyond the balcony turn into a maroon mirage. The confines of the gardens are deluged with blood. The woman's suicide. Her fall from Tunglo Tower's penthouse flashes to me. The crimson swathe left over on the sand from her head's collision with the ground is what I see now. It's what I saw the following morning when I went to Sebastian Inlet to surf with my father.

"Life is strange," he'd said.

I then, for whatever reason, think back to when I first saw a double rainbow. The fact that after this coming storm kicks the bucket one might appear and I might not be here to see it is sorrowful.

Why am I visualizing rainbows? They don't appear at night.

The mist disappears with it blurring into the background as my sight tries and runs away. But I still hear it. The shavings of mist pass over the fields of roses. Never thought there should be directions to smell a rose but to me, if I'm smelling them correctly as I'm dying, their wholesome smell projects the mellowness of ripe apples.

My heart stops racing.

Inflicted are the systems in my body that've halted blood flow to all my other bodily organs and are now gushing blood out of my back. Incomprehensible is the mind of the one who's placed a bullet into my back and through my chest. I collapse to the ground watching everything else fall with me at a slower pace than my tilting body.

In an undeniable position am I to state that I've just died as my eyes roll to the back of my head and my body collides with the sprayed ceramic tiles mimicking veined black stone. My whole universe suddenly fades into an unworldly spiral of darkness, though I feel something taking a hold of me as all memories slip away.

Did I really just get shot? Who am I? What exactly just happened?

I stray from what pulls me, grasping me as I yell at it to let go.

"Stop!"

Still conscious enough to know I'm dead but not conscious enough to know if maybe this is all a dream. The bullet that's shot me, the powerful force lifting me as I struggle to separate from it, and my thoughts still running despite my heart no longer beating. Should I accept this ending? It's just too restless of a concept to wrap my head around that this is the end and I'm indeed dead. Whether for it or against it...I'm dead.

Chapter 8

When you're dying the last thing you should think about is whether or not you turned all the lights off when you left home. For some reason that's what came to mind. Strangely enough I do remember that, but I can't recall my name. If ever I had a name and could choose it, it'd be Mansa Musa.

My mind starts sorting through useless information and I wait, still having some sense of a light around me. I'm transitioning into a deep sleep. Just as if my eyelids were sealed airtight and a lamp was turned on in the corner of a bedroom. I wait for something to occur and when something does occur, I wish I'd left the lights on at home because everything turns off. A veil of pure darkness descends; an oppressive shroud engulfing every ounce of light, mercilessly devouring what I named the last scrap of hope.

"God?" I call out but go unheard.

Where are you?

"Hello! Anyone?" Not a sound is returned.

My lips go numb followed by my body. I somehow lose my voice, forgetting a most basic way to communicate thoughts. I can't speak or feel but still I have the barest sense of uneasiness I'm getting tugged. Impossible to tell when you're numb. I blink and there they are. These things that're attaching onto me.

They don't possess the vitality of the living. They're nanoscale lumps of coal-black humans stuck together with contorted limbs that sprout spikes. I witness on me miniature peoples' conjoined shadows who look to have been pricked by a group of porcupines. If they weren't as close to me, nerved to touch my body, my impression from their movement and size would be they're spiders. They mimic them awfully well plodding up my body like it's a hill.

More shadows appear approaching me rapidly. The shadows that emerge from this thick darkness have an increased pitch-black hue. There's an essence of conflict to the sweeping darkness emphasized in them. So dark that they outgrow this chilling void of a backdrop. In contrast to their illustrious darkness that demands a person feel threatened, there's a glowing rainbow outlining their tiny warped bodies in the scene of this deep abyss. What could be my devious brain's trickery. They revolve by my side onto every patch of exposed skin on my body and I can feel them carrying me farther and farther away from the spot in which I'd just experienced my last breath. Their spikes can't pierce my skin.

I then stop fighting it. Whatever it is, these dark shadows with lurid tracings won't strain in taking me. Their handle on me has sapped me of energy and life. I feel like a prisoner chained by supernatural beings who are stronger than I. My limbic system and Broca's area have shut down their services. My occipital lobe follows the two parts of my brain responsible for memory and speech in completely abandoning me. They've packed their bags and left no trace in the limbo of this sordid space.

I'm not certain of who I am anymore. Just that I'm no longer on earth but a realm without a heaven or hell. Without a creator. A place separate from God; forgotten by him. A notion of utter desertion overpowers.

It's cold here. So cold that I can swear fog is coming out of my numb lips. These sheets of freezing shadows wrap me scrupulously like a Christmas present for a snug fit. I think of swimming in deep waters. But in a differing way I bet a fish feels when it jumps out of water and onboard a boat. A fish aims to get back in the water for survival. I want to drown assuring my own termination. Given the circumstance, I might as well be out of breath.

My time's up and the hourglass has spared its last grain of sand to keep me here. Aware but immobile. I feel as if it's these shadows' only job to finish what'd been started by the gun shot. To take me off to my final destination. Have I made it, or did I fail at life's game? I'm about to find out regardless and that is the truth of the matter.

Redemption in life is no longer an option. Deep in me I know I'm not ready to go. Something's missing that I still haven't achieved in this lifetime. Without this unspecified goal I'm incomplete. My destiny all in all has led me down a bitter road to nothingness. I've fallen into a pit of misery. Misery that carries with it the heavy burden of failure. Pushing down onto me and submerging me with shadows to get to nowhere.

But when will this nowhere become somewhere? The suspense is followed by alarm and fear overcomes my body. Just the idea that I could be spending an everlasting time with these shadows is cruel and disturbing.

As fast as the fear comes it goes. I can see again. The sound of a rattle has me shook. A rattlesnake, I imagine is here. I'm convinced it's come to help; curiously as a snake has never helped me before. My face is stripped from the shadows on account of the sound. The cracking whirring draws nearer. I'm liberated from the rest of the shadows in one fluid motion.

The shadows heave as I pant. They're a cow and this camouflaged presence turning out sound is a tornado. The shadows linger above me in a bizarre vat of foaming and seething liquid. In a heartbeat they're gone. They've vanished from this place they've brought me, bagging with them that rattle.

I'm set free, faced in front of a glaring light that shines from a far distance at the end of a steep rising hallway. A gloomy hall possessing many skewed rustic weathered wood doors. Only one of those doors straight-ahead at the end of the hall is open with a white light glistening in through the passageway.

Across the charcoal wood floor, this white light totes a pattern created by light reflecting off water. Something's disturbed the surface beyond that final door to get the water circulating. The light bouncing off it constructs these ghostly webs where I stand. Everything else is colorless. Gray without life or any knowledge of it.

The Old World doors are deteriorating. A result of abandonment has subjugated this hall to Mother Nature. I can't tell if the walls are made of paper or just look weak enough to tear. Conceivably caused by untended water damage. I raise my hand and swipe it over my eyes as I recurrently did when

I was a child. Whenever I was in a bad dream and wanted to wake up, the swiping of my hand across my eyes would get me out. It doesn't work this time around.

I'm in a building. Familiar but altogether unrecognizable. I cast a brief look behind me but there's complete darkness and another numbing sensation ensues over my body. I decide to go on and take a step forward on the ramp. One foot begins to flag before the other as I timidly walk away from darkness, hearing the wooden floors creak beneath my bare feet. I'm completely naked.

My skin is midnight black, almost indistinguishable from the dark color of the shadows. Still, I'm unexplainably vibrant giving off a whale of wavelengths from the visible spectrum of light. I'm effulgent. I don't shy away from it but just seek the exit with the new sense that my body is power. Be that as it may, I do feel like I'm being watched, and cold eyes are fixed on me. Something tells me I'm not meant to be here at all.

With every step the floor seems to creak harder underlining the decades this building has aged. Looking on about as I walk on, I notice next to the series of oblique doors amongst the walls there're markings. Illegible hieroglyphics slither on the tattered paper walls. Fluid and unpredictable, each character seems to writhe independently, as if possessed by a sentient force.

The writings and symbols sprawled across the wall appear to morph incessantly. What's happening here isn't drug related. It's drug fixated. This zone in between life and death doesn't make any sense. I can't sort it out for a second without feeling like I'm on a bad trip.

By the time I take my seventh step I reach out to open the first door to my right. The doors in this building open outward. I stand there staring at it. Mesmerized to say the least. If I wasn't already moved by the active drawings on the walls or my body emitting rainbow light, this sure does the trick. All I can see is stars floating in space but as I follow the stars with my eyes it only leads me into a never-ending spiral.

I wonder if this is what a subjective eternity looks like. An open door with an ongoing tunnel of stars, boundless and bright, all caped together in a timeless expanse, encircling me as my sight's guided through that which swallows all sense of my being. The weight of infinity presses down upon me, suffocating and consuming the last of my sanity, as I confront the terrifying realization of my own insignificance in the face of pure oblivion. It gives me a headache, so I keep on walking yet the open door at the end of the hall isn't getting any closer. When I finally begin to run toward the light, the door from whence it comes begins to close. As it does another opens to my left.

Startled by the unprecedented opening of the second door with no one there to open it, I stop in my tracks and listen. Out comes the voice of someone I once knew and I get a taste of melancholy. Perhaps my father or a coach. It spoke, "Just one more time son, you'll get the hang of it."

There's nothing past the door but a gray brick wall yet if I trusted that sound alone, I would've fallen for the deception that someone was on the other side of that brick wall. I pass this door checking for alternative exits and three more open with other voices slipping into the hall as I rush to get to my destination being that last door. They all have brick walls behind them and are spaced out sufficiently from one another. I can't make out what they're saying for I'm rushing right past them. I slow down at the sixth gateway.

A rusty metal door, heavy with ornate, wrought iron coils twisted like Celtic serpentine ropes. From the previous three doors that burst open came what only sounded like grunting and mumbles. The peculiar thing about this metal door is it's been bolted shut. Three hasps run down its center secured with vintage brass padlocks. There's a peep hole positioned at its far upper right-hand corner. Not where I'd expect a peep hole to be. I don't have time to speculate why. The door with the light is closing. The only words I make out with the interruption of a bang in between each as I pass it are,

"Stay." The first bang is inconspicuous.

"Koa." The second bang is tolerable.

"Help!" The third is desperate.

"Brother!" The fourth—unbearable. The last one damaged my eardrums.

The voice was inviting but the metal door was not. Something told me as I passed it that it could be dangerous to get close.

The seventh door opens. Just when I start picking up the pace, again, I get distracted. This voice is unlike the rest. It isn't human. A weak barking comes from behind the brick wall and a crying puppy is what I make out from the sound.

The indecipherable glyphs on the walls aside it slide onto the brick making it the only brick wall with markings. The unsettling script comes together, positioning itself in a systematic way. It spells out, 'Kill Tommy.' A barefaced command.

Impressed at the center of the brick wall is a child's handprint with luminescent white arrows pointing in the direction of the light. The arrows slide from the brick wall onto the paper walls and extend far out like shooting stars. I get the irrepressible sensation to touch. My hand glides through an arrow onto the brick. A smattering of the brick wall's matter gets on my fingers.

It's clay.

The brick is damp. I feel it out, letting it mold itself into the contours of my fingerprints. Its gray color withdraws before my eyes exchanging itself for an earthy yellow-brown. The color, it transpired, had been raw sienna.

I'm not stopping.

Sprinting past the doors, the hall expands tenfold and what were seven doors become hundreds with thousands of voices springing out from every direction. They're screaming at me, and I can't make sense of it all. It's like the screeching white noise of a broken radio growing louder than my brain can handle and process all together.

My gaping footsteps only add to this throbbing maelstrom of a headache, eclipsing all coherent thought. The stomping of my feet is exaggerated, possessed with an unbridled energy, meeting the ground with an amplified vigor. The floors respond with uneasy whispers of frail wood protesting under duress, with every few stomps manifesting in a loud symphony of snapping sounds that bounce off the walls mixed in with the indecipherable cries of these grieving voices. Despite the noise, one voice I can hear above all the rest. It's clear and reassuring.

It comes from the final door that immediately seems like a haven from this cursed place. It's like the voice of an old friend.

"Koa, a wave! Catch this one with me bra!"

The coming of that voice prompts a sudden change in equilibrium. It's so simple to defy human strength. I start breaking through the floorboards, punching in holes and yanking wood planks to make room for my hands and feet. The rising slope of this hall is no longer at an angle I can run on. It rises to the point of a ninety-degree angle and I'm forced to start climbing. I climb till a serious of deafening detonations push pause on the piercing cries from the doors.

The building I'm in starts to rumble. I look down as I've one hand and foot holding me up from the support of two holes I've punched through the wooden floor. The right side of my body is without any support leaving my other limbs to dangle in midair. A warm-beige titan hand, human in appearance from the wrinkles on its knuckles to the healthy fingernails on its ends, rises towards me. Following the hand is the reveal and enormity of the rest of its forearm.

What is that thing?! A human that size. That's Impossible!

I look on in horror. The thought sets in that at the end of that forearm, colossal in scale to me, is a giant. This fear propels me to the top. I punch and spring myself the rest of the way up.

Scared that I won't make it in the last ten yards I risk my life. I see the opportunity a floorboard presents by sticking out. I make a jump to reach that vital ledge and do the impossible—reach it. Holding myself onto the ledge with one hand for dear life, I get a quick glance at the floorboards around me. Amid pressure, my thoughts scatter, witnessing the haunting scratches of fingernails etched across the floorboards. Initially recoiling from the grisly scene, it grips my imagination, grappling with sinister scenarios.

Who or what left these harrowing marks? Was it a desperate struggle, a plea for escape, or something more malevolent?

It's a split second from the risky jump I made to the make-believe vision I have of someone's past struggle. Reckless in my climb, I lost sight of an opening door when I reached the ledge. It swings open from above me and smashes on my head. The fear that I wouldn't make it to the white light is my self-fulfilling prophecy.

I drop down twice the length I had left to climb when I made the dangerous jump.

I've dug my own grave in this realm.

I can feel a raw breeze beyond that final door and hear waves emerging with heavy waters.

Here's my last chance.

I return to the climb as a forlorn attempt to escape. The deafening thud of my heart reverberates through my chest, an ominous drumbeat syncing with the rising tide of desperation. I feel the colossal entity, a behemoth of dread, extending its colossal appendage, reaching towards me with an insatiable hunger. Every handhold upon the floorboards I rip through is a fleeting refuge.

    The next critical moments to the top are a flash. I make one giant leap to grab that last door right before the close. I grab onto the knob and fling the door open. The door breaks from its hinges and falls into the clench of the giant. It painlessly destroys the door turning its hand into a fist. Into the light I pull myself, shattering into an imponderable amount of inky particles that all merge together with remarkable precision in an area I'm more than comfortable with—the ocean.

Chapter 9

For reasons I cannot fathom I've always been intrigued by the mere sight of a wave. The effortless perfection of a wave gives me a sense of freedom, love, and happiness. That's why when I heard the sound of bubbles fizzing ever so quietly become an elongated tube of water, rolling intensely towards that final door, I couldn't wait to enter that world. I find myself reborn, nestled in a sanctuary of solace.

I behold the ocean before me in what still feels like a dream. I remember this. This is the day I...

Miraculously my memory starts returning. A glass of whiskey I can slug straight back would calm me right about now. My entire life is rebuilt within my head like a set of Lego blocks. Each memory stacking upon the former, flashing before my eyes with no longing for understanding the puzzling dimension I hardly escaped.

When you die your life's said to flash before your eyes. I suppose that's what's happening with me now. Yet somehow, I've become entwined in the netting of this singular moment. "Relax," I tell myself, splashing some water onto my face and cleansing my head of such ridiculous ideas. "I'm alive?"

I take a deep breath and then quirk my head to each side cracking my neck joints. I take notice of my surroundings, sitting on my hollow wooden Ubermotion surfboard. All wooden Ubermotion surfboards are made from reclaimed wood. This one in particular I believe was carved from a redwood hot tub. I'm sporting highlighter yellow board shorts that reach just an inch above the knee. My skin is no longer the pigment of a dusky fluid ink.

I can't help thinking that I might be in denial of what just went down. All of it, such as how I arrived here in the first place. After getting shot on the balcony and before pulling myself up through a door to get here is all a blur. That Lego piece is still missing but I know it's somewhere at the bottom of my memory. Under the rubble of a nuked city, locked within one of many coffers. Somewhere but it's surely there. I verily try to remember but nothing. I must find it.

This is the day I went surfing with my brother and some friends. It's about one week prior to my sister's wedding. Exactly five days before my death at the hands of an impenitent heart.

Here I sit on my surfboard, out in the ocean looking out at the western horizon as the sun begins to set. I think to myself whether this is real. Not the view but the moment of pure serenity. Lost within a moment in time, I look down upon the water that lay before me in the form of a divine all-seeing mirror, grasping my image among its surface. I reach out touching the reflection of my face upon the ocean with a single finger and the still water slowly begins to ripple into a series of expanding rings that's just impacted the image of me into the distorted reality of a bygone.

Is it possible that this whole life I've lived, a life that was mine to create, is at its end? I wonder if there're any similarities between my life and that of my ancestors. Looking back in time I often sought to understand who I am but now, staring at the image before me as it comes back into a poetic vantage point on this clear ocean skin, I see not who I was but instead I see a lifestyle with character. An image undeniable of a good vibe and seldom overcome by the anger and hate around which the people of this earth have assembled.

In the latest years of my life, I never once thought that living could be so simple. Being that for the last few years I was a con in a game of murder and war. No such bloodbath have I ever dealt with like Erik's experience in Iraq yet when I say murder and war, I'm referring to an inner struggle in which I'm at war with who I am. Killing off the parts of me I dislike and deem as bad. That part of me where I'm greedy, where I'm tempted, where I lie. An evil side that time and time again I believe every human must deal with and face. An evil side that I've conned myself into defaulting to when I'm weak in the mind.

Confronting that side of me is very conflicting because it's easier to get tangled in what the world is doing than with what my heart is telling me. I've lived in this world of war for so long that I figure I'm blessed to no longer be a part of it. I've no need to be perfect.

Being seventeen has had its company to grow and learn but I never let my age stop me. If I'm honest with myself, I was afforded whatever it is I desired because of my wealth. It's important for me that I live for every single breath I take and for every strife I face along the way. I learned at a young age that life can come with its own set of broken hearts and complications. Especially when you're exposed to people who just want to take from you and dispose of all you hold dear. Those are the people I try to keep from my life, cautious not to drink of their poison.

The cream archetype of these people is Luciana Barenclave. Our maid for ten years and reputed lover of my father, Daniel Califf, in the scandalous newspapers of my childhood. She had conceptualized a thought from the very beginning of her work in our home that she could turn her story into a rags to riches tale. In spite of their bruited romance, my father never put a ring on her finger. I'd got used to her youthfulness with her petite figure, auburn angled bob, and French maid outfit knowing her my whole life.

She'd begun working for the Califfs at the not so tender age of twenty-four when I was but a one-year-old. The French maid dress was a self-evident and ridiculous attempt on her part to seduce my father. Though her ostentatious caring and motherly nature, apart from looking like a slut when my father was around, would end the minute he died at the age of forty-three. Making her the only adult in a legal position to care for his three kids.

Three years later, when my sister turned eighteen, her decade reign as a stereotypical stepmother in fairytales was over. Luciana disappeared and the lengthy saga to secure the rights over our family's assets reached its conclusive end. Foreseeable, the year she packed her bags and ran away, she was convicted of first-degree murder in the death of Daniel Califf.

I forgave her for all those years of pain, but I can't be happy in that act of forgiveness because while she may be gone, I still haven't forgotten her. I admit that while the world has had its own faults, I too have had mine and I know...

It's a crooked path to heaven but I think I've made my peace with the person I've become. I may not consider myself a part of civilization but sitting here on my surfboard, just outside the city and out on open waters where no buildings are in sight back on shore and only black sand caresses the land, I come to feel sorry for those who are lost in the millions as a part of the wretched civilization our species has evolved into. A great mass of people who just can't see or progress from who they've become.

I take a moment to look up at the sky thinking about how close yet how far heaven really is. There in plain sight is the most beautiful rainbow I've ever encountered. It's layered with the most radical splash of bright colors. Each one bleeding into the next due to the saltwater in my eyes. Red, orange, yellow, green, blue, indigo, and violet lie upon one another. Above it is another rainbow. I'd never seen a double rainbow till this day, but it's magnificent and not only does it make me feel like flying but it makes me feel just that much closer to heaven and that much farther from earth.

Amazing what nature can accomplish, painting such a masterpiece on a blue-green velvet sky. I guess that's the outcome of it all after a couple hours of the heavens crying. This was one of the best surfing days I'd ever experienced that reliving it once more is no worry at all but a gift I've been granted and must cherish as one.

Earlier this day, on the spring of May 24, 2012, it'd been raining quite hard, and the waves were being harsh on my most modest attempts to tame them and ride them off to shore. However, I didn't grow weary of the powerful ocean because right there and then after catching my first wave that day, I formed a connection. A bond linking me to these waters. Something I couldn't explain but just grasped in the moment. The bond was unbreakable. The proof lies in consistently seizing every wave that had arisen, standing in my way and knowing them to be mine to conquer since their inception. I could swim out and catch a wave with my eyes sealed and not be scared to fall off my board because I was at balance with the water.

Truth be told is that I've felt this internal connection to the ocean ever since I was a little tyke. When I was four my dad sent me adrift on some three-foot waves with my newly begat orange-yellow octopus surfboard that'd never been ridden. While it took some time to stand up and learn how to ride the waves, I came to relish the sport for what it was. By that age my dad had already carved me four surfboards out of redwood and cedar. Those times were the best of my childhood. Just me, my dad, and the open ocean. I didn't actually catch and ride my first wave till I was seven, but bodyboarding is what I stuck with in my earlier years of learning the sport.

It became a habit of mine and since my dad passed away it's something I've always carried with me as fond memories. Looking back on it, I figure that everything happens for a reason and it's ok to move forward when life gets you down because I know one day I'll be with him, surfing the clouds of heaven with him right by my side. Maybe the day has come where I'll see him again.

The second door that opened. That first voice I heard. It was my dad. I remember now. He was saying I'd get the hang of it when teaching me how to surf. I believe I was five at the time.

I remember this day perfectly before arriving at this destination, looking up at the double rainbow. It was a tremendously challenging surf session I'd went through on this day. There I'd stayed catching one wave after the other as the rain came pouring in copious amounts. The clouds spit lightening out into the private grounds from which my brother, Kosta, stood and watched afar.

We arrived in Costa Rica before sunrise and broke into this private beach to get away from all the chaos back home. All the wedding preparations kept Jade in a permanent fit over everything. The wedding planner was fired just a week earlier as she'd proven useless. We figured we'd be deader the later we went back. The more time Jade had to soak in the thought her brothers had abandoned her, the greater the scolding we'd get. We were supposed to be sending out last-minute invitations to political bloggers and we hadn't due to brotherly laziness.

I, selfishly uncaring, wanted to enjoy four days freedom surfing. Hurricane Raziel wouldn't arrive in Florida till Sunday afternoon, so the ocean was dry of waves in that part of the world. Malia would bring the big news of our spontaneous trip to Jade. Come what may of her initial reaction, I could care less the outcome. Jade perpetually forgives us for our defiance for she loves us indefinitely.

I could hear my brother's voice echo through the strength of the wind, yelling loudly, urging hard for me to come ashore. He looked like a jumping springtail from where I was. Moving up and down, waving his arms and hands erratically to catch my attention. I could go back, I thought. But that'd be no fun. Besides there's no worries when it comes to a pro handling a little danger. I waved back at him, feigning a smile and acting as if I didn't have a clue at what he was hinting at.

The thrust of the ocean had a hold of me forcing my board and I to gyrate through the water in a series of twists and turns. The motion discombobulated my body. What looked to me like a jumping springtail before was now a total of seven springtails, all jumping, trying to snatch my attention. Still, I fought having little sense of coordination. I continued to paddle my arms in a swift but strong circular motion. I conquered the storm by overcoming what'd become its waters and launched myself in every direction a wave would push me.

I was able to glide atop a wave and pull back to prepare for the next one. After four hours of this routine, the rain came to a halt and the sun was roused from a deep sleep by the slap of God's open palm, out of the gray mass in the sky, giving off a lucid view of that wondrous double rainbow I've been staring at now for the past five minutes.

In the past, that storm was what had brought me to where I am now. Out here, about forty yards from land waiting patiently for the next wave to come into my reach. I realize I'll have to go soon. This memory of mine that I'm inexplicably reliving isn't real.

It can't possibly be real. Can it?

It's almost dark anyhow. Every world that's not tidally locked has a finite rotation before day's end.

The light warm heat of the setting sun compresses against my skin. I soak up the last bit of fresh air before night begins to approach, ending my day here at what I consider my second home. I look onto the beach to reassure myself that Kosta's still there. I laugh giving him a thumbs up as I already know he'd been worried, tensely watching me ride these waves the whole time.

I take on the smell of the salty ocean breeze with a gluttonous pride for all things clean before deciding to head back. The afternoon here at Playa Hermosa had been one of the nicest I'd experienced in my whole life. But why did that door lead me to today specifically?

I take my days as a blessing, and I never once thought I'd have another day to live life after death. That is if death has already found me. Maybe I was brought here because I'm meant to do something but right now my muscles are taking on the exact same strain I'd felt on this day after being at the beach since eight A.M. I'm beat. I want a hot shower and a good sleep.

"Koa, a wave! Catch this one with me bra!"

That voice. The same voice coming from that last door I'd pushed my way through spoke again with the same mollifying words it had before. I'm caught off guard by the sound of my friend calling my name.

The universal thoughts of the departed are interrupted by my best friend who I'd forgotten had been with me on this day, right by my side since this morning. Through the storm too. Lucas Farnham is just ten feet away from me in fuchsia pink boardies, lying flat on his white short board designed for down the line speed. He calls out for me to hop on the next wave.

Sometimes when I surf, I build a mental shield and get lost within my thoughts, forgetting the people near me. I'd like to think of myself as being the only person in the ocean when I surf even though that's rarely the case. I smile not thinking about the recollection of events that's led me here in which I've been dozing off with for the past few minutes. I decide to see how long this memory of mine will last and I'll appreciate the moment for every second I've left of it.

I start paddling on my surfboard towards the beach aiming to catch my final wave for the day and across from me is Lucas going at it, paddling hard for the same wave. When the wave first hits us, we both look to one another and nod as a sign that it's time to stand up. Keeping my balance, I grab the edges of my surfboard as I warily stand up and lean forward. Meanwhile, Lucas simply jumps onto his board and manages to catch the wave with me.

Bro along my side. My hands reaching out into the open air, he makes it so his arms are spread wide enough to reach mine. We clap each other's hands and hold onto one another by the forearm till the wave splits and shapes itself into a barrel. Inside the barrel of tunneling water, I bend my knees and keep steady exiting the wave. Behind me is Lucas with concentrated, saturnine medium-brown eyes staring out beyond the shore, into the abyss of the crabs that scurry inside. His short chestnut brown hair with blond streaks pushed back is evidence no matter which way the hairs on his head fall, the outcome is always as though intended by the most meticulous of studio photographers.

Stopping myself from riding the wave is going to be a difficult task. Lucas is taken by the wave onto the beach and I'm turbo-boosted in the direction of a natural rock barrier. Looking at the road ahead of me I maneuver my surfboard to the right, away from the rocks. As the wave begins to break, I start losing my balance. Reaching land, I see and hear my buddy Ramze Daji shouting, "Surf's up!"

I quickly spring off my surfboard and fall into the water before hitting the shore. Ramze reaches out for my hand and lugs me onto the beach. He's wearing his wonted board shorts that have a graphic print of lava oozing over the glassy black rock obsidian. Bound to his left wrist is a triple tier bracelet made up of spherical black volcanic rocks.

Ramze is a barrel-chested, bull-necked, tall and tan champagne blond with chin-length curly hair and deeply eloquent chocolate brown eyes. His full, thick, and ducktail caramel blond beard give the impression of an avant-garde homeless man; decidedly urban, gritty, and at times sophisticated.

His back is as wide as a barn door and the sinuous contours of his back muscles arch gracefully, resembling the poised stance of a scorpion ready to strike. His shoulders are boulders and his biceps—small mountains. It takes three of my quads to make up one of his and his thick calf muscles are a famous topic on his internet blog. An entire section of his blog he dedicated to his legs and what his ex-boyfriend christened the Hebrew hammer. That section of his blog he calls for grins, 'Between My Two Tree Trunks.'

He trims only his neck and lip above the mouth. His attempts to grow a beard throughout high school had never borne fruit but after bucking through the tough times of his teen fuzz, today people could mistake him for a Scandinavian Viking.

Shortly after getting on the beach, I see Lucas in the ocean paddling back out to catch another wave, but the waves have settled and with no more waves in sight we decide to call it a day.

Chapter 10

We call out for Lucas to head back in. Kosta pulls him onto the beach, helping hoist his board as Lucas unstraps the tea green surf leash from his ankle. Each of us, but Kosta, sit at the edge of the beach. Our boards are propped up in the sand behind us. We spy the horizon. The sun begins listlessly burying itself into the earth cueing its goodbye till tomorrow's workday.

Eyes closed, hands laid out behind him supporting his back, and his legs spread out wide in front of him, Ramze whispers, "Farewell Amaterasu."

"Ahh so you're speaking to the Japanese sun goddess now. Who's next, the corn god?" Lucas blurts out being a smart aleck. His back's scrunched over his legs, pulled in close to his chest as he draws lines in the sand.

Ramze opens his right eye, looking past me in the middle to eye Lucas. "I'm surprised you even know who either of the two are. Although now that you mention it, the Mayan maize god does fit my current focus on female deities. I've already studied the Aztec maize god, Centeotl." Ramze crosses his arms against his chest and plonks his back on the sand.

"Wait. You're telling me there's actually a god of corn?" Lucas snorts with laughter.

"The Mayans believed man himself was made from maize dough. Not so funny when compared to Allah creating man from clay and water. Buddhism teaches humans were once continuing beings shining in their own light who consumed of the earth and became the studs I see now." Ramze shifts to his side, facing me. With his right hand supporting his head, he ogles over Lucas in a waggish comportment. More or less, something expected of a playful gay prince. A warm smile and a light of wisdom in his dark brown eyes mince his tease. What's behind it is a show of real passion for his scholarship in religion.

"This folklore you study, have you adopted it or is polytheism custom in your family?" Kosta begs the question rudely whilst doing a firm handstand to the left of Ramze.

Ramze reverts his attention back to the ocean avoiding eye contact with Kosta; his upper eyelids raised in a stare. "I am human, so it follows I am prone to believe anything so long as it fits into my worldview; be it that it hasn't already had a part in shaping my worldview when I was younger and more impressionable. But if you must know my religion, I'm a Jew who just so happens to be like you—human. Don't forget the human part. We often do as humans."

"No shit you're human. Kosta's simply curious about your cultural heritage but what does any of that matter? Let the man identify with what he wants or nothing at all," I intervene, coming off rather coarse.

"Thanks, I guess, but I can defend myself Koa," Ramze lets know.

Lucas assures Ramze he's pulling his leg. He thinks it's cool Ramze is interested in religions besides his own and even suggests he study theology in college. He adds, "Although you should definitely maintain a career as an online personal trainer and pursue something along the lines of health and fitness." Lucas takes a sip of water from his milk carton inspired water bottle. "You know while some gods may seem ridiculous to me now, I admit that in time, my god might seem ridiculous to the future."

Kosta restores his feet to the surface with a look of lost faith. As he does, he neglects the dull, diminutive disc with patches of greenish-blue mold that whisks from his pocket and plops on the sand. "And what do you suggest to those who feel lost...say someone who thinks a god cannot suffice them?"

Ramze pauses, sighing in question of what to say next. "I'd say to them, if ever you feel lost or hopeless, think of what's important in your life. Could be a familial bond you have with someone, a pet, a memory or even a place. I find a person works best because we relate most to them. I'm a believer but what believer doesn't have doubts? In my time of need, I imagine my someone. I remember them at their happiest which curiously enough, was the first time I shared a Camarosa strawberry. So sweet was the taste, it ripened into a French kiss. And god, there's little more I love in this world than French kissing. Let the floodgates of joy from this, whatever special junk you choose to pull from a hat, open to drown you in its light," Ramze says smiling benignly.

"Hope can be derived from the weakest of places. The weakest place I've found is humanity's collective mind. What we fail to see is it consistently works overtime to deny itself the opportunity to approach things from a different angle." Ramze sighs again and turns his head, assuring he makes eye contact with every one of us, including the white crab who'd scurried alongside Lucas and attempted to blend into the attentive audience.

"Take this harmless example as a first step to stray from the masses when interpreting things not outlined outright. Some scholars believe the Tree of Knowledge in Abrahamic religions to be no tree but a vine. And its arcane forbidden fruit, depicted as an apple in almost all popular works of art after the 12th century, could really be any fruit that grows from a tree, vine, or something bearing the semblance of such. I'd like to imagine the fatal effects Adam and Eve incurred came from biting a strawberry. After all, what is more delectable than a strawberry? I can't fathom risking the damnation of humanity for any other taste in this world."

Sitting with the imposed thought of a strawberry vine, all but I avert their eyes to the dimming sun. I remain still, scrutinizing what fell out of Kosta's olive green swim trunks, trying to decipher what garbage he's collected this trip. Always being one to bring cheap mementos home from abroad. This fleeting sense of intrigue dies at sea. In part, due to the item's aura of decay and neglect leaving me unsettled.

Amaterasu is the Japanese sun goddess Ramze's currently studying the history of. Ramze has long had an affair with world religions, studying into various ones and taking with him life lessons from each. It's an experience he says that's fulfilling in a way only an open-minded person could understand. He's told me before that if you're predisposed to think a certain way it's hard to fully submerge oneself, without bias, into the topic of world religions.

His most recent focus are deities personified as women. It isn't a surprise to those who know him. Ramze studies a lot of things people wouldn't guess by examining him the first time around. The methods he uses to understand life can seem weird, but it is who he is. He finds peace in exploring customs unlike his own and feeding into what other cultures ascertain is the truth. I take it that if he's ferreting for the meaning of life, he's in the right direction.

"People just need to learn to read," Lucas says shrewdly.

"One must have the desire to learn in the Western Hemisphere or be forced to settle with what one denomination of Christianity has to offer. A small fraction of the world population," Ramze puts in his two cents.

"The Catholic Church has 1.2 billion people. That's not a small fraction by any means," Lucas defends his faith, finding comfort in numbers.

"By the means of time, I disagree. Compared to the 108 billion that've lived and died on this earth, fractured between the 4,200 religions and those lost that've existed on earth," Ramze gets up and repeats himself, "I disagree."

Lucas leisurely stands up next, reaching for the sky and then placing his fists on his back as he moves his hips forward. His gaze quickly fixates on the object Kosta had dropped. "Check this out!" He says enlivened, cupping the item over a small pile of sand in his hand. "It's some old coin with a mermaid. Nice tatas." He twists his wrist as he lets the sand spill through the gaps in between his fingers. A rich hue of copper gleams amidst the coin's greenish discoloration.

Kosta shoots up to retrieve it, angrily commanding Lucas to give it here. Kosta's request fuels Lucas to do the opposite. Kosta's eyes follow the coin's trajectory as it's tossed and passed among the group. Laughter and excitement reverberate through the air with our eagerness to keep it from Kosta only growing with his worry and concern. His pleas, despite their sense of urgency, become echoes bouncing off unresponsive knuckleheads. Alas, I end the childish game as I unintentionally crush the coin into dust in my hand.

Realizing the situation, I instantly apologize, attempting to squander the uncontrollable wave of laughter from the group. Kosta gives an indifferent shrug, clenching his fists and tightening his jaw. A faint smile forms upon his lips which only a brother knows belies a storm raging within. He gives a long sigh, loosens his tense body, and pretends to be ok with the whole situation. "Probably wasn't worth much anyhow," he says, his voice teetering between a sense of unease and frustration. He tries to match the joyous playfulness in the atmosphere by challenging us to a race back to the truck.

Lucas and I race him back to Ramze's busted up yellow pickup truck. A rust bucket with faded paint and trim in peculiar spots, bathed in the light of sunset. Dents cake the hood like broad craters overlay the Arizona desert. Its huge tires that howl when on move are passing flurries; most akin to the scouring of wind-borne sand just before maturing into a threatening cloud of dust. We put our surfboards in the back of the pickup truck. Once Ramze caught up, I whipped him with a towel repeatedly to draw all the sand from his back. I will one last sigh to my beautiful home.

"Hopefully I'll see you tomorrow sunshine." I wave the skies a kiss goodbye. Although not likely. Depression jabs me in the gut. Good things never last in this world. They fade away as we age which is why I can be content with the idea of being dead. In a position where age is unreal. The whole talk while we were sitting down got me to question, if I'm dead, why aren't I in heaven right now?

We all get in the car. Ramze gets the whole back seat to himself because of his leg. Lucas and I sit up front on our jungle print beach towels. Kosta takes to the open cargo bed with all our surfboards.

Lucas, in the driver seat, turns to me with a dumbstruck stare. He pauses for a second. "Phew that was a good one dude. Almost lost that last wave bro. Should've seen it coming from a mile away. What were you thinking about in that big head of yours?" he asks, turning his attention to the front view of the pickup truck and turning on the vehicle.

I too pause for a second. There's an even tenor of transcendental life disrupted by the mare's nest of rebirth. A true sense of déjà vu. As the pickup truck starts moving and we get on the road, I respond. "I was thinking I love life man," I say laughing.

It's ironic because I'm dead. That's why I laughed at my own comment which, in counter perspective, no one could understand. This outer worldly experience I'm feeling. Though I'm still confused as to just what my purpose in being here right now is. Surreal how I can be a visible ghost. Something that contradicts itself because ghosts aren't visible in any shape or form. No one notices them. Unless I'm in a haunting or a movie. I am whatever it is I am. A spirit walking among the living.

"You two up for tomorrow?" Ramze asks placing his hands behind his head, flexing his alpine biceps while lying steady straight across the back seat.

Lucas and I look to one another and give each other a dense stare. "Well duh?" we say in tempo.

"We didn't fly three hours from home last night, on the red-eye, to surf one spot," Lucas comments, staring at himself in the rearview mirror and plowing into his teeth with his fingernail.

Words of reason sneak into the conversation when Kosta comments from the cargo bed through the open window in the back. With his head nestled under a green fleece throw blanket he states that we nearly got ourselves killed in confining in me. He's being overdramatic. It was my idea to go against the law and sneak onto the closed beach. It'd be used as the location for a celebrity's wedding the following day. The only reason it was private for the day. Officials didn't want any tourists trashing the unsullied beach a day prior. The storm was just an added layer of concern. Lucky for us we managed to do it.

"Sure, we'll probably deal with it when Jade confronts us on why we left home, but the fact is we did it which means we can do it again," I suggest.

"If you're prepared to face Jade's fury that's your prerogative. By the bye, tomorrow I'm driving my Lucy," Ramze notes.

Lucy's the name Ramze has for his pickup truck yet since the incident he hasn't been able to drive Lucy. The three of us who can drive laugh and Lucas utters a sarcastic comment. "With that leg bra, you can stomp a crater in the earth and launch yourself to the beach."

We'd go through this all day and every day from here on out. Till his leg gets better we're not letting him do any leg work, including him putting strain on his leg by way of his foot, which pressing the gas pedal on Lucy would inevitably fall under. Ramze looks miserable as I turn partway to the back seat leaning my left shoulder against the passenger seat. He tells me he misses driving along the sunset and surfing with us. His whole body turns to face the back seat.

"Don't be upset man. Look out the window. You're missing all this attractive scenery," I say cozily, trying to get him to take his mind off his injury.

"I can't. I get car sick staring out into the uneven mountain range. This morning we were driving up for so long. I almost vomited when we were passing that ranch up in the mountains and saw what appeared to be cows walking straight up toward the sky. At that point gravity was irrelevant."

"You get car sick because you play your stupid videogames in the back seat," I tell him remembering I'd warned him before.

A small white light flashes from the back seat. The epic theme music of a retro adventure videogame starts playing. The sound of button pressing simultaneously follows the sounds of five exaggerated cartoonish action moves: Bam,

Yoink, Thwip, Wham, Kersplat! It's Ramze's handheld compact game system intended for kids.

"Really Ramze," Kosta says unamused.

From the back seat, a couple of clicking sounds follow our weighing in till the device is almost wholly mute.

"That's true. Staring into a computer screen while you're in a moving vehicle will make you sick," Lucas drawls, agreeing with me.

I plug my phone, which was in the pickup truck's glove compartment, to the auxiliary cord in the vehicle and play my Bob Marley playlist, knowing that his words will put Ramze in a good mood.

I can't quite feel the pain Ramze is going through. The thrill you get from surfing...it's not something the living can cope without. If ever I couldn't surf, I'd go mad. They'd have to put me in a mental asylum or slap on me a virtual reality helmet so I could surf. But then again while not being able to surf is my only fear, I stand by what Bob Marley said, 'My fear is my only courage.'

Stupid that out of everything this world musters to challenge me that's my only fear. Man, I love that stoner/musician/legend.

I recline my seat after putting on my favorite song of his—'War.' The inspirational lyrics Bob Marley derived from the words of early 60's Ethiopian Emperor Haile Selassie I. The song is a rallying cry. One for change in the brutishness of regimes across Africa. I apply the value of the song to everywhere there's war.

ALBERTO BONILLA

I take off my sandals as Joshua had when the Lord warned him, he was standing on holy ground. I leisurely roll down my window. I put my right hand behind my head and lay my left elbow on Lucas' shoulder. Everyone's shirtless in this pickup truck hoping that the cool mountain winds will dry us off. We drive off into the night heading towards unsung mountains for our next location on the map of light.

I stick my bare feet out the window before gently floating for miles on end, like a dandelion's tidy sum of plumed seeds, into unconsciousness and falling asleep.

Chapter 11

Lucas Farnham's a true friend. Since freshman year, this friend has never let me down. He shares my passion for surfing—the only sport we love more than Hawaiian pizza. He's become a part of my family, breaking down trust barriers I'd never known existed within me.

We met in internal suspension after some trouble we'd both gotten into back in the day at Pelican Island Econgregation. Otherwise known as PIE. A high school stationed inside of the cruise ship Mia Toucan. The white ship is anchored nine months out of the year at Port Canaveral. Thinking of school as my workplace made the hour-long commute by train a smidge more bearable. The lone peppy colors on the ship's exterior are concentrated in the upper deck, painted in nature's artistry of a toucan's bill. Orange railings, aqua floors, chartreuse steps and seating arrangements, and aggie maroon tables and bar tops.

The small lake the ship oversees back on shore and the school's psychoneurotic obsession with shoving economics into every subject, despite a mean fit in almost every case but mathematics, is how the school got its name—Pelican Island Econgregation. The nameless lake is inhabited by pelicans. Mischievous birds that'd wing their way in and out of school grounds whenever they felt like attacking the students. The island part of the name comes from the idea that the high school itself is a metaphorical island, not touching land and thereby a getaway from the world into the quieting but educational environment of an academy afloat.

To enter the high school, a student must walk through an orange tent that bears an angelic glow during daytime. Nicknamed 'the Tube,' the orange tent encircles a natural land bridge filled with white beach sand dredged up from the seafloor. At the fanned-out end of the Tube are two glossy red exterior staircases distanced one hundred meters apart. They're the Terminals that take students and faculty up to level five of the ship.

The private school has uniforms. Its dress code was narrow on style choices. Dark green or white polo with brown khakis. Girls were permitted scooter skirts so long as they represent the school in their colors. What once were the same colors of that murky lake.

As dark as the lake was, the sunlight would manage to penetrate its depths when viewed from the right angle on ship, revealing a pale sediment that'd cast a gentle white glow. No longer the school uniform colors, the lake now bears an acid green hue with a surreal luminosity. A ghost element that befouled the water my first year at the academy. Across the ship and back on land there'd been an investigation to pinpoint the cause of the lake turning that vibrant, almost toxic green.

No clues surfaced in my four years there from the limnologists studying it as to how it greened. With rumors circulating the cause was the illegal dumping of radioactive waste, it's no wonder why the lake was cordoned off and restricted from public access. It may also justify why the pelicans came onboard the Mia Toucan that day harrying like rabid zombies.

The school day started with a balmy breeze and ended in a torrid heat in the afternoon. People are expected to be peppery in this climate. It was during my second semester of freshman year that a flock of pelicans surrounded the outside of Terminal 1 at the ship's home port. In total, there're five entrances from the Tube onto the ship. Each but two boastfully display the school's crest on a pompous upholstery cotton blend fabric. There's no need for three banners. One's enough. They hang from the top of three closed entrances in between the two open Terminals: 1 and 5.

Terminals 2 through 4 had their individual staircases retracted. They're covered up by the school banners because those staircases are unused. Unless there's an emergency to evacuate, Terminals 2 through 4 will seldom open. Their single purpose was to serve as a base for the banners to rest on, intimidating our school's rivals—the Leafy Hyperions. The lionized hockey team of Quiet Lakes.

Quiet Lakes' mascot is an arboreous take on the Titan 'Hyperion'—son of Uranus and Gaia. Already an obscure figure in Greek mythology, Quiet "Lackey" Lakes took the idea of Hyperion and threw leaves at it. A strongly worded letter to environmentalize their mascot was sent by a prominent modern Greek philosopher—Lambidi Chopidi—who found their interpretation of Hyperion—a buff light-brown male in a long white tunic that likes to vociferously display his big hairy chest—offensive. Well, I never. Turns out, the order for change in their mascot's design was a fake outcry. Some doozy of a prank perpetrated by the high school's senior class of 2001.

The crest on PIE's dark green banners is an oblong medieval shield holding four sections with a thin white cross separating them. Each with an inventive, medieval representation of the academic criteria taught at the academy: language, math, arts, and science. Centered on the cross is our mascot—the Pelican Fatwa.

In the upper left section of each banner is a split tongue licking the Ancient Greek epic 'The Iliad of Homer' and a stack of historical logs from Juan Ponce de Leon accounting his voyage to Florida. To the right of that is a dystopian world as seen from space with the words 'Zero through Four is Five Numbers' written diagonally across it. Under the split tongue, in a section of its own, is a mermaid armed with a triton fighting a harpy—a bird-woman with sharp-edged claws. The capitalized word 'HERSTORY' rests above them. Both mythological humanoids have their breasts exposed on the banner artwork. The school thought it wise to show nudity at its entrance. High school students are mature enough to see past a female's breasts and take in the art itself for something more meaningful. Clearly.

On the fourth section of the crest, under the dystopian world as seen from space, is a cat eye with an upside-down image of the element gold at its center as shown on the periodic table of elements. If I were to flip the image vertically it'd show the letters Au and above it to the left, gold's atomic number 79. Above it to the right, gold's atomic mass: 196.97.

I happened to be on the port side of the ship that day in the classroom closest to Terminal 1. This part of the ship is home to all the sciences and pre-engineering classes. I had two classes that day. Latin in a stateroom below the upper deck and biotechnology on level five of the ship; right next to the Casino which isn't operational during the nine months the ship's docked.

Since biotech is held on level five where all Terminals are located, it's no surprise the birds would arrive outside of this area before getting beyond level five and onto balconies, the observation point, and the upper deck. Basically, any open part of the ship was fair game for the pelicans' exploration. Because the pelicans formed a blockade outside of Terminal 1, the principal was forced to put us on lockdown till the birds migrated back to their lake. Otherwise, we could endanger the birds with our presence, disturb them, and as they feed off each other's ensuing fit of pique, their first instinct to attack in self-defense would kick in.

On this very day I was put in detention after some disciplinary faults of mine from when I was encountered by the foreign exchange student Ramze Daji. I met both Lucas and Ramze during this calefaction of the school in what I call the dog days.

Lucas was as skater as they come. Long, light-brown straightened hair pushed to the left side of his face covering one eye, skinny jeans, a black t-shirt with the sleeves torn off and worn-out skate shoes that looked like he'd just trekked through the Amazon rainforest. He considered himself an outsider, spending most days in detention for not wearing his uniform.

As for Ramze, he had a rather bulky physique. The youngest body builder I'd ever met. He's a bright kid. Originally from Israel but the bulk of his life he's spent in Costa Rica. This happens to be where my brother Kosta was born hence the name he was given with the one letter difference from Costa. He and I never learned Spanish though. My family moved away from there to Sebastian before I was born when Kosta was two and Jade was six. It's understandable that only Jade had the benefit of acquiring a second tongue.

Ramze had just started his studies at PIE through their foreign student exchange program. He moved into town under the roof of the principal and his family. All he knew how to say in English were the words: blue horse and pizza. I'm unsure why those were his first words. It made me laugh at the time knowing that's all he could say.

Ramze has light-blond curly hair, dark chocolate brown eyes, and long eyelashes. You could tell right off the bat he's a surfer from the way he smelled. As if he'd come right off the beach with a superfluous amount of sunscreen imbued with a banana coconut daiquiri, unfailingly propagating from his dark-toned skin seen from years of exposure to the sun. He boasts that natural tan this generation desires. I later learned, in his defense, that it wasn't sunscreen I smelled but a water-resistant surfer cologne, 'Rongubōdo;' sold as a novelty item at the surf shop Moh down in South Florida.

He truly hasn't changed much over the years. Probably just a bit taller and wider at the chest than he was our freshman year with far messier curls in his hair. He lost his hairbrush at the beach and never bothered to get another. He also has a full, thick, and two-tone beard now that he maintains through regular grooming; taking better care of it than the tangled nest on his head.

Lucas, however, changed a lot. Both in maturity and in the way he carries himself. His light-brown wavy hair is kept pushed aside so that you can see his sharp, prominent medium-brown eyes. His skater days are far behind him. You'll only find him with gentlemanlike attire when in person and off the beach. Button-ups, dress pants, nice fancy shoes, golden watches, and things of that cocky, wannabe privileged kid sort.

When the pelicans filled the outside of the academy and got inside the Tube, I could already tell this was going to be a bad day. And when Principal Hollack sounded through the speakers in my class, his heeding of the birds also came with the announcement that they'd gained access to the school through Terminal 5 and reached the ducted air system. There'd be no air ventilation till further notice.

I was sweating. All I could think of was what a waste of time being stuck in one hundred-degree weather in a school with no emergency cooling system when I could be cooling off in a good surf at the beach. I realized that being stuck in a classroom was a hazard to my health for I was sweating intensely, and it could take hours before they let us out. The biotech classroom was amongst the few surrounded by restaurants. The shopping center was keen to parade their merchandise on the fifth floor.

Across from biotech one could view the Miss Hide accorded restaurant 'Sora and Litos' offering bona fide Greek cuisine with a menu of things I never bothered learning how to pronounce. The Polynesian inspired continental breakfast was just three apparel stores to the right of Sora and Litos. A pentagon window to the left of my desk created the connection between private school lectures and exterior life where I'd often watch students skipping class casually stroll by the hall.

My biotech teacher was Dr. Evanita Macenchi. Her black cherry hair would regularly be styled up in a doughnut bun. Towards the end of the day, she'd let it down to show off its wispy waves. Her blue-gray eyes were hidden on sunny days. Her disguise of choice—oversized black 80's style sunglasses. It didn't faze her that we were indoors. At work she'd blanket her willowy, lanky body in bright two-piece sets. That day she'd worn a long highlighter yellow skirt contrasted with a sharp-edged collar, navy blue long-sleeved blouse. Her two-inch black wedge pumps were invariably big and hearty. In other words, she'd big feet.

While the professor was off doing her own thing with her back turned, sharpening pencils and what not, I snuck out of the room and slipped past the bamboo door. An exotic and rich in design, environment friendly alternative to the profuse heavy metal doors found throughout the ship.

Though the classroom size was small, it was dead and either people were sleeping or too occupied in gossip to notice their classmate missing. The lecture that day was on a group of scientists who'd developed the darkest material on earth. Perhaps its most fascinating feature is its purported ability to acclimatize itself to foreign materials and become one. If ever on the market it'd be pricier than diamonds or gold. I harbored significant doubts regarding this assertion. The engrossing substance is made from carbon nanotubes and inspired by the triumphant adaptability of the aquatic plant elodea. Adequately named, 'Black Elodea.'

Developed in the UK, this material is under wraps. Scientists involved in its making decided they'd go public with Black Elodea once they could demonstrate its efficacy. The substance still had its kinks. Fading darkness with age and immediate breakage following human touch were amongst the few shortcomings. Strangely, the substance exhibited no flaws in its integration with bread, encompassing not only the conventional variety made from wheat flour but also diverse alternatives like rye, barley, and gluten-free breads. Dr. Macenchi was an insider on the project and even had photographs to back up the claim the material's indeed remarkably dark.

Her interest in Black Elodea was its possible application in biotechnology. Using darkness to reinvent food. Disease carrying insects ravage crops year-round, costing taxpayers billions. Crops fused with Black Elodea could possibly ward off these pests. The material swallows up all light. Insects would see its vast darkness as threatening, believing food's a predator.

When created, Dr. Macenchi will coin this genetically modified food 'Elodeas Pabulum.' An added bullet to her first point was that insects are attracted to bright colors. To them,

Elodeas Pabulum would be visually unappetizing. Allegedly, the benefits of Elodeas Pabulum expand to our own bodies. Black foods are healthier for the human body. They possess more antioxidants because of their high pigment content.

"Why Black Elodea? Why can't the crops just be dyed black?" one pint-sized, green-eyed brunette asked the professor.

Dr. Macenchi responded in her modulated voice. "Black Elodea will be permanent. Besides, insects as well as rodents, and many other mammals that delight in eating man's self-grown food, are exposed to black. However, they aren't exposed to Black Elodea. The material's alien to these deleterious organisms and before today it was alien to students. There's a special fear to be had from the unknown."

"What's to stop those organisms from learning Elodeas Pabulum isn't threatening?" the same girl asked.

"I hypothesize there's plenty of food out there from our own that insects will flock to. For a time, pesticides will continue their seasonal rotation with farmers. The hope is pesticides will be discontinued. After my theory is proven that Elodeas Pabulum is enough of a deterrent to halt pests, there'll be no need for further pesticides," Dr. Macenchi stated.

The lecture veered off into the European unity theories of economist Friedrich List. Dr. Macenchi could discourse at great length on the history of economics so why she chose to teach a class on genetic engineering is beyond me. But if she's a match for any school, it's PIE.

The sultriness of the air had the guys taking their white or dark green polos off. The guys and girls who wore long pants rolled their pant legs up to their knees. The girls who had on scooter skirts were the lucky ones. Most of them tied their shirts to their backs using an elastic hair tie. The shirts were pulled up to their lower chests so that their stomachs were showing. This let some air onto their dripping skin. They also tied their hair up in ponytails.

Apparently, girls have multiple hair ties in their possession. One for transforming their shirts from teacher's pet to naughty schoolgirl and another for fixing their hair up in case of a heated emergency. I wouldn't be the one to cavil about their crop tops. One outwardly nerdy girl did raise awareness by stating doing such is in violation of the school dress code.

'Shut up Patricia,' was the saucy clapback I heard before leaving.

Chapter 12

Security was up and about the entire school so I had to be incognito to escape these walls that contained me as they should a convict. I ran from hall to hall avoiding contact with any personnel till I got to the Casino. Every gold electronic gaming machine was turned off and the table games were empty. The layout of the machines had always been random with some in rows and others in semicircles. The table games were mainly off to the sides of the Casino with an exception for blackjack which had its own section hewed into the middle. Faint orange lights would glow in between white alabaster statues of Egyptian royals standing by the walls, watching over me. From life-size pharaohs to courtly cats and the royal guards, all stood but one.

At the center of the ship's Casino, Hatshepsut sat on a monumental throne alike the Lincoln Memorial in Washington D.C. Her seat is sculpted out of white alabaster but her body and two-headed pet snake that she flaunts as a scarf are distinct from the throne; both made from blue apatite crystal. The blue pharaoh is in the middle of four others, one at each corner of the white throne facing diagonally away from her. Golden leg cuffs on their ankles link one another through gold chains.

The white alabaster statues around her portray the male physique at its perfection. They're shirtless bodyguards with the heads of basenji dogs. Each guard is enhanced below

UP STRAWBERRY VINE

the waist with a metallic green snakeskin skirt. At the neck they sport a collar necklace in gold-tone with scale elements and small slightly smoked-colored rhinestones. Their only weapon is a gold staff with an ankh on top that they grip onto using their left hand. They've a pair of iron gauntlets trimmed with gold braid and turquoise rivets.

Above the pharaoh's head crown, on the ceiling, is the two-dimensional depiction of the goddess Isis kneeling on her right knee, face turned right, and wings extended symmetrically under her open arms; pointed to the east and west ends of the Casino.

Even with the low lighting, the Casino presents a sophisticated ambiance and captivating sights. Las Vegas' spirit screams to be freed in this casino where there's premium mid-century architecture with a nod to the ritzy scenery of ancient Northeastern Africa. Palm trees are carved around the walls of indents in the Casino where red contemporary sectional sofas mingle with the antique beige and bronze ivy sand of the trapezoid Sahara-dyed carpets.

I'd feel emotions that're unfamiliar to me every time I'd walk through there. I could imagine the winning high rollers who feel exhilarated in each game move. I could feel the depression of first-time gamblers willing to try their luck and discovering lady luck wasn't on their side.

Past the Casino of red and gold, I could see that there it was—the exit to the school. Terminal 1 was unguarded by security. The single barrier between the glossy red exterior staircase and I were two clear glass doors. I was thankful my class was on the fifth floor and not on top. Nine flights of stairs to get here would've given me heartburn with security guarding the elevators and all those waffles I ate that morning.

I heard angels sing. Cue the holy music as I made one final sprint to the exit before slipping on the wet Cairo brown porcelain tiles from the Casino floor. I fell on my ass and slid a good twelve feet on the smooth surface. Coming to a sudden stop, I'd bumped into Ramze. He was dressed in an extra-large white school t-shirt with a small embroidered pelican on the upper left pectoral. He made it look like a size small with his biceps bulging out of his sleeves. He had on light-brown khaki shorts. Long pants wouldn't fit him without looking like uncomfortable skinny jeans.

He too was trying to make an escape before I stopped him. The impact of my sliding up against him caused him to collapse onto the wet floor, falling backwards onto a Mafia-themed penny slot machine. His quick reflexes allowed him to break the fall with his hands.

"Sorry man. Didn't mean to get in your way," I said mildly.

As I tried to get up on my feet, he pushed me back down to the floor. I hit the back of my head on a round stool in front of some overly sexualized fairy-themed slot machine. He started bad mouthing me in his second tongue—Spanish. I could've avoided pouring gasoline on this altercation by walking away but I never let someone push me down and make me feel inferior.

I stayed on the floor and aiming for his knees I tackled him down to my level. He quickly reversed me and put me in a headlock. I missed the memo that Israelis are natural born wrestlers. This kid obviously knew what he was doing. He released me and before I knew it there were punches being thrown on both sides. I was fighting a crazy karate kid, twice my size, that could break me in half.

What the hell was I thinking? I thought to myself when suddenly, within seconds, came my savior. Skinny Lucas in a black tank top and black chain fleece long pants skated down the Casino at an angle, splashing water in every direction from his skateboard's wheels turning on the recently cleaned floor. He skidded after stopping and yelled, "Hey hotdog, you're messing with the wrong weenie!"

Ramze immediately turned to face him and screamed out, "Blue horse!" like a colorblind cowboy.

I initially assumed he was medial on a spectrum of intellect from the random words that'd left his mouth. Lucas dropped his skateboard and at lightning speed ran toward Ramze and I as if he were about to clash with us forming the next Big Bang. "Shut up muscles!" he came yapping. He jumped on Ramze's back and started choking him, wrapping an arm around Ramze's neck. Lucas' bicep pressed close against one side of Ramze's neck and his forearm against the other.

Ramze dropped to his knees, placing his hands on the arm choking him. I got up from the floor and began kicking Ramze with all my might, although I'm sure his muscles could take a hit. Ramze exploded and rose from the ground once his hands wrapped around Lucas' arms and split them like a gymnast's legs.

He took my leg in his hand, forcing me down as he got up on his feet. Gravity rammed my head into the ground and a headache would supervene. With one fist free and his other hand dragging me by the ankle on the Casino floor, Ramze began fighting Lucas. Lucas kept backing away from us after he was punched twice directly in the face. Ramze dodged the one punch Lucas built up the courage to throw.

I was dragged on my back all the way out of the Casino and outside of Terminal 1 when Ramze let go of my leg, side kicked Lucas' thigh and made him flop. I began to crawl away from Ramze, back toward the Casino, but he grabbed the collar of my dark green polo from behind before I could manage any distance between us. He then knelt by Lucas, checked if he was still conscious, and grabbed Lucas just under the neckline of his black self-made tank top. Lucas didn't react but I could tell he was playing dead. An amateur actor who'd probably seen one too many cartoons. Lucas' impersonation of someone who's been knocked out was sticking his tongue out to one side of his mouth whilst keeping his eyes closed.

Lucas awoke, tried to get back on Ramze's back and do the sleeper choke hold on him again but pathetically failed. Taking Lucas off him and seizing his black tank top again, he lifted us up with incredible strength. I swung my soaring feet at his stomach and swore he was about to turn as green as my polo. From the veins popping out of his neck, I knew our asses were about to get handed to us.

From just outside, past the round ship portholes and two clear glass doors, I could see there were pelicans obstructing all of Terminal 1. I made one final kick toward the glass doors pushing them open and like wildfire, dozens of pelicans flew into the school forming a mass army of hungry fiends. Ramze was fast to let go of my shirt but kept a tight grip on Lucas. After dropping me onto the floor, I grabbed the sides of his shorts from behind him and pulled them down to his ankles. Ramze had gone commando today with his dragon balls dangling in front of me in between his legs. He turned his head over his shoulder.

"Te gusta lo que ves?"

He released Lucas to bring his shorts up to his waist. Our shirts had been markedly stretched out that their form took on the style of Greek togas. Distracted by the chaos around him, I looked at Lucas looking disoriented back at me and told him to stay low.

"Follow me!" Lucas said crawling on the floor heading towards another hallway.

I used my hand to keep from the birds hitting me on the head. These massive birds were around thirty pounds each and possessed beaks that could poke a giant squid's eyes out. With so many in one place I panicked and got up as I lost Lucas in the crowd of pelicans. I made a dash for the fire alarm on a wall closest to me, sliding under the nine-foot wingspan of a dirtied pelican that stood four feet tall, and opened the clear case it was in.

A minor beeping began after opening the case. I pulled the fire alarm sending all the birds into a frenzy from the blaring siren noise. They quickly scattered out of the open doors from which they came. Right when I thought I was home free, I felt the ground shake. The siren had galvanized the student body into sprinting home. A stampede of students all came out rushing for the doors of Terminal 1 crying, "Freedom!"

That's what the loudest of students said, agitated at their imprisonment after school hours.

"Crap."

I looked down realizing I was about to get trampled. Out of nowhere, Lucas popped out from the disarray and stated the obvious, "There you are."

He grabbed my shirt at the chest and pulled me out of sight behind a wall left of the fire alarm. I gasped for air trying to catch my breath as the rush of it all had soaked up all my energy.

"You ok dude?" Lucas asked.

"Yea man. That big foreign kid beat the hell out of us in that fight."

"His name's Ramze. Sorry about him. He's new to the school and only acts tough to hide the fact he's a fairy. My name's Lucas." He reached his hand out towards me in a friendly gesture. I shook his hand and looked him in the eye. It wasn't necessarily a good handshake, but it was decent.

"The name's Koata but you can call me Koa."

We stayed behind the wall for five minutes making sure every last bird and student had dispersed so that we'd be out of harm's way. It was after the fire alarm was shut off that a cordial tone took precedence over any other distraction and we decided to move.

"Alright Koa, well I think the coast is clear. Let's ditch this joint."

We turned back into the hall outside of Terminal 1 and into the open came out Principal Hollack with his left hand gripping onto Ramze's right shoulder. A tall elderly man with strong facial features and gray hair that came down to his Elvis sideburns. Mr. Hollack had on a short-sleeved white button-down shirt with the first four buttons unbuttoned, giving the coarse white hair on his chest some room to breathe.

"Not so fast boys. You three are in trouble. Detention now!" he screamed at us and then blabbered on school rules in a guttural way, from the back of his throat. Flecks of spit fled his mouth as his loud lecturing on our transgressions got increasingly blurred. "I stated on the intercom that the exits to the school were blocked! What did you three expect would happen once you arrived at Terminal 1?"

"I didn't think that far ahead," Lucas was honest.

I squinted my eyes and scrunched my lips together, taking my hand and wiping the spit off my face. He pushed Ramze toward us and made us stand shoulder to shoulder facing him. He wanted to see the guilt on our faces.

"You, you, and you. Which one pulled the fire alarm?"

Ramze raised his hand and lifted his head from looking down to face Mr. Hollack. I remember thinking, either this kid is actually stupid or he's taking the blame for something he didn't do to get two kids which had just fought him out of trouble. Mr. Hollack then turned around and walked us downstairs to level four into the internal suspension room. A bland room with three white walls and one chalkboard wall, no windows, and a couple of broken desks that were the epitome of something out of a horror film. Scratches were pronounced all over their wooden surface and little spiders nested around the legs of the chairs. All that was missing was blood to convince me this was a genuine nightmare. My busted-up nose made up for that missing detail as small drops fell to the floor. I'd never been in detention before, but this was clearly a utility closet substituting as one.

Mr. Hollack handed Lucas a mop from the wall. "Here. You wipe all the feathers from the hallways upstairs as I suppose you had something to do with the birds getting in." He turned to Ramze and I and stared us down as we sat on the countertops of the fragmented desks.

"I'm very disappointed in you Ramze. We'll talk about this when we get home, but I warn you now, one more outbreak from you in school or my house and this exchange program to which I've kindly accepted a part in by letting you stay in my home is over. Got it? Overrrr. Now you two stay put. I'll be right back," he said with actual disappointment in his eyes, in the way you'd lecture your own kid for stealing. He walked out with Lucas straddling the broom like a witch.

I turned towards Ramze. "I guess the man caught us on the security cameras." Ramze didn't acknowledge me. "Look, I didn't mean to confront you the way I did. I know you probably don't understand me right now but I'm sorry. My intention wasn't to make you fall and keep you in school. Trust me, I was trying to get out too. This extreme weather's killing me," I said licking the sweat off my upper lip.

Ramze gave me a sidelong glance. "Ack!" he shrieked, looking sick to his stomach. He subsequently took his shirt off and threw it at me. He gestured I use it to wipe my nose, aggressively patting his.

UP STRAWBERRY VINE

Ramze looked at me trying to keep a straight face and then burst out laughing as I stopped my bloody nose from running, slapping his hand on his knee. He laughed with his whole body. I didn't think it was funny at all, but I shook my head in idiocy. There was a light in him I hadn't seen before.

"You didn't understand a word I just said, did you?"

He smiled and responded, "Pizza?"

With the assumption that there's a question mark after that which he'd replied, I thought he'd made a reference to hunger. He was inviting me to go eat with him. For good reason, anytime we'd fight since, we'd handle the aftermath a lot better than a sour compadre suing their business partner for breaching the terms of a contract. The bruises only take a few weeks to heal but holding a grudge, that never does heal. A grudge will always leave a deep gash in the flesh susceptible to infection. The longer you carry a grudge, the more damaged you'll become.

After that day, spending two hours in detention, Ramze, Lucas, and I went out for pizza at the 'We Don't Have Fish' restaurant. A local pizzeria on the beach, two blocks from where the ships docked. For the next month all we would do was eat Hawaiian pizza after an hour in detention every day. Considering I wasn't being put up for expulsion, one hour in detention every day was something I could cope with.

Chilling with Ramze and Lucas became more of a hobby for me. I never felt accustomed to anyone like I had with them. Being that I was forced to see them for the next three months in detention, I realized they were both pretty cool people. Within in a month or so of being in Florida and hanging out with us, Ramze had mastered English with the adornment of a rough, pensive Middle Eastern accent.

He'd been shy about admitting his polishing of the language behind the scenes. One day he startled us in a blow. Embittered as all hell, he was. As we waited for the server to take our order at We Don't Have Fish, his words cut through the solemn ukulele chords being played at the piano bar. 'Three root beers and one large Hawa—.' Ramze slammed his fist on the table, grunted, and raised his chin to the ceiling. He shouted, clear as spring water and as loud as the trumpet of an elephant, "I'm tired of pizza!"

We all laughed, including the server who'd mentioned We Don't Have Fish may be a pizzeria, but it offers more than just pizza. She let us reexamine the menu while she fetched us our drinks, giggling on her merry way. That was the start of me realizing I was actually building a friendship with these guys.

Ramze can fight for real, not just beat up his peers amid an embroilment. He'd taken an interest in the Israeli martial art Krav Maga which he'd just started taking classes for when we met. Today he's an expert at it and a deadly weapon without question. Anyone who can master such an intense fighting style can permanently injure an opponent in the blink of an eye. I feel safe breaking the law with Ramze by my side. That's sneaking onto private beaches. Nothing mad besides this. I miss the dog days when back in the day all we would do was eat pizza and go surfing.

Surfing—that's what made us closer and eventually what made us family. It's the sport we each had a common liking for and whenever I wished I had someone to chill with they'd always be there. Ramze somehow convinced his parents to let him permanently move to the US after only being in Florida for five months. His grandpa, who lived alone in Philadelphia, moved to Brevard County, Florida, to be with Ramze. Both could use the company of family. Ramze's an only child while Lucas has a younger sister and an older stepbrother, Welina and Demitres Farnham.

I'm not going to lie, having a skater and a buff foreigner as my pals never crossed my mind and before that I tended to keep to myself. I always felt like people didn't want to be around me or something. It was my nature of being since my dad's passing. Someone who's quiet and likes to surf is how I think my peers perceived me in high school. I'm deeper than most people think I am. I just never had the chance to show it.

I'm also quite the intellectual nerd having had a straight compilation of A's my whole life. Being smart has its privileges I suppose, like getting paid to tutor others and getting teachers to let me leave class early when I was finished with my work. However, I'd tutor Lucas for free.

Ramze's the antithesis of Lucas when it comes to academics. Exceedingly bright in his studies and Spanish isn't his only language. Along with English, he knows Hebrew, Arabic, and Portuguese. Hebrew because of his and his father's nationality. Arabic because his ancestry immigrated to Israel from an Arabic-speaking country. It's why his family maintained their culture with the second national language of Israel.

I think he has relatives from Brazil because he and his grandpa would take a lot of trips to Rio during the school year which is where he picked up Portuguese and got a better feel for surfing. His mom I'm certain is from Costa Rica where he'd previously resided and lived the longest. That's where he learned Spanish. He was adopted at the age of three in Israel and moved to Costa Rica thereafter. Lucas and I on the other hand are both Florida natives which is funny because we surf. Up in Florida we don't get much waves. You don't have to be an expert to surf in Florida. I got my experience from traveling with my dad.

My family used to travel a lot when I was younger since my dad's business required it. He built his own line of surf gear called Ubermotion. Uber standing for super in the German language. I don't know why he named it that other than the birthplace of the business being in Germany. Aside the almighty Isar River in Munich known for its hellish surf.

He'd take me with him to the river and I'd watch him surf for hours in awe. The business is still under the Califf name and one of the many entrepreneurial efforts by Jade to cash in on some extra money. She's given an undisclosed percentage of Ubermotion to a business partner who lives in Germany. The company took a big hit when Daniel died but this new business partner seems to be steering the company back on track. Jade's always busy and will not travel unless there's sufficient monetary gain to be made. She prefers to work in Florida, overseeing the business and soon to be franchise from home. Her primary focus remains She Core.

A second Ubermotion store is set to open in Malaysia by the end of the year at one of the world's largest water parks. This is another reason the week after my sister's wedding I would've traveled there; to inspect the chosen lot on which the store is to be built.

My other siblings never did have the zest I have for the sport. Jade would longboard every now and then but the older she got, the more disillusioned she became by activities that didn't lead outright to revenue. As for Kosta, he's an amazing surfer but he too lost a feel for it the older he got. Now he's a broker's shadow and his plans for college are nonexistent.

Jade never went to college either. A high school dropout. She became a journalist. Once an intern for some government affiliated agency in Florida. She transferred to a sector of that company which deals with amusement parks in recreation. That's where she was recognized by Rick Harford and later convinced by him to leave that government agency for a crucial part in She Core.

In truth, I don't get what her job is all about, but I do know with the time she puts into her work there's absolutely no room for the luxury of surfing. I'm not ever going to lose a feel for surfing. It's the clearest picture I have in remembrance of my dad and I bonding.

Chapter 13

Waking up to Lucas at my side in the driver seat, still driving, I take a glance at the anomalous map on his lap and ask if we're close. He's wearing an unbuttoned red Hawaiian shirt with a white floral pattern.

The sun is waking. I can see its red-orange light just beyond the Kelly green mountaintops of Costa Rica's ubiquitous tropics. He turns his head towards me with the weary eyes of a sailor who's spent months at sea and answers, "Almost bro. A couple miles ahead and we'll arrive at our next destination on the map of light."

I eagerly dump my head out the window, rubbing a fist against one of my eyes to clear my sight from a speck of dust that blew in. The arid cool air brings a calm. It careers through my skin as I get lost in my hunger. Hundreds of puffy white clouds in a twilight become a swirl of cookies and cream ice cream. I feel weightless and start thinking,

This is aerodynamics.

The sheer purple tinting of the skies evinces the dance between sunlight and molecules in the air. The bellafina orange baby bell sweet pepper light of a rising sun fervently pokes its nose into a radish purple sky. A beatific vision that needs a fair pinch of salt to make it feel real. Lucas remains torpid as he pulls over on the side of the road where there's a modest food store.

The pickup truck comes to a halt. He gets out of the pickup truck and says he'll be right back. I look to the back seat to check if Ramze's still sleeping and if Lucas closing the truck door might've woken him. He hasn't awoken and instead is curled up in a ball snoring. I'm the only guy that's still shirtless from yesterday. Ramze's wearing a large baby blue long-sleeved t-shirt.

The store Lucas enters is isolated with no other storefronts in sight; almost hidden amongst a therapeutic wilderness. There're lush red mangroves just off to the side in dark green waters. Where the still waters end and one white-faced capuchin monkey roams, the wind festively ruffles a community of southern cattails. Beyond them, the elevation drops, concealed by a dense tree canopy, though not far enough to muzzle the whispers of a river flowing.

The store's made of cut down oak trees, not counting its rusted metal sheet roof. Paper ads on store windows present deals on bread and milk. At the storefront, pub-like blue neon lights spell out 'Fundy's' in cursive. Under the Fundy's name, the entrance of a black chalkboard door lays out the sketch of a wee hand in blue chalk.

Conventionally, there'd be a knob where the sketch is, but the chalkboard door is an automated sliding door. Knowing Lucas, he's gone into the store wishing for a healthy Kombucha energy drink to quench his thirst and spirit. He'll need that extra boost for later today. I take the map of light from the driver seat where Lucas had placed it before taking it off his lap and getting out of the truck. I examine it viewing the route for our journey ahead.

The map of light is the name our longtime friend, Jake Gauthier, had given to some plots. This one pinpoints all the surf spots in Costa Rica, including those hidden from the public eye. It's a sizeable transparent sheet with thin blue ink outlining the topography of the land. The reason for the name was his take that we'd leave each of our destinations at night and just as the rose pink light of dawn would radiate upon the beach, we'd be arriving. Hence the name, 'map of light.'

Typically, we stay at a hotel and wake up to drive to the beach the following day. Before the sun bops the shore. Today's the exception. I'm sure Lucas parked somewhere, too tired to find a hotel, and we all slept through the night. I just so happen to have overslept and not even realize when Lucas woke up to start driving again.

Jake gave us the maps when we first came to him in the beginning of last December telling him about the crazy idea of a surfing world tour. It's crazy because it'd require us taking our first year off college to go visit some of the wildest surf spots on earth. An earth full of seldomly explored wonders. With beaches that're greedily locked away from the public for all time and guarded by environmentalists to protect wildlife.

This meant every place we'd visit would require us to conjure a plan that'd get us onto the beach and out without ever being spotted. Every country has a stringent set of rules on what places are allowed for tourism and those which are strictly out of bounds. Concluding that we only had one year to accomplish all of this before heading back to Florida, he feverishly handed us various maps of what he considered must-see locations when entering a new country.

I wasn't truly apprehensive on coming to Costa Rica because Ramze knows this place like the back of his hand. He also has a small house here which is where he retrieved his pickup truck, Lucy. My brother though was fretful, taking into consideration our timed schedule. Be back in Florida by Monday or Jade would have our heads for dinner. He knew once I got an idea in my head there'd be no amount of convincing to get it out. I told him to join us, to think of this short first trip as a return to his birthplace. He thought about it and the rest is history. Although, I'm sure the staple reasoning behind his decision to come is in protecting me from getting into trouble.

Throughout high school, Jake Gauthier had been the habitual sunshine of mine and Lucas' day whenever we'd get bored. Even though he didn't attend Pelican Island Econgregation. We met him during a trip to South Florida our sophomore year of high school for spring break. At the time we met Jake, Ramze was off touring Brazil.

Jake is the manager at a surf shop in Deerfield Beach, Florida, named Mermaid on Helium. Ramze was acquainted with the store before we'd been. He regularly ordered Rongubōdo cologne through their website. We tend to shorten the shop's name to Moh. Moh is stocked with awesome surf gear and skate gear along with some of the sickest clothes bound to make you the envy of any chill spot in beach place areas. 'Gillified Joe' is what Jake refers to customers as when they've bought all their surfing implements from Moh. The tacky phrase has worn out its welcome.

Jake's a five-eleven-foot surfer. His main sport of interest became skimboarding when he moved to Florida from California since Florida's only offer is moderately big waves in the winter months. Except during hurricanes. Florida would always surprise us with eight footers. Despite winter temperatures being just above fifty degrees Fahrenheit, we'd always go out in our Moh surf gear and catch the gnarliest waves. Our wetsuits championed the illusion of differentially warmer waters.

Jake's your typical stoner. He's five years older than me with long sunny blond dreadlocks about shoulder length. A glassy red film blankets his light-green eyes from smoking relentlessly. His Rastafarian style is fit for comfort in the island heat with light tone colors for playing up love and peace. He's surprisingly fit. He might not be completely built in muscle like Ramze but he's got the well-defined abs of a true surfer. The man's always tanning and only owns sleeveless shirts as far as I know. I've never seen him in a regular t-shirt. Not even at formal events. They're mostly tank tops he gets forty percent off of from his job at Moh.

When we surf, his eyes seal the deal for dates. He flaunts those light-green eyes of his so routinely you'd think his life depended on it. He'd persistently approach and smooth talk all of them polka dot bikini girls. They'd get lost in his eyes before he'd offer to teach them how to surf. Their first lesson in surfing: don't stop to talk to a shark. A simple joke.

Not as simpleton as the one airhead to always ask, 'Isn't that obvious?'

Jake has his way with the ladies. Then again, what girl wouldn't want to date a surfer? That'd go against our instinct to be loved by half-naked bodies dripping in ocean water with a gleam in their eyes. A chick would have to be an extraterrestrial not to go for a surfer.

Though Jake doesn't need any more girls in his life. He's been with Hawaiian surfer Malia for just over two years now. During high school summer breaks, Jake would drive up to the city of Sebastian and stay at Lucas' home. Although when we'd stop by my place to sit back and watch movies, smoke weed, and work out at my downstairs gym, he'd often be distracted. The reason, Jade's good friend—Malia Bixby. She and Jade went to the same high school with Malia graduating in the class that Jade would've if she'd kept an interest in her studies. The class of '08. Jake introduced himself not too long after first seeing Malia at my house. They've been slobbering all over each other ever since.

Malia is pretty chill. Can definitely show off any of us guys when it comes to surfing. We call her Fish. Her nickname comes from the fact that she's spent most of her life out in the water catching waves. She's been surfing her whole life kind of like me but unlike me she caught her first wave at three. It was four feet and she rode it for fifteen seconds without falling off her board.

Call me skeptical but I didn't believe any of it. That's until she showed us the photos and story from the Honolulu Ka'Nalu Advocate documenting her incredible outbreak in

Hawaiian surf history. Crazy that I'm friends with such a pro. That's our girl Fish. Sure, she had floaters and it was an insulated wave pool but she did what none of us guys could do at that age. The only girl in our surf crew. That's for now, till we find another to add to our clan with skills that match and maybe even surpass ours.

Malia is just one surfer in a group I like to call 'my people' which also includes Jake, Lucas, Ramze, and the newest member Erik—my brother-in-law. My people are those who've gained the same love for the sport of surfing that I've always had and because of it we've grown closer together.

Erik was a natural the first time he surfed. On his first attempt to catch a wave he stood up on his board without breaking a sweat, smiling and loving every second of it. From then on, he was one of us. Jade will soon be reunited with Erik. It's been three months since they last saw one another. Two years ago, Lucas, Jake, and I got him interested in surfing. We took him out to the waters of Sebastian Inlet thinking he'd fall ever so easily on five footers. Boy did he prove us wrong. I knew by the spark in the reverence he had for his first wave that he had it in him to be a great surfer.

I spontaneously entered him in his first surf competition, ignorant of how he'd react. It was back when we took an impulsive short trip to Hawaii while he was visiting Florida. His side of the family, and Jade's, all went to see his first competition. He won, clutching Hawaii's surf champs by the throat. Placed first in the Pipe Master's Cowabunga Competition. Every time Erik visits the US now, he never lets a competition pass him by; always ranking high in his category of other adults.

He's a twenty-seven-year-old, longboard inclined surfer, standing at a height of six feet with a blond crew cut and a military physique—one you'd expect every soldier to have. He's served in the Marine Corps for seven years now and remains on active duty. He sends me and my people letters every now and then from his station in Okinawa, Japan. Not because he has bad phone service but because he appreciates the antiquated gesture of sending a letter and his calligraphy is extraordinarily beautiful. This is why, unfortunately, he couldn't travel with us this year. His next break will be the coming week of his and my sister's wedding. He's allowed to return for a month. As for Jake and Malia, they too couldn't travel with us because they've plans for a wedding of their own sometime this year.

That left Lucas, Ramze, and I to have our own adventure with Kosta tagging along because he's my brother and watches over me. In any event, we're there for one another. We'll be there for Jake and Malia's wedding, and we'll be waiting with my sister back home in Florida when Erik returns this coming week. It's who we are. One big surf family never to be separated despite long distance across the world.

The map of light represents more than a series of forsaken locations to surf. It represents an opportunity to do something amazing before heading back home and returning with each of our lives. It was supposed to be the last time all of us would be together before heading off to college and not seeing one another for months at a time. For my people who aren't here with us right now in this Costa Rican paradise, let it be known that their hearts and spirits will be with my friends and I every step of this surfing world tour.

Internally, we as people are all connected to this wondrous planet and we're all a puzzle piece in this hectic thing we call life. The steps of life we proceed in have all dealt us hard times but there's love out there for everyone and I've found that love in my people.

Remembering my people, there's one now. Lucas returns to the pickup truck with a brown paper bag, folded at the head in his right hand, and what's a dead ringer for grape jelly scooped up by a hedgehog's crystal-clear party hat in his left hand.

"Sorry bro, they didn't have any of those pineapple peach ones we like. But hold on...the store's owner had these killer grape ones. Gave me his word they'd do the trick," he says getting into the pickup truck, closing the driver seat door, and unpacking more shots. "Here try one!" Passing a cone-shaped capsule with a cutting end onto me, he grabs another and throws it at Ramze, hitting him on the head.

"Dude what the hell. I was dreaming I was president," Ramze spoke awaking from his slumber with drool racing down the edge of his bottom lip.

"You sure this is an energy shot?" I inquired of Lucas, examining the small cone of purple goop.

"Nope," Lucas responds putting the car key in the keyhole. "But the owner at the back spoke English and when have I ever said no to free samples?"

Turning towards the back seat, I ask Ramze, pointing an accusatory finger at the cone, "Do you know what this is?"

Ramze takes the cone that Lucas had thrown at him from the back seat and rubs his eyes with his fists. Ramze's body does a sporadic jerk. He quickly snatches the one Lucas was about to drink. "Koa don't drink yours!" He stretches his other arm out and grips my wrist.

I freeze and look at him profoundly disturbed. I suppress myself from drinking it. Slowly, I hand him the full glass cone. "Guessing it's bad?" I figure.

"It's a hallucinogenic drug produced by the natives in these parts. It's meant to daze intruders so that they can be misguided into the unknown where they'll be forced to survive. It's something Jake had specifically warned us about in relation to this exact area on the map of light."

"Huh?" Lucas looks at him puzzled as do I.

"Well guys, this right here is the Costa Rican substitute for DMT. But worse. Gets a bad rep for producing exclusively horrific hallucinations. Damn dangerous with long-term effects. Psychological dependency and a lifetime at a psych ward is the common aftermath. Two things I'll fucking pass on. I'll stay here with my dick in my hand if you dumbasses partake. Oh, and its nickname's 'jaguar's spit' if its other faults aren't enough of a deterrent," Ramze recalled.

"Odd name. Sounds gross," I say. My mind hares off with unhinged thoughts. Man, the violent acts I'd commit if I saw the wicked store owner who gave Lucas this drug. I don't remember Jake mentioning it. We canvassed the issues Jake warned us about in coming here.

1. Beware of a man with blue hair, he'd stressed.

2. Keep the eyes peeled for the uncommon warthog. They'll keep you safe and sound.

3. Funny crocodiles don't tell jokes. Stay and listen at the cost of a limb or two.

4. Lastly, do not take unfamiliar substances from strangers.

The last point, something that should be fairly obvious. Jake's words bypass my memory's bodyguard to enter a gathering of quibbling thoughts.

'A stranger giving out barn red seeds, luminous perfumes, and other atypical freebies is most likely not looking out for your welfare. Especially, if they've a purple drink in their inventory. They will entice you to taste it. If you aren't beguiled by their efforts, they will haze you into drinking it as was I. And, I'm pretty sure I'll have cancer one day because of it.'

Ramze is adamant that the drink's toxic.

"Bummer dude. But why the hell would that guy give me such a thing?" Lucas grills Ramze, scrunching the muscles on his face together and lowering his brows.

"People around this specific area aren't too fond of tourists so they drug em. They usually wake up lost in the rainforest without their wallets or car keys, assuming they've a car," Ramze spoke cautiously.

"Whatever dude," Lucas says disposing of the topic, strapping on his seatbelt, and turning the key to start the car. "People are fucked." Lucas shakes his head in dismay.

Ramze takes the three cones of jaguar's spit and places them under the front seat where Lucas is seated. In cases like this Ramze tends to blow up and confront the people who hurt us. We weren't hurt though and I'd rather Ramze make a full recovery before engaging in any physical action. I'm more worried about my reaction than his. If only I'd seen the face of that store owner.

We drive off. Lucas pulls out another brown paper bag from his tall orange hiking backpack. He then throws the backpack to the back seat. He'd been carrying it with him when he got out of the truck back at Fundy's. From the bag, he gets three sandwiches all wrapped in plastic. "Eat up," he says.

"Are you crazy?" Ramze seriously questions Lucas' sanity.

"Relax. I got them from the counter and not from some guy in the back claiming to be the shop owner. I paid dinero for these so eat."

Ramze and I shyly grabbed a sandwich. From what's just happened, I'm not so sure I can trust anyone around this specific area. I hope that lampooner of a store owner unwittingly gave the cones to kind, gullible Lucas and not deliberately tried to poison him. I strip apart my sandwich making sure its contents are fresh and nothing I should be worried about. The two have already started gobbling their sandwiches and I've exhausted my aptitude for analyzing food, making sure nothing in this sandwich appears tampered with. I give in, relax, and revel in the meal while it lasts.

Taking a bite of my sandwich, I realize just how hungry I'd been. I nearly devour it, savoring every bite and chewing it like a wild dog. Clearly, I shouldn't skip dinner like I did last night. I finish my meal and ask if I can have another jokingly. Lucas pulls out another sandwich from the brown paper bag on his lap. My pupils must be dilating because I'm in love. "How much did you buy?" I ask, plucking the fresh one from his hand.

"I got nine. Three for each of us," Lucas says elated, as though he's won an Olympic medal. One for preparation. I'll give him gold for fat fuck.

"This is why I love you dude," I say unwrapping my second sandwich with covetous hands. I shove it in my mouth.

It's a regular sub, commemorative of what Ramze began ordering at the We Don't Have Fish restaurant after pizza got to be mundane. About a foot long with lettuce, tomatoes, onions, banana peppers, olives, buffalo chicken, pepper jack cheese and some sweet and spicy sauce. I can eat to my heart's content, but joy only lasts if shared all around. I bet Kosta would love one of these.

Wait. How come Lucas only got nine?

I turn around to see if Kosta's keeping himself busy, yet no one rests in the back of the pickup truck. The same fear that possessed me in that gray dimension approaches me once more. A chill runs up my spine. The fear that I'm no longer in a world with God feasts on my balls. I almost forgot. This is a dream of sorts. I'm somewhat dead.

"Um Lucas, where's Kosta?" I ask, stumped on his whereabouts.

"Kosta? Who's Kosta?"

Chapter 14

Lucas answered my question with a question as if inebriated.

"My brother," I reply. "He was with us on the plane and yesterday at the beach. He took to the open cargo bed of Lucy with all our surfboards. Where is he?"

"Dude, you don't have a brother?" he says impassively, contra the knowledge I have.

I turn towards the back seat to look out the back window. To my astonishment there're only three boards. Kosta's surfboard is gone.

We continue driving without a pitch of sound. I reach out to the radio and unplug my cellphone from the auxiliary cord. After that I stiffen, tapping my feet on the car floor till they slip into my sandals. My back sinks into the car seat and I unstrap my seatbelt. I bend forward to stretch. At the same time, I shuffle through some clothes on the car floor and grab a random black tee to put on.

No one's supposed to mind as it's our nature being traveling friends that we share clothes every now and again. The shirt's a size medium but it fits me by a whisker. Lucas is the smallest in the group, so this shirt is definitely his. There's a Jolly Rogers sign on the front of the shirt—a white skull at the chest and under it, two crossed white swords shape an X.

Silence can be heard from miles away.

What an uncomfortable situation.

I want to get out of this vehicle and run without stopping, not permitting my breath the liability it has to my lungs to catch up to me. If I stay, then I risk endangering a timeline of events which are all upheld in the past. My being here has made the very thought of living immoral.

If I did die at the wedding so be it. It's not safe for me to be messing with time. Especially if the occurrences that follow due to my living again are the disappearances of my loved ones. I know my brother. He is as real as the very blood that courses through my veins. He is my blood brother and the disregard Lucas and Ramze have towards him having been here previously is probably my fault.

Yesterday Kosta was in the back of Lucy. Today he's nonexistent. Forgive me brother. I will find you and get us home in time. It's not I who is crazy but rather my friends who are in a world of illusion. This is a separate universe in the multiverse sprouting from the timeline following my death.

Just a moment ago, this life I'm leading now was in correlation to the previous one. They were each aligned with near perfection from what I remember up to this point at which everything's due to change. From the subtle alterations scattered throughout my past, like the coin I inadvertently crushed at the beach, an interesting find from my brother, and the cones of purple goop Lucas was given at Fundy's, I sense I'm being primed to plummet into a cascade of misfortunes.

I sit there staring into the blank space of an empty road ahead. From the corner of my eye, I catch Lucas giving Ramze a heads up on something. They exchange nods. Lucas turns on the headlights to Lucy in defiance of broad daylight. I turn to look back at Ramze sitting upright and acting particularly uptight, clenching his fists. He takes his right hand and strokes his beard as if he's in the middle of a deep thought. He's looking straight at me, yet he says nothing. Finally, Lucas speaks up and asks if I'm going to finish my second sandwich.

"No, I'm fine," I say undeterred. "I'm suddenly not hungry anymore."

My suspicions arise the minute I no longer recognize the road. We make a turn up a steep rocky path. The dirt road is quenched by several adjoining waterfalls that fan out in segments. The track feels as if it's sinking. Some parts of land farthest of the waterfalls are covered in dried mud, protected by natural rock formations that lead the streams in different directions.

The path is devoid of life with no chance of locals or wildlife nearby. I get skittish as we're confined in a tight space hardly big enough for Lucy to drive on. There's a strong unspoken gospel in my heart that, though vague, makes me surmise something's seriously wrong.

Staring out the window on my side there's nowhere to go but down. Endless apple green and yellowish-green rock piles fill the bottom of the mountain in trenchant layers, like a reservoir of piranha teeth actively folding over each other. The brush of a ruthless wind, visible through the black dust it carries, is the spectral presence aiding the rocks make their journey.

Lucas' side faces the mossy cragged wall of a mountainside. I begin to realize what the headlights are for. The bumpy road. Altogether it fades behind this thick fog that comes rolling down the mountain's cap.

We're driving on a single mountain covered in inches of what appears to be snow. An elusive path made so by a mirage. It's the absurd thickness of this fog that compels me to see snow where there isn't. The higher we ascend, the more the low-hanging clouds swell, their ghostly pallor intensifying. The sound of waterfalls is cutback.

A series of lopsided leafless trees that've sloughed their bitter chocolate skin to turn white, with only patches of gray left behind, are now in place of the waterfalls. Silver dew starts to form on the car windows. The headlights come as two beams scuffling with the fog to pave a way for our sight. I can see mere feet in front of where this car's headed. The road is so faintly perceptible that even squinting doesn't help sharpen things.

The rocks we drive over get instantaneously larger in mass. Lucy begins to tremble and the whole interior starts to shake. Passing through mountains with this pickup truck is proving a gamble with our lives, giving me the sensation we're defying an overt unwelcome from the road we're crossing. I'm trying hard to remember where we're at but there's a vortex that's sucking everything I'm visualizing away for the simple reason that this didn't occur. It never did.

After Playa Hermosa we left for Jacobi. The first forbidden beach on our journey. A beach up in the mountains with an active volcano sunken at the pure depths of its waters. A beach with the impression it's stranded in midair. I can't pinpoint how a beach is suspended at such a high altitude.

At least from my experience, that was the first time I'd seen access to the ocean from a mountain summit. The mountain drive to get there was on a slim road but there were no major rocks or untraversable fog packaged in that ride.

Perhaps Lucas found a shortcut while at Fundy's a few miles back. Or perhaps I'm about to be drowned at the pit of Davy Jones' Locker where the remembrances of Kosta are now at. I get trounced with auditory distortions of tame buzzing.

Guided by instinct rather than prolonged contemplation, I reach for the wheel with no hesitation or remorse for the lives that could be lost. I get brushed aside by Lucas' elbow. "The fuck are you doing man?" Lucas asks, shifting uneasily in his seat.

Both my hands attach themselves to the steering wheel like a rancorous magnet taking firm possession of its polarity for the first time. One leg mechanically flies from my seat and fixes itself on the driver's side. I'm straddling the truck's center compartment. I will guide Lucy off track. With all this obstinacy rising in me, that end is absolute. The pickup truck drifts upon an upcoming curve in the course of the road. It manages to evade the damage it would've obtained from hitting some larger than life rocks.

After the turn, Lucy is impacted by a big bump on the road. The pickup truck hikes five feet off the ground. The hood flies straight up as soon as Lucy strikes the ground, blocking our view of what's ahead. Everyone but I is mandated into oblivion. Lucas yells out for Ramze. "Help!" he screams. "Help me you buffoon!"

Ramze jitters behind me, trying to unbuckle his seatbelt and unwittingly kneeing my seat. I let go of the wheel and dive to the forefront. Grabbing the screwdriver that was used to pin our fins to our surfboards, I quickly do a one-eighty, still bent ahead, and penetrate the screwdriver into Ramze's good leg. Ramze upbraids me for my bizarre actions, leading to his Olympic twister dive into a tangent of whys: why'd you stab me, why are you flipping out, why's this happening, why go berserk in a moving vehicle?!

An uncontrolled throng of screams commences as blood oozes from his leg. Overwhelmed with shock, Lucas becomes tight-lipped, keeping hold of the wheel in a quaking manner. Ramze detaches the screwdriver from his leg and lets it bounce off the car floor.

Struggling to cope with the upset of my actions, Lucas unfastens his seatbelt with fumbling fingers and pulls the handle to the driver seat door. He jumps out and I hear a splash of water a couple seconds thereafter. The car keeps moving without its driver.

The coarse spruce green wall Lucas was once facing is now on my side. The whole mountain seems to have flip-flopped from one side to the next. I'm dazed and jittery in my efforts to keep steady, trying to take back control of the wheel. I forcibly pull my leg from the passenger side to join its brother. Now fully in the driver seat, I close the swinging door.

"Where is he?!" I demand to know as I establish some sort of control over Lucy. The pickup truck, now being driven at a slant, begins just slightly tipping over the dirt road on the driver's side. Lucy's on the right side of a mighty drop with the left back wheel suspended in the air.

"Who? I don't know what you're talking about!" Ramze hollers.

"My brother. What did you do to him Ramze? Tell me! Or I swear to god I'll bear witness to your finale. All you'll soon hear are the sounds of this truck filling up with water and the bubbles from you retching trying to get out."

"I...I don't know what you're talking about," he repeats. "Are you insane?!" he vociferates with an intense cry. "Please don't do what you're about to do! This is a surefire way to get ourselves killed!" Ramze closes his eyes and finds sustenance in prayer. "O God, you know that with all my folly and wrongs I'm plain spoken. Why forsake me?! I've been aiming for change to the highest degree. Listen to my heart...it's open to you. I will change!" His mind buzzes with thoughts of regret in his final moments. "He jumped." Ramze's voice cracks. He opens his eyes—stunned like leftists hearing free speech—making a real doozy of a mind game in his head as he tries to work out what's happening. His eyes briefly pour themselves a cup of grief for Lucas in the rearview mirror before an ice-cold stare overtakes them.

My fear mongering isn't getting to him. I stare at the left wing mirror with the hood of the pickup truck still blocking my advanced view. Out of the mist comes a strange apparition. It's a mulatto boy, about five feet tall with curly black hair draped over his eyes. He's clothed in a white ascot wing collar at the neck. Below that garment, a Spanish bistre-colored dress shirt is worn. The shirt is tucked into his loose-fitting trousers, matched in color, with the ends of them tucked into beige over-the-knee-boots. Layered over his dress shirt, he wears an unbuttoned dark olive green greatcoat. Its length reaching down to his knees.

    Floating above the low clouds, beyond the veiling of the ground he lifts his hands. Both arms stretch afar in front of him as if to get me. I aggressively turn the wheel to my right getting the pickup truck's back left wheel onto the road again. The car balances itself out as I hit my right shoulder on the passenger seat. Unable to stop turning the wheel fully to the right, Lucy slams straight into a shelf from the mountain. The shelf crushes the right side doors. I experience a brief lapse of consciousness.

    A searing pain pierces through my neck. Glass shatters like heavy rain burst from a dark cloud. The jaguar's spit. Acting as a syringe fitted with a hollow needle, Ramze's injected me with the acid. I quickly floor my foot on the brake. The hood is yanked off from the head of the pickup truck by the force of the stop, detaching from its loosened bolts and breaking the front windshield into tons of disproportional pieces that persist in being intact.

    Again, the drastically white haze is in full view. Within its stir, per the running car, I see the boy's image split by every fragment of the windshield. He's in front of the pickup truck. Right away, I put the car in reverse. The boy starts to fly closer toward us. Between me and him appears in front of us a falling white tree limb and the boy vanishes.

    The truck is bound to keep reversing. Even if I prolong my foot on the brake pedal, the mud will continue to slide the vehicle backwards. In an effort to dodge the edge of an invisible road, I turn the wheel having the pickup truck shift to one side. We crash into a pile of bucked logs littering the side of the road, causing one tire to erupt and the pickup truck to tilt on its side. We break through a cloud, down a steep hill, tumbling like a die.

There's no hesitancy from Lucy about where she wants to go. We're tossed like numbered balls in a wire bingo cage, and I briefly see the transition from rough terrain to fast-approaching ocean. The pickup truck dives off the mountain, plummeting top first. Gravity takes possession of us and slams our bodies on the car headliner.

Ramze's head's under the middle seat in the back. He crawls dizzily behind the driver's seat and opens the passenger door. Exiting the car, he disappears and then reappears shirtless at the window to my left. Full-fledged, expansive burnt umber eagle wings span from the lengths of Ramze's large muscular back. There's a lucent buttercup yellow fire melting the chocolate in his eyes; so bright it blinds me for a split second. I see him rip the car door right off its hinges and throw it behind him like a frisbee. My line of sight is tilted.

He wraps an arm around my waist and flies me out of Lucy as it falls into an unclear, shadowy ocean. My defective vision realigns itself. I try and squeeze out of his tight grip, kicking the air and pushing his face away from mine. I manage to get loose but flip upside down in my success. He catches me by the ankle, raising me high enough so that I'm facing his feet. My other leg kicks. My foot skims the side of his chin. This shirt is tight enough so that gravity doesn't pull it down over my eyes.

Ramze ducks, using his other hand to clench the skin past the shirt on my chest. Once he gets a good, painful grip he lets go of my ankle and flips me over. Once more his arm's around my waist so that I'm facing him. Everything turns right side up. I see the 17th-century-styled boy at the rim of the mountain where I bungled my attempt to crash maneuver. His black hair is pushed to the side to show a potential scowl aimed at me—terrorizing me. Yet uncertainty lingers, as the height may be playing tricks on my interpretation.

He has electric green eyes that're brutally intensified on me. They're weighing me down. I look away nauseated and notice I'm alone in midair. My sandals are whisked away from my feet by the force of a wave.

It topples over me and drags me into an unfathomable abyss. I see here the car sinking. I swim back up but in the brief moment I resurface, another wave rushes to me. Before I'm able to get an adequate amount of air in my system, I choke on salt water. The unbearable lack of air takes its toll, impairing my lungs. I look around the cloudy water but the salty keen feeling of it in my eyes is so irritating that I'm unable to keep them open for long.

My heart's thumping, I'm lacking nerve, and I begin turning a bluish-purple in reaction to the icy temperatures I've been forced down upon. The murkiness steadily clears. Down here, in the bottomless pit, I'm amazed. Angels swimming in the ocean. There're hundreds, maybe even a thousand down here. Are my eyes willfully deceiving me?

In their pursuit for such beauty, they've launched their own.

Man and woman in the buff. All with sculpted physiques and the striking wingspan of a prehistoric white feathered bird. The longer I stare, the more that appear in sight. Not all have their eyes open but the ones that do have theirs blaze fiery orange burmite amber like exploding stars under a microscope. All are purposeless in their way of hovering in the water as if vast asleep. Under me comes a whole heap of them swirling in the water high and low.

The many faces of angelic peoples are crossed with the frigid expressions that come in being suspended within a wintry coral reef. To my sides are white exotic underwater plants. Below me is a crater of the darkest blue. Upon the stony bends of this reef are the reflections of beaming suns. The flashing array of ethereal light touches the angels. I trace the source of light that gleams upon the white coral and fish. It comes from the solid gold armor that sheathes the breasts of some of the rare clothed angels.

I swirl around and I'm in direct contact with an armored female angel. The lure of gold is clear cut, but this gold's seductive charm is even more so. Beyond its physical attributes is an enchanting mystique that pulls me in. Hard to resist, its worth supersedes that of the breath of life. The feel in my bones tells me one touch will drag me down somewhere darker than the pits of Hades. Should I engage the call, I'll no longer get the chance to weigh gold against life.

The angel's golden medieval cuirass shone like torches onto every curve of my body before it precipitously sank below, revealing a slew of clones behind it. All are gold at the chest with the centered clean-cut emblem of a peculiar cross elevated an inch off the front piece of their cuirasses.

Where have I seen this cross before?

A rod with three horizontal bars that vary in length, diminishing in order the closer to the top. If not armored with silver elsewhere, this clique of golden battle angels are robed in white and red mulberry silk.

On the reflection of one angel's golden chest plate, I notice a creature moving erratically. It could be a whale having a seizure but too many times have I mistaken flowing coral reef anatomy for marine life. I pivot like a figure skater, one leg extended behind me, and my arms swept back like a plane, toward a great black enigma. There's a strong purple fizz rising from its body as it convulses. It strains to move forward, seeming partly paralyzed.

If it's injured, I deem myself worthless to save it, but it isn't. It's one of them. It must be one of the shadows that brought me to the gray hall. I recognize it from the feeling of my stiffening limbs that'd happened upon my first encounter with them. An unmistakable feeling of defenselessness. No amount of weak mindedness will make me succumb to a pasting.

Chapter 15

I jolt into motion. As a frog does before a jump, I recoil my legs like a spring to propel myself forward. Through the water I swim bumping into several angels that've floated up above me. In the impact of hitting one and pushing off another I feel death right from behind. I'm not planning on dying again only to be reentered into a gray hall jinxed by insufferable cries.

The angel of death can't touch me for I'm already dead. My viewpoint changes into a far more traumatic sight where from a vantage point above the deep-blue crater I realize that the angels aren't swimming at all. Instead, they're drowning. I'm merely curious as to why it is so. How can something that looks so good and pure be a cause for expulsion into these cold waters? Many place their hands around their neck as the universal sign that they're choking.

Their death will come either from suffocation or that thing with a purple glow surrounding its body. I'm able to get a clearer look now. On its body lays a black cloak that in the water spreads far out like the chemical liquid petroleum. The same shadows that stole me away resemble the pitch-black color of that cloak. So dark that a human could not discern its shape or form. It's menacing, drawing in the energy of life from all around it. I know it's death but death's not alone.

The angels start warping into demons, sprouting horns from the temples of their heads and growing monstrous

UP STRAWBERRY VINE

lizard tails. They begin revolving around the giant as if it's the sun and the warped angels—planets. Why do I sense this heliocentric order of things will have the transforming angels turn to slaves beneath death's black garment?

From within its cowl, its mouth widely opens to where the jawbones crack. A powerful sonar, louder than a jet engine, lams its mouth. The pain it tholes with repose. Its jaw detaches itself from the root of its mouth. Its skin stretches to bind the detached jaw hanging loosely. The beast lolls out a mammoth sea salt white tongue. It could swallow one of the angels whole in a single bite if it wanted to.

Few of the fish around it that survived the lethal sound are quick to dash out of its way as it starts to prowl toward me continually being the center of the morphing angels. Long bony fingers leave the coverings of its cloak as it coasts. An oversized human hand extends out that isn't glowing purple—it's burning purple. Flames of God's wrath.

The giant from the gray hall.

It reaches above the head and around, whipping out scores of iron chains from behind its back. It uncovers the face of a model by delicately removing its cowl with its other hand. I'd expected an exorbitantly disfigured face above the mouth with bloodshot red eyes, but the face is of a man with soft features. Handsome but starved. Its eyes are linked in color to the flames, shifting from the pale blue-purple of a phlox flower to the hazy dark purple scenery of mountains viewed at dusk from afar. Its mid-parted mane is rose gold with scads of volume and a mystifying luminescence.

The chains shake and bullet their way through the water to every single drowning angel. Locking each by wrapping around their forearms, quads, and wings. Only to then tighten as death pulls back on the chains and brings every morphed angel under its robe.

What the hell's going on here?

The tremendous semblance of disorder hatched from this drug is insanely vivid. I feel as a lamb cornered by the wolf of torment. That thing is a predator and I its prey. Hopeless and still like a rock I ask myself, why the hell did I drive Ramze's truck off a cliff?

Maybe I'm crazy.

Every angel and demon forsaken by death transforms into a spiked shadow still banded by chains. I'm not about to become one as well. I continue to swim upward, swamped by the hands of angels and demons who're grabbing onto me, trying to save themselves from being pulled and transformed by the giant. Ramze's a short distance from me, fading away into the deep. I risk my life to save him anyways seeing as how this was my fault and drugging me was his. Taking a hold of one of Ramze's wings, I carry him kicking through the water.

The ethereal angels, tethered by chains, further contort into grotesque forms, caught in a glitch-like dance between their half-demon manifestation and their spiky, shadowy silhouette. Twisted and tormented, they reach out with clawed hands, tearing at my flesh. Ramze's wings bear the burden as feathers are ripped away in my struggle against the relentless undertow of the submerged abyss.

Their pursuit unwavering, I briefly let go of Ramze. I swiftly seize the opportunity to use the chains that bind them against them, twisting and maneuvering the chains with a dancer's grace. With a flick of the wrist, I weave an intricate pattern, transforming their own binds into a trap, momentarily ensnaring their glitched forms. I scoop up my unconscious, winged friend, and carve a path to the surface. The chains, turned allies, coil protectively around the dissonant entities. They hurtle towards the giant with unimaginable speed, disappearing in its vivid purple flames.

I pull myself and Ramze onto the ledge of some low rocks that together make up a narrow strip of land. They lead a path to some odd hole—a trapezoid opening exhaling cool blasts—pressed far ahead along a tower of boulders. A cave I expect has an exit at its end.

I need an explanation out of this guy as soon as he wakes up.

The cave is surrounded by flying seagulls and strange wriggling clouds. I sit down on a sub-rounded rock closest to the ledge I climbed after struggling to get Ramze on my back and dropping him off at the cave's entrance. I place my hands on my face and continue telling myself, "I have to come back from this."

Looking out to the clouds there's nothing but mist in the atmosphere and out by the ocean. Those purple flames. What was their significance to me if any at all? I feel as if that thing, that angel of death was more than I perceived in that state of fear. The second board I received from my father, carved and ready to ride before it was even known of my conception was truly for Kosta. It was only till I was born that Kosta's first ever two boards were repainted in my persona.

The first was the golden octopus surfboard from when I gripped my dad's chain as a newborn. To compensate for my father's taking of Kosta's first ever two boards, that'd yet to be used, he'd given Kosta that gold octopus necklace. Daniel was having money troubles and was superstitious about gifting his offspring a surfboard in their first two years of life. The deed would make the recipient a great surfer. He'd done it with Jade, he'd done it with Kosta, and then it was my turn to receive the gift of two boards.

The second board was repainted to portray a purple sun in which I remember my dad elaborating on the meaning once I was old enough to understand. A poetic symbolism that's aided in the color of royalty or spiritual fulfillment that's purple. The sun was a supposed male side of my nature in being driven without direction. Daniel recognized the sun as the great male principle. The ultimate yang as ancient Chinese culture did.

As a two-year-old I was told I showed superiority over my then four-year-old brother Kosta and curiosity followed me as I'd invest it into every little item I'd come across. The purple sun may be a melodramatic representation of who I was when I was two, but Daniel never overlooked anything about who I was growing up. Even as a child, character is a sign of progression through the years that mustn't be taken lightly. Especially if you see that same light that you had in yourself as a kid in your son.

What may've driven that thing to try and kill me must have a cause. If not, why did it and its iron chains chase me? A fire, somehow purple, burning over it. From a religious or spiritual perspective, it might've had a position of royalty in the kingdom of heaven and maybe it was looking to be fulfilled through a certain means of searching in its curiosity; not unlike my own. Curiosity then solicited its payment with punishment. That's what the fire represents.

I might be looking too deep into this, but I believe I'm right in the subject matter. Ramze must have delved into that vitality. If I can just get a word from him, I know I'd understand some of what I saw. It's not every day you see what I believe was a fallen angel garnished in a riveting purple fire. In any case, I should be worrying about how I'm supposed to get out of here and back on the road. I walk back up to the cave on the path of rocks with crevices in each.

"Wake up!" I lean over and shake Ramze with both my hands pressed rigidly against the sides of his shoulders. I kneel next to him and start tapping him on the cheek ruggedly till his eyes shoot open. He rolls onto his side, avoiding having to face me. His sweeping eagle wings are still intact, drooping from his back.

"I can't believe you! You know I'm deathly afraid of blood. How're we supposed to find Lucas now and get back on the road? What's gotten into you?" he asks broodingly.

"I don't know," I answer hesitantly. I really don't know what came over me other than defending myself in what I felt was a bad situation. But I can't tell him that. This isn't my friend Ramze I'm speaking to. It's a complete stranger who's never met my brother. Otherwise, why would he have tried so hard denying I've a brother when the cost of his lie would be his life on the line? I've omitted all possibilities that this newfound version of Ramze is a liar. All the sudden I'm second guessing my actions and my state of mind is in a dark place.

"I need someone to confine in. I need your help. Can I trust you?"

"What do you mean can—" he began to say.

"Can I trust you!?" I interrupt him.

"Yes," he asserts in a crude tone.

"I saw something in the water. Something evil. It was trying to get me."

"You're on drugs," he remarks.

"No! You don't understand. It was with us in the water, and I think it could find us if we stay here."

"For your own sanity calm down. I mean for fuck's sake you stabbed me in the leg. The jaguar's spit is in your blood and it's not leaving your body for another couple of hours so relax." He continues harshly after taking a deep breath. "You forced me to do it. Now you'll have to endure its effects."

Ramze's head's facing away from me but his body's facing the sky. His leg's bleeding, bent into his chest with his two hands covering the wound. Blood trickles down in between each finger.

"I'm sorry I did that to you."

"Cut the bullshit. Don't ever say sorry out of pity for something you've willingly done. It won't heal the wound," he says with resentment, then throwing up about two liters' worth of ocean water.

I feel a tension between us, but I proceed in telling him of the creature I saw. "It was a shrouded giant, youthful in the face with fulsome rose gold hair, a colossal mouth, and most, if not all of it, was burning in dark purple fires underwater. It carried chains with slaves that were once angels but as I saw them before my very eyes, became shadows of the deep."

"It's not an it," he speaks coughing out the rest of the salt water in his stomach and then turning fully to one side in order to face me. "It's a he and his name is Samael. You had a near death experience. What you saw down there wasn't real for people often see things that aren't necessarily there in a moment of fear. Not to mention you were injected with jaguar's spit. An extremely powerful hallucinogen. If what you're describing is true, then what you saw may very well be the angel of death but that was only your baked mind playing hooky with you because you assumed you were about to die. I can't say I haven't heard outlandish incarnations of Samael like the one you've just described. Usually from people on drugs who've a conviction they're going to die."

"Where does he come from?" I quiz him.

"It's a character from Talmudic folklore also known by other names such as the grim reaper. I'm sure you've heard of him."

Ramze is still the same visionary. His studies into a broad range of beliefs have come in handy. I'm at ease now that I know if I'm ever confronted by the image of Samael again, I'll know what I'm dealing with or at least what I'm hallucinating.

I feel a part of my head alleviated and maybe it's the drug releasing me from its clasp. I press the front of my hand over the side of my neck where the drug was injected and then bring it to my face to view my fingers. There's no blood. The ocean cleared what was an insignificant wound equated to Ramze's stabbed leg.

Ramze's wings become a soaked baby blue long-sleeved t-shirt pressed tightly against his skin. Each burnt umber feather turned blue, thinned into a single thread, and with exceptional sewing, all became one in the form of a shirt. He grabs the collar of his shirt and stretches it from the neck, getting it loose enough for deeper inhalations. Something falls out of the opening of his damp baby blue shirt.

A lambent gold is clamant to my eyes. I close them and dither in opening them again because of what I might see. Kosta's gold octopus chain encompasses Ramze's neck.

"My father's necklace!" I blurt out into the open.

Ramze quickly grabs it and pressures it against his chest. "It's mine!" he outcries. "Mine!" His eyes light up in a buttercup yellow fire as they had when he first grew wings.

It's weird how his reaction immediately put him on the offensive. It looks familiar, I say standing up and walking into the cave as if thinking nothing of it. Honest-to-god I'll find some way to get it back. I'm not sure how he has it in the first place but to whom I ask, is this crippled guy whose mind comes from another Ramze? It's unbeknownst to me who he is or where he came from. For all I know I was dropped off in the ocean yesterday by what could've been an alien spacecraft. That'd make a good story to tell my creator who's putting me through this.

"Ha-ha, you got me this time heavens! This is just how I planned to spend the afterlife. Reliving my actual life! In a weirder, detrimental way."

"What'd you say?" Ramze calls out from outside the cave.

"I'll be right back dude! I'ma go find us some help!"

At least I know he can't go anywhere now that his other leg is injured. I'm not sure I believe his story in how he fractured the right one. He was perfectly fine up to the plane landing. At arrivals he became distant. Then he took a taxi to what he said was a humble property he owned in Costa Rica. In the meantime, we went to go eat at a native restaurant a couple blocks from the airport. The best empanadas and tamales I've ever had.

After waiting at the restaurant for nearly two hours he came back in a yellow pickup truck and told us he fell running down the stairs in his house. In realizing that he'd passed out on his bed, he rushed to come get us resulting in the irrepressible fall down the stairs, leading to the probable breaking of a bone in his right leg.

He'd rejected any suggestion to be taken to a hospital. Lucas had to drive the pickup truck from the airport thereafter because he worried Ramze was unfit to drive. On top of that, he and Lucas spawned the most random argument once we got to Playa Hermosa.

As soon as the pickup truck stopped, Kosta and I left for the sand while they stayed behind. I came back to get our surfboards. They're on the other side of the large pickup truck; tall enough that they didn't even notice me arrive. I saw there was rope on the ground and Lucas' orange hiking backpack aside it. The screwdriver I stabbed Ramze with was creeping out of it.

A couple of unlikely tools I'd assume no one would bring on a surf trip were also falling out of his backpack. There was a jack knife, two seven-inch bayonet knives, and a disassembled AR-7 rifle. More so items people would bring on a hunting trip. Odd but fairly unsuspecting as I'm used to these two boneheads being enigmatic.

I'd heard the name Lucy and innocently enough I walked to the front of the pickup truck and hopped aboard the rim of the hood startling both of them.

"Who's Lucy? Huh?"

Lucas flat-out answered by saying it's the name Ramze has for his truck. Ramze was infuriated and he stormed off, limping with water droplets at the peak of falling from his eyes.

"Don't worry," Lucas said, nonchalantly. "He's just mad he can't surf. The dumbass probably just sprained his leg."

I started to snigger as Lucas grabbed his surfboard from the open cargo bed and we headed to the ocean. His arm tight around the back of my neck and his hand over my chest. I looked back once but Ramze had vanished and so had the backpack. The memory is fresh in my mind as if only yesterday it'd occurred. Although it isn't as if it'd happened last year.

As a matter of fact, it was yesterday. I'm currently living in the past. A moment which was just last Friday before I got shot. Today is Friday. Today was spent at Jacobi beach surfing. The only major nuance now is that Lucas took a

UP STRAWBERRY VINE

divergent path on our way to Jacobi from Fundy's where he got the jaguar's spit. Everything after Lucas and Ramze didn't know Kosta, and Lucas drove us into the fog, is rewritten history.

The end of the cave is an opening to a rock wall shielded with moist moss and jungle vines that fall as basil green brush strokes on a vitric black canvas. I start climbing the slippery wall. Up I go with a prudent approach to get a hold onto every possible grip. A steady thirty-foot climb shouldn't be too much of a delay. Halfway up, I bury my head inside a hole to take a breather.

I pull myself the rest of the way up by taking several of the vines around me and using them as rope to drag myself along the rocks. I've bloody calluses on my hands and a scraped knee once I reach the top, though I've seen worse on Ramze's palms from regular lifting sessions.

Out of the cave, into the light, and nearing a jungle. Alas, I feel free. I begin breathing in all the tropics and dance my head around a couple of times with my eyes closed to make sure I can actually breathe. A great deal of plant life arises from out of the ground making it my problem now to pick which trail I should take. Rather, make.

Green. Nothing but greenery for my eyes to soak in. So much so that I feel sick in spite of the healthy rainforest laughing at my defrayal. Karma for hamming it up when Lucas told me I've no brother. I can't manage to lose myself here. The risk of substantial blood loss Ramze faces every second I'm gone while in exposure to green would be one of my greatest regrets. It wouldn't be enough for him to depart but leaving him behind in that state as he writhes in pain, his aversion to blood intensifying, will haunt me. Especially since I'm to blame. Next, I find myself running like an idiot across the unbalanced terrain with sweat failing to cool.

Birds evaporate into the sun, peaking in on me through the cracks of widespread tree palms. With that, the escape to an open road gets darker as I glide deeper into the rainforest. I'm being exposed to something I fear and that's life taking away my chance at survival as night creeps in on day.

"Dreary minded specimen is I. No. I is maikaì."

Maika'i means good in Hawaiian. Fish speaks it aloud whenever she's stressed. I repeat the Hawaiian phrase out loud for several measures. One, to keep calm. Two, to stay positive. And three, to remember the friend who'd tell my sister we'd come here in the first place. As soon as Malia finds out my brother and I are missing she'll rat us out to my sister. They'll have a search party sent out to find us. Jade and Fish will be waiting to greet us back at Sebastian Municipal Airport, ecstatic at our arrival and relieved that we're chipper and able-bodied. Right? Everything goes back to normal and I continue to live my life.

Wrong.

Boy am I wrong. Nothing could be farther from the truth. I almost killed my two friends in an outburst. I hope Lucas found settled land and is safe so that he may lead the locals to come and get us. Then it rang in my head. What Ramze had stated the second he saw the jaguar's spit. Locals use the drug to guide unsuspecting tourists into the deliverance of the wild where they'll remain lost. If I do find someone and fast, I must be careful with my choice of words and manage to communicate with a language I don't speak in a friendly fashion.

There's partial light available where most of the plants ahead are smudged images seen through my doped-up eyes. I generally have crystalline eyesight. I see a definite boundary between the wholly illuminated part of the rainforest and its true shadow where things aren't meant to be discovered. The sun is out of sight but it's daytime. I realize this when I think back to when we drove up the mountain. It was only seven in the morning.

It can't be that many hours that've passed from then to now. I may've lost track of time but I'm certain night is beyond approach. I still have hours till dusk. It's this place I'm in that's making me believe in the day's end. The rainforest is quite fixed in who it allows in this intimate depth. Only night crawlers could fend where I'm walking now.

I stop, nodding my head down and positioning my left wrist with the attached wristwatch towards my chest. It's too dark to see the exact time but as I lift the watch to my left ear, I can't hear it emitting the fine-grained click beetle sound of its regular two second ticking. The polychromatic watch changes colors at different temperatures and has an atmospheric pressure rating of 40 ATM so it can be submerged as far as 400 meters underwater. I'm not sure how the currently yellow watch broke.

A rumbling of magnolia leaves become a boy incarnate as I stand there with a kid rising out from a bush. "You're the kid from the mountain," I say gobsmacked, stumbling back and staring avidly at the boy. "The boy who saw me fall off the cliff. Here you stand before me but how exactly did you get here?"

The boy begins to gravitate further into the rainforest by shifting his direction opposite me and sprinting away. His flowing dark olive green greatcoat and Spanish bistre dress shirt ensemble with baggy Spanish bistre pants and beige over-the-knee boots are unmarked by the woodlands. The clothes start to camouflage themselves with the nature around them. His greatcoat mirroring a cape as he runs.

"Hey! Come back!" I shout.

I start chasing after this itinerant boy questioning why he's in such an overcast, somber part of the area. Is it that I'm currently hooked on the drug and it still needs to leave my system? If so, why go after something that's not even there? In coming to my senses, I am cognizant that this boy appeared flying in front of the pickup truck before I was ever even stabbed with the jaguar's spit. Meaning one and one thing only...that boy's real.

Chapter 16

With bubblegum and lady luck I can blow a bubble big enough, hop inside it, and let it carry me out of this maleficent rainforest. I'm being over the top, but I keep getting wacked by big glossy leaves, dodging trees, running to this boy, and I'm to the point where I can't help thinking I'm on a wild goose chase. Ramze did say I'd a couple hours left of enduring the jaguar's spit. I start to walk, biting the air instead of gasping for it, letting it know how much I need it in my chest.

"Stay with me...please," I barely get out the strength to say. This little one's taunting me. The boy slows down every time I do, making sure to glance back every couple seconds in case I start running again.

I hear wild boars pass me by inches from where I walk. I can't bear in mind if I've ever seen something as menacingly ugly as these creatures being pulled from right out of a nightmare. They grunt every time their snouts touch leaves, releasing the sound of someone with a cold inhaling snot. I shiver with goosebumps at their squealing.

Thunder roars through the mountain skies, drowning out the pigs' insignificant cries. Trees sway in the wind, pulsating as if at any moment their trunks will snap. Sadly, I'm stuck in an incoming storm that wails over the deep environment in a blood-curdling rhythm. A crowd stomps their feet on rickety metal bleachers, gaining momentum as their college football game intensifies. With every crack of the whip, the crowd grows louder with feverishness. The befall of floods is promising.

Strident rains are summoned from the abode of Poseidon. Squalls of driving torrents bear the salinity and co-variation of nutrient concentrations; key to rejuvenate a primeval dry wood. Earth rejoices. She accepts the feast of rich minerals that the north-easterly trade winds carry from the offshore European and North African countries thousands of miles east. Plant life flourishes here without human intervention committed to deforestation. It's a lush, unruly landscape. Too bad I can't enjoy any of it in my situation.

Muddy terrain piled with continuous rain has flooded the ground turning it into a swamp with a slushy surface. The water at my feet gets warmer and I'm suddenly treading on layers of buttery pastry. The comfort is short lived. It's cold again and the pastry turns rough. The brush of my toes on serrated rocks, hidden by the beige stream I walk across, is tearing the tips of my toenails and heels of my feet.

I'd lost my sandals in the ocean after falling and getting swallowed by it; scattering through all the fuss of the morphed angels and the youthful Samael that choked them. The pigs ransack bananas from the palm trees above me.

Dim sunlight has found a way to come in through the tall trees and I can see a series of batches; batches of yellowish-green premature bananas falling into the mouths of these gray-haired pigs. One pig passes a stack of bananas to their mate as though it were a bouquet of roses. The mate delivers its romantic partner a slurping smooch from its neck to its ear.

They run into the trees, head-butting them till the food dislodges from their branches, becoming one with their foaming dark salmon mouths. Upon the ravenous clasp of their narrow black hooves drips any excess fare they fail to thoroughly chew. As I inspect their behavior, they stomp on any uncaught bananas, leaving sound spoors in the mire. The mushy combination of jaundiced rinds and starch rich banana flesh lies shoddily entombed in their salivating mouths. Vacate they do. Tis after their stomachs' content.

One of the boars has tusks that fan out from the rims of its mouth. It stands tall over the few surrounding boars that loom out of darkness. While the others stand low, the tusked boar keeps penetrating a side of the tree containing the last family of bananas. The little ones with their little hoofs and their giant heads, much larger in proportion to their compact bodies, move vigorously across the stream. As they push against the mud, I follow.

I locate where they head to for shelter. I stay far from it and cease from any venture that requires movement as the subtle scent of black pudding seeps in through my nostrils. The sound of a grumbling stomach rear ends me. The stomping of an animal progresses, digging deep into the ground. I swiftly turn, keeping eyes locked on the fair view of rain dripping down from the tree palms. Waiting for a bull to ram me but rather seeing a baby boar kicking.

Setting sight on the boar behind me, it shrieks with increasing yawns that show blood stains on its snout. Its body lays crushed under a fallen tree log that seems to have been stricken by lightning just seconds earlier. The end of the log is burnt black as the subdued fire from a lightning strike is put out by the ongoing rain.

I think twice before assisting this being in helpless need. I do hear the calls of pain, but that kid is close. Enough that I'd catch up to him in a matter of seconds. The boy is my only hope to find others out here. Some civilization that'll get me down the road to that store we first picked up food and drugs.

I hesitate, switching gears, turning my head left and right from panic. He mustn't want to be discovered if he's running so I let him go, leaving behind my existence to the saving of this pig meat. His mystery subsiding for now.

It must be starving. There're always consequences in doing the right thing. Just when I thought this animal would be grateful for getting this weight off it, it attacks me. I grapple it, taking a hold of the body and flipping it upside down. I latch onto its belly, but it squirms out of my grasp. It ends up bailing, running towards the safety of its clan. The shelter of a downward hill plastered with lanky grass.

The unclipped grass as I sneak ahead and come to view it from the top of the hill is next to a beryl creek with catfish jumping in the air. Water rushes into the creek and exits it in a linear formation. One end must empty into a riverbank but there're no rivers in sight. I think I'll find someone if I follow the water but how far? How long must I continue to walk in this downpour?

I'm lost. In a probable eighteen billion square feet of forest land. From the map of light, I might be able to conjure up an exit in my mind, seeing as how the details of this map were so eloquently drawn out to be everything one man may need. If those maps were to ever get in the hands of a thrill seeker or a government organ, the causation would be one of two. Ramze or Lucas. Keepers of these maps. Charted and designed by Jake. Sedately handed over to the three of us. So greatly instilled in our memory that losing them is an inconsiderable worry when navigating foreign lands.

Withal my sluggish activities, I didn't partake in the studious efforts of my two friends who did take the time to remember all of the maps. I mistook my memory's recognition of these surroundings for the only map I did study—Malaysia. As this was supposed to be a pit stop on our journey and not an enduring trap on common tourists.

The Malaysia trip would've come after the wedding. By a long shot, the maximum days we would've been surfing here was four so that we'd be back home by Monday morning. The day of Erik's bachelor party and then attend the wedding on Tuesday. I assumed that since we planned to be in Costa Rica for such a short time, I didn't have to remember this specific map but once again I was leaning on my naiveté. My inexperience in expecting the unexpected has bit me in the butt this time around.

How can these maps of so called light and secret access be obtained out of the knowledge of an average Joe like stoner Jake? I didn't think of questioning it till now. Another dispute I might add is what power can paper hold? There's a reason us three swore to Jake we'd protect them. We failed him because now one lies in the ocean missing.

Those loaded maps of a beautiful and creative mind. They've a tinting that makes glowing possible in the dark and contain multiple layers where one can turn the pages to see beyond the land of natives. In the sky and underground. Every ounce of water, every grain of sand in the database of this fey see-through map.

Its transparent attribute is the work of nano technicians who polish the fibers of recycled paper in order to make paper—vapor. Each piece of the glassy map is a sticky sheet written on with thin blue ink uncovering the dwellings of a particular altitude. The altitudes span from the deepest point in the surrounding oceans to the highest point on the highest mountain. When they're leveled over the other the reveal is a simulated eye-popping, downsized environment.

You need only use an eyeglass to reveal the rapturous degree of detail. The first one in the series of maps is now gone. Its three-dimensional graphics made it better than any navigational system that awkwardly talks in a robotic female voice. The mechanics of Jake's gift to our travels are too complex and perhaps too expensive to guide others.

It's something people have never seen. Something people aren't ready for. An invention that needs no introduction because it's simply a map with no patent behind its process. Its craftsmanship as unique as its maker. The maker who I'd compare to Andrea del Verrocchio.

The maps are truly superior to our time. Without limits to the use or wonder it can provide a traveler. Remote from sightseers' greatest wishes as these maps are unattainable and will remain with Ramze, Lucas, and I so long as Jake doesn't ask for them back.

The map's primary limitation is it only reveals the natural topography of each area we're in so there aren't any actual roads on the maps. We follow the land as most of the time, the reason these maps don't have roads is because there aren't any man-made roads from the populated areas of a country to the secret beaches. There's no point in including the roads that do exist outside the beaches because they don't lead us to the beaches themselves. Instead, we find nature's obstacles that keep the beaches hidden and decipher a way around them.

If only I had that first map now. I set sight on the tall grass as a screech is heard from within the singular. A line of blood cruises down from the pit of hidden boars into the stream. The group of them scramble out of the grass in opposite directions. I hear heavy munching sounds within their shelter thereafter. The baby boar is the only one that didn't come out. I retreat from the hill staggered, backing away from the stream as sleek as a black mamba. Once more, I miss the opportunity to find people.

Now that I've limited my source of flowing water who knows how long before I find another. I bulge ahead with blunt intuition. Searching to find the light again but at least in coverage from the rain. The trees here are thicker than past with colorful trunks of army green, marmalade, and maroon.

The Cimmerian forest with its damp tropics sees fit to provide yellow eyes in every outlying depth I perceive to be corners. Phosphorescent like the chemical gleam in the maps. I can tell they're eyes because they're blinking. They're tiny in shape. As small as a pebble yet as bright as a firefly. There're a couple dozen pairs up in the trees.

My foot gets caught on a tree's surface root. I do not falter to the animals amongst me. Instead, I reach to grab a mango off this smallest of trees that holds me with twisting arms dangling above. One of the yellow-eyed creatures is locking lips with it. I bring it close to my face noticing the short patches of bruising on the mango. Rotating it so that the fresh side is given to the animal, I take a bite of it with the umber furred creature sharing the bite.

Our eyes meet one another. This nocturnal I find has only one eye. Not sure if a birth defect or a fight with another creature cost it its eye. I ease the mango back on a low branch. It keeps its thorny teeth clenched to the fruit. It clings to the branch, flapping its brown wings upside down. I giggle as it starts swinging, making a scratching kind of sound through its wee fangs. In rocking itself it allows the fruit to fall from its mouth. Not certain if the rough sound it's made is echolocation.

I pick up the mango and put it back in its mouth. I swipe my forearm across my mouth wiping the mango juices from my face. I jerk my foot away from the curved tree root that rises out of the ground.

I return to the mudded grounds of this forest and drag my feet along with the modest wind current pushing the water against me. I hang low fearing that whatever ate that boar might still be near but glad that those fruit bats didn't have an acquired taste for blood.

The water I'm treading on is a marsh. The brown thick mud rises to my waist as I enter an area of little land and no trees. Not even at the borders I see. Finally, I've a good view of the sky.

The sun, partly hidden by two clouds, permits me to see better but the rain and lightning show no signs of retreat. The rest of the sky has a grand nebulous glow. The darkest of clouds distinct themselves from the glow. They're the two that cover the sun; the main concentration of heavy rain and lightning. Meanwhile on the ground, a low white haze floats above the water. It submits itself to the environment giving me little assurance as to where it is I'm headed.

My feet can touch the bottom of the marsh if I decide to walk but swimming will be faster. I swim towards a patch of land in the middle of this slough. About five yards in diameter, it's surrounded by water and home to one fairly tall tree, six times my height, with a thick base that tapers the higher it gets. I didn't see it from land due to the fog, but I see it now as I'm swimming up to it. The tree's crown is characterized by a shrub of mint green leaves.

Encircling the base of the tree are fat, fine-grained textured rocks that're wider at their center and angular at their ends. I climb onto land by grabbing onto the dangled, over the edge, tail-like end of one of the rocks. As I pull myself up, I'm rankled for I've the taste of bitter burnt rice in my mouth. I spit out some mud that'd smuggled its way into my mouth as I swam. All the same, it's made a home for itself in between my teeth. I inspect the similar rocks while standing but elect on kneeling to get an even closer look.

Crocodiles!

My hands swing to my mouth. One hand is highly pressured over the other to prevent the startled me from releasing inherent screams out of a concrete fear. I steadily rise from my bent position and take one step back. Jaws snap shut. A wheel of primary colors surfaces from the canopy above me. I don't catch on to what it is right away. It swivels deftly in the rain. A hellish squawk warns the flock of imminent danger. The psychedelic wheel breaks in a fracas. The scarlet macaws were sundered by panic. Alone, each multicolored red, blue, and yellow parrot sets flight from this minute island, evanescing into the fog. It's possible a cluster of trees awaits their union on high ground.

The birds take shelter in the opposite direction from where I swam. I rapidly turn to another crocodile behind me. I resort to ripping bark off the center piece of this land—the tree of jarring mint—by digging my fingers deep into a somewhat already tenuous part of it. The bark that's given onto me by tearing quickly is thin and soaked by rain. I, without any aim, throw it like a dart to the crocodile closest to me hoping it stunts it. It lands on top of the one that's now at my front.

A strike of blue light blinds me and leaves me with a repellant metallic taste in my mouth. I'm forewarned by maddened thunder of stronger to come. I'm so terrified that I must've missed the warning train as my tingling skin tried to tell me not to pursue a straight course through the water. I clumsily trip over another crocodile. I crawl hysterically on my hands and knees to the peeled tree, spin around and lie back on it, staring attentively at the reptiles for any subtle movements.

None dart to me for an attack. It's only seconds later that I can separate fear from fact and process—these animals aren't alive. They're formidable statues. "Rocks," I say aloud. I sigh with a nervous laugh but even then, I'm unsure if I've made a mistake. I'm put back on the offensive. My throat tightens, prompting me to swallow hard, waiting for any of the rocks to start moving. I push my feet deep into the dirt to get my back as tightly pressed against the tree as possible.

They're so realistically made that man must've sculpted them but surely not for art, out here where no one can see it. Unless that art's purpose is to provoke fear in local wildlife. The sound of jaws snapping was most likely a broken tree branch falling. Not sure how I feel about the inclement weather and being so close to an object that's a call for lightning strikes.

I loosen up a little. I'd rather stay under this tree however for I can't know for certain if there're any live crocodiles in the water longing for live bait. I'll make an effort to swim through the thickly muddied waters after this rain and fog dissipates. I'd feel safe with a clearer vision of the water. My state of mind need be at peace from an animal attack now that the thought of being torn up by crocodiles is sunken into my head.

I lower my head while sitting and wait, overwrought by the image of encountering people again. More so, I'm nervous about how I'll get to that point. A few hours from now I could be sipping whiskey on a one-way flight back to Florida. Surely, I'll cherish my sister's wedding to come. All that scrumptious food that I could use now, I muse as my stomach grumbles.

Steamed steak marinated in black pepper, soy sauce, garlic, and just a hint of lemon to give it that kick. Accompanied by a nice green decadent salad and crusty bread. And who can go wrong with roasted red potatoes and sautéed shrimp. A meal fit for a king and for dessert, colorful macaroons that're sweet, creamy, and share in the tasty blend of coconuts with pistachio. Being random, I also feel like eating chili lemon octopus with cucumber salad at the moment, even though this dish wasn't an option at the wedding.

The sound of rain is so pleasing. I mostly enjoy myself when I surf in the rain. It's the feel of water droplets falling all over me and then making them dance to my rhythm as I purposefully wobble that's invigorating. The oceans tend to move cautiously when there's a delicate rain and charge with an offensive tackle when there's a storm. Each experience of surfing in the rain reminds me of the high seas pirates endured in the 16th century when their presence was in the grassroots phase of leaving behind a legacy.

I manage to zone out the damning thunderclaps by zeroing in on the rain. I'm absorbed into each drop, resolving my trial.

Resolve...ha!

O this illusive conclusion on which I've dropped anchor.
Land, ho! I've arrived in the kingdom of forty winks.
Dare you close your eyes numb nut?

Chapter 17

In a gradual manner I open my eyes, blinking a number of times. My head swings up in a jolt. I lower it dazed and addled. I try raising my chin high, ready to howl in the absence of a full moon. My head is a wrecking ball on a crane. As it begins to lower itself defiantly, I think to let it go. Five more minutes and I'll rise up, high like the peak of a Portuguese wave.

From a bad inkling sprouts fear. The hibernating bear in me grapples with stout pushback from this fear. Neurotic about predators. Should I be this chary of a snooze? For there's a kicking horse in my stomach, I cannot stay. A vigilant self overtakes the fourth sin in me. A yen for survival. It's time. Wake up before you're comatose.

I circle my head as I raise it with purpose, jutting my chin out. I belt loudly. Not my forte. This, a beginner singer's ill attempt to hit that last soprano note. My throat's strained. Leaves dance to the beat of a blowing wind disseminating an unfrequented wood. Confidence in others out here wanes. I dread bright when it's a predator and not a sight purely glistening upon water. Brown–green swamp water kissed by the brightness of daffodils tinged with white light. Transfixing the greatest of heliophiles.

I'm unsure of how long I've been under the sun. I look at my yellow wristwatch. My eyes shift to its detachable compass on its yellow band, two sizes smaller than the case of the watch. The tree's shadow is pointed east, away from me. The tree's crown would've covered me had the sun been directly above it.

Without shade, my skin has secured a dash of red in its complexion. It partly hurts to move the sections of my body that've been exposed to a scorching sun. I get up at a leisurely pace, placing one hand on my chest. The other pushes off the ground with my feet. Both my dirt-ridden hands rush fingers through my hair letting it fall back. Only then do I notice a chub in my pants. Surely, I must've been dry humping a smoking hot female in dreams of better days.

I fell asleep but hopefully not for an entire day. It's 9:34 A.M. according to my yellow wristwatch. The black Jolly Rogers t-shirt I'm wearing seems to have shrunk from all the water it's taken to. Unlike me, it hasn't persevered and is now ruined. Pressed tightly onto my skin so much so that I find it hard to breathe. The once white skull and crossed swords under it, printed on the t-shirt, are now an off-shade of beige. As for my highlighter yellow board shorts, the forest inconveniences flunked out of the college of soiling performance fabric. The quality remains pristine.

I struggle to take my shirt off, gripping it from the ends and trying to get it up over my head. It puts up an irreproachable fight at the collar. After finally getting it off in a rage, I wrap it around my head like a clumsily made turban. I pretend not to notice my farmer's tan nor the marked red lines just under my shoulders from the tightening short sleeves of the shirt. I walk to the edge of the mud water and tap it lightly with my right foot. I shiver, shaking off nerves. It's cold but a mud bath seems a refreshing offering in this heat.

I get in at a snail's pace and without hurry, swim to the edge of highland where the scarlet macaws had flown to during the rain. My foot hits a pole as I'm paddling. I stand on the cruddy surface of this marsh and grab hold of an end. I lift the long wooden stick. Out comes a kabob with three white drones straight through it. The wooden pole's head that penetrated the drone quadcopters is hand-forged steel with a Clovis point. It bears the distinctive marks of craftsmanship—a fluted shape with finely serrated edges and a Damascus texture with its wavy pattern. I let go of the spear, letting it sink with the attached drones. I better not face off against any hostile tribes.

The end of the slough leads me to an upward, muddy, and hole-filled knoll. I try and climb it, wanting to reach the crest where the birds are unwinding. Only fourteen feet high, the knoll is putting up its own fight. I keep slipping halfway up, falling back first into the mud water. I start losing patience and the strength to keep trying. I decide to swim back to the island and maybe see from there if there're any other available routes onto highland.

As I get back to the small island I see and hear a shudder in the tree branches, rocking up and down like it's having a spasm. I grab hold of a crocodile statue's tail, hanging over the edge of the water, to get back onto land. I can't see any of the parrots from before hanging out in the tree but there's something stealthily moving within the coverage of mint green leaves that's the dull green color of roasted asparagus.

I walk right below the tree and stare from the ground up. A crocodile up in the tree gapes at me as if I were a new toy.

It looks to be about ten feet in length, but I can't believe my eyes. Crocodiles don't climb trees. The more I stare, the more I notice its physical characteristics are separate from that of a crocodile. As a point of reference, I do a double take at the crocodile sculptures next to me.

The head proportions are similar to that of a croc with a long flat top and round snout. The skin however is loose around its neck and stomach with it tightening around its four bowed legs. The end of the body has a huge muscular tail whipping from side to side alike a croc. Even so, this animal has more freedom to move its tail. More flexibility. Some sort of lizard.

Two black lily pads bordered by lava follow me as I step away from the tree. It runs vertically down the tree trunk using its large, black curved claws to grip onto the wood. It stops at the base of the tree and opens its mouth in which it reveals a bloody forked tongue and saffron rotten shark-like teeth. The teeth are so tiny they'd be nearly impossible to see if not for how yellow they are from what I infer is a recent feeding. It smells of mildew on meat or it's possible the decayed fat of an animal.

Two phthalo green and bright iridescent blue eye feathers fall from the giant lizard's mouth. Another feather hangs from its jaw in between its lower set of teeth. It reeks of raw sewage. The rapidity of the smell comes to me out of nowhere. I grip my nose tightly to spare my lungs. At the edge of vomiting, I stand my ground.

I'm getting desensitized from the jaguar's spit to the repugnant scent. I just know it. In a heartbeat I'd faint if it weren't for the drug blocking the smell. Only a smattering is getting through to me, but I know there's more to it that'd knock me out past what this drug allows me to sense. The power of the jaguar's spit is fleeting. The toxins that I can presently detect will increase. With it, their horrid stench. "Come at me lizard monster," I press for confrontation in a nasally voice.

"It'll make nice boots!" speaks a static voice through an electronic amplifier. The sound booms and frightens both the lizard and me. The lizard jolts backwards. I rousingly turn to the knoll I fell off previously and there at the top of the hill stands a thin, shirtless pallid man with a violet bowtie. He wears a white towel around the waist and a snow camo gas mask over his head with round chemical air filters at the cheeks that look like two glued on elongated cans of tuna. A pure gold double barrel shotgun is nestled in his arms.

I hear a breathy hiss from behind me. The turning of my body to it results in a quick, short bang. Thick red-orange blood peppers the side of my face. The lizard is tossed backwards in midair onto the tree. The duration of the shot was brisk. Its echo bounces off the surface of every crocodile sculpture surrounding my position. The shotgun fired leaves a trying ringing in my left ear.

"Don't move," the masked man orders in a stiff mechanical voice. "Komodo dragon blood is known for its toxicity. Something to do with the multiple strains of aggressive bacteria it carries," he nods absently as if concurring with himself. "Or perhaps it's its mouth that's the conveyor. Either way, let's avoid the discovery of what'll happen if it enters the body."

"A Komodo dragon?" I exhale through my mouth, letting go of my nose.

Don't know why things are frightening more so when I know what they are. I take the wet turban off my head and unroll it back into a shirt by whipping it. I use it to wipe the blood off my face and then hurl the shirt to the dead dragon, covering its guts. Failing to hide its upside-down head with an open mouth. A cringe inducing sight.

I stare to the man with a secret identity and still, I can't get any words of thanks out. The spectacular timing of his arrival not only saved my life but everything about this recent showdown is so random that I could've never expected it. "Help! I'm stuck down here," I yelp with a crack in raising my voice.

"Swim on over pool boy," says the guy who's wearing a towel.

"You said not to move!" I shout back.

"Well, you didn't listen, did you? You already used your shirt to wipe the blood. You'll be fine."

I plunge into the filth, breaking the surface of grime that floats atop of the water. I'm optimistic that this will be the last time I swim in these thickly mudded waters. At the knoll, the man puts down his shotgun and brings down a metal ladder. The ladder end sits at the bottom of the knoll and vaguely sinks an inch into the ground, just in front of the water. I climb on up.

My eyes nearing the top of the ladder, just over the knoll, hesitate in swallowing the sum total of the view. Recently mowed light-green grass is waving in a peaceful wind. The setting for a gothic castle with its walls overrun by trees—a vertical forest. An architectural feat, above and beyond Kosta's green project in our home.

The fortified structure is built of salvaged gray stones and has seafoam green shrubbery and neon green trees bolting upright from it. The sweeping, low lively branches are numerous and extensive, draping beautifully from all towers. The castle's surrounded by a land of evergreen trees, bald cypress trees with Spanish moss, and weeping white pine valleys. Trees unlike those I've seen in the rainforest.

"Is it a nursery?" I ask.

"Somewhat. We like trees," is his mechanized response.

Up high, pitch-black rectangular openings that round themselves out at the top accentuate the small blue birds perched on their ledges. The discreet narrow vertical openings on the castle are arrow slits. The highest tower on the inside of an outer curtain wall looks to be around six hundred feet tall. It's at the far back of the structure.

The outer curtain wall is in part destroyed. Bricks have fallen over that set way for an entrance into a bronze gatehouse. The turrets making up the crest of all towers look to have also been bronze once. They've since aged a greenish-gray color.

I finish the climb, one foot over the other on the steps of the ladder. Seizing the masked man's offered hand with my muddy fingers, the once-clean hand that pulls me up now bears evidence of a shared struggle in the form of earthy stains. He grabs the ladder and lifts it back up onto highland. Then he rests it on the grass at the knoll's edge, dangerously close to a precipitous descent. He picks up his gold shotgun and walks me down to the castle.

On these mystic grounds walk blue peacocks that drag their luxurious tails across pliant blades of grass. In a single feather, a glittering gold egg is painted with a light blue iris. Within that iris, a lily pad-shaped pupil the darkest shade of blue resides as was the crater in the ocean. It's not long before the dark green and misty teal expansion of feathers is revealed. Our steady stroll directly behind a peacock along our path gives it time to turn its long neck to us. It stares blanky at me, squawks, and fans out its aquatic colors, showing off its glamour shot before elegantly maneuvering through the space we've made between us.

"Stunning. The Komodo dragon you killed ate one of them you know."

"Yes. Baba Azul will rage if he finds out. Best to keep quiet about that sad fact." The static from the in-made voice amplifier of his snow camo gas mask leaves a tingling in my ears. Clear from the ringing of the shotgun fired that continues to curse my left ear.

"Take off your gas mask. I want to thank you but I'm afraid your seasoned, yet utile gas mask is a barrier between us getting better acquainted. The robot voice changer's also unhelpful in making this feel like your average meet-and-greet."

"We're all human here. To-a-moderate-extent," he pauses in between each word. With his elbows bent at a right angle, he animates a robot character using some mechanical dance moves in a silly fashion. "Ha-ha. Come with me into Neptune and I'll reveal my face. If it helps, I'll give you my name too." He stops doing the robot as we continue walking forward, closing in on the massive stronghold.

Further into land, we pass more of the delightful blue peacocks who faintly retreat as well as the scarlet macaws who restfully stand watching over us in the trees. "Not accustomed to new guests, are they?"

The masked man guides me to the bronze gatehouse. No, he says, stating this place doesn't get much guests because of the smell. That explains the gas mask he's wearing. I'm not in need of one because I'm drugged up at the moment on foreign narcotics. At least the drug isn't acting as a hallucinogen anymore. The grid gate opens upward by a simple wave of the hand on part of the masked man. A gust of warm air tears past two glass arched doors opaque with steam.

"You speak English. Are you from the US?"

Entering past the tall doors into the gatehouse, we come into a long windowless hall with fourteen portraits of men in wine purple suits and white top hats, donning proud expressions, each cradling a different human organ like it's a baby. The realistic portraits are lined on the left wall with magnified blurry photographs of ghostly white orbs framed directly across from them on the right. There's but one clear photograph of what looks like a full, greenish-gray cantaloupe, its rind possessing many rugged ridges, against a black backdrop. The cantaloupe hangs facing the man with the gallbladder.

Perhaps the most macabre portrait is of the suited man carrying a sheet of skin, folded like a blanket to look neat and tidy. A standalone frosted glass wall is erected at the end of the hall. A large monochrome Union Jack is moved ninety degrees to the right so that it hangs vertically on the glass wall.

"English. Native to Manchester," he states, putting his shotgun onto a hung wooden display case with a shamrock velvet inside to the left of him. Gripping the ends of his gas mask and lifting it up over his head, he tells me his name. "I'm Leonid!" His voice resonates with joy.

Beneath the gas mask is an older gentleman, perhaps around his late thirties with shallow and steady light-brown eyes. He's well-groomed with a slick vintage hairstyle that has the brown curls atop his head swept right. On his square face are thick eyebrows that could use a bit of a cleanup and a black handlebar mustache that's neatly trimmed with the sides not connecting to the rest of his facial hair—a triangular woolly goatee. The man's as tall as me and within his direct eyesight he asks for my name in return.

"Koata."

"I'll call you K. Do you have a lath name K?" The English accent is more prominent now without the gas mask. A slight lisp has also made an appearance.

"Of course, I have a last name. It's Califf," I say smugly. The glass arched doors automatically close behind us and the bronze gate is lowered over them, ending with a final plink.

"Wasn't thure if you were a bathtard child. Tho, K, how'd you get lotht in Costa Rica'th cloud foretht?"

"I was drugged," I respond somberly. His easily deciphered expression doesn't initially fit a concerned one but firstly it conveys interest. Then it switches posthaste to worry.

"Are you awright?"

"Yes. I'm fine now. What is this place?" I ask staring at the color-washed British flag. The ends of the single wall it covers are openings into another zone of the castle. I hear men quartered in what sounds like swimming pools from beyond the wall, laughing and conversing while splashing water.

"Thith ith a thanctuary for a group of men known ath the Immortal Jaguarth. Check it out." He points at the two-dimensional tattoo of a black cat on his right shoulder.

Its stocky, muscular body faces right. Standing on its hind legs with its feet pointed to the right and its upper paws reaching upward also to the right. The short tail is in the shape of a reverse S pointed left. The inflated head hardly manages to contain the cat's broad face within its boundaries. It has an overdone, elongated mouth so that its jaws are the foreground for the artwork. The round eyes above it have a strikingly demonic resemblance and are a touch squinted due to its mouth hung agape. I can only just make out its sinister stare—cold enough to forever bedevil an admirer of the tattoo should they look a second too long.

This two-dimensional tattoo is precisely identifiable as Abeni's black panther tattoo. Noted for its head's frontality and exaggerated features. Received by her from a tribe in Eritrea. Not even a negligible difference in the two marks. But how?

Chapter 18

I stare at the tattoo, inattentive to all else till Leonid lassoes back my center of attention by snapping his fingers.

"Hate to athk again, but are you awright there, mate?" Leonid questions delicately. My eyes aimlessly drop from the tattoo onto the ground. I'm embarrassed when I get caught off guard, staring off into space.

"Yea. That's a sick panther tattoo. That's all," I say dispassionately with my head lowered, staring at the gray lime-ash floor.

"Oh this? It's a jaguar. Common to get those two mammals mistaken for one another. Especially when this tat is missing the distinctive rosette spotted coat most jaguars have. Every man here is identified as a brother of this fraternity by this exact black jaguar on their right shoulder."

The mark is too thorough to oversight it as another feline tattoo. This is in fact Abeni's tribe symbol needled on her before adoption. She was nine years old when she got it. On the right shoulder too. "You good there, buddy?" I ask, keeping my head down, fidgeting with my hands and wringing them nervously. "Your speech impediment just left the chat."

"Ah, yes. Was hard to talk with this mouth guard in. Have a habit of grinding my teeth when I'm patrolling the grounds."

"So, is there a pool behind this wall?" I ask listening in on the splashing as I raise my head. Keeping my sight close to the floor as I pick my head up, I see that the white towel wrapped around his waist has a logo on a bottom corner. The logo stitched into the spa towel is the golden outline of a top hat within a circle.

"There're several. Come and see." He waves me over to follow in his steps. He leads me to the back of the frosted glass wall where a retreat is available for numerous men who're resting in Olympic-sized swimming pools. Two of which have steam rising out of them. Keeping close to the backside of the frosted glass wall, he stops at a white line. I stand with him over the line that splits this building in half.

"There're five pools in total. This room is a health farm for the Immortal Jaguars to delight in as they take a break from their arduous work schedules. Neptune currently houses over eight hundred men. A quarter of them being new recruits. About seventy men from Mercury—a sect of this fraternity—are always out on business trips. At any one time, seven hundred men shall be roaming the grounds. Any less would be bad luck. You'll probably never see more than a hundred brothers in the same place outside the health farm, besides at the theater or dining hall."

Nearly a hundred men are spread out, walking by and swimming inside the pools. Considering the size of this place, the number of men leave a glum emptiness to endure, like a bankrupt amusement park in talks to be closed. On the left-hand side of this building there're two pools. On the right-hand side there're three. Every pool has a distinct shape.

In between the two groups of pools, this white line we stand over continues forward and separates them. The white line comes to my attention. It's bright. The white radiates from underneath with the line acting as some sort of heavy glass structure, not more than a foot in width, able to hold our weight.

Brilliant translucent openings within oily black stone walls surround the pools and allocate a kaleidoscope of light from the sun to their pellucid waters. The colored glass on the windows measuredly plays with whatever sunlight it's given with an affinity to origami, folding light into decorative polyhedron and pentagonal shapes. Projected off glossy floors of ocean green, these colorful shapes embody a feeling of euphoria.

The polished marble mosaic tiles about the room, untouched by sacred geometry, are a frozen lake with an abundance of algae. The cracked teal shells from a slew of robin eggs sunken below it cry songs of subtle tranquility. Spellbound, I stare past the floors, through the steam, into the water. At last, the blocky shapes wiggling in the water come together in my head. I lift my head up from their reflections. Thousands of religious and historical symbols occupy the stained-glass windows throughout this enclosure with a peculiar stand-in for legs. Each character depicted here possesses a salmon's tail below the waist.

A particular window that stands out is magnificent in size and to my right. I only partly twist my waist to it, keeping my feet glued to the ground. On this right-hand wall, a window boasts the shape of the capital letter H—a balbis. On the left stem of the stately-sized balbis window is Napoleon Bonaparte in his imperial throne with a rose pink salmon tail.

The bar of the balbis connects the Napoleon I icon to another icon. But not only is it there to serve as a bridge between icons. The bar displays the words 'Per vitem fragum sursum,' elegantly spelled out with hundreds of sapphire and baby blue glass shards in each letter. The right stem, congruent to the left, concludes the shape of the balbis and presents...

"Is that the prophet Muhammad on the right line of the H?" I ask lamely, pointing to it.

Leonid fails to hide his contempt in my foolish assumption. "It's actually Jesus K. Unlike most interpretations of Jesus, that one there portrays him not as an altered European version with blond hair and blue eyes to resemble perfection in the eyes of the westerners who worship him but as a historical depiction of a dark-skinned Middle Eastern man. What Jesus would've looked like in the past according to what most scholars believe to be his origin. I'd say he looks much like the Middle Easterners of today; minus the bright orange fishtail of course."

I turn my body to Leonid from behind. "For me I can appreciate a genuine art form. Seeing this icon on stained glass. The craft. The great artistic skill it must've taken to conceive all of this. Well, it's just mind-boggling." Raising the muscles under my brows I exaggerate my blink as if I'm dreaming.

"I personally find truth to be more beautiful than lies. Don't you think so too?" Leonid asks, content on the information he's provided me with.

Rapid grating honks ring me in at an end of the health farm. Below the large lancet, cathedral, and rose windowpanes of tinted glass at my front are big fat geese running around chasing one another. Around forty frolic with their white feathered bodies not minding the heat from the steam that rolls past them.

I notice they're actually chasing a man in green and white swim trunks. He has a fairly young face, short shaggy red hair, and is of tall but chubby build. A black smile fills his whole face. One that'd run up the dental bills fixing to put his house in foreclosure. Charred breadcrumbs leap from his palm with a flick of the wrist behind his back. To my surprise, the few skinny geese are the ones being left behind. The fat ones interlock their long necks in a scrimmage their own. Those lucky to get in front first bearishly peck at the breadcrumbs using their orange beaks as weapons and guards.

The red head misses a step in running and begins to stumble on the wet floor. He saves himself from a fall by staggering to the edge of a pool and confidently flipping into it, causing a rowdy splash. His eyes steadily peep out from the surface as though conducting reconnaissance for a profile about geese. His disembodied arm shoots next to it and he throws the blackened loaf of bread he had in his pocket, now soaked, at the skinny geese while the fat geese peck away at the breadcrumbs he'd left behind. Good arm he has, having thrown that loaf of bread like a football all the way to the slow geese, still far from catching up to him.

"Who's that?"

"That's David. New member. He turned eighteen just a few weeks ago." Leonid gives me an engrossed look when he says this. He wants a response out of me, letting him know when

I'll be eighteen. I wonder how far off his guess on my age is, solely based off my appearance.

David too possesses the mark of a black jaguar on his right shoulder. As Leonid said before, that mark identifies a person as a part of their club. Everyone here has the label that comes with a sense of belonging.

"Now I'm no philistine but isn't this a little too much? The graphics of it all, in this tinted window swamped health farm are breathtaking but I can't keep focus on any one visual. What's the point?" I ask, still astonished I'm here having been in the wild just moments ago.

"Art's functional and beautiful to all men. Rooted in man is a deep symbolic pine for art to unveil meaning in otherwise meaningless signs. The soul can derive inspiration from nothing if that nothing's name's Art." Leonid sighs, staring approvingly at the many still icons flattened and reimagined through colored glass as if it were his life's work.

"The pleasures of Neptune soon cloy all men's senses. So, I suggest you observe your surroundings. For when your time here goes sour, you may find that the need to get some creativity put back inside you, is right in front of you. You'll have more than plenty of time here to focus on these icons. And you might even begin to remedy boredom by shifting your focus toward some of the more flavorful, active features Neptune has to offer. Try looking up for example. It's almost seven," he signals with his index finger pointed up to the ceiling. I trace the gray powder from his shotgun's residue sprinkled on his pale finger, discernible despite the mud I transferred to him, raising my head tall to the ceiling architecture.

At the center of the health farm's ceiling, a large circular gap leads way to an even higher end. Inside the gap, a cylindrical stone wall extends several yards above the average height of this area, beyond the four stories already housing this acre and a quarter sized health farm. The upper limit of the cylindrical wall is a bowl-shaped ceiling. Below the bowl-shaped ceiling, the lowest part of the cylindrical wall is bedecked with a clerestory. High windows above eye level so clean that they look to have no glass inside their stone frames.

The clerestory's infested with intertwining thick reddish-brown branches outlining their lower borders. Along the thick branches, full-sized jaguar sculptures constructed of smooth black metal lie leisurely with their heads bowed. They're a conversation starter for sure. Why, what masterpiece wouldn't sulk that their beauty be imperceptible at night? And in the day, as they perpetually peer down at those soaking below, what if none look up? Sad. I would've missed them had Leonid not spoken.

Above the clerestory, the oily black stone wall continues up for some yards and then ends with a divide. It's a hollow in between the wall and the bowl ceiling. An empty space that cunningly convinces anyone looking up that the bowl ceiling is separate from the rest of the tubular structure; thereby it's perceived to be floating.

Not only is it a ceiling though. It's an enormous annular clock, separated from the cylindrical wall by one ongoing circular windowpane. This is the perceived invisible divide. From outside the castle, this clock would look like half a sphere and its base—a tower. It's as a monolithic dome church that has its roof form a convex surface.

The clock is awry in comparison to flat clocks. Not uncommon to Gulixua watches alike the one I'm modeling. It's distorted in shape as though I'm looking up into a legit cereal bowl awaiting milk. Mighty in comparison to what I'd use for breakfast. I'm no giant but if I were, I'd flip this place upside down and fill the dome with Zombie Surfer Crunch.

With wandering eyes, I glance at the watch on my left wrist. It's just grown a spec of green on its yellow rubber strap. This caved into the ceiling clock is made of iron wood and holds a high gloss shine among its exterior. I know the same wood to be the material for what Erik's yacht is made out of; firm and shining.

Around the inside edges of the bowl clock there're openings. Twelve roman numerals to signify the hours of the day. But there're no other graduations on the clock nor hands on the clock denoting minutes for an exact time. The Roman numeral seven is instantaneously lit up in strawberry tangerine flames.

A line of fire shoots out to the center point of the clock where a minor square aperture slurps up the flames. The source of fire comes from inside the holes that shape the digit VII. The square hole at the center of the clock must be a vacuum because the fire changes direction once it reaches the center and shoots up, vertically into the hole. It'd seem the fire is shipped by the vacuum out into the open. Depending on how often the fire is blasted I would've seen it. If frequent, I'd seen it when we were still walking amongst peacocks and scarlet macaws towards the castle.

"How?" I speak, turning my head immediately to Leonid with the wide eyes of a child having just experienced their first magic trick. I'm simply stunned as to where this fire goes and how exactly it's being produced.

"There's another floor above us that shields the tower and clock. From outside Neptune, one cannot see the outer clock or tower because it's housed in the above layer." He looks up and asks me if I hear footsteps on the second floor.

"I do."

"A monster lives on the level above us, roaming that floor and crawling around the tower, climbing to the top of the dome. The twelve roman numerals are openings. It burns fire through the openings with each hour of the day to let us know time." He smiles and squints his eyes, letting out a short laugh from behind his shut teeth.

"Um...ok?" I take a step back muddled. Could it be he's referencing a mythical dragon? I reckon that's the only monster that can conjure a fire.

Bet my reaction was expected. How am I to believe this? The clerestory on the base of the tower shows white daylight and so does the 360-windowpane separating the tower and bowl clock. I know the difference between artificial light and broad daylight. There's certainly no other floor above us covering that clock tower. Not to mention that all wood burns and not a single streak of ash is on that iron wood clock. Those aren't real flames. Can't be.

I glimpse at my yellow wristwatch with a green spec. Its time doesn't double the time on the wooden clock above everyone's head, currently spitting out flames from the Roman numeral seven. It's not even seven P.M. and it's definitely not seven A.M. My clock...I'd forgotten it's broken.

When I checked the time back in the waking heat of the sun from a small island it read 9:34 A.M. It remains stuck on that time. My watch has been fixed at 9:34 A.M. ever since I saw that mysterious boy from the cliff come out of the bushes, when I couldn't hear it ticking anymore. It's been hours since Lucas, Ramze, and I drove into the solid mist.

The fire above us clears on the minute.

I wonder if the drug has anything to do with how much time's passed. The drug that has 'jaguar' in its name. Just like the people in this castle have 'jaguar' in their club name. Jaguar's spit and the Immortal Jaguars could be correlated. The jaguar's spit might've somehow led me right to them, but correlation doesn't equal causation. Correlation doesn't model cause. It models relationships. I'll test that statement.

"You know that drug I said I was struck with?" I ask looking away, pursing my lips, praying he doesn't respond.

"Yes. Jaguar's spit, right?" he says in uncertainty as I look to him arching my brows.

"Strange. I don't remember ever stating the name of the drug."

"And I don't remember you ever thanking me for saving your life," he quickly counterblasts raising his chin up at me, rolling his eyes along with his head as if he just saw a fly pass by.

"Touché. But to be fair, it's because you had on that gas mask in your left hand. Sketchy behavior won't get you no thanks from me."

He shifts the gas mask behind his back.

"We'll continue this conversation later." He lays his chin on his violet bowtie. "I'll send him your way."

The violet bowtie has a small portable black mic on it. A stainless-steel button protrudes six centimeters from the core of his violet bowtie. In his left ear is a tiny crescent-shaped listening device. It's the pale pigment of his skin.

"But—" I mutter.

"No buts. We'll talk more after you change your shorts. I don't want you dragging any Komodo bacteria further in here."

"Bacteria's everywhere. You can't stop it," I murmur, slouched over, releasing an exasperated sigh. I must change my shorts when they don't even convey dirty. Is this all a joke? Is the person on the other side of that listening device telling him to make a mockery of me?

I'm too tired to do anything about it except think of how long I'm going to be here. This place is a fanciful surprise but I've no business here. There're other matters to attend to. Number one is saving Ramze. At the same time, I don't want to get arrested for veering off the road and almost killing my friends.

I'll eventually have to come clean, tell the person I get help from how it came about that Ramze and I became stranded, and why he couldn't tag along with me looking for assistance.

Ramze is in trouble and my mission after a good talk with Leonid will be to get his support in a rescue. In order to get my friends back I'll need him. I can't do it alone. Not like this.

"Better safe than sorry when it comes to lethal germs. Go to David over there. The second row of pools right at your front. The row with only three pools. All the way at the end."

"I'm sorry. Which?" I ask, attempting to relocate David.

"The one shaped like a blotch of splattered paint. Ask David to take you to the locker room where you can change. He'll let you borrow one of his many lively swim trunks."

We part ways. Leonid walks off with his clear mouth guard in one hand and his snow camo gas mask in the other toward a far-off exit at the end of the health farm. The exit leads to the outside from what I can tell. The arched passageway has geese wobbling through it to get outside. They're clearly seen to be following the natural light from a mid-morning sun.

I walk past the first pool in the second row of pools. A Venetian-style pool. The diamonds suit in playing cards is its shape—a rhombus. The pool decking is flamed Italian granite. Four steps lead into it on its side. There's a grotto across from me at an end of the pool. A waterfall gracefully falls over the opening of the grotto, distorting the figures inside.

The men in this pool are racing slowly through the water. The color shifting fuchsia to powder blue metal bands linked to their limbs I assume are the cause for their downtempo swim. The spirited bands must be wrist and ankle weights.

No swimmer takes notice of me. They mustn't care much for who visits this castle.

Some of the guys are hanging out on top of a long, wide Venetian bridge. It's curved six feet over the water, going across the middle of the pool and serves no purpose in my eyes but to jump off it or swim under it. It only gets someone dry across the first pool before they get to the second pool so that they don't have to walk all the way around it.

The next one over is a rectangular pool. It's understandable no one here takes notice of me. They're playing an athletic game of unofficial water polo without any caps or a referee. A yellow ball is in play with men in speedos bashing each other across the head to get to the ball. In front of this row are the first two pools which Leonid walked past to get to the exit. Those are truly the only ones releasing steam. Some of the steam overflows onto the back ends of the second row of pools. The pools are so large that for this sport active pool only a portion is used for the game, closer to the back end by the steam.

Then there was one. The paint blotch. More of a leisure pool with David being the only one who's making a fuss, doing continuous backflips into the pool. The surrounding men deviate from him and corner themselves at an edge of the pool. All the geese had followed Leonid outside with no more bread available to them.

As he's about to do another backflip, I interrupt him, and mention Leonid sent me followed by an introduction. "My name's Koata."

He does a quick jerk of the head to face me with gritted teeth in what could only be called a smile if I was dangling on a tree limb upside down. His plump body's dripping wet and his red shaggy hair's drenched but fried in some parts, like there'd been a plugged-in toaster swimming too. "Pleasure." He reverts to doing a backflip, ending it by compressing his body, pressing his arms and legs inward into his chest.

Cannon ball.

Now for my first encounter with this guy I already have a bad feeling about him. His teeth are disgusting, and he pays them no mind. He swims underwater to the edge of the pool and rises from it. Once out of the pool, he shakes his head like a wet dog. Water droplets go flying from all sides of his head, out of his inextinguishable hair.

He takes four steps to me and places his right hand on my left shoulder. He then pats the side of my shoulder, telling me to lighten up. That I look stiff. "So, you're the guy everyone's been talking about. I'm David Collins. Your chosen herald. I'm here to give you some good news but my message to you won't come easy. Not quite yet. So, you've met our groundskeeper, Leonid Vandever." He spoke a mile a minute.

"Come again. Did you say you're my herald?" I turn my cheek to him with my left index finger on my left earlobe.

"Yes. You don't suspect you stumbled upon Neptune by chance. Do you?"

"Would it be crazy if I said yes? How was I made known to you? Everyone you say has been talking of me, how're you going to start off a conversation like that when I only just got here?" I try to regress to my previous line of inquiry as

I notice David's different colored eyes. His left eye's a deep blue and his right eye's a light green.

The people in the sport active pool clamor for attention. One team in the middle rectangular pool scored against the other team by getting the yellow ball into the floating hockey-type goal net. The shouting men must mean its game over and the losing team isn't happy with the results. On the other hand, it could be a celebratory rumpus from the winning team. I go back to David and I's conversation. "A herald? As in you're my messenger. How does that work?"

"Slow down there kid. You're about to crash. I've already said too much. Don't grass on me or I'll kick your ass. I'll have plenty more to explain and talk to you about once you emerge anew from round one. Kapish."

"Capisce?"

"No not Capisce, Kapish," he says, the two words synonymous in their phonetics.

A rugby fit, hairy-chested man with a pecan brown man bun and a Spartan beard, in what must be a red speedo stuffed with a sock, comes up in between the two of us with his right brow bleeding and a white towel hung over his right shoulder. His merry and child-like cocoa brown eyes hopscotch past me to greet David. "Some game huh? You see me score the winning shot?" he asks David with a swell of joy.

"No. I was busy talking to Koa over here or do you prefer Koata as you said your name was?"

"Koa is fine. That's what my friends call me."

"Perfect. We're all friends here. Isn't that right Kapish." He looks affably to him as Kapish awkwardly stands there glaring at me. David throws a soft punch to Kapish's left shoulder and Kapish responds nonplussed, rubbing his shoulder with his right hand.

"Sure. You play any sports kid?"

His voice has a slight rhythm to it with the stressed vocalization of his vowels. David and Leonid are both British. Leonid with his English accent intact and David's an obvious Welsh. The Tudor colors of green and white separated by a horizontal line on his swim trunks gave it away. It's the Welsh flag and on his butt stands the flag's red dragon incorporated into its design. Strictly going off his appearance, I'd say Kapish must be Greek because he looks like the descendant of a Greek god.

"I surf."

"That's not a real sport," Kapish contends with arrogance projected on his face.

I clench my fists but rather than instigate a debate, I smirk. My odd, fake, closed-lip smile fades as I ask for his nationality.

"I'm Swedish."

"Ever been to Varberg? Doubt it. You wouldn't get past the cold surfing in Sweden. When you decide not to be such a bloke in defining a sport, I can introduce you to some of the hot, fit, friendly Swedish girls only we surfers get. Something this place is in dire need of."

"Thanks, but I don't need to *get* any girl. I prefer women who aren't into snuskhummers." Kapish grits his teeth thinking I only objectify women.

"So, this is probably a dumb question but if everyone here isn't British, why's there a variant flag of Great Britain hanging from that panel of frosted glass as soon as one walks in through the gate?"

"We expect it to be the first thing people see," David responds.

"Our founders are British," Kapish adds.

"If from that region, why settle here, away from all towns?" I ask, looking up again to the sound of monster footsteps coming from the supposed second floor.

"Costa Rica's cloud forest provides a beautiful hideaway, and we don't like being bothered," Kapish says realizing I'm looking to the ceiling as he's talking. He roughly punches me in the chest forcing me to take a step back. "Pay attention when I'm giving a response to your vapid questions."

David tries clearing the ferocity in the air by offering up a tour of the premises. I politely decline and suggest stalling the tour till he shows me the locker room where I can change my board shorts before Leonid gets back and has a fit. He concurs that's the better plan. We turn from Kapish and walk to a corner of the health farm parallel to the archway Leonid went through. I can't help but look back and see Kapish cynically watching us.

What did I ever do to him?

An equilateral triangle with stairs running down one side of it is what we arrive at in this corner of the health farm. The path downstairs immerses us in an underground man-made cave. There's a mixture of black shale and light-blue slate rock formations that're the makeup of the ceiling and walls. Midway into the cave there's the bending of glass that becomes the wall to our left.

David notices my interest in it. There're legs at the height of the glass wall kicking their way through the water. One man dives deep to retrieve his gold aviator sunglasses.

"It's a look inside the White Oak Leaf."

"The splattered paint blotch pool?"

David glances at me. His eyebrows shot up in judgement.

"That's what Leonid called it anyway." I felt the need to state.

"The White Oak Leaf is that pool's official name."

"So, what's up with the gas mask Leonid had?"

"The gas masks are an item exclusive to the Aedile and the Praefectus because they're the only classes that spend time outside. I'll explain more on why gas masks are needed later but I'm sure you got a hint from the smell walking outside."

"Boy did I." I nod my head with a look of repugnance.

"As for the strange labels I just told you about, this fraternity is divided into classes. Those are just two out of the fourteen we have here. The Aedile, which Leonid is a member of is the groundskeeper class. We only have three brothers in that class, but more can be added as time goes on if an appropriate candidate is found."

We turn into another hall.

"Our brothers in the Praefectus, there's a set number of eleven members allowed in that class. There'll always be but eleven Prefects. They control the prison system composed of two buildings which just so happen to be connected through an outside path. The Praefectus class and the Caesar class, composed of one individual, are the only classes with a set number on members that can join them."

"What's the Caesar?" I try and keep up with the information overload.

"Why that's God of course," David says with ease.

Chapter 19

This is a cult.

I've had my bad experience with a cult. It's disturbing how people who fall into cults lose their ability to think critically. They cannot tolerate dissenting opinions and will push away those closest to them to protect their ill-founded worldview.

"Hang on. That's not possible," I chuckle in disbelief.

"What's not possible?" David pushes open a blue rock wall that subtly fades to black—a hidden entrance to a bathroom.

"Maybe what you define as god isn't what the rest of the world defines as god."

"I'll have you decide that for yourself," he says holding the rock wall open for me. "All yours," David says to an empty bathroom, shoving and enclosing me inside.

This bathroom is what I'd expect to see at a gas station, not a castle. It's about as clean as I'd expect any New York City subway station to be. Four urinals and four stalls run parallel to eight rusted mirrors. Their surface is touted by the overall low lighting of an antique kerosene lamp sitting firm in the second sink. I walk forth to stare at myself in the first mirror and challenge its strength in reflecting light; a match to the dull side of tinfoil. Weak. I run the side of my fist across the mirror in an effort to clean it but it's not unwashed, simply primitive.

A shadow sails across the mirror and I quickly turn my back to it, glancing about the bathroom aisle and ducking to check if anyone is under the stalls. In the last stall is someone, sitting on the toilet with black python skin cowboy boots and light-blue standard denim jeans at their ankles.

"*Hello boy,*" speaks a gravelly voice deeper than I've ever heard.

"You've no need for a voice amplifier like Leonid. Your larynx amplifies your voice enough." I return my stare to the mirror. "So, you must be the god giving orders on the other side of that listening device Leonid had."

"*You're mistaken. Vandever was born with a hearing impairment in one ear. That device in his left ear is a hearing aid.*"

"Oh yea? Then explain the microphone in his bowtie."

"*That's to communicate with Collins. If you haven't noticed, he gets orders from Vandever through an earpiece in his left ear. I would've had Vandever bring you to me, but he has other matters to attend to.*"

"Such as?"

"*Death of wildlife has reached epidemic proportions from a group of illegally imported Komodo dragons. We're not sure how many are roaming around loose in the cloud forest, but Vandever has been hunting them down nonstop.*"

"Why him?"

"*He was a hunter before joining us. Selling pelts in the streets of Munich to get by.*"

"Can I ask about David? What was he before joining?"

"Backstories are as ample and sufficient as rivers. We'll be here all day if I swim upstream to recall the tales of individual trout. You're lucky to be here son."

"Don't doubt I am." My back faces the mirror. I toss my arms backwards, grabbing onto the brink of the sink from behind me and getting a good back stretch. "I'm grateful to be here but David told me some things. Evidently, people here are aware of my identity. He said they've been talking about me. The news that I'm so popular in a stranger's paradise can come as a bit of a shock, wouldn't you say? He's also mentioned his assignment to me as a herald and your title as Caesar."

"Late last night a dangerous individual escaped our castle's prison."

"David mentioned a prison."

"We have a maze and a zoo too."

"Continue."

"Thought we'd lost the prisoner till you showed up. Prefect Majdick saw you on a live feed driving some yellow pickup truck off a cliff. Video provided by one of his drones."

My heart sinks to a depth below earth's crust into the hell of my own assembly. "I can explain that. It was nearly impossible to see the road. I veered too far in the wrong direction and lost control," I maniacally try and justify my self-induced calamity.

"Collins and several others in Mercury asked to be your herald once they caught a whiff of the story. Majdick has a big mouth. Wasn't long before the rest of the classes heard the news. The drone that scavenged the area searching for our guy caught the whole thing on tape and along with your little car accident, one thing Majdick missed that his drone didn't was prisoner 1313. On camera at the edge of the cliff you drove off."

I hear tissue paper tearing from inside the only occupied stall.

"Collins had been eager to meet you because he believes you may have a link to the prisoner but since the only members allowed outside are Prefects and Aedile, and Collins is neither, he had to wait for Vandever to come fetch you."

"I don't know anything about your lost prisoner."

"I agree. I don't believe you do know anything about the boy, so I denied Collins' request to have a Prefect bring you in for questioning. However, that changed when I had Vandever go investigate some drones that were pierced by a spear. In danger of a dragon, he saved your life. I figured, destiny you'd show up at our doorstep. I told him it was time to bring you in and here you are."

"How do you know of the lizard that cornered me? How'd you even command him to bring me here in that instant? He doesn't have a listening device. You said that was a hearing aid in his left ear."

"Correct. You're a good listener. I often communicate with him, and everyone really, through telepathy."

"You're an idiot."

"How do you think I'm communicating with you now?"

"Um."

"I read his mind like I'm reading yours. His exact thoughts were *Baba it's the crackpot.*"

His voice changes mid-sentence, persistently deep but bagging with it a new Southern American accent. The toilet flushes and the stall door creaks open. As he makes his way toward the sink, the rhythmic thud of his boots against the floor resonates, resembling the sound of a horse navigating a concrete path. A tilted forward black Dallas wool cowboy hat with a silver bullhead medallion is perched tight atop his head. His storm gray retro western-style shirt flaunts a winter blackberry floral embroidery on the cuffs and around the neck.

He turns on the faucet, grabs a mint dome surface oval-shaped bar soap from a corner of the sink and washes his hands. After which, he begins rubbing the bar soap against his face. The bar soap is gently dragged across his small, pointed, and berry blue 'Van Dyke' beard. The tips of his zany moustache and goatee are sharp and symmetrical. Fairly dense, bulging out from his weather-worn skin.

He returns the bar soap to the corner of the sink where he got it and splashes water on his face. He turns the sink's right metal lever to stop running water. The crow's feet next to his brumous eyes have been exfoliated. Full body towards me, he turns.

"I ain't blind. A bit feeble, yes, but still able to walk like a good ol' stray dog prowling the area for its next snack."

He knew I'd question his vision thus he's milked me of words. He really can read people's minds. I was just thinking why his eyes look like they've been bleached, and his beard looks like it's been dyed in dried plum, blueberries, and eggplant extract.

"Hey Collins, your god's thirsty!"

"I'll seat you guys in the Wolf's Den," David says, his head popping out from the cave wall he's opened again. "But first, go on and change." David throws me a pair of Union Jack swim trunks. I cling onto them as they hit my stomach.

"We'll wait for you outside," their god assures me, tapping my shoulder and walking past me toward David.

As the cave wall closes, I undress and begin focusing on the power to redress. Those grievances Lucas and Ramze must own from my grody stunt are heartbreaking. They're pulling at me like reindeers leading a sleigh. I put on these swim trunks, unmoved by the national flag of the UK on my groin and buttocks publicizing me as a patriot of foreign lands. I turn to the cave wall for an exit and in my view rests a yellow ladybug in midflight with black spots on its open wing covers. It's frozen. Unmoving till I blow some air its way. It glides a short distance ahead remaining in flight. I take a step forward to inspect it.

"Curious little critter. What's caused you to be paralyzed in this manner?"

My attention's absorbed by a knock.

"Be right out!"

I delicately pinch the ladybug and place it at an end of the first sink. Then I look to the antique kerosene lamp, thinking it best to put out its flame before I go, preventing an undue disaster from transpiring. I walk to it and turn on both the sink's valves. The water instantly puts out the flame overfilling the lamp's glass vase in a chaotic surge. A dingy room materializes as I turn off the faucet. Dark but not big enough for me to lose my way.

Walking back toward the cave wall, I see the first mirror glint. My full sight returns to it. Within its aluminum surface there's a screwy shape. The mirror reflects a beast. A splay flat face and elongated snout emerges. Black marbles are planted high, wide asunder on its head. Four tusks rise low at the head's base. The first two tusks are large, unfolding from the sides of its snout in a semicircle. The two right under it are small, honed like curved blades.

With a wrench, I see nothing behind me. I slowly face the mirror again with discomfort. I think after jolting my head over my shoulder and seeing nothing, this pain in my neck is deservedly pronounced. I'm just paranoid. But no. There's the blurred beast staring at who knows what from within the sullen rusted mirror. The largest of the gray boars in the cloud forest, which I'd followed to a steady stream of water, is a mold for this beast. I've been thrown into a rabbit hole of demented realities.

I avoid it, head turned from it, like trying to tiptoe around a shadow in the dark, afraid that shedding too much light on it will make it loom larger and more terrifying. I hastily exit the bathroom joining the Caesar and David Collins. Surprised to see Leonid Vandever will also be joining our group. He walks to us from a distance carrying the head of a Komodo dragon within a clear, frosty shopping bag.

"I left the other board shorts in the bathroom. Hope no one minds." The two ignore me watching Leonid arrive.

"I lunged at it with my drop point. Managed to slice its throat straight through," Leonid confidently notifies us, spinning his knife in one hand. Two sloths with emerald stone eyes are carved into his knife's rosewood sheath.

"You're a prime cut butcher. You should use the silicon containing wax I gifted you to keep that blade from rusting," the Caesar advises him.

Leonid tucks the knife by his lower back, using the towel around his waist to hold it in place. He turns the light metal dial at the core of his violet bowtie. "Zorian, meet me at the Wolf's Den in ten minutes. Bring your father too."

Turning the dial changes the channel with whom he communicates. He had it set to David. I notice the cocoa butter beige earpiece in David's left ear now. After the Caesar mentioned it in the bathroom, it's only fitting I verify its position. Now the metal dial on Leonid's bowtie is set to radio some guy named Zorian. I wonder how many people he can command through that mic. He must cherish that power to give orders, have people directly follow them, and not be able to question him back.

"Hungry for the power?"

"I'm not hungry."

Leonid and David both peer at me with distaste.

"No one asked," David chuckles.

"But we'll have some cheese and crackers at the den if you change your mind," Leonid halfheartedly adds.

I actually am hungry, but I was responding to the question about power. Once more the Caesar has talked to me telepathically. I know I should be awestruck but hardly a day ago I came back to life. I'm feeling primed for the next shock wave in this series of atypical events. While the three jaguars casually discuss Zorian Majdick's repeatedly struck drones, I keep my eyes pried open for any possible exits. Not for an escape but to inwardly wander aimlessly into another world.

A net of tunnels interweaves at every high gloss jet black lamp post. Not one pole is straight. All are a spiral shape like a stretched coil spring toy. Two sculpted jaguar heads have been sited, one at each end of the pole with the lesser inverted. Their wide-open mouths carry a lit mint green orb. Their powerful jaws and impressive sharp canine teeth contain the spherical bulbs, lighting the way. From every lamp post, someone could point out another. They're placed in a precise path.

We walk past one tunnel where the cave essence of the other halls end. This descending tunnel had a light-gray concrete ceiling curved over a polished golden honey onyx slate floor. At its end, a circular steel vault door. There's a smaller circular hinged glass panel at its center for viewing both ways. I'm a keen believer that's a nuclear shelter similar to ones I've played through in apocalyptic video games.

We get to a hall where an elevator awaits behind a bronze vintage Otis scissor gate. Just outside the elevator, two talkative men are leaning against a cave wall whilst sharing a cigarette. The chatting stops as soon as they notice us arrive. David and Leonid at the Caesar's sides and I lagging. The brunette clean-shaven men are costumed in Roman soldier attire.

One's outfit includes a white tunic, black body armor with a skirt of leather strips, an attached ruby red cape, a golden medallion above the right pectoral cast with the two-faced God Janus, and brown leather gladiator sandals. The other man, while similar in dress, lacks the white tunic under his black body armor and the skirt of leather strips to protect his uppers legs. Rather he has on blue briefs and to substitute for the absence of Roman footwear, he has on white calf-high socks with red double contrast stripes and brilliant white tennis shoes. Wrapped around his left wrist is an aviator watch with a black stainless-steel case sitting on an army green canvas strap.

"What're you plebs doing smoking underground?" Leonid asks the two, frustrated as their faces toughen to contest his.

The authentically dressed Roman gladiator parts the cigarette from his lips, puffs smoke in Leonid's face, and passes the cigarette to his buddy.

"Who doesn't want cancer?" the man asks unenthusiastically, locking eyes with Leonid.

"Smoking on site is forbidden," Leonid warns, unamused as though he's reminded them before.

"What's the point of living forever if we can't live up to our deadliest impulses?" the other man notes languidly.

"Eternity isn't a gift that can be taken back but it's a promise that can be broken," the Caesar jumps in.

I stare to the half-dressed Roman gladiator and notice his watch isn't working. The black hands of the watch avers the time's nine o'clock.

"Baba, it's just a little smoke. We're taking a break from rehearsal." The first gladiator denies any wrongdoing. He drops the attitude present with Leonid when talking to the Caesar.

"I'm not buying it. You two have been caught smoking down here—on duty—before." The Caesar deepens his gaze, made more frightening by his eyes' purely white color.

The half-dressed man drops the cigarette and puts it out by stomping on it. "The show must go on," he playfully comments.

The Caesar bites his lip in vexation. The two try and scurry away. David blocks their path by extending his arms. "I believe the Caesar wants some reassurance this matter won't happen again."

The two men look to one another, back to David, and nod. They clap their hands once, then raise their arms like Frankenstein till they're parallel to the ground with their palms facing us. A commanding gesture meant to convey stop or halt. Together they recite something in Latin. "Per vitem fragum sursum."

They relax their arms and offer their sincerest apologies for breaking the rules of Neptune. David purses his mouth in a self-satisfied smirk. The Caesar points his thumb behind him. The two are allowed to leave. I check again before they go and still no motion from the hands of the watch. Leonid slides open the Otis scissor gate. We all step in, and he closes it once more. He taps the first of three white buttons vertically lined on a bronze plate. We ascend onto the third floor.

What did those two quote?

"*An axiom of the immortal jaguars,*" the Caesar telepathically responds.

It's as if I have two separate minds now that the Caesar has access to mine. An axiom remembered by all to show their respect and loyalty to this brotherhood. I took Latin in high school but well-versed in the language of Ancient Rome, I'm not. The elevator stops preceding a vibration that tickles my feet. Leonid opens the gate, and we enter a canary yellow home.

The quaint country cottage has antique China displayed at four corners. The white porcelain tableware boasts roses in medallions, green scrolls on cream edges, and heavily gold gilt trims. The trays, tea sets, and cutlery are exhibited in dark brown hardwood curio cabinets with mirrored backs and low halogen lighting, granting all crockery a gleam around gold rims.

Floral and checkered prints coat a small dining room set and a mint green coffee table. The whitewashed wood chairs at each table are layered with chipped paint. I push a chair forward out of habit of touching things at a store. Succulent cactus plants rise from dirt packed turquoise metal pails. The plant holders sit at open windows; their white lace curtains split apart. We pass black beans that overfill a burlap coffee sack on the floor. From outside an open window, there're white geese bathing in a pond among tall grayish-blue grass.

The rustic touches and shabby chic décor continue into the Caesar's office. Leonid and David each place a hand on a shoulder of mine as we enter an expansion of these canary yellow walls. Its arched opening leads to an impressive, freakish workspace. They put a driving pressure on my shoulders as my eyes comb the room with the strong perspicacity to recognize an unhealthy obsession when I see one. I'm sat between two pastel paisley pillows on an espresso polyester loveseat. This office is overcrowded with exotic animal head mounts hung on walls. The head mounts reach far up, seemingly reaching into an additional floor that exists as an open expanse.

The longest head mount is the giraffe, extending two yards. There's a gazelle, a zebra, a lion, a cheetah, a moose, an elk, a crocodile, a gemsbok, a hippopotamus, a nyala, a gerenuk, a wildebeest, an eland, a baboon, a jackal, and many others that resemble antelope and buffalo but that escape my knowledge of genus and species. The largest is the head of an American bison, three feet long and two feet wide. The reddish-brown thick mat of hair on its forehead matches the cowhide rug at my feet.

The glass top modern executive desk with white drawers is accompanied by a black leather conference room chair. A half-full burnished black museum bookcase stands behind it, trash bin beside it, and dangling oatmeal mushroom drum shade above it, suspended by a mangy beige rope. A solid walnut desk plate with gold engraving and a shiny gold border sits atop the desk. It reads 'Rilextus Sagert' and under it, in a smaller italic font, the title 'Caesar.'

"Where can we hang this one?" Leonid asks, proudly holding high the frosty shopping bag with the head of a Komodo dragon.

"I'll get the taxidermist to fix it up. Then we'll talk," the Caesar replies, inching closer to his desk. He sits upright on the black upholstered rolling chair behind his desk. Leonid and David take a seat at opposite ends of each other on the loveseat's arms.

"So why am I here?" I ask dull-wittedly.

"You're here because you lost two friends in the cloud forest. Lucas, who cowardly exited a moving vehicle and fell off a cliff and Ramze whom you last saw before entering a cave and fatefully finding your way here." The Caesar wastes no time in showcasing his power, further revealing I've nothing to hide.

"You know my story. You know I need help finding my friends. If you can read my mind, then you must also know I've no idea who that boy was that you asked me about downstairs."

"Your thoughts are hard to catch. The boy led you deep into the cloud forest. Where did you lose him?" he asks, wiping down a speck of dust on his desk with the backside of his bare hand.

"I can't remember. I told you I don't know anything about your lost prisoner."

"I know that, or I think I do, but there're others like you or unlike you, depending on where you stand. I haven't decided yet where you stand. Others who've trained their minds to be immune to mine and its meddling mind reading."

"Though my thoughts are innocent you believe them to be insincere. I don't think I can give you what you want," I tell him ruffled, crossing my arms over my chest.

"We'll see," he mysteriously counters.

David looks to me with his legs crossed. He slides into the empty seat next to me. "I wanted to be your herald because I thought you and the escapee were working together. There's a big reward for the jaguar who captures the boy. Plenty of others though, wanted to be your herald because simply put—you're badass. Driving a car off a cliff and surviving." David makes it known he's only my herald—whatever that entails—because he mistook me for a crook and thought he'd get rewarded in using me.

Was that supposed to make me feel better?

"You all are wildin."

"Downside is that because you're closely associated to the escapee," David assumes.

"I'm not."

"Well because people believe you are, jaguars like Kapish dislike you dearly."

"What did that prisoner even do?" I ask David, compelled to know.

"Can Califf and I have a moment?" the Caesar genteelly asks of David. David hesitantly gets up and leaves the room. Leonid stays seated.

"*When a baby is born it can change the course of history in which this world sways. That boy you encountered is a lethal weapon, destined for chaos since birth. A harbinger of malignancy yearning to proliferate.*"

He's just a boy.

"No. No he's not. He's a clever trap. Help us find him. Please." His quivering tone is desperate.

I can't.

"I must go," I say aloud, getting up.

"*You mustn't. Need I say can't.*"

Leonid forcefully pushes me with an open hand back down to a sit.

"*Get the boy. I'll personally assure your friends' return.*"

A woolly-headed black-haired boy with bemused and vivid brown eyes, a long face, round cheeks, and a high forehead enters the office from the arched opening. Dressed in a solid white wrestling singlet. Scarlet lines the edges of his straps and leg openings. At his chest, red lining zigzags around a yellow backdrop. The capitalized go-to word for when there's a knockout in comics, 'POW!' appears in red within the animated boom explosion. He has on standard black wrestling shoes with a breathable single-layer mesh body and red suede outsole.

Leonid gets up and turns to stare. The knife, tight on his back, held in by his towel, comes loose. It drops on the rug, hampering its sound once it hits the ground. I'm surprised he doesn't notice. I cover it with my barefoot and then drag it toward me making sure neither Leonid nor the Caesar are watching. I occupy my mind with a rock song to keep the Caesar from noticing.

Shells slowly shatter upon a grueling romance.
Tandava's trying. I hope this is our last dance.
Enough is enough. I'm the most brisant.
You may detonate me if that's the show that you want.
Love hurt you so deep. I'll put you to bed.
You can kiss my rocket. Have love you'll never forget.

No more pain in your day. Best to cop out.
All smoke's faded away!
You'll never, never, never. You'll never, never, never be her!
What a bogus display!
You'll never, never, never. You'll never, never, never be her!

"Zorian!" Leonid calls, delighted. "Meet K. The guy your drone caught driving a truck off a cliff. K!" Leonid turns to me, right after I kick the knife with my heel under the loveseat. "Meet Prefect Majdick. The genius behind our drone program here at Neptune."

"Hold up. A kid engineered those drones you were all chatting about underground?" I'm shook.

"Yes. Brilliant minds come in all ages," Zorian makes known his modesty in a genuine way.

"And where's your father?" Leonid asks, staggered. Raising his chin, he inches aside to see if anyone's going to follow Zorian into the room from behind. Leonid must expect his orders to be met on command. If I were his desk jokey, I'd prepare a good excuse after failing to meet those demands.

"Bo got lost in the maze again," Zorian responds, ashamed.

He refers to his father by his first name like me. That's interesting.

"Ok. Well, here." Leonid hands over the frosty shopping bag to Zorian. "Have him take care of it when he finds his way out so that we may add another showpiece to the Wolf's Den."

"Are all of these your game?" I ask Leonid, astonished if my belief that he's hunted every animal in here is true.

"All are indeed. If I recall, there was one above that window." He stops and looks around the room searching for something lost.

"It wasn't your intent to stupefy our special guest, but you did just that in opening your big mouth," the Caesar lightly scolds Zorian.

Leonid remains dazed at the revelation that a head mount in the Wolf's Den is missing. Zorian apologizes to me. There's no harm in telling others what he saw on camera. In his shoes, seeing someone do the impossible, I'd probably jump at the chance to tell all. At least now I know the Immortal Jaguars discovered me through Zorian and one of his drones.

The drone program, from what I've learned, is a security measure executed to find people. In this case, prisoner 1313. This lost prisoner who can fly, while eldritch in person, didn't give me the impression of lethal weapon as was disclosed by the Caesar. I always thought seeing someone fly would be more breathtaking, less creepy.

The Caesar's desk plate reveals his name to be Rilextus Sagert but I've yet to hear people call him that. Rather, I've heard people refer to him as God, Caesar, or Baba. One of the smokers below called him Baba.

One of the first things Leonid told me after we met was that Baba Azul would rage if he discovered a peacock had been eaten by a Komodo dragon. Is the Caesar Baba Azul? The only Caesar I know of is Julius. A Roman general, father, politician, and author of Latin prose. Most know how his iconic story came to end. He was assassinated. Death found him through Roman senators who inflicted him with multiple stab wounds.

"You there! Quit your morbid squabble. I can hear your thoughts debating with themselves over what to call me. You may call me Baba Azul. Also, Vandever, when were you going to mention one of my peacocks was slaughtered outside these walls? Do you think our friend Califf here was just gonna let that slip from his mind after meeting the precise person you told not to tell? Every jaguar knows I can read minds and you as my Vicarius should know better, you subordinate imbecile."

David comes in with a round silver plate of assorted cheeses and crackers as Leonid said there'd be. Baba Azul instantly gets up, pushing his chair back, and raises a finger over his head. "Let's have an alfresco luncheon!" Baba shouts ebullient and happy as if he's presented the room with the proposal of the century. A most incredible idea.

Chapter 20

Baba's idea flies in the face of David having brought food. He's just come back from getting cheese and crackers, decorating his round silver plate by arranging them in a happy face. The cubed buttery-hued cheeses are stacked up in two square pyramids for eyes. The square saltine crackers are lined at the edge of his plate in a curved smile.

"God your insatiable," David puts it nicely. Not sure if he's calling Baba god again or using the title senselessly.

Baba tells Leonid never to withhold cognizance from him. Then makes it clear he's saying it aloud so that everyone present knows not to be so foolish. He then sends everyone out into the Dome of the Plebeian. As I step out of the office, behind the others, he asks me to stay. I oblige.

Baba warns me that I mustn't tell anyone I saw prisoner 1313 fly. Should I decide to talk, he'd know. It sounded like a threat without baggage. He aimed for it to sound like an afterthought. Even so, my ears caught the weighty nuance. He ends the cautionary advice with a wink and a cheeky grin. I wander off, catching up with the others.

We exited the country cottage through a white wood door. It's composed of black metal on the side facing out. I look to the one-story cottage with what looks like a fat chimney on its roof belonging to a separate house. Perhaps Goliath's. It's the Caesar's office, clearly distinct as it's the only unevenly taller section of the cottage. From outside, I'd never guess the cottage to be so quaint. It's of the same stone bricks that compose the outer castle walls with a more washed-out gray color. Approximate to a dolphin's dry skin after hours bathing in the sun.

The cottage is centered in an overgrown Aegean blue grassy square. Massive white empire columns line the square. Across from the cottage's front porch is the health farm. Its gripping stained-glass windows are visible past a row of the Olympian white stone columns. Two white-washed wood rocking chairs attest to the only furniture in the square. What little lush vegetation this square has is to the right of the cottage's black metal door. Bright blue boy cornflowers rise above the soothing faded blue grass.

"Nice touch, this painted grass." I look about the square in approval of its artistic design, deserted by all but a few geese.

"That's no paint," Zorian casually states.

Before he can say more, David gives him a nasty glower. His unsavory reputation for a bigmouth precedes him. Leonid tells him to move along and to go give the dragon head to his father. I felt as though Zorian was in the midst of telling me what it was that's made this grass blue. If not paint, what more? A fiddle, a banjo, a harmonica? The makeup of classic American roots music.

"Baba wants me to stay here and eat. We all have delicate matters to attend to—together." Zorian is emphatic his place is here with us. He firmly takes a hold of my hand, certain I'll embrace. Without delay, I instinctively slid my hand right out from his grip, turning it into a fist. "We're brothers. All four of us now." Zorian attempts to grab hold of my hand once more. I combatively bounce back, compulsively turning my other hand into a fist.

"He hasn't even accepted the bid yet git," Leonid sternly reminds Zorian.

"A bid? If it means finding my friends, I'll accept willingly. The plight of them surviving in the wild gives me notice that…I don't even know if they're alive anymore," I state anxiously. With a doleful look I bite my thumbnail. I assume Lucas is ok, but Ramze is a different story. I left him out there bleeding.

"God will find your friends. Don't worry." Leonid tries to calm me. He nearly places a hand on my shoulder, but I dodge it histrionically like a 100 mph foul ball.

"When? We're wasting time!" I shout frantically.

"Calm yourself. Breathe. You're the one who drove a truck off a cliff putting your friends' lives in danger Kamikaze. Zorian's drones are probing the rainforest for them as we speak." David gives me a nickname and a reality check, at the same time wrapped in ridicule.

God I'm embarrassed and saddened. What happened to me in that truck? It wasn't me. Well, it was but it wasn't. The third grader in me is telling myself to take responsibility for my actions. The fifth grader in me is saying fuck that. It wasn't me! I know how bad this looks. For now, I can't prove my innocence nor explain what went down in that vehicle. I swallow my pride and apologize for getting frenzied.

"I regret what happened. I'll stop asking for everyone to mention my mistakes," I sigh, defeated. I don't want to be remembered as a screwball. Imagine having to deal with people who think you're nuts. Having to get strangers to do what I want is difficult enough. Meeting Kapish was a regrettable short encounter. There're far worse encounters to come. Some jaguars will want to use me. The lie that I'm associated with a bad guy, a jailbird of all things, has hammered in this idea they'll get rewarded.

I'm no lead. Not even close. To help catch this super boy they're after I'm going to need more than just the promise of my friends back. Chiefly because if Baba's firm in his belief that boy's a lethal weapon, I'm no buckler. And I won't be a decoy duck. Some jaguars will befriend me for being a daredevil. All naive. Trusting this fraternity in helping my situation might haunt me. But until there's a more attractive offer on the table, I'll stick with them.

"Where's this dome Baba wants us to dine at?" I ask the group.

"You're standing in it," Zorian answers with a half-smile.

There's something strange about the sky. A gloss hails over it. We're in a fishbowl but the notion I'm trapped just isn't there. David sits down on a rocking chair and begins picking at the cheese cubes with a toothpick. He offers the guys some. Leonid sits in the rocking chair next to him and gladly helps himself, prodding two cheese cubes on a toothpick. David asks me again if I'd like some cheese and crackers. I deny the offer. He incentivizes me with, "Are you sure? You never know when your next meal will come along."

I shrug, confused, and grab a toothpick off David's round plate. I stab a cheese cube and eat it, tasting the sea. The cheese is salty and sharp. Another few minutes go by before the Caesar comes out to the dome. A lot of blather in those brief moments we waited.

I learned that Zorian at age twelve is the youngest member in the Praefectus. A class that's stagnant on its number of members—eleven. He's also the youngest member ever to be initiated into the Immortal Jaguars due to what David call's 'his savant brain.' And just for kicks, he's not a wrestler but tells me that as the night progresses, he won't be the only guy pretending to be something he's not.

The conversation takes on a morbid tone when I ask Zorian why his father went into the maze in the first place. Zorian talks despondently of the future. He makes it known his father Bo suffers from brain damage, incoherent speech, paralysis, and delirium. He blames it on his father's high exposure to inorganic mercury working in a factory below. Located a level under the tunnel system with cave walls. He worries it's too late for him to recover and mentions it's his fourth time getting lost this week, every time running into the maze.

I ask him head-on what exactly people are doing working with mercury down there and the safety provisions, if any, that're taken for precaution. I'm not allowed an answer. Zorian's speech is nixed by someone else's ego. The need to make oneself needlessly heard.

Leonid, unmoved by Zorian's bitter life, moves in, swanking about his hunting past. This recent intrusion by Komodo dragons into a tropical part of the world where they're no more wanted than snow has allowed him to reignite his passion—hunting. A once notoriously profitable profession. The overweening way he blabbers on and on about how great of a hunter he is, the glut of certitude I have it's for the fame and bragging rights. I warn him, "You wouldn't want to go around bragging so hard outside these castle walls. Whether you're hunting for sport or using it as your main source of income, exotic hunts aren't something many people take lightly in the Americas."

He did what he did to survive in Munich. Making just enough to live above the poverty line. When the opportunity presented itself to sell more than pelts on the black market, he snatched it. He'd be compensated for travel and no longer would he have to hunt to eat. Still, he'd have to work above the law.

He began getting a seductive, much more lucrative paycheck as he puts it. The buyer who he indirectly sold to through some shady henchman he wouldn't know for another ten years. It was none other than Rilextus Sagert or as he went by then and now, Baba Azul. And yes, without any word from me, he tells me forthright that God's beard was blue then too. "Don't ask me how or why. That's none of my business and you'd be wise not to make it yours."

"Don't plan on it," I respond, casually checking for Baba Azul to come out of his dwelling. I ask Leonid how he and Baba Azul met. The short story is he got busted. On an assignment that require he hunt and deliver the buyer's henchman the head of a fully grown African male lion. The henchman set him up. Leonid had returned to the henchman with his order and was arrested on the spot. Coppers were onto the henchman and had previously settled on a lesser sentence for him if he were to turn in who he was working for and the person providing him with the illegal game.

In a twist of fate, after one hundred days in the clink, Leonid was moved to a different cell. His cellmate, prisoner 1313. An old man by the likes of a cowboy nicknamed Baba Azul. While Baba instantly knew Leonid, he kept his identity a secret, befriending him and telling him he was the buyer a whole month after they met. The revelation incited a brawl as Leonid blamed his entire misfortune on the man who'd hired him. He refused to place any blame on himself.

After that first fight, and it certainly wasn't their last, Leonid was punished. Put in an inferior cell for three days with far worse living conditions than a prison should call for. A punishment Leonid felt was unjust considering it was a dark hole for criminals that misbehave, committing heinous acts in prison above those they're convicted for. I trust he wasn't talking about a literal hole he was put in for three days. I don't get to hear what happens next, how they escaped from prison, or if they're both pardoned.

Baba joins us in the dome. A white picnic blanket hangs over his shoulders. It's embellished with a quilted fog gray elephant silhouette motif. A bulky matte red spiral notebook is suspended on his left pinkie, hooked into the top two binding spirals. He's ready to discuss the—unknown to me—delicate matters Zorian broached.

Chapter 21

Contrary to what I thought would be the driving theme of this brunch; instead of talking about finding my friends, their escaped prisoner, or the potential bid Leonid brought up—insinuating my future involvement with this brotherhood—we talked about girls. I did learn the escaped prisoner's name, so I guess that's a plus. I'm not one to complain about the topic of girls but no delicate matters Zorian teased were touched upon whatsoever. And while the lack of women here is alarming, I'll see and talk to plenty once I'm out of this web of blunders. Or so I thought.

If not the biggest wakeup call that I've got to get the hell out of here, I don't know what is. Sure, I smiled and conversed, clenching my jaw and grinding my teeth as if what they discussed out on the dome was childish prattle. Completely delusional is this gang I've asininely stumbled upon. Where to begin as these thoughts are being juggled around in my head.

"So, let me get this straight. Everything that was said out there is true?" I ask David disconcerted.

Out of necessity I ought to take everything he says at face value. We're alone now, inside a locker room underneath the health farm. He's getting ready, slipping into a fulvous and white striped spandex clown costume. It has a wine ruffled collar, white ruffled jester cuffs, and candy apple red pom-pom accents.

"Collectively, no. Broken apart between speakers, yes. Truth is just a gravitational pull you can bend."

"Fibbing is still a whopper whichever way you dissect it. How can anyone be scared of a child? This isn't just a spoof on a playground horror film, is it?"

"I'm more into rom-coms. Don't focus so much on the details of it all. Worry more about the next step. Then again, I'm not the one who chooses where you go from here. God does."

"Please stop calling him that. It's discomfiting," I beg with a wistful smile. Knowing that in some measure Lucas and Ramze are being scouted is on par with having a warm purring cat resting atop my lap. It's de-stressing.

I is maikaì.

"Don't take umbrage in my remarks," he chortles.

He pauses as he notices I'm on the verge of a full-fledged panic attack. I divest this facade of composure. I cough and wheeze as though this locker room's been bulldozed, buried in ash. His spandex clown costume is halfway on when he grabs onto me by the shoulders. He reminds me to breathe. The best exercise to unwind is to take a deep breath. He takes one with me to calm our brains. David's counsel is to relax and have fun tonight. Reassuring me things will be better tomorrow morning.

"I'm not exactly thrilled to be spending the night."

"Well, you don't have much of a choice there do you. Now zip me up Kamikaze."

He finishes putting on his costume and I zipper him up from the back. I struggle and tell him he needs a bigger size.

Committed to it fitting, he readily sucks in his stomach. The mass force I pull the zipper up with causes the zipper to snap. The skinsuit would've covered his face had it not been down-market sourced. At least he'll breathe easier now without it bestriding his face. He doesn't appreciate my insight on more air coming in through his nostrils being a good thing. I guarantee him I can fix it as though I'm the salesperson that sold him the wacky getup.

I snatch a random white towel in the locker room that'd been thrown over a butterscotch yellow microfiber bench. The standard towel of this castle. An ultra-soft, super fluffy white bath towel with the golden profile of a top hat within a circle at a corner. I tie the towel around his neck, just under the wine ruffled collar so that it falls over his back like a cape, covering the unzipped portion of his spandex suit. I tuck the head portion of his skinsuit from the front, at the neckline, within the skinsuit itself, puffing out his chest but a tad. "You don't need a clown mask. You already have Siberian husky eyes and red hair."

"Clowns don't wear capes," he says so naturally.

"Didn't know you had a bachelors in clown school, but your god might. He sure does know how to tell jokes. For all the bullshit he spews, his jokes are horrifyingly elaborate."

"Hey, you're getting the hang of this. Starting to call him God too." He wags his finger at me with a sly smile.

"Look, I'm about as freaked out by the idea of cults as I am by the fake smiles on clowns. You're throwing the word god around to describe a man who can read minds. That's by far the single stupidest claim to divinity I've heard since Krishna Tusshar said I am God because I walk on water."

"You're smart enough to know that we don't use the word in the much more macro sense the church does." David opens my eyes.

The narrative of using god as a word without any rationale behind it but to label someone in command, unfiltered for people who might take offense, is quite audacious. A lot of people hide behind their god but never question their interpretation of God as personal and therefore strikingly different from someone else's, even in their own faith. I don't respect this fraternity's decision to use the word god in the manner they have but does it bother me? No. When so many people do the same worldwide, across every religion, why should it?

Today the Immortal Jaguars celebrate Halloween. The brothers follow a different calendar from the others. Anyone who's not a jaguar is called an *other* and their lives carry on in the otherworld. David told me this. When I asked if I was considered an *other*, he replied craftily with, "Not for long."

On the white picnic blanket we'd sat. Four male servers in synthetic light-aqua wigs and full glamourous makeup looks arrived dressed as women. A playful French maid came with ruffles and lace around the neckline, shoulders, and hem. Complete with the classic maid dust wand. A green-skinned woodland fairy with tiny gold wings and a black wand arrived shortly thenceforth, gracing us with his presence.

Accompanying him was an enchanting witch in a slinky black corset fixed over a black tee with draped long sleeves. A slit skirt put on view his skinny thigh muscles. A studded zip accent leather belt kept it from falling. Scanty in its crack at keeping the skirt above his waistline. To top off his imitation, he donned a pointy black hat with a green buckle and clasped a thick branch, brandishing it like a sword. One I'd advise be best left to a cavalier.

Behind the witch, a circus ringmaster appeared splashed in cardinal red from the tuxedo tailcoat to the oversized top hat. His white bra, red metallic spandex pouch shorts, and silver wand—gripped tightly near his crotch—were the only incongruities posed to the vivid red.

Each carried out a plate of food hidden by silver dome plate covers with finial. The sophomoric humor in their costumes should only appeal to prepubescent teenagers but I couldn't help but giggle. I wasn't alone. David and Zorian let out an inescapable chuckle. Baba turned to look at the men capering about the grass. At once, his jaw dropped, in sync with the inner corners of his eyebrows.

At first it seemed he was mortified. Then I got an odd hunch of what was going on. Leonid paused, abruptly got up, and escorted the man dressed as a witch away. The witch left his issued platter on the grass. David was eager to fetch it.

I thought they'd dressed up as women to amuse me—the guest, but they'd only done it to amuse themselves. When David got back to the picnic blanket, he'd let me know the day—All Hallows' Eve. I was charmed, breathing in the air of befuddled unworldliness that fenced me in. I knew it wasn't Halloween, but I felt a rapport with the jaguars for they're as kooky as my dog. That explained Zorian's wrestling singlet and the Roman soldiers downstairs.

I asked to anyone who'd answer if women here also found it comical to dress as men for Halloween. Baba, at a glacial pace, replied, "Negative. Women aren't allowed in Neptune." From my understanding he doesn't like witches, women, or flying children. I stopped myself from thinking so and thought up a slim apology.

Sorry. Just a thought.

Baba either read my mind and didn't respond or was too busy reading someone else's. After dropping off the platters of mystery, the three crossdressers retreated to a zone of the castle left of Baba's cottage. I wanted a costume now that I saw everyone but David and Leonid garbed in droll textiles. Baba, I reckoned was playing cowboy, but I quickly remembered Leonid's tale. He'd met him as he is now. A cowboy-esque cellmate with a blue beard. No longer in chains.

"The white eyes. They're contacts. Am I zombie enough?" Baba asked, looking at me with a rueful grin.

He was back at it again, prying into my personal thoughts. I couldn't help but think, what a dumb costume. He didn't respond to that private insult. He did, however, nod. Figures he'd agree with me. It's dumb. It's a middling act most elderly put on for Halloween. At least he's making an effort.

From what I discern, he's the oldest man here. Baba's probably tired of his followers' carouses. I anticipate there's alcohol somewhere to be had. Men need it to forget there's no women. What a sad decree. I'd volunteer to be exonerated if I was a brother knowing it'd mean I get to see Abeni again.

"Who's Luciana?" Baba grilled me.

The French maid outfit patently evoked unpleasant memories of my family's caretaker. Yup, he'd brought up the nasty woman who murdered my father and evanesced when convicted. I told him who she was in my life. Unafraid to hide from the past. I knew he'd pluck it from my mind regardless of if I spoke.

He accused me of being wildly overemotional. Whilst I didn't show it, I did stockpile tears. I had them set at liberty in my mind's eye. I sought to confute his view, telling him at least I've the balls to sit through a parody of someone who arouses in me negative thoughts. On the other hand, I'd said, you can't bear to be served lunch by a witch. I'd asked Baba, "Where's the poignant reminder of a witch present on your face? It sure is easy to call someone out for being emotional when you can inquire impertinently their innermost thoughts. I wonder what you're hiding. Having had a brother of this fraternity leave just because he was dressed as a witch."

Baba raised a brow. If upset, he hid it well. No one in the fraternity dare speak to him in the manner I'd done. Zorian and David decided to eschew from talking and opted for looking bovine instead.

The conversation ceased until Leonid got back. When he did, Baba lied. He'd told Leonid I thought it'd be rude to start eating without him. Leonid thanked me under the first alias I was given since entering Neptune—K. A nickname I'll never get used to yet can dote on more so than Kamikaze.

Leonid had brought back five champagne flutes as an insouciant bride would carry out a bouquet. An unlabeled green glass champagne bottle was in his other hand and a carton of orange juice, pressed tight against his ribcage, was being held in by his bicep.

In concert we lay bare what hid under the silver dome plate covers. It was a neat and fishy surprise. Chili lemon octopus alongside cucumber salad. What I'd wanted before I zonked out in the company of crocodile statues under the tree of mint green leaves. This welcoming gesture on part of Baba is relatively disconcerting. How long this man has been reading me is forevermore going to beleaguer me. Only he could've known I was daydreaming about this platter.

Coincidences aren't an element of a great story. My story is being manipulated. Access into my safe space—my mind—gives Baba an edge. He's making things I want come to me. The doyen of persuasion. He's going to do everything in his power to precipitate catching this boy he's after. If I'm the one to do it, he'd better start playing his cards right. The Luciana, trying to break me down affair wasn't a good start. What's his hand? He clearly instructed someone to cook this dish for me.

Everyone else had a slice of pizza with cut pineapple and sliced ham. My favored pizza—Hawaiian. This can't be coincidence. His tactic's working. I felt comfortable eating amongst strangers because I'm accustomed to eating Hawaiian pizza amongst friends. The scenario captured the warmth of the dog days when Lucas, Ramze, and I were strangers in cahoots to pass time. Through detention, pizza, and surfing we fared.

"Great food. I wanted this dish back in the rainforest. Though I'd be just as content with what all of you have on your plates."

Baba chomped on his pizza. Irregular in size. One slice was the length of my two hands, one at the fingertips of the other, and the thickness of a good stack of money. Being the only misfit that didn't get pizza, I was the only one given silverware. Of course, I was mannered enough to use it.

"Does everyone agree it's not actually Halloween or am I the only one?" I posed an inconsistency with their calendar.

"The holiday is contingent on people's acknowledgement and approval of the day," Zorian replied serenely. The excess melted cheese on his pizza slid from his hand and plopped on his plate.

"I like it here because we have our own rules. One pertaining to the order of days. It just so happens you found us on the day we celebrate All Hallows' Eve," David briefed me.

He grabbed four of the champagne flutes Leonid had brought out. The champagne bottle had previously been opened. Otherwise, there would've been an audible pop when David twisted the cork off. David filled the glasses with three quarters of champagne and a quarter of orange juice. Then passed them out to all but Zorian.

"Found? I didn't find you guys. You found me. Leonid, you brought me here. Baba, you've admitted why. That boy you're after. I'll be ready to look high and low for the boy once I'm done with my plate. I expect my friends will be waiting for me here at the castle when I get back. Shouldn't be a hard find with your drones rummaging the place." I glimpsed Zorian, patently challenging his drones' effectiveness.

Zorian reached for the last champagne flute which'd fallen over the blanket when David grabbed the four. He filled it to the brim with orange juice. I chew the tender meat of an octopus done right. I've had bad octopus before. The overly tough and chewy meat ruins the taste which is similar to that of an overcooked lobster.

"I'm afraid you won't be helping our search for the boy tonight. We won't stop looking for your friends but, in the meantime, you'll be prepped to help our team," Baba let know.

"How so?" I countered.

"By partying with the fraternity. It's clear you don't trust us, and trust is imminent if you're going to help us catch prisoner 1313. What better way to establish some trust between us than by joining us in the festivities!"

Baba knows I find myself at a crossroads. I can't leave yet. The uncertainty of finding my friends alone is too great. Yet to stay and party seems irresponsible. "What's to stop the boy from getting beyond reach and can someone please give me a name to identify this boy? Four numbers aren't going to serve me. I need a handy duck call. To attract the boy when in my proximity, I'll need his name."

"Tommy. He won't get far. He forgot something back in his cell. He's bound to return sooner or later for it." Baba's certain.

"In my life I've lived in five cities before Jacó but only here do I feel the sun," David randomly professes. A goose strapped for food approaches him. David blandly feeds it a piece of pineapple.

That city we're in—Jacó. It's a resort city Ramze spotted on the map of light because of its vicinity to Jacobi beach. The closest city to our first destination on the map of light. A place I've been to in my previous life. I can't imagine a city being nearby. This forest is boundless. I marveled at this castle having divulged its existence when it seemed no man had stood where I stood.

I focused on what mattered. To get my friends back I need Tommy. The name jogs my memory. In the gray hall there's an open door barricaded by a brick wall. A barricade was nothing out of the ordinary in that dimension. But from beyond the wall came a crying puppy. And on the wall came the arrangement of foreign letters and symbols ordering me to kill Tommy. There's an uncanny feeling I'd got that whoever or whatever was telling me to kill is sinister. No other brick walls had markings. For me to kill someone is unfathomable.

"*But you already have killed or at least showed us you're culpable of intent.*"

What're you talking about?

"*Your friends, the truck, the cliff. Ring a bell?*"

Baba was goading me onto more daring revelations about my inner psyche. This was his way of punishing me for calling him out in front of his brothers. He'd prompted me to mention his emotions. It's very remiss of him to bring up Luciana. I'd to defend myself in his attempt to break me so I pointed out a simple observation: the man dressed as a witch triggered him.

There's no use in fighting Baba as he listened in on me collecting my thoughts. There's no way he could possibly understand what I was thinking. I myself can barely crack what's happened to me. I ignored him telepathically taunting me. By and by he stopped.

I was all but done with my meal. Everyone else still had three quarters left to grub on. Their faces were relaxed and stomachs replete. Baba laid down the unfinished portion of his pizza on his plate. His hands were smeared with grease having left apricot-stained fingerprints on his champagne flute. He wiped his greasy hands across the white picnic blanket. It wasn't a surprise for they'd let a guest who'd swam through mud to get here sit amongst them in all his grubbiness but his new shorts.

Baba opened the red spiral notebook he'd brought out. In it were taped leaves of varying plants and seasons. He scrolled through the pages and stopped at a pinnately lobed pickle green leaf. He pinched a side of the tape and delicately pulled back on it so as to not rip the leaf. The leaf was then offered to me.

"A gift from God," David announced.

"Best to take it. Go on, accept it," Leonid urged.

My addled brain went with their game. I took the leaf and exaggerated my gratitude, bowing while sitting, offering Baba multiple thanks. I'd nowhere to put the leaf so I kept it in hand. A full circle in conversation we'd went. Back to the topic of girls. Zorian asked me if I'd a girlfriend. I was honest. David asked me if I'd any siblings. I'd said yes and specified—an older sister and an older brother.

It's safe to assume Baba knows everything I do. I'd drove Lucy off a cliff partly because I'd lost my brother and blamed my two friends. Thankfully, he didn't brusquely mention it aloud as he'd done with Luciana. It'd only make me seem crazier trying to explain my brother having been with my friends and I last night, waking up to find he didn't exist this morning.

Zorian welcomed me to a double date in fifteen years with his girlfriend. Prompting my curiosity, I asked why it'd be so long. I'm told by David he's yet to find one. I told him not to fret for it didn't have to be so long. When his drones find my friends, and I'm hesitantly buying they will, I'll help him score a gal. Finding them I indomitably sense will lead to finding my brother.

Without question, Abeni would treasure our time here. Wild beauty is something we both value. I wouldn't necessarily bring her to Neptune but if I end up being friends with Zorian, why not accept his clement invite? We'd take our girls to an amusement park. Something appropriate for both age groups.

David was able to finish his pizza and we excused ourselves. He'd said I needed a costume if I was to join them tonight. My daft thoughts exactly. We walked through the tall blue grass, past the white stone columns, back into the health farm.

In the health farm David had said a lot of the workings of this fraternity have cabalistic significance. How this brotherhood runs is arcane to the others. Others? I'd asked. So, he told me. Others are the people on the outside. He's referring to the outer boundaries of this castle. They're a part of the otherworld. Apparently, when people enter this castle, they let go of the otherworld. If I'm going to make it through the night, I too will forget the otherworld.

Chapter 22

David decides to keep the cape. People will have to come to terms with this version of a clown. The costume he proposes I wear is his costume from last year. It's no bombshell what he has in store. It's a striped poncho with multicolored earth tones and a festive woven straw hat. I ask for something a little less insensitive.

"You don't like my sombrero?" He asks, reaching for another costume inside his locker. After shuffling through a pile of cheap textiles and trinkets, he pulls out white cat ears splashed with glitter on a headband.

"That'll do," I tell him. He's floored I've accepted what he clearly brought out as a joke.

Like everything else I've seen in this castle, there's a harmless anomaly to this hall's style. A locker room this fiery and flavorful should be situated in a funhouse. I stand on its visually gelatinous floor. A pale-yellow rubber surface—as smooth as a neutron star—I crave badly to sit on. The tall rectangular metal lockers throughout the spacious hall are limned with lime green and numbered in white up top with the finesse of a paintbrush. Between banana yellow walls are butterscotch yellow backless microfiber benches with button tufted rolled ends. Some benches bear shades of yams. The colors used to paint the hall make sense of the name the jaguars have for it.

"Ta-dah, the Lemon Room!" David had spoken with grace when we first walked in here. The sort of flair one must have to develop this design is well recognized in its intricate details. The scarce ginger marigold stamps on the walls and ceiling, the polishing of steel lockers to a mirror finish—that which has sealed their shine—and the modern iceberg chandeliers.

Inspired by the natural beauty of icebergs, these crystal chandeliers float freely in the air as icebergs would out on open water. Each is a slight variation from the next. All blocky flat-topped shapes with steep vertical sides. Their spectacular inner light source shifts in color. Fading in and out of kindred shades of lemon chiffon, lemon meringue, and lemon glacier.

David told me not to worry. That what I was seeing wasn't witchcraft. It's physics. The chandeliers are lightweight, sitting on a cushion of air produced by downward directed fans inside them. At the chandeliers' underbelly, several inconspicuous openings allow the running fans' airflow to escape. Air pushes down and out, chandeliers are lifted and moored.

Their bulbs need only be changed every ten thousand years. Wireless charging pads run through the base of the floor. The chandeliers are constantly charging when the room's not in use. Zorian programmed them to rise solely when the Lemon Room's in use. This keeps them charged at all times. Their fans also serve to keep the temperature in here cool.

Much like a standard walk-in closet, the Lemon Room's lockers are something a person can step into. Each locker contains a boudoir for jaguars to change in. They're more akin to storage units than lockers. David's locker is filled to the brim with clothes. Sedimentary rocks deposited as strata aren't far in looks to what lurks inside his issued locker.

He's organized his wardrobe in layers. One layer somewhere in the middle is designated to swimwear. A vibrant stash with all the hallmarks of a drunk rainbow. A few layers under that, amusing costumes and props are squeezed into the mix by the narrowest of margins. A great way to organize if you want to keep your clothes as far away from being wrinkle-free as possible.

It's impossible to deduce the depth of each locker. I've only David's to go off of. Each locker is an arm's length to the next. The long side of a common foosball table is the width of each locker door. In terms of how far deep each locker stretches, David tells me they range in size from utility closet to cavernous warehouse. The Lemon Room itself is a sizeable room so it's hard to imagine a warehouse inside a warehouse.

The locks are notches on the lockers themselves. A thin platinum rectangle, the length of an average house key, was inserted into the slit at the locker's center when we arrived. The locker automatically opened, lowering its door a level below us. Anytime a locker opens or closes, it emits a short bloop like a river otter blowing bubbles underwater. David had placed the platinum key under a bench leg. It's easier for him to hide it and know where it's at than to lose it and have to ask some wally financiers to replace it.

"You'll meet the Quaestor class when we get you a locker. Till then, borrow whatever it is you need from mine." David's quite the optimist to think I'll say yes to a bid I've yet to receive from this brotherhood.

I'm welcome to share his clothes since I've none of my own. So long as I remember to put the key back under the bench leg. I appreciate his offer but one night in Neptune shouldn't call for a fashion haul. "Can I get a shirt?"

David closes his eyes. At random, he pulls out a red tank top with ribbed trim at the neckline and armholes. Destiny's spoken. It'll go well with the Union Jack shorts I've on. I hold off on putting it on. Till scrubbed, I'll remain shirtless. I don't delay sliding the headband over my head, behind my ears.

"You guys should really consider changing the rules of Neptune so that girls have an in at least this one time a year. Then someone could appreciate how adorable I look in these sexy kitten ears." I most likely look like a dimwit.

"Didn't you say you had a girlfriend you dog?" David pokes fun at me.

"I'm a cat and yea. The next time I plan on getting lost in the rainforest and finding a horde of lonesome men, dawdling in swimming pools, I'll bring her with me."

"Have you got all you need?"

I nod my head yes. David stomps his foot twice in front of his locker. In a flash, the locker door rises from below with a bloop, securing its contents once more.

"Where to now?" I ask gleefully. It's obvious I'm an ignoramus who'll follow David like a puppy dog.

"Hit the shower." David leans his back against his locker and raises his left foot, planting it on the locker door. I turn from him and start walking down the hall. Foxed by my course, I spin my body to him.

"Wrong way. Front of the hall to your left. It's the only chamber with a beaded door curtain."

I nod, changing route and idly salute him. At the front of the hall there's a light wood beaded curtain. A pale khaki matching the sands of Hyams beach, Australia. There's a fair amount of light through the curtain. You can see past it into the other room. Its tree design is a makeup of leaves depicted as mint green whorls and a trunk depicted as a tower of irregularly stacked russet brown cubes. If real, the cubes would certainly tumble. I fling the red tank top over a bench outside the curtain.

I delicately approach the curtain and push aside its wooden strands constructed of spherical, cubed, and cylindrical beads. At first glance I'm in a white room with dark, rich stained wood floors. The hanging quirky LED light fixtures birth the stark white light of a hospital unit. Their black beams follow the outline of a chicken's footprint. One circline fluorescent lightbulb sticks out at the end of four separate cutoff points. Three face out where a chicken's front claws are based, and one's popped into the rear where a chicken's back claw bides solo. Each black beam is held aloft by two fine iron-black cables hitched into two steel-gray metal plates on the ceiling.

The walls are a powder blue satin. All the ring lights work in unison to subdue their blue hue. Dark green flowering plants, nearly two feet tall, cover opposite sides of the illusory white room in concrete round pots. The pots' texture parallels the natural oak bark in Neptune's nursery with their deep, nearly black ridges.

To be used for firewood when camping.

I dispense an expendable thought to the universe. To my right, obstructing the pathway to the bathrooms, is the backside of a shirtless platinum blond gentleman in heathered medium-gray loose-fit joggers. He has a heart-shaped café au lait birthmark on his right upper lat. He's fidgety, idly kicking his bare feet in the air and shaking his arms at his sides. A method to cut loose. I do so sometimes for mental preparation or to relieve stress. I wonder, is it something significant that yearns for him in due course, expecting of him the utmost readiness?

Just ahead, a long egg-shaped room with soft-green glass mosaic tiles—iridescent on the floor and matte on the walls. Two freestanding stainless steel shower panels are stationed parallel to one another inside. Each shower panel has five shower heads powered on by five nozzles around their center. Several lit antique kerosene lamps circle the room on protruding non-uniform glass shelves; safe from the trajectory of the five running curved streams.

Hard to pay no heed to the nudity at my forefront within the working showers. Never have I had to use a communal shower, though I've been privy to them in the men's locker room at Pelican Island Econgregation. The five men washing themselves are all familiar with one another, carrying on a conversation about battle. All of them have the color shifting fuchsia to powder blue metal bands I saw on the men swimming in the diamond-shaped pool. One strapped to each wrist and ankle without the ball and chain you'd envision on a 17th century prisoner. Buffed enough to reflect the dour flames within the antique kerosene lamps but strong enough to deflect a 9mm bullet—nix, nix.

The platinum blond outside the showers stops kicking imaginary soccer balls and stiffens his arms, taking a deep breath. He turns to his side towards the beaded exit revealing an unmarked right shoulder. The first man I've seen without the black jaguar tattoo. "Hey!" I call out wishfully. "Are you new here?"

He points to himself and looks around as if there's someone else I could be talking to. His near silver hair's short at the sides and tousled at the top. Pieces fall in every direction like sloping swords. In this light, his ice blue eyes appear lucent under his hard-angled burnt umber eyebrows. It's almost as if I can smell fresh spearmint leaves getting waded over cool salmon. His semi-transparent irises can't be igniting the smell of winter blasted gum, for all the aqua ivory they equip. I savvy it's the soapy men showering. He's hawk-nosed, lean and long, faintly freckled at the shoulders, and harbors an athletic chest.

"Naaaaah, not exactly. Whoa-ho-ho! See ya accepted the bid! Wahoooo!" he says in a zany, unique tone of voice like a cartoon voice actor. He prances towards me with his chest puffed out and asks if I've had a taste. I realize that fresh mint breeze I smell is his breath that billows, breaking upon my face. I taste the spicy and invigorating air approaching.

Is this what he means by taste?

"A taste of what?"

"The mochi leaf," he says, reaching for my right hand and taking from me the pickle green leaf Baba had given me outside. "Oh, my oh my! What in the wacky world happened there?!" he asks, taken aback. He grabs my right arm and tenderly traces along the long, thin vertical scar on the ventral side of my forearm with the tip of the leaf. The leaf glides from the end of my bicep to the start of my palm. He looks me straight in the eyes with unbound curiosity, still holding my hand. He brusquely lets go, leaving me with the leaf once more. I close my grip on it and let my arm rest.

"I tried to kill myself," I announce with a stone-cold grave face.

One of the nozzles in the showers is shut off. The overall pitter-patter of falling water dies down. A nude man in the chameleon metal bands walks past us into the locker room. The unmarked platinum blond stands awkwardly, grabbing his left shoulder anxiously and crossing his legs. He's debating an appropriate response.

"I'm kidding. Surfing accident."

His face calms and he releases the long, high pitch whistle sound of a boiling kettle pot—his variant of a sigh of relief. A line appears between his brows. He didn't have to say anything. I knew what he was asking himself— 'Does he think he's funny?' Without expressing it aloud, I do.

Another nozzle is shut off. The man walking out, physically small but generously built, is stopped by this platinum blond when asked, "Ay, what was your name again? Hehe! My memory's playin' tricks on me! Was it Tom? No wait, John! Oh, can you give me a little reminder? Pretty please?"

"Billy," the man replies, squinting at him as though his vision's briefly turned fugitive.

"That short for William?"

"Sure is," the man says gruffly, now standing moodily, watching as the inquisitor prepares another dumb statement.

"Ya know, I never understood why that is. Names like Billy short for William and Chuck short for Charles."

Within earshot, the rest of the men showering laugh aloud. The compact man tires of their short interface and swaggers off. I too decide to hop in the shower and get back to David at a gallop, inattentive to slippage. I make a beeline for the showers. Two more men walk out as I get inside. One, having left a shower running. I grab my sides searching for a pocket and detect a cool donut zipper located on my right butt cheek. I slide it back with a pinch and stuff the leaf inside, halting it from making a sly getaway.

I step into the stream, not needing to turn it on. My cat ears bow under the water pressure. I leave my trunks on for they're swim trunks. If there's any need to get naked, I'm ignorant. This will be like the dog days running late for school. A rushed sponging. The water's warm but not warm enough for steam to spring long like a kangaroo or mushroom toward the edge like my mother's bad decisions.

"Polka Yankel," the lone man in the shower across from me introduces himself with a jovial wave of the hand. A black man with a brush cut and gray eyes that're as flashing as his metallic bands.

"Koa," I reply, not needing someone else to choose a nickname for me. I grab a crescent-shaped golden bar soap from a tray attached to the shower panel, mid waist. The bar soap slid in and out of my armpits, into my swim trunks, round my crotch, and down my crack before I could regurgitate Polek Yankel in my head.

"So, you American, English?" I ask airily as the foam whipped up by the bar soap is cast off my skin in dollops.

"Eh, just because I speak English doesn't mean I fall in line with those two categories. I'm Australian. Born in Brazil. If you manage to pass the rounds maybe you'll be put in Celeres too. Oh, I'm a Celer by the way. The pro-gravy vambraces and greaves probably gave that away," he says gloatingly, clinking his metal bands twice in tapping his wrists. A smug smile wedges his full lips. My eyes scour the corners of the room, heedless of what he means by rounds, Celeres, and pro-gravy.

"Unless you're new here. Oh, you are new. Not just new but fresh off the boat new...I see." His proud expression dims as if telling me what he was—a Celer—had gone to waste. "I pay no mind to when things start around here."

"I know not what great honor that must be. A Celer. But I'm sure I'll learn. See you around Polek." I turn the nozzle right ending the jet of water.

"Polka, Nihil." I catch a trace of irritation in his voice a step away from the boundary between iridescent green glass tiles and dark rich stained wood floors.

"What did you call me?"

"Nothing." Polka returns to washing himself.

I walk out smelling like freshly squeezed lemonade. Not far from my steps into the bright yellow locker room, Polka passes me in a flash. His bowling balls of an ass make me quail as they roll down the hall. Each cheek giving the other a chance to project, bouncing with every long stride.

I look back to the light beaded curtain realizing I missed the platinum blond as I'd zoomed out. The only other 'other' I've seen thus far. As I stare back into the shower room without a touch of the curtains to push them aside, I see the platinum blond. Now alone inside the green room, he walks about pounding the walls with clenched fists. He whops at them like a street fighter, sticking to a double punch for his go-to move. He waits a second, breathes heavily, and then pressures an ear fast on the matte green walls. The antique kerosene lamps scarcely tremble on their glass shelves every time his fists make stark impact with a wall.

What on earth's he doing?

I neglect my chance viewing of his tantrum and look to David. He's still waiting in front of his locker, carefree, with a fluffy white bath towel in his hands. Polka paced a bit further past David into an open locker with dazzling cyan blue lights as four more men walked out of that same locker, slipping by him. Each dressed in an elaborate costume.

A semi peeled banana, split cleanly down the middle. A blue-ringed octopus that resembles the half-peeled banana with twice as many peels for tentacles and dark blue rings omnipresent on its body. A gray wolf wearing lavender night-gown pajamas, a pink shower cap, and large gold aviator reading glasses. And lastly, a fantastical brown jungle cat with a smooth and polished spring green paw glove on his right hand and a brown furry paw glove on his left hand. A white gold hoop earring highlights his left ear—long, pointed, and facing forward. Most beetling of all are the six broad angel wings extending from his back. They're spray-painted silver and made up of what look like real feathers.

"Wow." I watch in confoundment.

"Hurry up you! Don't start lagging now," David calls out to me as he's twiddling the towel.

"Aren't we leaving?!" I bent slightly to grab the red tank top, which'd almost fallen over the bench, and race lazily to him, pointing behind me with my left thumb towards the entrance.

"This way!" He nodded to where the costumed men were headed.

Must be another exit.

He pitches the towel to me and I catch it, drying myself with it before I reach him. I slip the red tank top over me, tilting the cat ears on my head. We're moving so fast now I neglect centering them.

"Drop the towel," David orders. "The plebs will get it later."

The end of the Lemon Room is its entrance's twin. Broad mustard yellow swinging saloon doors one could look over and under without tiptoeing or kneeling. As we push aside the swinging doors, we enter a gray room. Sizably different from the dark and narrow wet cave walls across the Lemon Room. This gray room is airy, round, muted, and aglow with white light issued from an undulating cloud sculpture overhead. It's well-contrived from what's suggestive of heavy-duty bubble wrap.

At the room's center, three Asians are lounging on glossy white egg chairs with cobalt blue plush interiors. They're surrounded by the echoes of our footsteps. There's one empty egg chair alike all the others and a large, rounded ash gray chabudai with a one-by-one-foot square hole carved into its center. The short-legged table is commonly the dining room centerpiece in traditional Japanese homes. A hill of smooth black stones rises from the floor through its square opening leaving no gap but a square outline to be seen.

Unsure of what the sitting men are supposed to be, my best guess is gay popes. Their long lavish robes all have a shoulder cape and are raffish in their select color when put against this gray backdrop. There're no dippy hats to add to their religiosity. One's in crimson red. The many black hairs on his shoulder cape alarm me to the fact his hair's been recently chopped to a short French crop with straight lash-skimming bangs. Another's in chocolate brown. His pointy and whacky raspberry wine hairstyle that's straight and short at the sides almost outvies the joshing nature of a thrift store wig. The one currently rising from his chair is robed in buttermilk yellow with jazzy medium-length messy black hair.

"What's taking Baba so long?" the man in buttermilk yellow asks the two in repose.

"Izumo, if I have to teach you the essence of patience, I'll sacrifice my own and have to seek refuge in Buddha all over again," the one in crimson red says bitterly, looking extremely sulky.

"The crux of the matter is that we all have places to be," Izumo splutters, watching beadily as we pass them by.

"Ah, some levity in this most taxing day," the one in chocolate brown says optimistically with shadowed eyes.

"I do jibe with the eight-armed cephalopod." Izumo now smiles, goggling at the blue-ringed octopus.

At the end of the gray room, I look back. The mustard yellow saloon doors, culled out of a Western art flick, pop vividly next to these looping gray walls. A disturbance at the center of the room shifts my focus. Without warning, the pile of black stones totters. A single stone torpedoes from inside the mass, knocking over several stones across the chabudai. I didn't see its collision with a wall, but I heard a thud, managing to catch its fall from the corner of my eye, ending in another thud. I see the lone black stone reeling on the floor. A convulsive possession of something inanimate.

How batty.

It spins uncontrollably, jerks an inch off to the side, flips once, and continues to spin like a machine assisted dreidel. David ushers myself and the other guys off. There's nothing to see here but a living rock. We enter a gray hall at the end of the room, walk for about five minutes, and turn through a gap.

We wend our way across more gray halls, getting sootier by the moment, snaking and sloping as gales of laughter come approaching. At last, we reach a dark room. Its doorway's a literal hole into the earth. The ground here is weathering rock—frore and coarse-grained. The ceiling's untouchable by sight. Mounds of dirt have compiled here over time.

Where's a broom when you need one.

I step on a mound and my foot sinks into its cold, pebbly depth. I'm filthy all over again but I don't feel like dirt. Tall golden candelabras with vaguely visible thin black candlesticks border the room. Their flames appear to be floating as their base is only palpable through squinting. The borders of this room are also unclear. Darkness runs mocking revolutions over light, though in theory nothing's faster than light.

The energy in here is both tragic and comic. On one hand, there're men dressed in costumes that took a light and witty approach to the holiday. On the other, there's something genuinely disturbing about those who've chosen the fear component of Halloween to play up. A polestar for evil in the flesh. There're gruesome monsters here and there.

Hybrids. A lion-eagle, a rooster-snake, an owl man, a donkey-camel, an elephant-fish, and a hippo-goat. The ultimate bloodcurdling front for me are the human portrayals scarred by illness and war. Men who look to have reworked skulls, unrecognizable as human. Those coated in blisters and boils. My stomach churning as they shift into the candlelight. Men bringing to mind the harsh realities of war. Fake guts spilling out of their stomachs, blood-stained head to toe. At least it's all an act. A calming thought.

"This gathering is a conceptualization of hell. A drove of demons in their untold forms. Jesters in amity with damaged humans. Earth's animals all thrown into a blender to see what newfangled nonsense is spat out," a paunchy construction worker with a yellow hard hat to my right voices boastfully so with a slightly rugged and hoarse quality to his cadence. He wears a confident grimace.

"And here I am as a cat," I say dully, looking around at the mass.

"Ah Swamidoss, a great work of art it is. The best yet, I'd say!" David says amiably to the construction worker, not meeting his eyes but in awe of the scene before him. The banana, octopus, grandma-wolf, and angel-cat disband, one by one tapping Swamidoss over the shoulder, each with passing praise.

"Nice one!"

"I dig it."

"Never fail to impress."

"You sure outdid yourself this year."

Swamidoss' fierce black eyes, though small, speak frankly of the delight his work's being bestowed.

A blinding white light bursts from ahead, quickly filling the gaps of a large rectangle. It's a movie screen. The stately size of this subterranean theater's no longer suppressed. Dusty black walls are crisscrossed with a network of golden boldly delineated squares, rectangles, and triangles. A sleek Art Deco room with a twist of abandonment and to that end—grunginess. Ahead, I count them. Eight chairs to my left and eight to my right, split by a wide rift—the descending path towards the foremost seating. The lot of monsters and dead men walking scramble to their red velvet padded seats before being called to do so.

A grainy black film is projected onto the screen. Darkness swallows all men beyond the distance of candlelight. As the film progresses, I register, it isn't white specs that're making the film grainy but stars that come into focus. Billions, making a spectacle of the cosmos. Suddenly, it's a swirl of them in high definition from a remoteness that makes them seem small. The pure white hailing from the stars—fresh as an untouristed village subsumed under a snow blizzard—manages to make the falling rows of seating visible. Murmurs of excitement spur in the dark.

What's there to be excited for in this roundly underlit and humdrum ambiance?

"Jaguars take your seats!" an orotund voice echoes over us as if next to us.

"Go on Kamikaze. Pick a seat. After the performance, go ahead, mingle a little. I'll be here at the rear. If you get lost, don't dither. Come and find me," David informs me in a strangled whisper by cause of a show starting.

"Ok." I become taciturn with no plan of mingling.

I wander through the center aisle as some men begin taking their masks off and placing them on their laps. Eight rows in, I'm halfway through the theater. I scoot my way through a row to my right, picking a seat in between a decaying pale blue zombie with his nose hanging to his face by a thread—a good chunk of his pink brain being aired—and to my right, a solid yellow Lego man in a plain red tunic with a block head and one plastic claw hand. His second plastic claw hand is settled on his lap as his right hand's holding a peach drink cast with a pink bendy straw.

How's he—

My question's answered before I can think it. He inserts the straw through a mouth flap in his block head, slurping the peach drink from his glass.

"Nice costume doofus," a man sitting directly behind us remarks snidely, stoutly pushing the Lego man's block head forward with the heel of his palm. The Lego man's peach drink spills a titch. Few drops trickle over his bleach-washed blue jeans. It looks as if he's tinkled himself after making a quick stop at the urinal. I spin my head round.

The bully's a seaman in a white sleeveless top with a striped collar, gold button detailing, blue necktie, and white pants with blue stripe accents at the sides. A white sailor hat with a dark blue embroidered anchor on the upturned trim covers his molasses brown hair; seen through his long, moderately thick mutton chop sideburns.

"What're you looking at bitch?" he says grumpily with near vacant eyes.

I face the movie screen. The Lego man seems unbothered having kept still. The stars recede from view as the screen's lifted. Behind it, a stage is occupied at warp speed with three clashing figures. White chocolate next to dark. Dark chocolate next to pumpkin spice. All chocolate but a one-off flavor, each is. A spotlight follows the three.

A lavender impression of a man, purple from head to toe owing to a skinsuit and brash single-toned full face makeup. To his left, an angel in a shimmery silver satin loose-fitting t-shirt, a golden rope tied in a reef knot at the waist, and bare feet doused in sterling silver metallic paint. Two crystal stakes are fused to his back—the main stems to a wealth of white feathers.

To the right of the two, a shiny black glob—the very picture of melting burnt mozzarella cheese. Detectable are two black gloved hands—the glob's sole human properties. At its midsection is a bulbous half sphere like an igloo discharging flashes of white light. An overt flickering light bulb in need of an electrician. They know a thing or two about loose wiring.

Sideburns back there must be looking for trouble, picking on block head and calling me a bitch.

A sad melody begins to play characterized by a piano's dalliance with a violin. The sad music quickly turns eerie as the chess pieces begin to move on stage. The spotlight breaks into three. The angel and glob ballet their way to the foremost corners of the stage. The glob reveals its black human feet for the first time in its pointe work. The two figures kneel on their right knee. The glob does so by extending its left leg in a black stocking, springing from its insides and stomping its foot flat on the stage.

The two turn to face center stage where the lavender man stands facing the audience. He bows his head. From either side of the stage, two rows of lavender men come waltzing in in rapid shuffling steps. They form a line at the original lavender man's sides. Every one of them but the man in the middle faces the audience. The spotlights fade away. The entire stage is lit in clover by a screen behind the lavender men, showing those same men but from a vantage point overhead. An inward light, like that of two warm cozy hotel room lamps, inhabits the screen and in turn the stage.

The line of lavender men curve inward till they form a circle, then shift to face each other's backside. Now all bow their heads and begin to walk steadily clockwise like zombies in a computer programmed loop. The circle rotates for some time till one lavender man awakes and exits the circle. Standing alone on the outside, he's become a glitch in the system.

He desperately runs counterclockwise alongside the rotating circle of men. Eventually, the lot of lavender men walking turn to stare at the black sheep, halt, and two men fiercely pull him back into the circle. The circle closes in on him, getting tighter and tighter till he disappears in a huddle. No longer a circle but a clump of lavender men fighting or stacking themselves, one over the other.

The uncanny melody shifts tone and becomes one with a glorious tune played in the art of drums. Fired up slapping of rawhide vibrates from under the stage, into my soul, and oozes down to feet.

I want to dance. Maybe after business. Should I let sideburns' comment fly, or should I grab it by the wings? Screw magnanimity. Have at it!

As the huddle breaks off, the stage's lit brilliantly as if the sun's cropped up underground for an unnoted visit. The lavender men return to their rotations, switching gears and walking counterclockwise with their heads lifted. As the circle enlarges back to its previous size, I look to the screen behind them. In the center of the circle is one lavender man in a...bridal gown I suppose.

The lavender man in the middle of the circle is in an unfussy white dress with flowy, long bell sleeves and a skirt that's quite broad. On his head is a club-shaped white hat most relatable to a bowling pin. A gap within the circle effortlessly forms and the bride exits looking lost. The gap closes instantly.

A sign of guidance appears to the left of the stage in the form of four angels. Not one differing from the frozen knelt one at the left foremost corner of the stage. Not having moved since falling into position opposite the glob. Each forthcoming angel carries an object of intrigue to the bride. Pumpkin-shaped glass vases with an element inside. Dry dark brown earth, a black liquid, nothing (I reason this typifies air), and fire.

The bride looks longingly at each vase like I would a menu of seventeen distinct hamburgers. At last, he chooses the pumpkin vase with a black liquid inside. The drumming intensifies. The three angels whose gifts were unchosen retreat saddened from where they came, leaving behind their pumpkin vases on the stage. The remaining angel embraces a hug from the bride and he too leaves, but in style, taking flight above the stage.

The bride looks round for anyone outside the circle. The coast is clear. He pulls three lavender men from the circle. With his pumpkin vase at his side, he directs the three to pick up the unchosen pumpkin vases. They're beholden to the bride, falling to his lavender feet and kissing them. At full tilt they gather themselves, take the pumpkin vases, and retreat to the right side of the stage, out of sight.

A gap in the circle forms to let the bride in. He enters, bringing his chosen pumpkin vase with him. No sooner does he enter that the gap closes. He gets in the middle of the circle, lifts the pumpkin vase high over his bowling pin hat, and starts spinning clockwise. His broad white skirt rises to his waist as he spins like a bat out of hell.

On the screen past the lavender men, the image of them walking jointly in a circle with one white-dressed man whirling in the middle looks to be an eye with purple eye shadow. The black liquid swirling in the pumpkin vase could be interpreted as the eye's pupil.

Five minutes go by. The Lego man takes another sip of his peach drink. As he does, the bride becomes lead-footed. Under a spell, he takes the pumpkin vase from over his head and starts spilling the black liquid on his every side. Splish-splash! Aiming it at the lavender men's feet. One by one, the lavender men slip and fall till there're no more standing, laid like rag dolls across the stage. Some men, up to four, stacked themselves on top of each other flattening those underneath.

Mashed potatoes.

No more black liquid's left within the pumpkin vase. Thus, the bride stops pouring. Leaving the empty pumpkin vase at an end of the circle, he resumes spinning amongst the fallen lavender men. This time, counterclockwise. Another five minutes go by.

What an outrageous concept for a show. What's the message?

The drumming draws to a close. At last, as the bride is spinning, he lifts the bowling pin hat off his head. Loads of red paint come gushing out of his hat, forever staining the white dress. The fallen lavender men get bespattered with red paint from drops flying off the ends of his long skirt. An abstract scene quickly turned militant with bloodlust. Before another five minutes can pass, I seize the Lego man's peach drink and throw what's left of it behind us unmistakably hitting the seaman.

"What the fuck!" an adenoidal voice yells outraged.

That wasn't the seaman I heard. Expecting everyone behind me to be angered with me, I turn. But everyone's gaze is fixed on the wet seaman's left-hand side. An orange-suited astronaut, also sopped by the peach drink, with a globose white plastic helmet and tinted gold visor sits there silent still. From the bemused looks of those unmasked, close-by, I can tell they all know what I know—that voice is female.

Chapter 23

"Could be a spy from the Chinese," a caveman to the seaman's right-hand side suggests sternly.

"I'm Chinese," the pale blue zombie to my left tersely points out.

"Not you, one of Huan Keung's girls," the scaman interjects pompously.

A trio of jam red monkeys, a row behind the seaman's, peer haughtily over the stirring commotion. The astronaut lifts his gold visor eliciting a chuckle from the seaman.

"Man's just got a fruity voice is all," the seaman says in a level voice.

"Huh, that wasn't me?" the mellow-brown man with outmoded long sheeny black Jheri curls says looking reasonably morose from inside his white plastic astronaut helmet.

I crane my neck over the astronaut and seaman. A dark pewter gray warthog in a tawny tattered cloak, directly behind the seaman, is rising from its seat and quickly sliding past those seated towards the right end of the theater. The attention rapidly falls back on me. The seaman, caveman, and two others—a mime and donkey piñata—stand up.

I'm impulsive but not stupid. It's plain I'm outnumbered. I duck and hastily crawl to the left end of the theater. I pounce on some feet with my left hand, knocking some knees aside with my left shoulder as I worm my way toward the middle passageway, away from the hollers.

"Come back pussy!"

"Sit down jackass!"

The second of which thankfully wasn't directed at me. A vampire's leg jolts up and kicks me firmly in the stomach, thrusting all wind out of me for a good minute. The rough blow checked in with one of my ribs. If I'm not mistaken, I saw that warthog within a rust-covered mirror in the grubby bathroom I met Baba. I get up at the end of the row and hobble up the slope with one hand clutched to my stomach. The warthog exits the theater through a black hole. A different path from which I was shepherded.

The unseated men who stayed standing when all jaguars were called to be seated quietly converse amongst themselves as the show progresses. The stage has been cleared of the prior scene and is transitioning into a hunter green forest clearing with rustling foliage coming from the stretched away faux trees at the sides of the stage. The screen at the back of the stage has been replaced by a scenic construction of an ancient, abandoned campsite made of straw and live branches with spring leaves. Three stuffed deer dyed reddish-brown with white fur around their black eyes, muzzles, and the underside of their short puffy tails are rolled out onto the stage on grassy circular dollies by camouflaged men in green paint and bush-like overlays.

David is speaking to the construction worker, Swamidoss, which I know is not really one but some type of special effects makeup artist responsible for a lion's share of the costumed men here. He must've spent so much time transforming the jaguars he left no time for fashioning himself a showy costume. David's white towel cape faces me as I continue into the black hole of the warthog's choosing, taking with me a lit black candlestick from a golden candelabra at hand, abreast of the black hole.

The other holes of the theater are the main forward-facing entrance and the two at the head of the stage; one on each side. This black hole at the back right end of the theater, aside the theater's hindermost seats, is conspicuous. Or at least for me it is as it's rectangular, not round like the rest of them.

I enter it gingerly as the hurt on my abdomen melts away with the wax of the candlestick. Ahead there're two red doors with classic bathroom stick-figures upon them—a silhouette of a person and a silhouette of a person in a high waisted skirt. I open the men's bathroom to poke my head in. It's brilliantly lit by refined silver wall sconces with flourishes of swirling vines with thorns and what could be a tiny dragon perched amidst the vines in the ornate metalwork. The sinks are aligned along one side and feature intricate gold and marble detailing. The oval mirrors above them are rusted to the point that denies a mirror its purpose. Plush royal blue velvet benches line the opposite wall. There're several stalls and spotless urinals toward the back. Yet, beyond those, my line of sight gets hindered by the corner angles and curvature of the room. There may be additional rooms or stalls further back and off to the sides.

At my feet, upon the intricate floral motif of delicate petals in shades of bluish pink, ivory, and soft greens, crafted by hexagonal mosaic tiles, lie sooty Polaroid snapshots of naked women. The photos litter the bathroom floor up to the first sink and while their subjects' features are crisp, an unusual effect surrounds them—a subtle, ethereal tinge of colors that seem to dance and shimmer. A breathing halo, blending shades of iridescent blue, soft purples, and deep grays.

I press on to the women's bathroom. Similar to the men's, except the lighting from the silver wall sconces is subtle and therefore more ambient and soothing. There's a lavish circular vanity equipped with cosmetics and perfumes, all meticulously organized at the center and delicate rust-free mirrors that look to have been intentionally shattered into irregular pieces upon the vanity and marble sinks. Each shard reflects what fragments of little light they can muster in different directions, casting a mosaic of fractured mini white triangles around the space. The stalls toward the back end provide an added layer of privacy with royal burgundy velvet curtains separating the space. I hold the door open before unwittingly taking another step forward, leaning slightly to see if there's any movement among the curtains.

My foot floats above a dark pit in the ground. There's a disruption in the bathroom floor's pattern with a large section of mosaic tiles shattered and blown around the edges of this gaping hole. I boot a pebble in with my big toe. A second passes before a plop answers a question I had. What's down there is water. Brassy footsteps flounce in behind me and two hardened hands, flat against my back, encroachingly shove me onward. Water bursts through the hole as I make the splash of a million reasons not to go wandering alone in the dark. I shimmy my head, narrowly shifting the white cat ears back into place on my head. Above me, the red door's steadily closing with a large yellow block head peeping in through its crack.

Motherfucker.

I let go of the put-out candlestick and shift my awareness to where I'm at. Only six feet down from where I was. The arch of a rainbow catches my eye as if a flashlight was shone through a glass prism dispersing its light. In the left corner of the room, the band of colors dies out but with it a different light buds. From the darkness emerges Lucas in his fuchsia pink boardies and open red Hawaiian shirt with a white floral pattern.

"Lucas!" I shout exuberantly.

"You see me?" he asks in a quiet voice. He grabs me by the forearm and pulls me out of the water onto where he's standing.

I instinctively hug him. "I see you," I say sweetly.

From behind Lucas is a bright bulb, no bigger than a one-year-old's fist, fitted on industrial metal pipes that're bent into a miniature stick-figure with eight arms flung skyward and two legs spread wide. I can internally hear it shouting 'Hooray!' I try and tug the comical figure upwards to shine its light elsewhere, but it won't budge. The teeny pipes are rooted deep into the ground.

I convince Lucas to follow me though there's not much convincing involved. He says no more but gives me a lost boy's wide-eyed stare. Instead of climbing up the six-foot pit, back into the theater, we walk the length of the spoon-like room searching for another exit. I become a chatty Kathy without even realizing Lucas might have a lot to tell me too.

I tell him about being injected by the jaguar's spit and how I saw a boy fly. How I lost Ramze but miraculously found this castle—Neptune—home to a group of men known as the Immortal Jaguars. How they stupidly refer to their leader as God—a blue-bearded man who can read minds. How they're currently celebrating Halloween despite it being months away and how I think they want me to join them.

"Somehow, maybe I'm being primed to become a member. I already have a herald. Though I'm unsure what that entails here in Neptune. I haven't received any news essential to me. His name's David."

It's only moments before I find a trap door on the ceiling. A dim white light outlines the square. I wave Lucas over and hop onto his shoulders, able to stretch my hand out wide enough to push open the trap door. I lift myself up through the door and then wrench Lucas on up as I lie on the floor, keeping myself grounded by pure luck. I all but slid back through the trap door just as Lucas got his elbow up over the opening. It seems we're back in the unvaried gray halls of the castle.

"We best walk away from the noise," I tell him coolly, knowing the amped-up classical crossover music is coming from the jaguars' poppycock theater production.

I continue talking about things transpiring after the truck fell to the water, ignoring the fact that it was my fault and doing my best not to bring up the topic about him and Ramze denying I've a brother. I'm so busy babbling as we walk further away from the theater that I nearly miss Lucas drearily chanting something under his breath in a funny, detached from the here and now sort of way.

"Lucas, are you alright?" I ask meekly and smile. "We don't have to talk about everything now if you don't want to."

He gives me a curt nod and asks, "You see me as a human being talking as my own individual self?"

I stop and turn to look at his expression beside me. His mouth's gaping stupidly, his eyebrows are up a notch, and his eyes are bulging like a red-eyed tree frog's. He's inspecting himself meticulously, pinching the fine hairs on his arms.

"I'm not sure I understand," I say warily.

"We are oneness at its core. We are here to bring you home," Lucas says in a deadly tone, beaming at me.

"What's the meaning of this? Why aren't you with...who's this?" Baba Azul strides over to us looking perplexed. Baba's in a wine purple robe with a shoulder cape. He tips his black Dallas wool cowboy hat over his forehead, lifting his robe a jot off the floor. He stumbles before stopping in front of us and takes a hardy gulp of air before instructing me to—"Stand back from it," he advises warningly.

"This is my friend Lucas. He's a bit rattled seeing as how I don't know how to drive," I say looking quite unabashed.

"I said stand back fool!" he shouts menacingly.

"Ok! You don't have to tell me twice. Just don't do anything brash," I tell Baba, looking quizzically at him, wondering what's got him up in arms. I smoothly step back, away from Lucas and Baba.

"Behind me now Califf," Baba commands pleadingly.

All this time Lucas is standing there absent-mindedly. I study Lucas suspiciously and do as Baba says. The shock of it all, my actions and him finding his way here like I must've really fucked with his head. Lucas is acting as though he's just smoked the dankest weed on the market.

"Welcome Lucas," Baba says eyeing him intently with moon white eyes.

Baba leans in to hug Lucas with his left arm extending across Lucas' back. Baba steadily reaches into his robe's right pocket and withdraws a seven-inch black plated cylinder. He flips his wrist at his side and three telescoping shafts extend from it making it a three-foot-long baton. Baba's index finger taps the baton as he's holding Lucas unbecomingly tight. The top two shafts light up in a police strobe blue, producing a rumbling sound as though the baton's viciously vibrating.

Lucas stares at me with a sorrowful look. Baba steps back and in one spurt, plunges the baton through Lucas' heart, coming out black on the other side. I gasp, not far off from fainting. Baba whips out the baton from Lucas' chest. With a simple twist of his hand, the three shafts retract back into the black plated cylinder. "Now that that's done..." he says dropping the cylinder back into his robe's right pocket.

Lucas is standing, frozen with an after-dinner starlight peppermint candy sized hole in his chest. From the tiny hole comes out a black daddy long leg spider radiating polychromatic light. Following the one are a dozen alike. And then his whole body gets inundated in black starting at his chest and expanding beyond the total volume a human body can occupy.

I hear a muffled cry and look down to my right. Baba is crouched on the ground against a wall, flagging me. His mouth is moving in exaggerated yawns. His cries become apparent as I read his lips. The message materializes in his deep voice once I've already spun myself from darkness.

"Run boy!"

How'd these shadows find me? How'd they make a copy of Lucas?

I race to the beat of raging violins, violas, cellos, horns, trombones, a piano, and organ heard from the theater. Their weird, tension enkindling sound motivates me to run faster than I've ever run. My legs glide over the floors that changeover from hazy gray, on the face of it granular rock but at the touch of it smooth landings for my feet to buss, to autumn blended cobblestones.

I venture into a red square, equally nescient about what's trailing me and where I'm headed. Three doorways, one on either side of me and one straight-ahead triple my options for an escape. Embossed atop each doorway is a stodgy emblem with poor paint retention.

To my left is a juniper green snake. Its body's curved into a spiral. At my front is a cream yellow apple. The faded paintwork on its leaf consents to it blending in with its cinnabar background. To my right is a black elliptical shape with pointed ends like a caiman's vertically slit pupil.

Within polished glass boxes, golden crowns lie flat upside-down or right-side up on top of antique purple wooden pedestals featuring central columns, which stand on a circular base. Ten are spaced out irregularly across the room wherein at the heart lies a sheeny white sarcophagus. I focus in on the doorway straight-ahead, dodging the exhibition of crowns.

"*Turn left!*" Baba's voice echoes in my head.

Too late. I'm already bounding down the stairs at the end of the hall I chose instinctively. If I can find a way to loop back around into the red square and make a right, I'd be headed where Baba wants me to. I turn back once out of toxic curiosity for what's chasing me. There's not one nick in the union of black spiders barreling over stairs. They mirror a black creek tumbling over rocks but parrot the scuttering of a thousand rats. As I jumpily jerk my head around, another pack of shadows hits me with a—'Surprise!'

A jumbo black bloom with overlapping petals flitters on the ceiling in the background. Like a beetle darting a swatter, it won't stop moving evasively.

Well I'll be a monkey's uncle! Never thought a flower could scare me.

Its short center petals curve inward and revolve around a scooped-out center. Their revolutions expedite, one per second. The bloom's core zaps an unbroken ray of kaleidoscopic light in my direction with the smooth whoosh of a flying arrow. The dazzling light shoots into me, right through my stomach. I'm unaffected.

I feel unaffected.

The cup-shaped center widens. The black petals ape its growth, maturing into carbon copies of a monster truck's overblown tires. So widened the core has become that its light reaches my eyes. As if to derisively say, 'feel unaffected no more,' I'm put in a fugue state. Forthwith, I wish I were blind.

How is this real if I know real? Why does life exist if this is real? Where am I if it is real? When did it become real, or has it always been real? What is real? Who am I if I'm real? Is this reel of questions a proof insanity's real and if insanity's real, did I make it so?

The cataclysm of doubt is unanswered because there is none. What's revealed to me is a nether world overrun by silver tufted dandelion puff balls. They're blown apart by great winds. Their seeds dislodge and parachute to far-flung corners of this world. A graphically inept world. I'm a clunky representation of myself with single polygon sunburnt hands and feet; involuntarily making jerky movements in a flat landscape and drab habitat.

Colors have no depth here and are limited to silver, red, green, yellow, blue, black and white. The silver of dandelions. The red of my skin. The green of the land. The yellow of dinner plate sized coins, stamped with crooked faces, afloat in a monotone blue sky. And the black and white of magpies, raucously cawing after popping their heads out from the earth. A common behavior of moles, most peculiar of magpies. Their raspy chatter is oddly pleasing. Beautifully unabating like a newborn's cries to a mother straight from the womb.

I'm making tracks on a downward sloping conveyor belt. All the while, witnessing the evolution of video games. From pixelated graphics with zero texture to choppy animation and a limited color palette, to the manipulation of 2D objects impressing upon me 3D visuals, to a senior realm of significantly finer graphics, to the scale of a whole-hog Hollywood production.

Ruby dandelion seeds, carried through the wind by their platinum umbrella-like extensions, explode with the heft of a diamondiferous supernova. The ruby seeds fly past me like sparks from a bonfire. The simulation of ghostly white smoke dances and curls on their tails. Flaming cumbersome gold coins execute a figure skater's scratch spin from above, reflecting and blurring flashes of an ultramarine sky and a fluorescent green, sedgy earth.

Velvety black and white magpies with photorealistic red jasper eyes shoot out of the earth like rockets aiming for the cosmic distance record. Wisps of feathery silver residue are left abaft in their atmospheric escape. Eye candy so chiseled, so intense, so unbelievably squeaky clean that I'm sweating. Ultimately, it all ends at the doorstep of reality.

It'd be rude not to knock before it lets me back in. I've no patience for waiting. "Let me in!" I shout in a thunderous voice.

My reality welcomes me with open arms, and I remember everything.

I'm in Neptune and I'm in danger.

Turning back now is perilous. The prospect of evasion's unlikely. At the foot of the stairs, I find myself stranded.

Moss has grown amidst grooves in these great slate gray cobblestone walls. I find myself in a space with cathedral high ceilings—superficially ancient—and three-inch hexagon lilac gray mosaic tile floors that extend into nothing. Yet I continue to sprint full-blast toward what I hope whole-heartedly is an unassailable end. Half this exhaustive space is remarkably gone. A wide opening ahead with a beachy sky as turquoise as the Caribbean Sea lets in aureate light. I hanker for the golden shore.

An earthy fragrance only familiar to me after ample spring showers rings me in. A thunderstorm's ghost loiters in the face of spring. A large chunk of the ceiling crashes down behind me with a resounding boom, nearly pulping me into fresh blood and bone marrow juice. Beyond peradventure, this architecture's been lost to time.

I've put an equitable distance between myself and that abstruse show's clash of instruments. It's appropriate 'memory' be the marker on its tombstone. If I elect to ignore my advancing footsteps, having barged in on this nearly quiet place, the solitary sounds are the melodious repercussions of chirruping birds.

Abandonment has left but ruin in its wake for another species to occupy, from wherever these birds may be squatting. Stealthy as they are, fallen emerald statuettes counter their furtiveness, lying shadowed by black dust on the ground. Even so, they glint. Small patches of withered grass rise through cracks in the tumbledown floor. Some mats of grass, in shaded regions, do discreetly hide the precious gemstone figurines.

I've reached a dead end so early in my run. A few steps forward, below the turquoise blue sky, billowing clouds drift in a cold light. The turquoise around them—blanched, rendering the distinction of their boundaries elusive. Should I choose to jump into this morbid blue, how long would I fall? Above me is a side of this castle. From where I stand, my eyes falsify its walls going on for miles, not nearing an end.

I look behind me at the black alien anatomy bathing me in flashes of psychedelic light. I swiftly look down, flinging my left forearm over my eyes as a barrier between its light and me. My chest's rising and falling rapidly. I raise my arm, only slightly, to watch for its next move.

Its form thins. I glance up for a second to see it remains three times my height. Veins spring from it like a healthy tree root system, each root a springboard for droves more. The root caps become as slim as pine needles. A loud rattling disturbs the birds' song. The light wanes at my feet and I restrictedly lower my arm. Inches from my eyes, its septenary roots ice over.

From behind the skeletal being steps out a stubby man, much older than Baba, in an airy calico print mustard yellow kimono layered over a magenta berry tee, tucked into olive green carpenter pants, and ending at tobacco brown leather boots. He has a low hairline, chimped out ears, and arms shorter than a stack of pancakes in a short-stack competition. He's furiously shaking two fuzzy brown coconuts, struggling to keep them high above his bushy white helmet hair.

His rounded belly's an act. By lowering his right hand, whilst maintaining a firm grip on both coconuts and continually juddering them, he's able to whip up his shirt. A third coconut falls straight onto the bridge of his right foot deflating his faux stomach. He kicks it forward in an arch so that it's caught by my alert ready hands.

"Shake coco," the man says shortly.

I complaisantly begin wobbling the coconut in great circles, trying to spread the rattling sound all around. I can feel oodles of pebbles bashing against the inner walls of the coconut acting for the steady thrum of rain on windows. It's at this moment I know I've been here before. In this situation, as it'd happened once before, the entity gets liquidized. Gravity abandons it, changing its mind partway. The being rises, then becomes static, a pinch too close for comfort above our heads. Its melted body bubbles throughout, clamped in an invisible saucepan that evenly distributes heat.

Rapidly, it's vaporized.

"Afuera!" shouts the man in an affronted tone.

"Thank you," I say, my breath constricted. "Have you any idea what that was?"

We simultaneously lower our coconut noisemakers.

"Bad juju. All here in Church Apple bad. Baba said protect and I try. I live just round corner in vestry where organ kept. Plenty I improvise with," he says in broken English, pointing a coconut toward a hall to my right between two stone pillars.

Atop each pillar are the effigies of two shirtless, stupidly muscular men ferociously grinning at one another like aggravated lions. One's grasping a spiked club with a rounded knob in one hand and the other's wielding a double headed battle axe. Both weapons are cartoonish in size and from their strategic positioning—are in for the kill.

"I take you back now. Where, Baba?" the man asks with his eyelids clamped shut, absorbed in his own thoughts.

We walk the sweeping grounds of Church Apple back toward the unremitting red cobblestone stairway. I look back at the gaping hole in this church and laud at heart the ethereal gold light from the sun. I've solace in my ability to eschew evil. I look to the elderly man beside me, a head shorter than I, dull and worn out. I wonder how long he's had to put up with this hooey. He was so primed to jump into my disquieting situation. I can't be the only one he's saved.

"I Felix Valor," he says benignly. "Hold breath." He raises a coconut to my lips and subsequently lowers it. "Know you from stories jaguars be spreading."

A fraught silence proceeds.

"I'm completely lost. I feel like I'm in a nightmare though I know it's not so. I've seen things yesterday and today miles past the fringe of dark fantasy," I spoke with a brooding expression hoping to one day make sense of it all.

"We become overwhelmed when we see what is unknown. We must realize the scope of existence beyond our own is vastly greater than we'll ever know. You can choose to be absolutely terrified by this prospect or do as I and accept we are not alone," Felix says with a pitiless gleam in his honey brown eyes. His voice had become erudite and low pitched as might be had a college professor spoken through him.

He could care less what I don't understand. That's my prerogative and from his callous expression, I be damned if I drag anyone else into it. I pocket this quick-change personality of Felix into a memory log. Could past trauma be the cause for his fragmented identity? If it is fragmented, into how many pieces? Two or more distinct personalities are vexing. I'm afraid I'll cause him distress should I say something out of line, so I won't ask.

Chapter 24

Mountaineer, Tusked Keeper and Scrappy Scuttler

Koata and Felix hike up the stairway and pass from sight. They've been out of sight now for some time. A hand in a pineapple yellow and tan goat leather glove grips onto the edge of Church Apple. Their body's obscured by the veiling of clouds. They haul themselves up over the golden shore and roll clumsily onto the three-inch hexagon tiles. The mysterious individual's in a carrot orange nylon high-altitude climbing suit. The mini lilac tiles around the stranger appear etiolated in comparison to their arresting orange figure.

Clipped to a carob brown eleven pocket tool belt is an acid yellow gas mask with two cobalt blue Xs distinguished at the cheeks. One of its clear dual eye inserts is cracked in three. The single filter gas mask elongates the face of the wearer as though they've an aardvark's snout.

Its late wearer's head remains stuck inside. One of his brown eyes is eerily frozen in shock past the three-way broken frame whilst the other's half seen. Its droopy eyelid's pinned in a mid-wink. Blood gushes out in ropy doses from the underside of the gas mask, leaving a mounting crimson puddle to form aside the stranger's waist on the ground.

The carrot orange individual unclips the stainless-steel carabiner from the gas mask as they stand up, letting it drop and roll three paces to the right. From a hall to the stranger's far right, between two stone pillars decorated with two armed musclemen statues, comes a bipedal six-foot-tall dark pewter gray warthog. Its extensive tawny tattered cloak flows gracefully, covering its hands and feet as it ambles. The warthog creeps in on the stranger never letting its guard down.

"Is it you?" the warthog asks blithely in a girlish voice.

The orange-suited individual chokes on a deep breath. Their stomach gives a jolt before turning. The creature continues to daintily approach them as they analyze the creature looking fixedly at them. The stranger determines this warthog's no stranger. They dramatically stomp their foot in its red neo rubber bandages like an insolent child.

"My god, I could've killed you!" a gent's voice shouts maddeningly from within his orange suit's inflated hood, passably low so that it occludes his gaze.

He tucks a throwing knife back into a pocket from his carob brown tool belt. He'd been so quick to snatch it, the warthog missed its glister as a majestic ray of light bounced from the silver bluffly making it gold.

"You're uglier than I remember Hajibala," the man says bluntly, spitting into the clouds out the chasmal outlet from which he rose.

"As are you, I'm sure," the warthog responds crossly, sliding a tactfully placed katana back into the depth of its lengthy sleeve. "Where have you been?"

"I'm back from Paris. Hair's a bit longer. I'm a little more rested," he says breezily, raising an arm up to shoulder height and crossing it in against his chest. "If I'm honest, I've never been so eager to get back to work after a vacation," he confesses. With his left arm, he pulls his right arm close to his chest and solidly holds it there, letting out a grumble expressing somewhat of an intense sentiment amid tension and allayment.

"Because of Koata I presume," Hajibala says in a bored voice, at arm's length to the man.

"That goes without saying. Where have you been? You look like you just burst through a pound of cocaine," the man asks casually, fixing his eyes on Hajibala's only screened body part.

Dark pewter gray bristles with a bad case of dandruff carpet her plump, screwy face. All the man visualizes the longer he stares is an oversized, abhorrently grimy toothbrush having just rammed through a salt mine. Her long and sparse rhino gray eyelashes have the same visual effect of chalky corn husks at the end of a broomstick, hedging her wideset black eyes. Dark brown, mighty moist nostrils flare between two large and curved off-white tusks, extending like midway cut curly fries; powdered enough to sate someone's appetite for beignets. At the end of her elongated snout, inferior to her two larger tusks, two acute smaller tusks match the shape and luster of ice cream cones dipped in a cinnamon bun's vanilla glaze.

"I was snacking on a cookie cake pie when I heard you blundering about the floor. I wiped my snout on my sleeve before coming out, but I expect some frosting's still on my second pair of tusks since you won't stop looking at them," she says piqued, uncloaking a rosy pink and transparent human hand, the feigned consistency of strawberry mousse gelatin, from her sleeve. She grips onto the base of one horn and slides her hand out toward the edge, heaping up all the white frosting from it. "I've been hiding out in the white dunes with Luly," she says, using the same frosted, pink glassy hand to swipe clean her other horn. She wipes the smooth sugary remnants on an already visibly whitened sleeve.

"You crazy bitch. Since when is Luly a domesticated house cat?" the man asks, astounded by what he's cocksure is a pure lack of judgement. The man proceeds to do a shoulder stretch on his left side, balancing out the stretches.

"I've been observing and learning her behavior. Should I perpetuate this positive trend of her acclimating to my presence, I can be her keeper. She's yet to attack me because she's content. The jaguars have been maintaining Luly by feeding her their own. Particularly plebs. One every three months," Hajibala conveys in a scandalous, almost childlike voice.

The man becomes chafe at her way of relaying this info as if it were a juicy primary school rumor. He sifts through all possible reactions he may employ and curbs his feelings deciding it best to press on. "The plebs? Has anyone caught on to this?" the man asks dumbfounded.

"No. These jaguars are as blind as bats. They still think the raffle is fair. Every jaguar's name is put in a white top hat and, without notice, someone's taken to Luly the last day of every third month. These past nine months it's been a pleb each time."

"So, three plebs. That ain't too bad," the man says fairly, tugging on his hood a bit lower so that his snub nose vanishes behind it. The swollen orange veil induces Hajibala's speculation about a potential new scar the man may be masking.

"The last time anyone from another class was chosen was twelve months ago. From the Governor class and that's because that member refused to convict Koata for a crime he didn't commit."

"Reckless driving?" the man asks assumingly.

"No. Collusion with Tommy to overthrow Baba Azul," Hajibala states in a waspish tone.

"How long's it been since Koata found Neptune?" the man asks curiously.

"One year...I've been waiting for you since last Halloween," Hajibala unfolds anxiously.

"Shit. An underestimation of time on my part. I never thought I'd be so long. Any progress on round one?" the man asks, frazzled by how long his journey had taken.

"The boy's yet to start. He's spent the year in prison," Hajibala notifies, glancing past the man and over her shoulder thinking she'd heard a noise. Her spade-shaped ears rotate from their sides back to their forward facing, slightly slanted angle.

"First of all, he's a man. Let's get that straightened out." The man draws a breath of exhaustion. "Guessing he was convicted for the crime after all."

"I never discovered why he was locked up and he's only seventeen. Is not seventeen still a teen?" Hajibala asks, becoming unglued, thinking she'd heard a sound again, flinching and hopping forward. "Sorry, thought I heard something. It's been a long day."

"We don't determine men by age but by responsibility."

"And by *we*, do you mean the wiped-out branch of your fellowship?" Hajibala asks, getting snarky.

Ignoring this, the man strolls away from the edge of Church Apple toward the armed musclemen pillars. "And his herald?" he questions, attempting to hide a patent snoopiness in his tone.

"A ginger named David Collins. He lives in Baba Azul's pocket," Hajibala says, haltingly turning towards the man behind her.

"That reminds me. I have something in my pocket," the man says from under the spiked club and axe of the musclemen statues.

He withdraws a stainless-steel travel mug from his left most tool belt pocket. He snaps open the mug top and jiggles it upside down above his palm. A mahogany red Madagascan hissing cockroach plops right side up on his palm. It's frozen till he brings forth a clear, cone-shaped vial of purple liquid from another tool belt pocket. He delicately tilts the vial to sprinkle the insect with a few drops of the substance. Its three sets of legs bustle about the man's palm, tickling him and evoking a snicker from him. The cockroach begins break dancing upon his palm, rolling over and spinning clockwise on its back. Its back's as smooth as polished wood. "Soak it up Gideo," the man says placidly.

"What's in Paris?" Hajibala splutters from behind.

"My grandfather," the man responds gently, watching the cockroach's convulsions intensely.

"Laslonto's alive?!" Hajibala dashes to the man's side, kicking the gas mask on the floor forward. The clatter of the gas mask rolling briefly steals the man's attention. In the process of its movement, Hajibala notices the lone head inside it for the first time.

"Of course. He's only thirty-three," the man says shrewdly, bearing down upon the cockroach once more from inside his goodly hood.

"I wasn't aware the elixir had worked," Hajibala says robustly. "Was murder really necessary?" she asks in an undertone.

"Now you notice. Did you think all that blood where I lay was cranberry juice?" the man asks sardonically.

"Why though?!" Hajibala restates boldly.

"I did no such thing!" the man counters offensively.

"You expect me to believe you found a Prefect's head lying around in the jaguars' backyard?" Hajibala lowers her tone, grappling with anger.

"Could be an Aedile's for all I know. And yes. It was most likely one of your kind. Savage beings you lot are. I found it at the scene of a far nastier crime than this head bespeaks."

"Very well. I won't push for more," Hajibala abates knowing her kind is capable of such. "What're we to do about the Califf *man?*"

"We'll need a distraction to bail him out. Any bright ideas?"

"I've been steadily releasing warthogs and Komodo dragons from the zoo, into the wild. They still think they're being brought here by other means. I could release other species," Hajibala suggests.

ALBERTO BONILLA

"Release them all," the man directs with a glittering smile as Gideo the cockroach's spasms subside on his palm.

Chapter 25

It's November 4, 2013, or if I go with the otherworld's calendar—my world's calendar—then it's May 29, 2013. Not for one day has it escaped me all the loss I've endured in going missing. What Jade must endure however, is far greater for she doesn't know if I'm missing or dead. And that worry doubles for my brother. I hope Kosta makes it back home ok if that isn't already the case. As far as I know, it's both of us out here surviving.

It's peculiar…I'm still sunburnt and I've yet to hunger for food or thirst for whiskey since I last dined with Leonid, David, Zorian, and Baba out on the picnic blanket inside the Dome of the Plebeian. I can't sleep either. My last nap was upon the tree of mint green leaves. The why to these questions are nominal to the questions I pose today. They shift in importance every day.

Today, the main questions I ponder are what attacked me that Felix rescued me from two Octobers ago? How's it possible I died and woke up in the past? How can Tommy fly and if Lucas and Ramze are still alive somewhere?

Then I get to thinking that the inexplicable nature of all these things might simply be answered by the fact that I'm dead. Therefore, this path I'm leading isn't one of the living. It's one of a zombie's futile existence. The only other rational exit I see to understanding is to admit that I've lost my marbles.

I'm not quite ready to accept any of my marbles are missing. Not because I can't face denial. I just know something's amiss and in my acknowledgement of such, I am mentally engaging with my circumstances, working through a problem that can only elicit retrospection from a sound mind. This isn't what's supposed to happen when you die. You either go to heaven or hell. That's what I was taught and what I have faith in is true. I've prayed for answers every day I've lived in this cell. I've yet to receive clarity. Only further questions have arisen. I've used bravery to overcome these questions since enlightenment isn't a possibility in hell.

I came into this cell the same way I'm leaving it, with a will to fight and with white cat ears, jazzed up with slathers of glitter, anchored on my head. They've become a part of me like addictive human enhancement technology. Once you're improved by way of tech, you'll be afraid to let go of that improvement foreboding you'll be less than.

To claw my way out of this ditch, I've been channeling my feline energy and storing it for the day I'll need it. If my jailers thought they'd squeeze the anger out of me by keeping me imprisoned, they're terribly mistaken. It's only percolated into my consciousness. Every fiber of my being yearns for revenge. Make me a ketchup bottle and see how fast I sell.

The devil and angel on my shoulders keep watch over my cat ears round-the-clock. A reminder that I'm an animal and it's only a matter of time before I bite. I've already bitten myself twice today. The red arched marks prominently seen across either side of my left forearm can be traced back to my initial confrontation with a wavering sense of sanity and an escalating desire for tactile sensation.

One of my cat ears is no longer as pointed as its twin. I nearly shed a tear this morning as I felt it grow flimsier than an onion skin, rubbing it in between my thumb and index finger. I sometimes flatten the tired one out so that it's not flopping about like my Johnson.

The pitter-patter it makes while I meander gently through the four corners of this cell can get so irritating, I become lost. Into a harebrained swimming pool, I submerge.

On sunny days, I let the worn cat ear flop, counting how many times its tip taps my head. I'll pace back and forth one hundred times from one end of my cell to the other. The number of taps varies depending on how fast I'm pacing. The record thus far is 951 taps.

Flip, Flop, Thwack!

The sounds repeat in my head like the infinite recycling of energy. Long after I've stopped moving, the sound of the cat ear's tip bouncing on my head still rings with a zeal for healing. A therapeutic song that guzzles me down deeper and deeper into the stomach of the almighty. I've yet to dip into the harebrained pool today. I may find in doing so clarity will come out.

Fli, Flo, Thwa!

The trial was a mockery.

I find you Mr. Pitter-Patter in contempt of court.

Mr. Pitter-Patter tries to be frank with the jury. He has a family but Mr. Pitter-Patter's pleas go unheard. They sink back into a wonted quiet. I follow each vowel into a trap.

It's quicksand!
A third-party's reconnaissance reveals who queues for blame. Not for fame but by guilt. That third party is my mind which I've misplaced time and time again in one of four corners. Mind against body knows just any quicksand won't suffice. Why should all quicksand be blamed for the crimes of one?
Why it's purely Mother Quicksand who's responsible for kidnap.
The prosecutor would like to remind us all this mind I call mine no longer belongs to one.
Order in the courtroom!
As I tranquilly allow myself to sink with them all, vowels a to u begin to float, bidding their farewells like a harmonic chord progression with a descending bassline. The quintet: a, e, i, o, u whisk away higher and higher into the chromatic jazz blues of a beginner's piano lesson.
My mind slowly becomes a naturally composed sensory deprivation tank.
The familiar sound of a pet breaks through the fourth wall by having Mr. Pitter-Patter refer to the script on his own stage show in muddled meows. The audience falls silent.
It's a fiasco!
He's forgotten his lines!
Mr. Pitter-Patter, you're a cat's soundboard. Now please take the trill away.
I hear Caligula trilling without so much as an ounce of reason. For expecting Kosta's cat to show up and purr in this cell is as desperate as waiting for life's punchline to drop.

The last comic on earth should be here soon. I need to know this prison game's a project in reflections of the ego gone south. I rove ceaselessly in my cell waiting for someone to come and save me. Save me from my incessant laughter in which I find myself every now and then maniacally spouting into the void. There goes another laugh I could've shared with someone; gone until it hits the wall, boomerangs back into my voice box, and disgorges every few hours.

I've become the last comic on earth.

I exit the harebrained swimming pool, drying myself under the ventilator of reason and flicking off the last few drops of lunacy from my fingertips. Too many gibberish fish have taken occupancy in the pool for it to still be metaphorical.

David told me when I first met him that he'd a message for me and that it wouldn't come easy. I assumed later that day it'd be an offer to join the Immortal Jaguars. I was mistaken. My enrollment into this fraternity was a given.

In accepting the pickle green leaf Baba had given me out in the Dome of the Plebeian, I purportedly accepted their bid. This I realized after recounting my meeting with the platinum blond blessed with minty fresh breath in the Lemon Room showers. He'd looked me in the eyes and what he labeled the 'mochi leaf' I was holding, stating, 'I see you've accepted the bid,' in his own funny way of talking.

The news David was to tell me was spilled by Zorian. Predictably so. It doesn't take a detective to work out he's a trumpeter. He'd acquainted his brothers with the truck episode and I starring as lead. I'm disconcert with my performance. An episode that will inevitably flop should it premiere like my left cat ear or that infamous pancake that landed right on Kapish's face the day I unguardedly entered this cell.

I strongly believe he was on the verge of telling me why the grass out in the Dome of the Plebeian is blue. Not a particularly pressing concern of mine but nonetheless it's odd. He got scolded by David through a single glance as soon as he voiced, 'That's no paint,' in reference to the blue grass. The words seemed to die in his throat after David's nonverbal cue. Though I'd be wrong not to think they're still clutching onto his trachea.

He'd also mentioned his father's inability to fight off adverse effects in his day-to-day functions. High exposure to inorganic mercury working in a factory below has left his father's brain bedridden, leaving the door open for another malfunctioning brain to move in in its place rent free.

Unable to ask Zorian why the chemical mercury is present in the underground factory, I've sprung up my own theory. I believe that the peaches and cream reputation Baba's trying to uphold is but a lie (as if his paranoia's not the sole reason I'm here) but I also believe that the jaguars are using mercury as a catalyst poison.

Chemists use catalyst poisons to reduce the potency of chemical reactions. If so, their science is of goodwill. I've trouble leveling sound intentions with the need for secrecy. It's confidential why mercury is being used by the jaguars. Otherwise, Leonid wouldn't have been so quick to cut off Zorian unloading his worries about his dad with a remissive nugatory tale about hunting.

I was meant to earn David's news in completing the first of four rounds the jaguars put their newcomers through before admitting them into one of their fourteen classes. All the same, Zorian couldn't hold his tongue. The string of events that ensued after Zorian relayed David's message to me are an explanation for...

Well, for starters this prison isn't your run-of-the-mill prison. The Prefects who oversee every aspect of the prison system, from management to design, have a dark sense of humor. My cell is located in cellblock 13. Otherwise known as 'The Housewife's Corner.'

Each cell at cellblock 13 is modeled after a room from an old hat home décor magazine marketed at the quintessential 1950's housewife. Cellblock 13 is either a picturesque flashback, a nightmare found at the base of an Irish whiskey bottle, sights reminiscent of a foregone childhood, or an unfrequented atomic test site never made use of.

My individual cell is 'The Center of Your Life Kitchen.' A replica of a kitchen with the reputation of the kitchen par excellence for the perfect fifties' housewife. A highly subjective claim. I believe it to be an imperfect nook in the deepest of holes harboring fruitless creativity. Perfect only to the interior designer if the interior designer in question is downright colorblind.

It comes with a salmon pink vintage dishwasher, an aqua green state of the art stove and oven, a banana yellow retro fridge, goldenrod cabinets, periwinkle walls, red and white checkerboard vinyl flooring, orange-red curtains over a sky blue kitchen sink, and a pink frilly apron with white polka dots hung over a silver hook in the wall.

Next to the apron, a red chrome high pub table with two red chrome high-top chairs is set with polyurethane foam dinner chow. A rotisserie cooked ham, mashed potatoes, chicken and mushroom casserole, garlic parmesan roasted asparagus, fruit salad, and an angel food cake. All elegantly displayed on six pink and blue China plates.

Colorful peonies and butterflies dance around the plate rims making me seethe. Perhaps because I'm the jealous type. Fun in art is real to me. The joyful plates so fiercely contradict my emotions that I can feel them stomping out my last hopes for freedom with football cleats, gleefully relishing in something I'll never have.

I don't know why I haven't smashed any of them yet. Maybe that's how I'll kill some time today. I make a one-eighty pivot from a corner of my cell, ceasing poking the synthetic squishy ham, to the body of a woman lying dead on the floor.

...the dead body of the woman I've been coexisting with for one year and almost four days now. A body with a mutilated face, lying partway on its side with one hand laid flat over a blade and the other outstretched toward me on the cold checkered floor. Her legs, bent in a downward bending frog pose, are as wry as her neck—bowed unduly over her right shoulder. So bloodied, even to this day, that I've become immune to the presence of blood.

Her body's as fresh as the day she died. A deep brunette with wisps of auburn hair stuck to her bloody neck. Her gray long-sleeved shirt dress, black footless tights, and green single strap thong sandals might as well be fitted on a mannequin. Although two months into my imprisonment I could've sworn I saw a toe wiggle. Excessive staring born of boredom will make you see movement where there never was.

One year ago, Felix led me from Church Apple, past the crown room, through the gray halls, and back into the theater. The show was in intermission when we arrived. Burgundy stage curtains concealed the ending scene of Act One. The music playing had an austere art rock sound from the 80s. All jaguars were back to standing now, mingling cheerily amongst one another. This time around, the theater was lit by soft white ambient lighting so that not one jaguar was stowed away in a dark toy box.

My eyes immediately fell upon the large yellow block head in the center of the room. His mask was the largest of them all, floating plainly across the theater. He wasn't the tallest jaguar but his consistent bobbing to the beat of bells and whistles, mastered within the 80s drum sounds, allowed for enough breaks in the crowd to target him. I felt I should introduce him to the thick coconut in my hand. A slick whack across his yellow block head should teach him a lesson or two.

Somehow, Felix sensed my rage and held my arm back. He snatched the coconut from me after stuffing one of two he already had into his shirt. He pulled his magenta berry tee over it and tucked the shirt tail deep into his green carpenter pants so that the coconut lay snug against his belly. After a minute of searching, he located David and passed me on to his watch, winding down and offering a huge exhalation of pent-up breath as if he'd rid himself of a thorn on his side.

David was still chewing Swamidoss' ear off but excused himself to attend to me. Before the question escaped me, I asked Swamidoss, beginning to stammer, "B-by chance, have y-you ever created a warthog costume or something resembling the likes of for one of the brothers?"

Swamidoss looked disinterested in my eagerness to know. "Why no, I don't believe I have." He crinkled his eyes as if conceding to himself I was up to something.

Felix and David grabbed a hand each. I was led away from Swamidoss into a quieter section of the theater. We happened upon a black baby grand piano occupied by a werewolf, a ninja, and a zombified gingerbread man at the keys. We lingered across the keys, adjacent to the propped open lid. Felix gave David a quick run through of what'd occurred in hushed tones. I leaned in, resting an elbow upon the piano's widest curve. I doze off, harking back on the warthog I'd seen. It just vanished.

How did it just vanish?

David seemed just as confused as I once Felix concluded his version of the tale, having described the shadow creature that attacked me as a herd of sea urchins. David gave me an unnerved look and decided we needed more privacy. He grabbed my wrist with a rocklike grip and led me out of the theater, into the gray hall. Felix trotted along behind us. I got in a question before I was briefly reprimanded by David for leaving the theater.

"Do you know if the missing head above the window in the Wolf's Den belongs to the body of a warthog?"

"A warthog? It belonged to a black bear," he answered irate, thrown off by my sudden interest in warthogs. A topic he'd thought ended with Swamidoss. "Now you listen to me Kamikaze, I may not be able to exercise punishments, but others will..." I began getting forewarned of nameless punishments should I choose not to listen to him again, which I was fortuitously doing again.

Who was under that warthog mask?

"Oh, I listened. I just didn't obey," I admitted snippily as I noticed David pause, staring at me beady-eyed, awaiting from me an admission of guilt.

David crossed his arms. His nostrils flared like he'd wanted to sock me right then and there. His better self persevered. He drifted back into the theater to finish off his conversation with Swamidoss, mentioning to Felix whilst acting immaturely derisive towards me, turning his back on me, "There're whispers for what round one might entail. I must find out what I can if I've any hope of helping this rebel here." He turned his head over his shoulder and shot me a vilifying look, making no mystery of who he tagged rebel.

His scorn didn't sting in the slightest.

Who is he for me to care? My herald. Big whoop.

"That Minwoo something huh?" Felix said beaming toothily at the sea of costumed jaguars inside. "Minwoo Swamidoss. Prosthetic Makeup Technician. My old age makeup thanks to him."

"What do you mean?" I asked as I recalled countless behind-the-scenes featurettes of actors getting made up to look older for movie roles and comprehension set in on me. "You're not really young, are you?!"

"I kid, I kid," Felix said with a tinkling laugh. "Talent, talent though. He need use that skill on me. Make Felix young and pretty again."

"Felix, what's up with you and coconuts?" I asked kindly, trying to make conversation.

He held up the two coconuts on either side of his head and whispered ominously, "They live in the coconuts."

From behind Felix, Zorian strode over to us in his white wrestling singlet with great urgency in his pep. At the same time, a voice shouted from inside the theater with clear-cut aggression, "Hey kitty, you have a problem with us?!"

I turned to face a mime. The mime that'd been seated on the right-hand side of the caveman, two seats to the right of the seaman—the only one I intended to wet. I could see the redness swelling behind his white base makeup with a painted black teardrop under each of his eyes. He had a red paisley bandana tied around his neck, a black and white horizontal striped shirt, red elastic suspenders, black poplin pants, and a skewed black wool beret.

He pulled forth his suspenders and let them snap back onto his chest. "What's all the hubbub with ghost?" Felix asked, surveying the mime's livid body language: chin forward, lips compressed, and fists on his hips.

"That's a mime," I enlightened Felix as Zorian and the mime coincidentally reached us at the same time.

Zorian tugged on a side of my moist red tank top. His mannerisms alerted me he'd a scoop of garden-fresh news. He was tugging on his bottom lip and his eyes were twitching from side to side. Any attention I had was hereupon drained from the mime and sprinkled over Zorian. Scanning the scene, he drew his lips inward and out he blurted, "Ramze's alive!"

I barely had time to register the news when a white gloved fist came flying at me. A rigid forearm with a coconut at its end materialized in front of my nose. It halted the blow and the mime braced himself for impact. Another hand with a coconut swooped into him from the right, bashing his ribs. I heard a crack and the loud moans of pain that sparked from the mime told me Felix had shattered his ribs.

The animated boom explosion on Zorian's wrestling singlet might as well have been auditory because Felix's jab made full use of the word 'POW!' He deserved a follow-up background chime roaring 'K.O.!' The mime fell to the ground, onto his side, trying to save face by pulling his black wool beret over his eyes. Surely his black tears had become genuine under the beret. He clutched at the shirt over his ribs, not needing one to escape and be made into a woman.

"Fuck, Felix! I'm going to have to punish you now," Zorian said looking crestfallen.

"And?" Felix breathed nonchalantly.

"We'll discuss your punishment later. I may be as humorous as my coequals tend to get called out for when handing out punishments but trust, I'm not as tough on those who use their strengths to defend others." Zorian dabbed Felix's nose and rumpled his face, smiling coquettishly.

Felix turned sour.

"I must borrow Koa for a bit. Tell his herald we're with the Celers on Baba's orders," Zorian said, shunting me forward away from them. "And do me a favor will you? Take the pleb down to the Elysian Springs. He can recover there in peace."

Zorian and I walked side by side down the gray hall. Felix raised the mime behind us, over his shoulders like a log that wept increasing louder as we advanced from the scene.

"Zorian, before we get into what you just told me about Ramze, assuming you're not an evil twat who raptures in grim humor, what's a pleb?"

"You needn't worry about them but since you're asking, a pleb or Plebeian is the second to worst class in the hierarchy of classes here. Just a notch above Servus in importance. They get dealt the worst hand of bullying. Plebs have the stigma of laziness unfairly thrust upon them and no one likes a bum," Zorian said dogmatically. "That mime should be used to it by now. It's common, picking on the slothful, but that doesn't mean they don't fight back sometimes."

"You recognize him, even behind all that makeup?" I asked disbelievingly.

"He's a mime every year. The only one I might add. Poor kid. I've seen him around, working hard down in the factory when it's my turn to patrol that sector. Never getting the recognition for a job well done because of his class." Zorian sympathy was transitory, to the point that it came off as phony.

"Now back to business. David was the one who was supposed to tell you about Ramze. We've known of his whereabouts since before you arrived here but, keeping up with his duties as herald, any news of the otherworld he gives you need be wheedled out of him in proving yourself. I expect he wants you to pass round one—the greatest sign you're equipped with what it takes to be a jaguar—before he tells you what I've just told you."

"You're a kid just like that mime and why're you telling me this?" I chided him.

"I may be on the outside, but my mind is by far older than the mime's. And I'm telling you this because I've compassion...aaand because I need intel. We stopped near a mischievous-looking grinning gargoyle protruding from the gray wall. He turned to face me, grasping the sides of my arms, and manhandling me, making me trip back a step against one of the gargoyle's jutting bat wings. "Tell me how you know Tommy. You don't have to tell me where he's hiding. I just need to know the link between you two."

"Ay, lay off!" I pushed Zorian off me. "There is no link! He flew when I first saw him, I panicked, and ran the truck off a cliff. I saw him again briefly in the cloud forest, but he ran when I chased him." In that very moment, I regretted the words that'd tumbled out of my mouth.

"He flew?!" Zorian boomed genially. "Do tell!"

I felt I'd just made a grave mistake in telling him that I saw Tommy fly. Of all the people to confide in, I'd let myself slip, not to a priest but to a bigmouth. Baba would know I'd defied him in no time. The news would arrive to him with expedited shipping, either from Zorian himself or myself the next time he picks my brain. Considering I can't reverse time, I might as well use what I know, or don't know, to my advantage. Zorian won't know if I lie to him about Tommy. This may be my only bargaining chip to extract information from him.

Zorian noticed my hesitancy to speak, whether for the sake of protecting my image in the eyes of inculpability or to hide something far more sinister—my connection with Tommy of which there's none.

"You know, I overheard Polka talking to some of his fellow brothers about you. I knew the minute I saw you you'd be interested in Celeres. So, I've set something up on my own time. No need to thank me now. Perhaps after meeting with them you'll be more inclined to speak," Zorian said elated.

"Perhaps not," I countered in a gruff whisper.

"The Calling isn't until round three, but I've rounded up some of the best Celers there are to give you an overview of the job description. You'll have a head start on the other Nihils if you decide Celeres is where you belong. You'll be getting a one on one—correction—" he cackled. "A one on twelve introduction to what Celeres is all about," Zorian said jubilantly, separating his hands in the arch of a rainbow to emphasize the grandeur of the opportunity he was presenting me with. "Your intro to the other thirteen classes will have to wait until round three of the Gauntlet like the rest of the newcomers who'll join in on the fun but no matter, no matter. Celeres is right up your ally and, worst comes to worst and the two of you aren't a match, at least you'll be able to cross out this class from the list of those you wish to fight for a position in. Come now."

Before long, we were no longer in the gray halls of Neptune. Zorian had led the way through the autumn blended cobblestones, past a tortilla beige panel door, into a room much like a classroom setting. Soothing dark gray-blue walls had several long-running, blackened steel wall-mounted cabinets. The largest space in the room was devoted to cranberry desks lined in neat rows. There were both well-lit and dimly-lit areas due to a non-uniform, multidirectional bronze ceiling track light. Some spaces optimized shadows whereas others fell directly in the target range of the track's white socket bulbs—blanketed in open amber glass shells. Posters were few and far between. But all had the harmony of being black with white hand-drawn rabbits in suits.

Twelve men sat atop some of the countertops of the cranberry, laminated L-shaped desks with tubular steel frames and grayish tan chairs welded to the backs of the desks. All but one man bore the shiny metal bands I'd seen before on the men in the diamond-shaped pool and in the Lemon Room showers but none were costumed. Instead, they're unified in their casual wear. They reacted instantly to Zorian's call for them to line up in alphabetical order at the head of the room.

I followed Zorian's lead as all men rushed past us to line up. It was now Zorian and I who sat side by side atop two cranberry desks; waiting while the twelve men gathered to face the back of the room. Looking over us, they stood rigid, awaiting their next command with their chins held high, arms crossed behind their backs, and their feet pointed forward, shoulder width apart.

One by one they took a step forward, crossing their wrists over their chests with clenched fists as Zorian called out their names authoritatively. Barring one, their bands whistled through the air before breaking impact upon one another, precipitating a reverberant 'shiiing' like the clash of swords.

"Absumo!"

"Arturo!"

"Lugulo!"

"Leto!"

"Macto!"

"Conficio!"

"Caedo!"

"Effligo!"

"Ferio!"

"Neco!"

"Percutio!"

"Sopio!"

The last name came with the return of the men's original stance—arms crossed against their backs.

"As you're all aware I've summoned you here today to introduce to you...a special guest. Koa is our most recent arrival here at Neptune and a little birdy told, not me but someone else I lent an ear on, that he wants to be a Celer. Brother Leto, would you be so kind as to show Koa what the Immortal Jaguars require of a Celer?"

All men but the one without metal bands stepped back a pace, leaving him to stand alone. A lean and mean man in a green alpaca printed polo, navy blue chino shorts, and white sneakers. Starry-eyed, he swept a hand over his short, tailored golden brown hair. He'd faint whiskey brows over a prominent brow ridge, rather cunning green eyes, a bulbous nose, thin lips with a black tinge, and a square jawline.

"If I may say so myself, a Celer is the best a man can hope to be in this fraternity. That's not to say it's by any means easy. You must perform well above the standard in the Gauntlet to be qualified for this role. After which, it's only the beginning of your assessment. Once in Celeres we require of you three things: ethics, grit, and gravitas." Unlooked-for, from the other hand he'd drawn forth from around his back was an ivory egg. He cracked it open over his head letting the fall-yellow egg yolk streamline down his head from all angles, down his neck, and into the collar of his polo.

"Why is it no matter where I go things get more gaga?" I piped up.

Zorian nudged me with his left elbow and keenly whispered, "Watch."

Unbelievably, the egg yolk was surging back into the egg on Leto's head, flowing over his face. The egg repaired itself once all its insides were home but the cracks from its split remained an imprint on the shell. Evidence it'd been broken. It rolled off his head and landed nimbly on his left palm.

"I can't do that nor does my name end with an O," I said flatly. "Celeres and I must not be a match."

"Don't be absurd. Of course you can't. Only Leto can. He and Baba...*and Tommy*" he mumbled from the corner of his mouth so that only I could hear his mention of Tommy. "Are our desert spoons."

"As you've just witnessed, you can attest to I being gifted. Baba and I are alike. We are who we are—desert spoons—because our gifts radiate from our core like the leaves from a descrt spoon's apex, in all directions," Leto said in a high, clear voice.

"The desert spoon plant grows spherically and so do Baba's and Leto's range. Baba's sphere is larger than Leto's. Leto's sphere can barely reach me," scoffed Zorian. "He can reverse time in split-seconds within a surface area of 78.54 feet squared or 2.5 feet from where he's standing. The volume of which is 65.45 cubic feet."

"That trick is something I like to perform for the Nihils when introducing Celeres. Something silly that wakes them up before taxiing on from the nitty-gritty. And it goes hand in hand, rather poetically, with our motto: ethics, grits, and gravitas. E.G.G.," Leto said pleasantly.

"So, you just carry an egg around all day waiting to do a doltish magic trick? Nitty-gritty?" My voice dropped to a harsher tone. "You haven't even scratched the surface of what Celeres is. All you've said is that it's difficult to join and you must have E.G.G."

"I'm not much of a public speaker. Anyone feel free to butt-in at any point." Leto looked behind himself, almost as if he was about to do a backflip, for any assistance from his fellow brothers. "Let us pretend I can use my gift to forward this moment. I'll save myself the embarrassment, then we'll hit the basics." He cranked a fist forward as if he was a beginner fisherman reeling in an Atlantic Bluefin tuna, blank about causing line twists. "Where were we? Ah the basics." He steadily stopped cranking his fist and looked behind himself again, desperate for a helping hand.

A man with curly brown hair in a gray head sweatband, white shirt with 'HALEGIANUM' written across his chest in navy blue university lettering, black sports shorts, light-blue calf-high socks with a pink glazed donut pattern, and white tennis shoes stepped forth. He was heavy and strong with spirited but soft blue eyes and a guileless smile that spoke, 'The moon is made of cheese because grandpapa said it was.' He dipped his hands into his pockets but quickly retired them against his sides when addressed by Zorian.

"Effligo, what've you to say?" Zorian asked pointedly.

"I merely have the suggestion that we let Koa ask the questions in a freeform setting. He can come up to any one of us in the room as others dip into plans for the coming battle. That way we don't waste precious time on discussing tactics and Koa won't have to listen to things he cares not," Effligo said, all the while talking with his hands.

"That's a fine idea. I'll leave you to it." Zorian assented cheerfully.

Zorian exited the room through the tortilla beige panel door. I quickly followed suit. All men disregarded me the second Zorian hopped off his desk. They began conversing in groups of three as if no one but them existed in the room.

"Zorian, I'm sorry but Polka was talking out of his ass when he said I was interested in Celeres," I revealed as the panel door shut behind us.

"Oh my," Zorian said with a tone of delicacy. "Well, I guess I'll have to find some other way to persuade you to pour me a glass of more info on Tommy. I acted so fast on what Polka had said I never bothered questioning if it was true. Although, you could've intervened at any moment," he said rather cross.

"I wasn't thinking really. Mind was elsewhere," I said honestly.

"Perhaps I can help lead it towards the light. Is there anything you wish to know? I am an open book after all," Zorian said compellingly.

"Not really. There's nothing more I wish to know or want apart from finding my friends. And you've already told me Ramze's alive. I assume you have nothing on Lucas."

"You're correct in assuming I have nothing on your friend Lucas, but don't you have an itch for knowing where Ramze is?" Zorian asked circumspect.

"I do."

"You don't seem too eager to find out," Zorian stated, analyzing my inexpressive demeanor.

"I'm a mess Zorian. As you can imagine, I'm talking to a twelve-year-old who's brighter than I and currently floundering through a world I know little about," I told him, furling my brows.

"Ask away then. You're only impeding learning by not."

"Ok I'll bite." I clenched my teeth and smiled. "Let's start with where Ramze is and how desert spoons have super powers," I said falsely confident, feeling obtuse in my admission such things exist. My smile—a poster child for the know-nothing club of stupid town.

Chapter 26

"That I don't know. I just know he's alive and that desert spoons are gifted," Zorian said defeated.

"So, you can't tell me nothing?" I asked, my deceptive smile fading.

"I can tell you about the inner workings of Baba's mind and how he's connected to us all. If that's something you long to hear," Zorian said, moving sinuously back and forth across the hall.

He shiftily pushed open another tortilla beige panel door a bit further down the hall, adjacent to the room where twelve Celers were plotting an ill-defined battle. I followed him inside a room much like the one we'd just visited. This room, however, was a mirror image of the first and had white hand-drawn Ferris wheels on black posters instead of rabbits in suits.

"Up until you arrived, Baba would've had us believe the incredible gifts he and Leto possess are something innate in an individual since birth. Set free by chance. No explanation on how this profoundly isolated event can occur. Now I'm not so sure Baba's verdict's correct," Zorian said, internally debating whether to have a seat or not atop a cranberry desk as I kept still by the door. "He never mentioned Tommy's a desert spoon. I wonder why he'd withhold such intel from us. Unless Tommy knows something he shouldn't. He's a very curious thinker that boy. It wouldn't surprise me at all if he stumbled upon something Baba was attempting to conceal and if so, he might've not been as keen as Leto to play ball and keep the fable of *innate ability* within the select few desert spoons."

"How many are there?" I inquired.

"Three if Tommy can fly. How sure are you he flew? Did you verify he wasn't lifted by the mechanics of a jetpack or rocket boots? Were you under the effects of padda divinorum when you saw him?" Zorian asked, sticking to standing.

"What's pad of devil-doorknob?"

"*Padda divinorum* is what the locals call 'jaguar's spit' as a way to disparage us. We make it in-house," Zorian said in a levelheaded way that made me feel he was confiding in me. Not because it's a secret the jaguars produce drugs but because the cards upon which Tommy being a desert spoon fall have dire implications.

If Tommy is a desert spoon, it only follows he knows how to become one and if Tommy's anything like Zorian, that imperils us all. Is Baba really wrong for wanting to suppress knowledge, serviceable to the weak but parlous to the horde? For any power as simple as rewinding the bust of an egg could be dangersome in the wrong hands. What if that egg had been a person, most recently dead, 2.5 feet from him? Could he reverse death? Make a zombie?

Could he reverse his death? Be a zombie?

I'm unsure whether Zorian and I are on the same side of this rift keeping Baba and him at odds. He could mistrust Baba for keeping this secret amongst those already exposed to it. But I know gifts, the likes of which people in the otherworld are accustomed to seeing played up in theatrics, will be abused by the routine knavish people who preach virtue through grating megaphones on college campuses. That's why if Baba's purpose in going after Tommy is bringing him in before talking up a storm, I'm aligned with his efforts.

"I saw him fly before I was drugged. This I'm sure of but..." I boldly raised a finger to Zorian, eventually lowering it as he got pestered, twisting his face. "Whether or not Tommy's a desert spoon, I agree with Baba's claim that the gifts are innate. And say they're not, so what? It's best not to know. Where today a gift is rebuilding an egg, ground up from its shattered pieces, tomorrow a gift can mean climate manipulation—the tilt that'll knock the human race off its high horse. I only tell you this, not to put you off with my blunt emotions coming through about people and farcical powers, but because I trust your drones are still helping find Lucas. I see no reason to lie to you about how I feel as long as you're not lying to me about your drones on the hunt. That is how you know Ramze's alive, correct?"

"Yes, but we lost him. A mysterious spear penetrated the drone quadcopter just as we obtained visual. We've a general sense of where he's at but that doesn't mean once we find him, he'll want to come back with us," Zorian said in a clipped voice.

Zorian's opinion struck me as honest. Above all, nothing's impossible. "He may not want to," I agreed. "The Ramze and Lucas your drones are after are not the same friends I flew in with from Florida."

They don't know my brother.

"I'm not your therapist but people do change. Without further ado, allow me to brief you on the complex nature of Baba's telepathy. Please, sit down."

"I'm all ears." I sat down on the tan chair of a cranberry desk, slamming my hands on its surface and producing a quick drumroll, directly in front of where Zorain stood, steps in front of a black glass dry-erase board with an empty aluminum marker tray.

"Baba Azul's mind reading powers are wild. He can translate different languages from his own through emotion. Emotions are all the same across language barriers. So, through sadness, happiness, etcetera, he's able to assign meaning to foreign words. This is a tricky facet of his telepathy I've yet to fully understand but I know it to function because I myself have tested it. My native language is Russian you see." He said something in Russian which flew over my head but after disclosing his native tongue, I startlingly began picking up on the subtle accent. I might've just overlooked it till now because he's a kid and ashamedly, I never really listen to kids as intently as I listen to my peers or elders. This changes his narrative completely.

I giggled under my breath.

How funny would it be if he's a spy? I am frrrom Soviet Rrrusia, I thought in a bold accent with heavy rolling R's. I'm a callow impressionist of a Russian man.

Zorian got in close, his face inches from mine, as I promptly sunk deep into my chair thrown off by his explicit disregard for my personal space.

"He can read your mind, tap into any emotion you have at that point in time, and be able to intercept any other memory of yours in which that emotion was held. The same goes for sensations. Anyone in a memory he's reading is also vulnerable to being read. So, you thought of Luciana after seeing a jaguar dressed as a French maid and he was able to connect to her through you. He found out where she was and brought her here. When you were hungry, he was able to connect to every memory in which you've expressed hunger and from what was brought out to the Dome of the Plebeian, my only guess is my best. Your most recent food craving was chili lemon octopus alongside cucumber salad, was it not?"

"L-Luciana," I said dreamily, my chin tucked into my neck, not having heard a word after 'he brought her here.'

"That's right. The criminal long having evaded arrest for your father's murder is here, right now, in Neptune," Zorian said, backing away slowly.

"Take me to her," I ordered, my fists tightening, chewed-down nails piercing into my palms.

"I will but I wanted to soften the blow before I did," Zorian admitted, carefully treading on treacherous waters.

I felt the superheated steam of a great western locomotive pulsating inside me, ready to rush from my ears for the 400-meter dash. After all this time, she's here. I'll finally have closure. Can I stare directly into the eyes of the woman who murdered my father without strangling her? The woman who cut the most important person in my life out of existence, denying me a father through the whole of my adolescence.

UP STRAWBERRY VINE

I thought I'd forgiven her. That I was at peace. A compulsory invention of a mind driven astray. My foolish sympathy after having been hammered in this idea by my middle school counselor that we're all human and we all make mistakes. I've always known I never truly forgave her. To forgive is the ultimate act of maturity. I'm a cut below mature but more so than she'll ever be. As a human, I embrace my mistakes, not run from them. Had I truly forgiven her, I'd see a beast of betrayal. One who spits on my father's grave every time I look in the mirror.

Pardon me my Lord but today I take from you vengeance.

"Believe me, I'm trying to follow here. Baba managed to locate my father's murderer through me having simply thought of her?" I questioned, my voice cold.

"Thought of a memory with her in it, yes. He infiltrated her mind and found she's been living in Tipitapa, Nicaragua. I've discussed the matter with him. She'd been thinking of visiting Lake Managua as she paid for groceries using the córdoba—Nicaragua's own currency. She'd counted five banknotes of one hundred córdobas each. More than enough to buy a twelve pack of beer which she'd been planning on doing. However, the cashier notified her the beer she was thirsting for—Saarland Frost—is only sold at one convenience store in the entire city—Pulpería Saxony." Zorian retired his hands behind his back and held them there, speaking without blinking.

"Having exited the store, she admired the bright orange-red color of its exterior. By the time she'd made her way through town into Saxony, Baba already had a brother from Mercury waiting for her outside. She was taken in broad daylight. This, he's done for you. He's extending an olive branch after he'd foolhardily brought up her existence in conversation at the Dome of the Plebeian, admitting to me he knew how much this pained you."

"That's nice and all but how? If she was taken today, sometime after we dined in the dome...it all happened so fast. How could a jaguar get to a neighboring country that fast, then return, smuggling in a full-grown adult without being spotted?" I asked confounded.

"Mercury has its ways. They bring us messages from the otherworld, but Baba's found uses for them beyond bearing news," Zorian said, grazing the subject lightly.

"Kidnapping people at warp speed? That doesn't make fucking sense! Nothing here makes fucking sense!" I said, rising in frustration and knocking the desk aside so that it nearly toppled over.

"And yet it's happened," Zorian said, meeting my glaring eyes with mild scrutiny, enough to gainsay my attitude.

"Fine! Then it should be easy to relocate Ramze and find Lucas. I've been thinking of them the entire time I've been here so Baba should have access to their thoughts by now too," I said, moving hesitantly towards the door, donkey kicking the desk back into its column along the way.

"It doesn't always work like that. Firstly, it can't simply be a thought of the person. It must be a memory involving that person in-person. There're people who can bypass Baba's mind reading. For example, say someone has recently inhaled, consumed, or injected themselves with padda divinorum. It'd be hard to read them because what they're seeing and currently thinking is nonsensical. He can't control thoughts and actions, just read minds and communicate telepathically. As of now we know Ramze's alive and have some sense of where he's roaming based on his thoughts about the forest scenery. Lucas on the other hand is unreachable. I think it's because the effects of the drug haven't worn off on him yet," Zorian said, hurtling towards the door. "Where do you think you're going? We're not finished talking!"

"I was the only one injected by the drug," I said dropping my voice and squaring up to Zorian behind me.

"I don't know what to tell you. Maybe Baba has found him, but I promise, he's told me otherwise. Baba may have his reasons for telling me this just as you believe he has his reasons for concealing how to become a desert spoon," Zorian said, averting his eyes.

"You're the one who doubts him, not me. I said if he is concealing that information from people then it must be his sound judgement. You think many of your brothers would be cracking eggs over their heads with the power to playback time like a cassette tape? Shit, if I could do that, I'd have endless redos in life."

Zorian guffawed. "Oh please. Leto can rewind things that happen within his cramped sphere and only seconds after they've happened. He's so limited in his ability that I wouldn't even broach the term power when describing what he can do."

"How big is Baba's sphere?"

"His reach is far. The exact volume of his sphere I'm unsure of but it's enough to reach anyone in this castle. He can't read us when we're outside Neptune's boundaries. He doesn't have permanent access to your thoughts. In fact, he has zero access when you're outside of his sphere, but he does have unlimited access to your thoughts, present and past, and anyone within a memory, when you're in it. Once you're inside his sphere, you're fair game. Leave his sphere and his access into your mind lingers for about a half an hour before it wears off," Zorian said, restraining his irritation, either from my lack of grasping outrageous concepts or for my urge to leave, pressing my shoulder up against the door so that it stayed ajar.

"Luciana. Now," I demanded nastily in a voice I did not recognize.

Zorian nodded, taking in my edginess without reservations, and traipsed past me back towards the hall. To get to the prison, we returned to ground level. From autumn blended cobblestones to smoothed out gray halls and into the Lemon Room. Then back through the black shale and light-blue slate rock configured tunnels, into the health farm teeming with jaguars, and out to the blue springy turfed dome. Past the Wolf's Den, there stood a monumental moving glass door amidst two Olympic white stone columns. Behind them, a quartet of Tudor living rooms.

The glass door separated us physically but not mentally from the Dome of the Plebeian with its large panel of high-performance glass maximizing the views outside. Inside, the space could very well be the layout of a medieval hotel lobby with oily black stone walls and polished black marble floors. The seldom seen guests of several white geese can be found waddling about the glass door waiting to exit or lounging within an indoor waterway under a short bridge at the far end of the space.

Where we were exactly was the living quarters for the last four classes in the jaguar hierarchy—The Honeycomb Lodge. Though I'm sensible the name comes from the building's shape, there's nothing giddy or bright about the lodge such as a honeycomb bespeaks for bees.

The building's a hexagon rising five floors. Each floor's visible from the first. A consecutive black railing on each floor allows views from a stratum of loci and heights. Servus live on the second floor, Plebeians on the third, Tribunes on the fourth, and Vicarius on the fifth.

From the fifth floor, Vicarius have a level view of four large hanging cones, hung from the tip by industrial stainless-steel chains on a fan vaulted ceiling. The translucent cones are half full of purple goop splashing about their insides in hoops like mini typhoons; despite the cones sitting motionless above us.

The cones are similar to the ones Lucas got from Fundy's, with the same substance. Still and all, these cones' glass is less clear, they're enlarged enough to double Zorian's height, and their base is bulbous, a smidge less than a hemisphere. An incomplete hemisphere I'd say is nearly finished loading.

According to Zorian, that purple goop is padda divinorum. Its term of rancor is jaguar's spit—the name I'd been familiarized with first. They hang directly above the four corners of a scopious square oriental rug with an ivory background. An imperial blue, rose, and teal floral design envelops the rug. The single round medallion motif at its center gleams with supreme verve. It has a pearl white top hat as its focal point and silver ferns, superimposed like tentacles around it.

At each side of the rug is one commodious living room set. All together the four sets bond in their similar voices from the past. For them to suggest horror and mystery would be an embellishment but their settings do recall the Middle Ages. Or at least some offshoot of it.

Delicate wood carvings course like wind shaping zebra stripes over sand on the Sedona red bench, four armchairs, and two coffee tables to our left. To our right, there're four cappuccino-colored hardwood boxes with small-scale carvings of pigs playing musical instruments such as harps, fiddles, and drums. Six cherry wood oval cane back chairs, three with arms and three without, are intermixed amongst the whimsical boxes.

The living room set nearest to us is of chocolate brown walnut wood with violet streaks. The four armchairs and couch in this set are upholstered in chintz with gold, burgundy, and navy floral prints. Two armchairs have massive growling lion heads as their arm stumps whereas the two others have open beaked, goggle-eyed owl heads as theirs. Parallel to one another, the two owl heads face the two lion heads. A cleared trapezoid coffee table with claw feet stands between them. The coordinating couch aside them.

Beyond this set, the furniture embodies geometrical foliage carvings on four mahogany round side tables. The crisscrossing crooks and flails and regal falcons carved on two light oak cumbersome couches, and two equally cumbersome armchairs, invoke Horus. Their tan bulging cushions, decorated with ebony and khaki beige snakeskin print, look to be the most invitingly comfortable next to the chocolate brown walnut set.

All sets have been run through a foundry to append aged premium black metal on every side. If their wooden cores were stripped, a black metal framework would abide leaving behind a ghost of the furniture to idle.

The four living room sets are set atop navy Persian style rugs of their own. The rugs' mint-cream complex outlines differ only slightly from one another in their kaleidoscopic patterns. Despite no winter in sight, a warm fire blazes within a rustic desert brown and tan sandstone fireplace. The Dragon's Throat, as they call it, occupies an entire side of the first floor of the hexagon. Two rows of six whitewashed wood rocking chairs are empty, facing the fire.

We took a semi-long route to get here because Zorian fell head over heels with Dilly-Dally. He made a pit stop at the Lemon Room where he retrieved a platinum gas mask. His locker had a heavenly array of suits, muted dress shirts, florid ties, and black and brown leather dress shoes. The interior was composed of oak barrel floors and a fully stocked bark gray corner piece.

The piece offered chests on either side of it with plenty of shelving space throughout. The shelves were glutted neatly with folded dress shirts or lined with classic dress shoes. A built-in silver bar hung Zorian's various suits in the widest and longest space. A square shelf where his gas mask laid rest below them next to more casual wear—a small niche in an overflowing haberdashery.

At the center of the space, adjacent to his closet system, was a revolving tie display, around my height with eight sides, fifteen tiers, and three columns each. Tortoiselike in its speed. Each tie was neatly rolled up in its own cubbyhole, resembling a collection of stacked scrolls dyed in vibrant hues. Every side had its own refuge for a particular color with only similar shades occupying the one. Patterns, however, were a free-for-all, crossing boundaries between colors.

"I didn't take you as one to spruce up so well outside of wrestling." My genial compliment was one he'd shrugged off with humor.

"I was born in a suit."

After the Lemon Room, a second delay was gifted to me from a hell where the sole punishment is waiting. Zorian spontaneously ran into another Prefect at the health farm. A man with icy platinum black hair, cut sharp with a low fade and a long fringe. He'd ironically innocent brown eyes given their conversation. He'd on a mellow yellow hooded long-sleeved t-shirt, distressed white denim shorts, and two-strapped white rubber sandals. An acid yellow gas mask with two cobalt blue Xs at the cheeks hung over his chest on a solid gold Cuban link chain.

He talked to Zorian as though he were just another man in his forties—what I presume was his age bracket. Their adult conversation hinged on the upcoming Gauntlet. A game, I picked up, consists of four rounds that Nihils are to play be-

UP STRAWBERRY VINE

fore becoming an Immortal Jaguar. I interrupted imposingly with the question of what a Nihil was as Polka had first called me so in the Lemon Room showers. I wish I hadn't horned in because after the brightly clad Prefect answered with Nihil literally meaning nothing, Zorian got tetchy. Perhaps he was afraid he'd said too much about the Gauntlet in front of me.

I knew what nihilism meant but somehow, I hadn't put two and two together. Zorian explained that a Nihil here means a male on the path to become an Immortal Jaguar who's given up all worldly possessions and forfeited their right to freedom. Before getting into the specifics of each round, Zorian asked me to wait for him outside in the Dome of the Plebeian. I'd overheard the mention of a feather as I was turned away. Until I'd spoken, they hadn't looked at me once and had I not, I wonder if I would've learned more about the Gauntlet.

A game composed of four rounds with each round's difficulty open to debate. The two Prefects were in unison that the rounds would start with the most mentally challenging task, followed by the most frightening, leading to the most arduous. The game ends with the most honest task. I don't believe the game they spoke of was a game in which losers get a pat on the back for trying. I don't know what the alternative to winning is but I'd a strong sentiment regarding such an ask. There is no alternative.

From the way they talked, as if every word concealed pride, I knew the Gauntlet was a game I'd no interest in playing. The word death escaped their lips a few times and while each time it did it was in a joking manner, their condescending smiles said otherwise. I can't remember who said what, but their words are as clear today as the reflection of a periwinkle ceiling on the slight portion of steel, forged on the handle of an astonishingly sharp knife untainted by blood in my cell.

'Death will wiggle its way into one of the four rounds.'

'It always does.'

'Death will eat em' up like Yankees gobbling up Sunday supper in the middle of July, Oklahoma 1939.'

'Ain't that the truth! And when it does, heaven knows they'd have died in good service to God.'

'Which round do you believe death will take a liking to this Gauntlet?'

'It's obvious, isn't it? The first.'

'I say the third.'

'Death is slutty. It can make love to all four.'

'I see potential in this group of Nihils more than years past to curb its advances.'

'Let's hope none come for our jobs if they sidestep it.'

'You as well as I know perfectly well that can't happen. An opening in the Praefectus will only occur if one of the eleven dies or retires.'

'Still, you never know. With that prisoner on the loose, anything can happen...After what he did.'

'We have enough to worry about without Tommy running amok. For us, the Gauntlet takes precedence. Let the Celers do their job and coddle that artistry of a baby that is their battle plans.'

'And should they fail?'

'Should they fail? Have you lost your mind brother? Celeres is a disciplined fighting machine poised to destroy our enemies. Don't you ever doubt their skill in combat.'

I'd waited for what felt like nearly half an hour in the dome. A close estimate I believe, no thanks to my watch. My anger had not yet abated. Seeing Luciana would unchain the demon in me long serving as a dormant sun bear. When Zorian arrived, I'd asked the specifics of what the two talked about inside the health farm to which he'd replied, "I take my position as Prefect seriously and if there's one thing I'm quiet about it's our plans for the rounds."

"Don't involve me in that game of yours. I'm here for a helping hand in finding my friends and that's that," I said in a querulous voice.

We charged past the monumental moving glass door into the Honeycomb Lodge. Before it closed, two geese shuffled past us into the dome. The lodge was empty apart from some geese under a short bridge straight-ahead. Not long after, some jaguars on the fourth floor leaned onto its railing to look down at us.

"We found her in a catatonic state you know. Luciana. Once she exited the store, she dropped her case of beer seeming only capable of moving her lips. It's like she knew karma had arrived. She told the herald we'd sent for her that her husband and daughter were missing, though we've found no evidence she has a husband or a daughter. We had to sedate her of course," Zorian said inconsequentially.

"I bet she lied," I said unremorsefully.

Zorian's lashes fluttered. I speculate he knew then that nothing he said or did to moderate my rage would read as more than waffling to me. He shunted me forth, expounding upon where we were. The name, the four classes housed here, and the fireplace. He didn't indulge me with how the purple goop in the cones above us was twirling. All he validated was that the goop in them was indeed padda divinorum.

As we crossed the black marble short bridge at the end of the lodge with purpleheart wood railings, I noticed the steel blue brook under it was bubbling with a touch of steam coming through. It couldn't be heat that's the cause for geese floated in it uncooked. Zorian put his platinum gas mask over his head imbibing Leonid's static voice—the one he'd possessed in the nursery when under his snow camo gas mask.

Zorian pulled out a blueberry floral tie from a secret compartment on the backside of his gas mask. He placed it over my eyes, tying it tightly from behind so that everything for me went black. He affirmed this measure was temporary.

Zorian led the way with a hand on my wrist and the tug of an ardent dog on its leash. The muddling of our path was a form of precaution taken by Prefects to prevent newcomers branded as high risk from pulling a fast one on them and releasing a prisoner.

We walked over the bridge and meandered for a bit, coming to a stop near the Dragon's Throat. The gentle heat waves and sharp crackling stylings of wood virtuoso Cherry Wood welcomed us. It smelled of vanilla. The treble beeps of button pressing went off like they hailed from a microwave's keypad.

After eight beeps, came the chinchilla squeak of a path unveiled.

Audibly, a doddery door creaking open. Its low scrape fizzled out with a flurry of subzero winds. I received a cool kiss from the winter solstice. The reversal of atmosphere smacked me silly. Never would I have expected the threat of a blizzard. Zorian pulled me into a room too gusty for a picnic. Besides the biting cold that gave me shivers, a knot of people clustered around either side of us as we stepped inside, bawling,

"That motherfucker's a goner!"

"Ay Russki, I've got some syrniki for ya!"

"Oye papi!"

"Whip that ass good!"

"I'll get you one day motherfucker!"

The shouting came bundled with a clangor of metal bars—what typifies older jail cells. I kept getting pulled forth, expecting Zorian to respond. Zorian never gave into the yells. Instead, he breezily talked over them, letting me know we were entering cellblock 13—The Housewife's Corner, in which every prison cell is a parodical take on a room pertaining to the perfect 1950's housewife's dream home. Luciana would be waiting unexpectantly in the 'The Center of Your Life Kitchen.'

The floor was a carbon steel grid texture. What'd be a slip resistant floor had I worn the right shoes. We turned into a hall and Zorian paused within a few steps of what ought to be an entryway since an access code was entered into a keypad.

Four beeps later, a door groaned at the hinges as it lumbered open.

Zorian easily pulled me in as I was awfully ready to go—blood boiling and nearly a decade of repressed enmity at this point unchallenged. He fleetly let go of my wrist. "This is where we split. I've some dealings to get to outside. A warthog got into the prison yard and somehow that's above Leonid's pay grade. You may take the blindfold off once the door shuts behind you," Zorian said dutifully.

I waited a whole minute after the door banged shut before untying the knot of the tie at the back of my head, setting free the silk to mingle with the floor. Perhaps it was the nerves encroaching on me as the confrontation with Luciana became all too real.

I was in what could be construed as an edgy elevator shaft. The walls were a thick white plastic agleam in the sun, seen high above through a glazed skylight. An angelfish-shaped cloud easefully sailed past, swimming amongst lumps of bleached coralline algae. Slim transparent plastic trays and deep square bins were suspended in layers on the wall in front of me, ending a foot above me. My insides writhed as I grabbed hold of a plastic bin and delicately pushed open the white plastic wall.

Chapter 27

There she was. The French maid succubus from Hades—Luciana Barenclave. Forever pretty. Now at the cusp of forty, she'd dyed her long wavy hair with full bangs that graze past her eyebrows, a rich, deep, cool brown hue. Only glimpses of her past auburn locks flit as stray hikers at the heart of a dark wood, disappearing under darker strands as her neck turns towards something sizzling.

Luciana was sitting warmly at a red chrome high pub table atop a red chrome high-top chair. She'd traded in the inane ensemble that came with her past stint as a French maid for a gray long-sleeved shirt dress, black footless tights, and green single strap thong sandals. Not an ounce of remorse for my father's killing had been reflected over the years on her youthful guise.

"You've got a great ass. Now don't slip and leave those pancakes cooking on one side for too long. I like em fluffy. Crispy at the edges and tender in the middle. And don't you dare add a drop of macadamia oil to that batter," Luciana ordered, shooting a dubious glance to a man standing over a gleaming, restored vintage aqua green stove and oven.

The man's fit out in a denim apron and an oversized white chef's hat with a puffy mushroom top. His posterior's completely bare and an orbed hairy ass is what sticks out. A brown cat with a mondo head turns to look at me on the man's left shoulder with atypical red jasper eyes. All three sets of eyes in the room convene on me.

I was at a loss for words for I was in a room with her. Though Kapish seemed to think he was the cause for my silence.

"My punishment for knocking some teeth out of a pleb. Everyone who enters Neptune receives their final meal upon arrival. She chose pancakes. What did you choose?" Kapish asked eerily serene.

"I was given chili lemon octopus alongside cucumber salad," I answered in a surly voice.

"Who's this cat?" Luciana questioned, sniffing out the delicate smell of bananas with vanilla from her order.

"You really don't know do you?" I asked sounding shaky.

"I can assure you anything I ask is my truth in not knowing. Being in the dark has ripened into a more unnerving experience than was when I first found out I wouldn't be able to bring my beer with me." Luciana's faint eyebrows slanted inward and her glossy orange creamsicle lips pursed terribly tight. "My kidnapper travels light. The closer to the hour the clock ticks away, the closer *im* gets to patient. All the abduction shenanigans I endured in getting here would drive a trigger-happy hysteria out of anyone. So, since my chef de cuisine for the day won't entertain my meek curiosity, are you here to give me some solace?"

I was speechless once more, but my eyes said it all, whether she read them or not.

"No?" She shrugged, remissive of me and rose from her chair to stand by Kapish.

UP STRAWBERRY VINE

As does every good pirate share his shoulder with a parrot and no care, Kapish too was at an ease of mind with his special friend. Not even a flinch from the uncommon Nordic man as the brown cat that fit well on his shoulder nibbled his ear and sequentially licked its paw. Kapish's right brow that'd bled earlier was now only marred by a red vertical slice—no more than an inch—set amid a white butterfly bandage.

"It's funny. I remember the day you left us for good. I try not to think about you but that stupid French maid dress of yours really became your signature style, much to no one's amusement. Who would've thought a brother of this fraternity would dress just like one prompting my last memory of you? Your last words to me. That memory is what brought you here. Do you remember me now?"

"I can hold my tongue no longer. Hate to spoil the surprise but I'm short on time. The better you two get acquainted, the faster I'm out. Espy this cat! For it's your murder victim's son—all grown up," Kapish said, his tone biting. He returned to pouring the pancake batter into a black frying pan; already having amassed a neat mini stack of hot steaming pancakes on a red dinner plate to his right. The biscotti-shaded stack was not yet big enough to tilt over the yellow Formica countertop; of which had laid out six other courses—spongy and glossy.

"Koata...?" She drew a blank on how to proceed, until she drew her next words from a poisonous supply and handed me the box jellyfish of gibes. "So sad what had to happen to your father. So sexy what you've become. Do you cry when you look in the mirror and see Daniel's eyes or smile in favor of a hereditary godsend?"

"You're going to hell for what you did!" I erupted.

"There is no hell. Maybe a heaven. But for now, it's just now." Luciana was all too calm. She slid her hand coolly across Kapish's upper back before walking past me to shut the fridge door. That's when I'd actualized, I'd come into this clean-cut suburban kitchen through a banana yellow retro fridge made of heavy gauge steel, beefed up with a high luster finish.

"You and I have unfinished business. I don't presume you'll understand why I did what it is I did. But given that this forced opportunity to reunite has fallen upon us, I'll share exactly why your father is dead and why you're here." Luciana had the nerve to speak to me at a distance of neighborly familiarity. Her gray eyes speckled with gold and brown protruded from the rest of her glazed facial expression. She was leading onto knowing more than I knew about why I was here.

"I do not claim innocence for my crimes, but I am a prisoner just as much as he was." She casually flipped her hair and retired to inspect Kapish's progress. The brown cat jumped off Kapish's shoulder onto the red and white checkered floor. Kapish had lifted a pancake off the pan's surface to flip it over, but the cat's sudden jump led Kapish to overexert the liftoff. The undercooked pancake landed flat on Kapish's face with a flop. With a leniency towards the heat, Kapish laughed haughtily, cleaned himself off using his apron, and returned to his mild punishment.

The cat strut toward a pink frilly apron with white polka dots hung over a silver hook in the wall and began scratching at it on its hind legs. Two thin silver stripes ran parallel to each other, vertically down its back. Kapish instructed Judas to stop. When the cat gaily ignored Kapish's command, scratching at the apron more belligerently, Kapish thrust down his spatula. He'd put a terse brake on cooking to bag the cat under his arm, chock-full of exasperation.

Luciana and I had an in-depth heated discussion about why she killed my father. An implausible story that started with a mother. When Kapish finished making pancakes, he served them to Luciana on the red chrome high pub table. What accompanied them was an eight-ounce teardrop glass bottle with a thin, roughly straight sided neck. Its dark amber fluid insides were the delectable peach syrup of New England states, communicated by an enlivened fuzzy sticker of a peach and the motto 'An appeal to Heaven' on the bottle's front side.

As Kapish fussily washed a few dishes over a sky blue kitchen sink, Luciana enlightened me to a screwball's murder story—one living with a schizoaffective disorder. A barbarous chewing here and there scourged her story with limes. The unshared hearty serving of banana pancakes delighted in tottering about in her mouth as though they were set on the fastest spin cycle of a washing machine. It was hard to listen to her at all, made much less easy in between each bite. What choice did I have? It was either now or never.

I knew then—my annoyance in her rabid chewing snowballing—that only one of us would leave this room alive.

"The last year of your father's life, my mother disappeared. Gabrieli Barenclave—my beloved mother—was a woman whose pride knew no bounds. Her ability to overcome the greatest obstacles was her life force. She'd climbed to the top of Mount Everest, wrestled a bear, attained certification as a helicopter pilot and contributed her skills to wilderness search and rescue operations, headed her own honeybee farm, and opened a Georgian restaurant with my father, Monato, in New York City. All before the age of fifty-one. An unbelievable summation of deeds. Even to my father. Can you believe?

I spoke with her every day over the phone. Then one fine sunny day when she didn't call me, I shook in my boots. Like employing an ancient sewing gauge riven with cracks to evenly space out buttonholes, I knew something was off. I tried contacting her but strangely enough my call was connected to a nonworking number. I then contacted my father who made it seem as though he knew nothing of the great woman I described."

Luciana was pegged with a roused, very uneven, rough-hewn accent, catered with an unusually long pause between sentences when reciting her father's response to her burning distress. Almost as if overthinking her next words would cede validity to her claims.

"'Your mother...? You've never known your mother...' he told me worriedly. 'If you're curious about who your mother is, we can discuss that, though before now you've never expressed interest in knowing anything about her... And I say, just because I raised you as a single father doesn't mean you weren't loved... Are you alright Luci?' At that point, I'd thought he'd done the unimaginable. So, I did what any concerned daughter would—I contacted the authorities.

Lo and behold, the authorities had no records of a woman named Gabrieli Barenclave or of a Gabrieli with my mother's surname, Gogoladze, having ever stepped foot in the sunshine state. My father had also provided the authorities with documentation of my adoption leading them to think I was insane or seeking attention. I had to find her. A mother is the spring water that runs miraculously in arid land, a nightingale in choked desolation, the last known reason in a world of madness.

I wouldn't expect you to understand since your mother was never present in your life. I tried to be that for your family but was never given the chance to fill the shoes your birth mother negated. Although, I'm sure the Jade we both adore got it into your head that I was no good for your father when you were too young to cook up your own opinions about me...

I loved your father, and I would've taken you and Jade under my wing. I did try. But your father never let go of the love he had for your mother. Your father was a prisoner of his love for your mother. I am a prisoner of a blood curse.

I confined in your father what I'd never conceive of telling anyone else—my mother had been erased from existence. As crazy as that'd sound to any thinking man, your father was unsheltered from such. Therefore, more open to such-and-such.

Despite being quite the brilliant ball of fire, Daniel was an experimentalist on the fringe of a crooked science known as aeternumology. The study placed intent focus on proving Rainbow Gravity theory. He also believed our minds' capacity, when pushed to its limits, would be triumphant in curing mortality. He was always doting on outrageous concepts.

A whole lot of crazy, he'd been exposed to. Daniel spent half his life as an intimate affiliate of a secret organization known as the Immortals. He belonged to a branch of that organization that call themselves the Immortal Octopi."

"And he shared this with you why?"

My back had melted into the wall across from her. Kapish, having finished washing his cooking utensils, had been fixedly watching us as he cradled Judas blissfully in his gorilla arms.

"Get me some milk will ya. You've been told how I like it." Luciana ordered Kapish, briefly breaking eye contact with me. Kapish dropped Judas, allowing him to wander freely. "While he may not have loved me as I did him, Daniel and I had an impenetrable friendship. In fact, if it wasn't for him, I would've never gotten my precious mother back."

Kapish brought Luciana a silver-plated mint julep cup laden with milk foam on top and fresh milk tucked tamely below it. He'd served up two separate consistencies of milk. An oddly pleasing fusion. The airy whipped milk he'd obtained from a glass jar. The purely milk-milk he'd obtained from a square quart glass bottle—archaic, like those the milkman delivered when such men existed. I caught a glimpse of more of the same stowed away in one of the upper goldenrod cabinets.

Wintertide was the first to enter the silver cup. A warm light body of milk tiptoed behind it—a cloud of toothsome proportions. It floated smooth and velvety atop its chilled counterpart. The two managed to coexist pleasantly. The base never supping the elevated.

The cup was exhaustively sweating from the cool milk that'd first been introduced into its residence. Luciana tussled to pick it up at first, nearly letting it slide from her grip twice in one go. Judas now mingled with the legs of the two red chrome high-top chairs, skirting Luciana's legs with every turnaround.

"Daniel introduced me to a special book his branch regarded as sacred. I initially assumed the texts in its black leather boards and spine—embossed with a mature pumpkin on the front cover—were satanic in nature as your father was a Satanist. Now before you get your panties in a knot, he didn't actually believe in Satan in the literal sense. Lucifer, for him, was more of a literary figure—the ultimate symbol of insurgency against authoritarianism."

"Liar! My father was a Christian man. He instilled in us the morals of Christianity."

"Did he? Or did he let you choose what to believe in and you simply mistook his support in accompanying you and your sister to church as his own support for Christianity? What was it your father used to say all the time? Something along the lines of, 'Don't thrive off stupidity.' Stupidity—the cardinal sin of Satanism. I wonder why Daniel would try so hard to instill such precept and not—say—one of the Ten Commandments?"

I felt uneasy but I quickly bounced back, standing erect and becoming one with the confrontation at my door. My security blanket in knowing all that I know about my dad—a man I aspire to be like—was being pulled from right under me.

"Shut up! You may have killed my father, but you will not kill his honor in my eyes. He now resides among the heavenly embrace of the Lamb of God—Jesus Christ—where his spirit finds eternal refuge, beyond the reach of any earthly torment."

"Look around you Koata! This is reality! Wake up! You've been lied to your entire life, starting with your god. Generation after generation of fools. When your holy text was translated what was added were specific teachings to push an agenda and what was omitted was reason. The real teachings of Jesus were never preserved while he was alive. People manipulated and defiled them for personal gain and sadly—they succeeded."

I wouldn't listen to any further ridiculousness. Luciana only knew how to spout lies. After years of hiding, she'd created a mendacious reality about a man who never returned her love to cope with an unforgivable sin. She knows nothing of what she speaks. A murderer, once a murderer, lives only to cause pain. "No, you're just a looney murderer. Incompetent to stand trial but a waste of society's resources to admit into a psych ward."

"I can't rationally explain all I've done. What I can say is sorry. And what I say to you next will sound like all but sanity. But I beg you listen closely. The book your father showed me had a ritual in it. If I were to complete this ritual, allowing it to live up to its full barbarity—to the detriment of my aching soul—I'd get my mother back. A part of that ritual that mind you, your father was the one who showed me, was: take the life of the love you so choose to sacrifice everything for. For me that life was your father's."

"You're going to wish you were dead!" I lunged at her but like greased lightning, she hopped off her seat, knocking it back with an elbow. From her back, she'd brought forth a hunter's knife with a glistening silver blade, stopping me dead in my tracks.

"I won't give you the satisfaction." She pointed the knife to and from Kapish and I, her eyes flashing dangerously.

"You plan to take on the both of us with a hunting knife? How'd you even get that?" Kapish asked cool and collected, slowly sidestepping along the wall towards me.

"When I was thrown into Baba's office, I saw the glittering eyes of two miniature sloths staring back at me underneath the loveseat. I stealthily reached for it, overplaying my pain from being thrown on the floor. Now this knife will give me my freedom." Luciana holds the knife shakily at us.

"Cool off. You may've once been a hotshot killer but let's not get so confident you forget two men can easily overpower one woman. Your heyday as a butcher is over." Kapish got in behind me and grabbed me by the arm to pull me back aside him. My lower jaw was thrust forth in anger. I be damned if I didn't avenge my father here and now.

"We're all entitled to our own adventure. Where one ends, another begins anew." Her last words to me before disappearing eight years earlier were her last words to me before disappearing now. Except this time, they weren't accompanied by the orange smudge of her lipstick on my forehead.

I witnessed her soul leave her body as her head rammed head-on into the knife. All the hatred in my heart regressed into a dark corner of my mind in which I kept asking myself, why do I pity her in this moment? Was it because she'd confirmed my suspicion, she's insane?

Benumbed, I'd stood still as the knife made its toilsome path into her skull searching for a life to claim. Judas lifted his mouth agog to catch the shower of blood. The brown fur on his head converted to red and enraptured, Judas dipped his tongue into the mounting crimson puddle at her feet. After nine jabs had carved a crooked hole into her pretty face, her body gave into death. Judas slyly dodged Luciana's falling corpse. What followed was a laugh. The likes of which sent shock waves throughout my body like no other instance had in my life.

Kapish took pleasure in watching her die in an act I felt nothing for but remorse. I wanted her to die. This was justice but justice felt cold. He paused his laughter, momentarily suppressing it, like a hyena catching its breath before returning to its raucous chorus, to exclaim, "Fuck, I wish I'd brought popcorn! Who's next on the chopping block?" The grating sound of Kapish's laugh struck me like a bullwhip across the face. Its very crack is embedded in my darkest daydreams to this day. It haunts me in a deeply rooted, subliminal way. I've assented to it never going away. Let it be a reminder to me that death is no play to applaud.

As the maniacal laugh faded into the background, Judas skirted past me. Kapish crouched down, inviting the cat to leap into his arms, murmuring to it, "Thought I'd seen it all with him allowing the inclusion of a female on these grounds. Surely, he foresaw her short-lived tenure. Who'da thunk it? The instance that warranted an exception in the eyes of God was a crazy bitch." The fridge door opened and closed before the numbness in my body had come to pass. I found myself alone in a deafening quiet. I turned for the fridge handle, pulling it with the full force of my weight behind it. Unavailing. Kapish had locked me inside.

Chapter 28

The antiquated square quart glass milk bottles had been empty for months. I poured them down the sky blue kitchen sink for I did not thirst in all my sorrow. The quirky polyurethane foam foods had been rearranged around the kitchen several thousand times on their pink and blue China plates. As for Luciana's nourishing final meal, I could not stand the banana, vanilla smell.

Knowing that when the autopsy's performed that'll be what's found undigested in her stomach made me want to vomit. So, I threw it all out. The dishes, the unfinished pancakes tinged by her orange creamsicle lipstick right where she'd taken her last bite—chomping through the full stack—and the bottle of New England peach syrup Kapish had put out all went flying out the window. Between the red-orange curtains over the sky blue kitchen sink, this small window quenches my aching lust for freedom.

The square window's no bigger than Judas' head. It grants me breath through its casement door, ever appeasing as it whisks open every morning with a glim ray of light. I can't see much from the open window but a dirty gray cobblestone wall with a little over ten feet between us. Daylight announces its arrival from a wee crack in between cobblestones—the sole way I know night's handed over its shift to day.

A white poster with the image of a purple cone and two floating zoomorphic cherry heads hangs from the wall. There's a peppy bold font on the poster. I can't make out the phrase completely as it's too dark. Just the capitalized words 'SUP INTO THE EXTRAORDINARY' in purple are discernable over the purple cone and the orange-beaked cherries.

Someone must've discreetly cleaned up the mess of shattered dishes and spoiled food from the other side as there're no longer remnants of what I threw out. The keen weapon has had a tireless vacation from its last kill moving here and there, getting more attention from me than the pappy squishy dinner foods. It's spent time in every goldenrod cabinet; all empty but the one full of emptied antique milk bottles. Though, after eight months I felt it looked best under Luciana's right hand so under it it's stayed.

The bloody hunter's knife leaves her hand only to help me register time. Counting the days has been an easy task with this tool. Behind the pink frilly apron with white polka dots hung over a silver hook in the wall there're tally marks. They transition to five-pointed stars after the one-hundred-day mark. Each star represents five days. I'm surprised not a smidge of blood has soaked into the apron from the periwinkle wall of fifty-three bleeding stars.

Baba kept me some company for a few minutes, not long after the shock of getting locked up had settled. I was not yet delirious enough for Baba's voice in my head to be indistinguishable from the little voice in my head. He'd explained to me that I'd be here until Tommy's found. He'd hoped seeing my greatest foe die would ease the pain of waiting for bailout.

I hope he knows now this sick gambit has only caused me day terrors.

He'd apologized for casting a question mark over what I told him was my intent here—to find my friends. Because I was seen within proximity to Tommy and my thoughts seemed so ludicrously contrived to throw him off, things ought to be the way they are. For the safety of the jaguars, he believes desperate precautions must be taken. As desperate as stealing my freedom for a chance I'll let this *act of innocence* die.

He'll get his due.

My wristwatch is still yellow. However, the green spec on it has flourished into a dime-sized patch. The time on it no longer reads 9:34 A.M. It reads 9:46 A.M. The small window flies open and a wistful ray of light peeps in. I meditate on the blazing sun on the other side, preparing myself for another gut punch of loneliness and like so, a new day has begun.

I net the hunter's knife from Luciana's limp hand and walk spiritless to the white polka-dotted pink frilly apron to add some two-bit change on the twenty cents of a star. I whip the apron aside and carve in the second to last part of Star Fifty-four. It's sad. The writings on the wall are already three stars past the American flag.

The faint hum of a song breaks through the open window. I drop the knife bewildered, release the apron, and scurry towards something untrodden. The heavenly voice of a woman singing creates a roadblock to my year of desolate gloom, releasing dismissed harbored feelings of wanting human interaction. My heart could burst with the joy of a pardoned turkey.

Upon the poster that lay partnerless amongst cobblestone, a new font emerged. The word 'POISON' is graffitied aslant in a self-luminous chartreuse green. The fridge door squeaks open and a cool gust of air presages what lies behind door number two. I turn and run for the exit. My feet get stained by the puddle of blood I'd so long avoided.

Has Tommy finally been found?

A beaming sun beats down upon me through the glazed skylight. It energizes me to kick open the white wall in the elevator shaft. Freedom comes with the sense of being buried alive in a glacier. And while I'd forgotten the path to get here was a frozen one, I'd not yet forgotten the pesky yaps of prisoners attempting to intimidate Zorian. An uncommon greeting erupts. Presumably from those same comic, vengeful prisoners I'd only heard, not seen. The psyched-out cries of grown men reverberate throughout my escape.

The hall just outside my prison cell has mortared stone walls fashioned by an astronomer. A luxurious assemblage of stones made holy by the pale gold of Saturn and the pale blues of Neptune circulate an unearthly calm. I feel visited by a dream—a woman's song is calling to me, the rowdiest of men are doing their darndest to wake me, and the stretch of space is gaily tuning me into its vibrations. The floor I'd blindly traversed was exactly what I'd imagined it'd be. Once again, I felt its bitterness in the stomp of my naked feet.

Past the spaces in the carbon steel grid floor, I could see two floors below me. Two men a level below me are sprinting, gasping, and fraught with death. An adult arctic fox gracefully bolts after them. One man artfully trips the other with a will to survive. As the fallen man struggles to turn his body around at the speed of which his head turned, he stares petrified at the white beauty who's gaping mouth of get 'er done teeth releases a high-pitched howl.

Had I not seen where the sound came from, I'd have thought it was a woman's screech signaling bloody murder. The artic fox bounds and clamps onto the man's lower jaw with its mouth, slicing facial flesh and cracking bones. Baffled, I run from the beastly sight. My eyes wished too soon for comfort. Around the corner, lies a fixed prison guard, sat against a wall with an off-white rat tigerishly exiting his mouth. It joins its family of about a dozen others, bite to bite, prick to prick, scudding about his cushioned moldy-green bomber jacket.

A walkie-talkie and desert eagle handgun lie next to him on the floor. The static voice on the other side of the radio calls desperately for Croxteth. After a third attempt to reach the dead, the radio goes silent. I reverse my path till I'm face to face with my prison cell. Across from me is the stalking gaze of a black wolf with yellow eyes and a salivating mouth perfect for shredding Belgian endives or piercing flesh. I don't think twice before pushing a head-on collision with the wolf.

I attempt to scare the wolf by yelling at it but I'm much closer to an intoxicated hobo arguing with a telephone pole than with the opioid market and its intimidating epidemic. My yells are drowned out with the bodyless screams of fleeting life. The wolf darts to me in a short burst showcasing its maximum speed. Its long snout faces the ground with pint-sized spurts of steam absconding its nostrils and getting left abaft, disappearing at the thrust of its hind feet.

The yellow eyes of the wolf meet my neck. It forcibly pounces atop of me with the nerve to dine freely, not expecting a fight. In spite of my headstrong rigidity, I fall, unlucky as spilled salt, on my back. I yank it by the testicles as I hedge its attempt at biting my neck. My neck sinks into my shoulders, my knee jerks to bump its bum, and my elbow swats its face as it pivots to cover mine. Its slobbering mouth returns apace, outstretched to catch a giant cannolo filled with fifty smaller ones.

I release its testicles to glom onto its neck, thrusting his head upward. It repeatedly bites the air with spasmodic lurches to get his head lower. Inch by inch his bite gets closer to exchanging my consciousness—sending out Mayday calls to my operating body—for a fresh meal. Its wet, cold nose kisses mine as both our fog-ridden breaths dance to form a lukewarm blanket between us. Naturally, choosing to confront the wolf rather than the prison cell was a fatal decision. And yet, the howl of another wolf saves me some time.

The black wolf raises its head high enough so that a peanut could balance itself at the tip of our noses. The slow waltz of vapor that lingers long enough to blur the wolf's features make of its slobber—a syrupy rain. The cloud dissipates as that one surging howl becomes a growl, becomes a shriek, becomes a revised lesser growl that filters out the last of a lone wolf's strength. An ailing dog's whimper loiters ahead.

Had it not been for that other black wolf I see now, fat as a cow, pierced at the jowl, no ifs, ands, or buts about it—I'd be dead again. Its whimper carries on in a marathon cry for help as the wolf atop of me plucks its front claws from my chest and negates I ever existed. The wolf reunites with the dying member of its pack. I waste no time in seeing it pull the arrow that caused the second becoming.

The breakneck cracks of gunfire sound off from where the rats chowed down. It's here I encounter the only other 'other' I've seen putter around in the private grounds of Neptune. Standing over the dead prison guard, admiring his work, is the platinum blond I first saw in the Lemon Room showers. He's decked out in a slim black pinstripe suit with a white dress shirt, red satin tie, and white rose boutonnière over his left lapel. His hair's been slicked back with a heavy-duty wax that's stiffened to emulate a skater helmet with a matte shine.

He's reaped the desert eagle handgun from the bulwark of rats, carrying a black recurve bow with a shoulder strap and a red quiver on his back. Several silver arrowheads peek out from the quiver, too long for the tubed carrier bag. He peers tensely at the dead man with warring ice blue eyes. I feel colder staring into his eyes than this prison's already succeeded in doing; testing my limit beyond Iceland's surf. Three rats have been disemboweled with bullets across the prison guard's moldy-green bomber jacket. Another was shot at the foot of the guard. The overspill of its rosy intestines slips through the carbon steel grid floor with a splat.

While I'd like to think I'm smart enough to make sense of how he got a hold of the gun, he relates that miracle through his actions. The sharp mobster pulls an arrow from a rat that'd been covered by the right thigh of the guard, on the opposite side of where the gun had been. One arrow wasn't enough to stunt them, but it managed to distract them with a fallen member long enough to procure the gun. By then, it was too late for all to scatter. I walk to meet the mobster and there upon the prison guard's right thigh is a nauseating bundle of executed rats.

Another splat is heard further below. Most likely the same intestines from the rat blasted at the foot of the guard having reached the lowest level. Before we can speak with words, a pack of wolves pine away from where the fat one was struck. Our eyes need say no more. We run from their cries interconnecting with the fading shouts of men and the swelling sound of a woman's song. Now clearly distinguishable as being an operatic aria sung in Russian.

Her song's not at all chirpy but dreadfully sad and somehow markedly beautiful. The power her voice carries emboldens this feeling of dreams where anything can happen. The typical things I encounter from now on should be questioned for being other than what they lead on. God forbid they all be glittering simulations.

This dream of mine is not yet processing as nightmare. One year with a corpse dealt me an armor that ricochets grisly stimuli. Which helps as we pass the mauled victims of beasts. Neither prisoner nor guard has been spared the wrath of the wolfpack or mischief. All torn, indistinguishable to the crude chuck roast beef I had at Jeffrey's Bay in South Africa.

Above us, the grid floors interlaid with halls of Saturn and Neptune's palette paint a tower of waffles beat in steel. I can't perceive how far up this prison goes. I do know we're currently roving the third floor, speedily passing other cells' open white steel doors; made to look avant-garde with a convex-concave square pyramid pattern. A preemptive second door rests open behind each; all probable harbors. Sense strike me sane if ever they cross my mind as an option for refuge.

The mobster alerts me he only has one magazine left with five rounds. He exhausted the first and most of the second on those ferocious rats. The timbre in his voice has lost its goofy pizzazz. It may very well be the situation we're in that's changed it as his tone strictly denotes seriousness—what shouldn't surprise me but does. I'm still under the warped mindset that everything bonkers that happens will precede festoons of tomfoolery. Should we survive, I hope to hear that comicalness in his voice again.

I see a boisterous orange glow on one end of the grand rotunda we've arrived at. What could only be the Dragon's Throat. Thirteen access points reign around the room with wine purple banners above them, snapping snootily in the cold breeze. And yet I see no windows. Every banner possesses the centered insignia of a white top hat with a ring around it. Under the carbon steel grid floor that extends to the grand rotunda is a deep basement occupied by tiny cages. A wad of prisoners remain trapped inside them. Sat in their individual cages, they're still as a fly off guard of a swatter.

Some frailly raise their heads to the footsteps above them. They'd seemed so eager to see Zorian but not us, bawling and banging on their cages rabidly enough that I'd once thought they were aside me. All but one partake in the yogic practice of observing complete silence. The dissident can't help but snivel uncontrollably. I would too, had the same anaconda that's leisurely wrapping itself around his cage now been as deathly close to me in my cell as it is to him.

The snake needn't be modest in claiming the record for largest reptile. Looking to be near forty feet long and as girthy as a steel drum barrel, this snake's an authenticated B-movie monster. The cage disappears under its army green skin prettily blotched with hickory brown. I can't imagine how but the creaking sound of metal bend rings under its exerted pressure, tolling the knell for the prisoner. The snake wraps the remainder of its body atop of the cage in swirls of pulsating muscles, laying bare the smoothest Christmas tree.

"Where're these animals coming from?" I ask with a thievish glance at the tightening snake.

"My guess is they all from the zoo, but something's made em go mad."

He draws from his left inner coat pocket a brain-shaped royal blue glass bottle with a short ribbed white plastic propellant—barely visible amid the bridge splitting the brain's left and right hemispheres. He pressures two thumbs with great force over each hemisphere and like that of a can of spray paint, the propellent pops up and expels a steady flickering blue mist aimed at the ground. The brain is not glass at all but a darn good mock of it that squelches as its squeezed firmly. A hole briskly appears in the carbon steel grid floor where the mist laid its hands.

"Abraxas Blue. Impressive, wouldn't ya say?"

I nod blankly.

"Time for the rat to eat the snake."

He stows away the royal blue brain back in his left inner coat pocket and draws forth the silver arrow he'd used on the rat meant to divert the others; recognizable solely by the curved pinkish-purple organ still stuck on its shaft. From his shoulder he whips the bow and equips it with the arrow. Without hesitation or fault, he shoots the arrow into the hole and straight through the anaconda's left eye.

From the entrance of cellblock 13 comes another archer wheezing rabidly. Upon him are the same black recurve bow and red quiver the mobster totes. The young man has a square high flat top from the early nineties, pouch-shaped ebony eyes, a broad Nubian nose that's a near perfect triangle, and a stubbly upper lip that's intemperately sweating. His mustard long sleeve plaid flannel with faded pine green overtones has its sleeves rolled up to his elbows and its black buttons buttoned up to the apex. An oversized lavender puffer vest rests upon it, calling attention to his hale slenderness. His twill khaki joggers are torn at the knees and his sulfur suede low-top sneakers have their burgundy shoelaces untied.

He pressures us to move in a highly exasperated voice, asking vehemently what the holdup is, letting know he didn't waste an arrow on that fat dog to see me dead. At once, we all turn towards the fire. It eagerly wags its red-orange tails, concealing what lies ahead. A shimmering in the air blurs the ground at the foot of the fire. Collected we stand, probing its looming light.

"A trick of the eyes," comments the second archer.

I tactlessly follow the two archers into the flames and before I can blink, we come out unsinged on the other side. The instance of heat was brisk, offering no real threat. Incomparable to a baking dish fresh off the oven. The fire's heating potency was less than that emitted from a freshly turned-on lightbulb. An exhibition that'd ward off by mere looks but lay to rest any aversion through interplay.

Within the Honeycomb Lodge, the menace of the wild levels up, putting us in line with the Far East. Two Herculean tigers are roaming the first floor while an army of black armored beetles pester a legion of brothers above. "Careful," speaks the mobster brusquely, holding me back. A jaguar on the fifth floor tumbles over the railing while fighting off a swarm of beetles intent on pricking every inch of exposed skin. Having landed mere feet ahead of us, his arms twitch and voice dies with a feeble moan.

I was distracted by the thousands of black papers lettered in gold scattered across the floor. Inferably, a neglected announcement. They capture the vein of tawdry New Year's Eve party invitations. Feasibly dismissed for a better design. The second archer bends over to snatch one but negates reading it till an appropriate time is won. The black armored beetles scatter from the fallen jaguar's contorted corpse and amalgamate with the black papers, fleeting our vision. I start hopping from one foot to the other to avoid any that may be lurking at my feet.

The two archers simultaneously turn their backs to me, raise their bows, and direct an arrow toward the same end of the lodge. The silver arrows fly cohesively, cutting the air for a microsecond before branching off. The arrows hit one of the wandering tigers at the neck and left forepaw. It topples over like a toddler learning to walk. The muteness coming from its end tells me it's been fatally wounded.

The surviving tiger leaps across furniture to its mate's aid, jumbling tables and chairs whilst roaring offensively. It attempts to move the fallen one's struck paw with its nose and then through use of its jaws. When nothing comes of it, the tiger lays inert against the dead, bellowing a low-pitched groan. As we progress into the Dome of the Plebeian, the mobster declares our finest fighting chance is to attack first.

"These animals have all been raised in tribes pertaining to their species. Make a distraction of one of their members either in injuring or killing em and the rest will come to its aid, until their serotonin deficiency exploits their rage. Whatever is causing em to rage, we must not refrain from killing. Act on an impulse—survive."

Raised in tribes?

For being a non-member, he seems to know a little something-something about the zoo. I guess it makes sense since most captive animals are grouped amongst their species. But do all animals care if one of their members is injured or lost in a fight? Based on the reaction of the wolves, rats, and tigers, I'd say certainly. I fiercely agreed with the mobster though it took me a rickety short bridge to get there.

The soaring glass door into the Dome of the Plebeian had withstood several blasts from a potent firearm. The imprint of bullets and their rippling faults were stark upon the glass, tearing apart the image of blue grass and a fortified cottage behind it in fluky spots. One spot in particular distorts a person like a Picasso original standing at the cottage's highest point—Goliath's chimney. Once the glass door shifts open, an awestriking storm of gunfire's broadcast from the opposite side of the cottage.

At the summit of the cottage is Zorian and oh my god—that's the woman I thought I heard singing. The heavenly voice coming from Zorian packs a mighty blow to my attention span as I briefly lose focus on the gunfire. It showcases a benevolence native to him, to be so kind as to share his gift with us. It's a complete and utter privilege listening to him. I just wish I knew Russian.

Zorian's in a plaid dark blue suit with the blazer unbuttoned, a white dress shirt, navy and gold floral silk tie, and midnight blue leather lace-ups. A black microphone firmly held against his lips echoes his voice as though nothing else matters. Hidden speakers are the only basis for which his voice must be flowing throughout Neptune.

Has he sung himself into oblivion?

We maintain a low profile given exceptional concealment by the tall blue grass. As we head into the warzone we duck and begin low crawling toward the health farm. I turn my head to the left confirming the platinum blond is still with me shifting hastily through blue lines. I turn my head to the right. I see nobody but the blue is being questioningly parted in two. Keeping up with the increased pace of the bullet storm overhead, a set of jaws is in route, snapping in my direct sight where the second archer was a second ago. A scurrying freshwater crocodile is a meter from rending my head off my body.

Thrust through its snout and pinning its jaws shut is the cold steel of a notably sharp katana. Perfect for the cold-blooded. Amid the katana, standing over the curtailed reptile who's aggressively whipping its tail and cutting itself further in gaping its mouth, is the bipedal warthog who'd once been air under the nose of an oxidized mirror. In its tawny tattered cloak, its body hides. Within its watery black eyes I cry, for monsters, in the most basic sense of the word, are real.

No artist could penetrate the wall that divides what's real in nature and what's a carbon copy of it. How the warthog bearing down on me is standing as men do, I leave a stirring cabbage soup of a question to the narrator of this world. The katana's withdrawn at a speed that cuts the air with the swish of a thousand whips. The warthog turns its back to face an opponent.

"Kookaroo! Kookaroo! Kookaroo! Why awen't you cowewing!?" By the likes of a lisp that kicks, I know that's Leonid behind the bizarre cries. I poke my head out of the grass. Sure enough, it's him. Must be wearing his mouth guard to stop himself from grinding his teeth as is his way to cope with tension. The warthog makes soft chirruping noises in response to Leonid's frenzied rooster impression. They begin to spar. Gold shotgun against katana. A pair as common as pickles soaped in peanut butter.

Meanwhile, baboons rain on men contiguous with the fray. The baboons leap from the tall blue grass, scratching and gnawing at the jaguars. The fraternity fires back at the baboons with gold Soviet style small arms but there's a militia of around thirty making gains on the jaguars. Two baboons manage to take possession of an AK-47. While unaware of how to use the weapon against the unarmed jaguar they've stripped, they use the buttstock to bash in the face of another. The unarmed jaguar attempts to pull the baboons off his brother but it's too late.

The warthog's agility is sufficient enough to evade the shotgun's blasts, darting in and out of the tall blue grass with nimble footwork and swift parries. Leonid adapts his strategy, utilizing the shotgun's powerful blasts to send shockwaves through the grass, attempting to disrupt the warthog's precision and balance. With every swing and slash, the grassy terrain becomes more refined, evenly trimmed to a precise and uniform level. The warthog leaps from the grass and twirls with its katana extended, creating a whirlwind of steel that slices through Leonid's shotgun, outfitting it with a shorter barrel. Leonid ducks and rolls as the warthog lands beyond him, leaving him without a scratch. I observed a momentary deviation in the katana's trajectory upon contact with the shotgun, suggesting a degree of flexibility or resilience in its steel blade.

Nearing the health farm is the second archer running in zigzags. The grass behind him is being parted, mimicking his trail by none other than another crocodile out of sight. He loses his footing and vanishes into the blue. The mobster and I continue to push forward in a high crawl. We bob up at the edge of the dome where the grass shortens. Our nearest option for cover is an Olympian white stone column. We lurch to the column and hastily duck behind it, wide enough to cover our backs side by side. A nightmarish growl swells a long climb above us, heavy with gripe, then lost in the gunfight.

A baboon driftlessly falls from the capital of the column to the tips of our feet. It twitches twice before going black. Its death prompts a capricious spike in gruff hissing sounds. The mobster peeps our six. The face of a hare scared stiff palls his once lively expression. I mirror him and watch the rich blue grass searchingly as dozens of baboons unmask. All the baboons amass to bum-rush our column.

Any weapon in play has ceased fire, Zorian's gone, and his entrancing melody has dug itself into the ground; enabling the feverish hisses to prosper. The jaguars retreat toward a yet dirt-poor security posture, provided by the Honeycomb Lodge, courtesy of the one tiger and the swarm of beetles serried inside. The abashment from their lack of aim, to have only hit one baboon out of the troop of thirty plus, is reason enough to fall back. As a bumbler of a psychic, I think it useless for them to stay and roll the dice. Chances are high another jaguar would die. From the looks of it, there'll be no ammo resupply.

The final stand in this fight is a sight. The mobster, the warthog, Leonid, and I remain unbroken with no sign of the second archer rousing from the tall blue grass. Though I never learned his name, I hope he lives to fight another day. The baboons pay no heed to the uncommon joust between Leonid and the warthog. They starkly whiz at us, their lion-sized teeth bared wantonly.

A baboon whips his head back, struck by an arrow in the mouth and the troop evenly splits like a railway comprised of two paths. Half attend to the stricken and half continue to gallop at us, beaming a feral, maniacal front. Their sole purpose is to take us. Their devoir right to avenge their brother. The mobster tightly grips onto his recurve bow, content he's stalled them at this juncture. Even so, their nearing hisses wed by prolonged wails tells us it's in passing.

"Don't have enough ammo or arrows to save our asses. Keep silent still. Do not smile or show them a glimpse of yo teeth. Don't dare look em straight in the eye and be prepared to follow ma lead, bar none," he says, his tone dire.

I'm unaware of what he has in store, but I won't place my fate in this stranger's hands. Not when I've a spectacular idea. A light bulb is anchored over our ordeal, bright enough to sway, say his decisiveness on an undisclosed plan.

"The brain!" I erupt.

His eyes survey me through wonder.

"The blue liquid with sparks and the cloud and the poof! Hand it over!" I say, my face in utter despair. He's complacent once he understands my request. Though I know better. His expression reading man at sea is an SOS distress signal signaling he doesn't trust me at all.

I exact a steady flickering blue mist from the brain against the column providing us with cover. I push the column forward as a whole section near our waists disintegrates into the atmosphere. The baboons scatter directionless as the column falls. It's too late for most to reject the divine decree—they will be the newest feature on Neptune's Fall 2013 menu.

"A baboon cranberry flatbread sandwich," I say with a wry smile.

"Very well Koata. Ma name's Arnold in as much as that offers some positive identification," he says approvingly.

Chapter 29

The column had smashed a great many baboons. The rest lay stunned atop of it or hidden within the tall blue grass contemplating what to do next. Arnold and I were quick to exploit the opportunity to get away. Through the arched opening into the health farm, we arrive at the scene of a ghost resort. Not a jaguar nearby.

We head down into the underground tunnel system through the triangular hole aside the White Oak Leaf. I attempt to relocate where it was that I first met Baba Azul—the hidden bathroom I'd left my highlighter yellow boardshorts in. Reaching at the cave walls with little recollection as to where the bathroom lies is fruitless.

Nothing's wedging open. Arnold inquires about what I'm searching, and I reveal my bid for safety is a secret bathroom on the other side of these walls.

"Safety?" he says carpingly. "We won't be safe till Tommy's gone."

"He did this?"

"I'll bet ma writing hand he did."

Arnold assures me he knows where he's going. The calmness from the health farm quickly dissipates underground. As we push onward, the hulking tread of a beast stomping the ground and the loud strung-out breaths of the uncommon kind follow closely behind. We rush ahead attempting to lose the pursuant stalker. Perhaps we have but the echo from its movement lingers uncomfortably tight. Through guidance from the spiraling jet black lamp posts, with sculpted jaguar heads at each end, and glowing mint green orbs to light the way, we manage to find the Lemon Room.

The stalker grows silent as do we. We each nudge open one of the mustard yellow swinging saloon doors. From outside the doors nothing looks unchanged. However, as we step inside the chandeliers rise to greet us and an optical illusion turns our bodies, our clothing various shades of gray. Something about the yellow lights from the floating crystal chandeliers does seem off. The lemon shades they'd once emitted have been overturned by titanium yellow. We are transported into a monochrome world where any object is a bleak canvas for black and white to tame.

I begin wildly kicking over every bench lined up in the middle of the hall for I know there's a key under one. I promise Arnold we'll be safe if he follows me through to the end of my violent wreckage, but he's bound to the notion there's no safety while Tommy's around. Arnold stops at the Lemon Room showers at the front of the hall as I bulldoze my way to David's locker.

A thin platinum rectangle skids like a fidget spinner from the leg of a bench as the bench tumbles like an IED blasted Humvee onto the wall. I snatch the key and emplace it into the slit of the adjacent gray steel locker. When I eject the key, the locker door lowers itself a level below. Ahead of me is a mountain of gray clothes with spectral traits to tell its units apart, but their size for a start.

UP STRAWBERRY VINE

I cast out heaps of laundry into the hall till I'm a foot deep into David's locker and a pile the size of a termite mound has formed all around me. Arnold shouts he can't find it, though I can't imagine what he can't find or what anyone would expect to find in the showers, but a seedy drain clogged with friable hair.

"En route!" he hollers.

"Get your ass over here! Help me plow an entrance through these clothes will ya!"

As his footsteps approach my position, his voice dials-in an annoyed tone with some waggish gibberish to remind me there's a comic persona trapped somewhere inside him. "I don't get it. Magumga should be here."

I blindly throw a motorbike finger glove behind me at the scaling pile of gray clothes. As I turn to face Arnold, tittering with the question of why someone named Magumga would hide in the shower, a silverback dons the glove on its left shoulder. Its frown tells me I'm done for. Its rumble of 95 decibels nearly rockets me into the hereafter. Its thickset fangs facilely pierce my grit.

The ounce of grit I've left climbs lickety-split from six feet under once Arnold fires a gunshot at the gorilla's right arm. The silverback owns its aggressive stance, settled on all fours, with no sign the round or its sound's made impact. I bring forth the brain, aiming it high at the gorilla's widening jaws.

The steady flickering gray mist pecks the gorilla's face only slightly before its giant hand backslaps me a breadth away. I grip onto the Lemon Room's satisfyingly rubber floor. I focus my blurred vision on the tall shadow above me. I must've been in the black for a minute too long because another voice has entered the space.

"You fired five shots! How could you miss?!" a man cries in a high-pitched voice.

"With all due respect laddie, I fired four!"

Arnold takes his final shot at the spine-chilling gorilla. Its facial skin has been stripped back to reveal its skull, animated despite the death penalty common sense would entail. Alive and well, the gorilla beats its fists on the ground like a toddler on a drum.

How could the brain serve me as a bomb?

I search the ground for where it may've rolled and find it at the foot of a new man. His profile's as gray as an actor through the silver screen in the era of silent films. He's short and beefy with a neat comb over and undercut, abruptly serious hooded eyes, a button nose, and an unbroken circle of heavy stubble; within which a twitching smile reads nervousness. There's a darker hued portion of skin with irregular borders over the right side of his cheek and neck—ever imperceptibly slight.

His active wear is that of a pro runner who's done well enough for himself to be endorsed by the most lucrative brands. The highly burnished silver metal bands clamping his wrists and ankles claim him as a member of Celeres. If I'm to believe their reputation, touted by Zorian, this man's basic training has prepared him to fight and win against anything under the sun.

The man picks up the brain at his feet, winds his arm, and throws it at Arnold, driving his whole body into the throw. Arnold instinctively drops the gun, exchanges it for the brain and aims it at the gorilla, extending his right arm and squeezing both hemispheres with one hand. He squints in a slump, away from the protrusion of mist that rockets out of his hand. At the same time, a bench leaves the gorilla's hands and flies straight above us hammering three crystal chandeliers. The gorilla's skeletal face, barely a face but a savage grim remnant of one, zooms through the flickering gray mist toward Arnold, swiftly deteriorating within it.

The chemical undoing of its skull is not fast enough to stop the gorilla from taking one last token with it into the grave. Its massive jaws clamp down on Arnold's fist and Arnold's right hand is plainly separated from him. Amazingly, it continues to grip onto the brain. From the disembodied hand, the brain's aimed low. The gorilla's headless corpse sways from side to side momentarily before it decides to tumble down toward me onto a bed of clothes. I roll from the falling body and lucky I did so. The gray mist eagerly attacks the ground where I lay, where the gorilla now lies.

Arnold's gone into shock. Cowed into silence, he pales at the sight of red blood gushing from the stump where his right hand just was. I briefly see the red too, made possible from the gray mist exposing a network of conductors underneath us. The entangled wires near the headless gorilla are throwing up electrical sparks that interrupt this gray illusion indecisively. The blue-gray mist works to snip some of the clutter out of existence. The Celer puts an end to the hazard by stomping on the frigid hand and forcing it to loosen its grip on the brain.

The hole the mist has made, however, engulfs the lower half of the headless gorilla. Its upper body is instantaneously lit up in high flames. The fire bounding over it, working to touch the ceiling, works overtime to craftily defeature the creature into a spongy texture suchlike burnt marshmallows.

There's no longer a gray filter to mask the lemons from which we must make lemonade. From behind the Celer, where three crystal chandeliers had crashed upon the jelly-like pale yellow floor, three explosions occur successively emulating the gorilla's blinding blaze. I retrieve the brain and shoot its flickering blue mist into the wall of clothes in David's locker. From the corner of my eye, something unhurriedly floats over the tips of the fallen chandeliers' yellow flames.

It's Tommy. His eyes as threatening as ever, flashing electric green in the presence of a burgeoning thick black smoke. The boy remains in his olive green greatcoat and colonial wear with a white powdered wig now carefully fitted to his noggin. He paddles and kicks through the air as if suspended in water. The Celer madly tells us to hide but I'm already two steps ahead of him, lifting Arnold from under his armpits, and dragging him toward David's locker where a path now stretches to the end of a blonde wood room.

"See this!" The Celer rotates his wrists in front of him to show off the chameleon metal bands, no longer silver, encompassing half of his forearms. "You can't hurt us anymore! You're feckless without power!" he shouts with a wan smile.

Tommy snorts with laughter. Now floating at the edge of David's locker, he performs a breaststroke in the air and glides toward the wall opposite the locker. "Get a grip Percutio," Tommy says triflingly. He bores into the Celer with annoyance riding his clenched lips. His stare briefly leaves the Celer to unemotionally eye Arnold and I—shaken but unpacified—inside the locker, then drops to the burning headless gorilla evoking a gag from him. "That's disgusting."

For the chance he'll be the first to ring in and answer the milestone question on a hit quizzical game show, Tommy slaps the air downward with his right hand and abruptly halts, suspending his hand smack above where the big red answer button would be. His hand compacts into a fist. The ground below the Celer promptly collapses and he looks stunned, eyes widening as he attempts to pull himself out of the incidental hole Tommy's fathered. Tommy slowly raises the palm of his hand toward the ceiling. "Egregious. Grievous. Garbage." In front of his eyes, he firmly rotates his palm to face the ground and clutches the air.

In a flash, the ceiling crashes over the Celer and blockades us inside David's locker. Scarps of metal and flint rubble tumble riotously into the room, forcing us to retreat further inside. I've dragged Arnold deep enough to where all around us—as the cloud of dust irritatingly tickling my throat settles—a floor-to-ceiling coconut white bookshelf says, 'Stay, read, and sip some dark roast coffee...*forever and ever.*' The shelving bows outward like the mainsail of a schooner tackled by the whirlwinds of a supercell thunderstorm.

David's library is a rare conglomerate of books in Sacramento green hardbound covers that mosey in the tens of thousands range. Ending an inch above the bottom of each book's spine is a crosshatch pattern of sleek black dots, gleaming faintly as if freshly painted on.

The rocks upon the locker entrance form a still wall momentarily. The actions happening on the other side of the wall start to gently topple the foremost stones with grueling anticipation for the reveal of a mole. I leave Arnold at an edge of the high bookshelf, sitting upright with no sign of life roaming the winter wasteland that's his eyes. Walking up to the breaking wall on the balls of my feet, I near my head to a copper sheet of metal at the root of some tremorous movement. The sheet belts my face and slumps on the floor. Tommy's head pops in through the hole behind it, perfectly crafted to include the fit of his wig.

"Meow," he murmurs unexpectedly, making me think it's time to retire these cat ears of mine shining like trillion brilliant cut diamonds by virtue of the library's telling white light.

Stupefied by his eyes, I might as well be in an inverted armlock. The electric green, radiant light emanating from his eyes, burn into mine. Though never blinding. Tommy's face retreats into the hole and a swirling collage of debris follows him out. Any significant barrier was emptied from the entrance hall of David's locker. A small ruin of ravaged clothes and a scattered trail of Arnold's blood sits tight, signing the path into this library.

Tommy peeks his head in before floating on by, bent on what I feel is our hellish demise. I continually stumble backwards till I can no longer fall back. I'm aside the disturbing visual of Arnold getting paler by the moment as he can't function or think to stop the blood loss in his right arm.

"Oh, how I've dreamt of this...since I was three," Tommy says winded as if pain suddenly struck him. As he approaches the last few steps toward me, he daintily lowers his feet to the ground. His eyes center on mine—at no time straying from them—till he's in my reach. I cautiously circle him at the center of the room as he stretches his fingers and then makes a gentle fist, one hand at a time, with his thumb wrapped across his fingers. His left hand is scabrous and lumpy whereas the fingernails are fine and sharpened like arrowheads. I position myself with my back purposely facing the entrance as I hold steady.

Make a run for it, even if it means leaving Arnold behind.

"For thirty-nine years, I believed you to be dead and for the past twenty-five, since leaving the otherworld, there'd been whispers you may still be out there. How Koata? How does one mysteriously vanish at the drop of a hat? You must've been taken, tortured even...for the knowledge your father passed on to you. But you weren't, were you? Here you stand perfectly fine. Say it's truly so!" he bawls snappishly.

"I'm only eighteen. One whole year I spent trapped in a kitchen," I say filled with gall, restraining with a head gate my urge to squawk, 'The sole reason I got booked in the first place is you!'

"You do seem quite young to be him but, I see him in you. The same face captured in photographs surfing mere days before disappearing. I pray you've a better explanation than I can muster, blessed father," he says longingly, turning to face me.

Tommy jumps at the chance to hug me. Before I can tip my head to the side in confusion, I'm cinched in this boy's arms, unable to stop squirming. "We must destroy magumga," he says delicately, releasing me with a sigh of disquiet. The look of torment in his eyes beclouds his overbearing thirst to meet me.

Arnold, suddenly cognizant, grabs a book from the bottom shelf. He attempts to knock out Tommy while his back's turned. His left hand rides the air forward with his grip on the spine of the book. Midway into the throw, the book holds onto him. A slimy thick teal secretion from the book's cover has sown itself to Arnold's palm, causing the book to dangle merrily from it.

Tommy nearly turns his head round when I grab the sides of his shoulders and half-wittedly submit to calling him—"Son!" His eyes flash and through the window of a child's imagination, I see a glint of hope—bootless hope. For what his eyes speak is a malady of the mind—the tooth fairy is real.

Baba is to the jaguars as I am to him.

Whatever I am to him, my response seems to have affirmed all his notions about me.

"I burned to embrace you the minute I saw you on the cliff but the jaguars—they're after me. Their drones have had their prying eyes on me ever since I escaped Neptune's penitentiary—Cabrini Dream Khayhím. When I found you, I couldn't let them think you had anything to do with what I'd done."

"How do you keeping finding me?" I ask hard-pressed.

"The face of your watch and compass are made from the lucid body of an aluxo-tez. Something that if you saw in person, you'd mistake for a species of snail. When ripped from its shell, its body slowly hardens, and its white spots dissipate. People tend to flatten the body, then use their fingers or small bursts of air to stretch it out into an assortment of shapes." Tommy rhythmically taps the bulbous case of my Gulixua watch with the lengthy fingernails of his left hand.

"For centuries aluxo-tezes were used as hardy glass in jewelry. Your father repurposed them as trackers. You see, I have three receivers here under my lapel—pearly orbs extracted from under the shell of three separate pregnant aluxo-tezes." He turns his greatcoat's lapel inside out flaunting Orion's belt against a dark yellowish-green cloud of ionized hydrogen.

Pinned to it, the aged blue hair pin fitted with three white pearls my sister wore on her wedding day. Or could it be a replica? "There you have it. Three fossilized eggs from an aluxo-tez. For the longest time I couldn't get a reaction—not one out of these cuties. That's until I came here to Neptune. Then, miraculously this middle one started to work. I've been hot on your tail ever since. The center egg must come from the exact aluxo-tez your watch and compass are made from because it's led me right to you. I can always teach you how it works later."

I never took the watch my father gave me to be anything more than a watch. But how else would Tommy have been at the cliff, in the bushes, and here now—at the same time as I—if not for a tracker? Of course, there's the possibility of coincidence. Or if not coincidence, some other reason I can't reason to smoke out right now.

"I couldn't protect you then, but I can now. This is our chance to get out," Tommy says with urgency.

"I can't leave Arnold here," I answer inimically, staring blatantly at Tommy's corroded left hand—a complete parity with crispy buttered bread. Except the bread's skin and the butter's acid.

"It's a fresh wound from when I attempted to take back magumga," he says in a fearsome whisper. "A deterrent was emplaced around it. An unquenchable blaze. Though it didn't dissuade me from trying to steal it again."

"Where is it!" Arnold cries petulantly, unable to hold his breath any longer.

"*What* is it?" I pine.

We naturally form a close triangle with our bodies facing each other based off Arnold's position on the ground. Tommy's gaze falls upon Arnold's absent hand, and he casually remarks, "Rough day, huh?"

"So, itching to find out what it is?" he swiftly shifts focus. "The strange fruit I stole from Felix after its prior guardian, Leto, was fired by Baba for biting it. It's now in the hands of Pilot Dice, who consecutively stole it from me using slick talk, approximately forty-eight hours ago when I returned here to rescue you...and to retrieve my Sir Isaac Newton wig.

Felix originally kept it in the communal showers' subbasement."

"The wig or the fruit?" Arnold asks stubbornly.

"The fruit."

"My premonition was right," Arnold whispers under his breath.

"It hasn't been in the subbasement for over a year because of organ traders like you," Tommy says, peering haughtily down at Arnold.

"Organs?!" I question agog.

"Yes, organs. You possess the brain," Tommy nods to the Abraxas Blue cradled in my palms. "Magumga resembles another organ but in fact, it's more akin to a fruit. I guarantee that fruit is the reason all these animals are currently going berserk. How they got out, I stand to reason. No one who's held onto magumga for more than a minute can resist squeezing from it its nutrients and absorbing them, either through skin like lotion or plain ingestion. I've firsthand experience with it and let me tell you, there's no getting by what that fruit wants and what magumga wants is to get inside you."

An odd shriek, as loud as a car horn, comes from the book holding tight to Arnold. Arnold's furiously ripping its pages with a fervent gnashing of the teeth. The book tremors and sings horribly to the tune of each tear. I instinctively attempt to stifle the noise from Tommy's ears with my palms. He isn't as surprised as I at the selfless gesture. I reset and worry about my own hearing as Tommy reasons to protect his own.

So close is the sound to the mating call of a greengrocer cicada—the autotuned conception of a wailing monkey and the rattling noise from an accelerating vehicle with dangerously low levels of transmission fluid. Arnold wraps the loose pages over his stump with his mouth to soak up the blood. He does this until there's enough paper encompassing the wound to resemble a maroon papier-mâché cast. His blood manages to dilute the words on each page, making them impossible to relay.

The booming wails die out as Arnold slams the book shut. Its heavy teal goo doesn't letup to free two birds of incommensurable feathers. For it to release him, Tommy informs Arnold he must return the baby xoder to the exact location on the bookshelf where he got it. As Arnold does this, the sticky teal substance recoils itself into the book cover like a hoisted mud turtle retreats into its shell. The slick sheer residue left on his palm, he squeamishly transfers onto his tuxedo jacket's left lapel.

"Feel better?" Tommy sneers at Arnold, ready to get a move on in explaining this *organ*. "I hate fruit and I devoured magumga like a panda guzzles bamboo. Impossible to resist. Felix is the only person known to have bypassed its possessive allure. The consumer who ingests it, like I, involuntarily gargles the juice in their throat, tastes around twenty-five exotic and plummy flavors I relate to the native plants of the Congo, before swallowing pandora's box. The box opens itself in about a day after its digested."

"*The organ is power*. That's the root of Baba's ability and yours!" Arnold accuses.

"Am I missing something?"

"Magumga. It translates to Triton in Saul Tails. The language mermaids use to communicate with other species who like us have developed speech," Arnold says, his face paper white.

"Triton's one of Neptune's fourteen moons. The jaguars imitate life in their hierarchy of fourteen classes which all house one organ fairly named after each one of Neptune's moons, given their keepers state of residence is a place called Neptune. A place that was once inhabited by mermaids after the great flood and abandoned after the basins sank," Tommy says, his voice sharpening.

"Magumga, or Triton, is the Caesar's organ. A golden fruit framed like a gallbladder. A week before you got here shit hit the fan when Newton here sprung up the theory there's a burglar amidst his class Mercury, after their inherited organ Despina disappeared." Arnold's tone hardens. "Despina's the form of a compass rose figured on the lid of a miniature wooden barrel, engulfed in a clear gel-like substance that retains the shape of a human heart. It leads its possessor to their heart's desire. Tommy believes it may be in the hands of a herald or group of heralds seeking the other classes' organs."

"Am I wrong? Only a jaguar from Mercury could've taken Despina. We're the only ones who knew of its whereabouts," Tommy says in a low voice.

"These organs were inherited from who?" I ask, locking eyes with Tommy, then Arnold.

"The founders," they echo cohesively.

"They've found us," I say aglow as I hear David shout from outside his locker, "My clothes! Christ's blood! Is that a burning ape?!"

The locker's subsequently occupied by David and three Celers armed with pure gold M16s, distinctly aimed at Tommy. Among them, Leto and the Celer who'd just been buried alive by Tommy, shrouded in soot. Before any combative phrases can be exchanged, Tommy manipulates the galore of books in the room to come hurtling at the Celers like shuriken. At the same time, David's body erupts into scraps of red meat that forgather in a beastly pile at his disembodied feet. Everyone alive in the room is bespattered in David's blood.

Thousands of books continue to spring from their shelves as one Celer's impounded in their pages and teal goo. One of his arms struggles to slip past a crack in the cluster. It moves in the open, in the same fashion Tommy wound his arm to manipulate the books, as though he were spinning a lasso in preparation to restrain a wild horse. A reversal of time sends every last book flying back onto their shelf. David's body's rebuilt like an arena housing a mosh pit for pink clay. His blood upon us—withdrawn. Under the vanished cluster of books is Leto gasping for breath.

His sphere's grown.

Irate, Tommy prepares to repeat his attack, raising his arm till Baba's voice derails his train of thought. All but the Celers and David seem to be aware of the transmission. David's cognitive functioning is on pause. He gives a shuddersome stare denoting zombie to the exposed ceiling of interlaced white duct work and yellow piping above. A thick stream of saliva waterfalls gracefully over his lower lip. His nose appears to be broken, his left shoulder's been dislocated high and aside his neck, and his right foot's been reattached to his body backwards. Unsettled, I listen to what Baba has to say. Meanwhile, the Celers scramble to retrieve their weapons scattered about the floor.

"I've been privileged to have served you as the twenty-sixth Caesar of the Jaguar branch. As you're all aware by the melody Zorian's sung, a new Caesar has been chosen to take my place. Effective immediately, Baba Mora will succeed my position as Caesar in this most unfortunate of circumstance. A word of caution—Koata Califf, as suspected when seen conniving with prisoner 1313 at the foot of the cliff on which he murdered his two friends, is not to be trusted."

"They're not dead!" I shout as if every jaguar would hear me and side with me. The nerve of him to single me out. A beef between us, created solely by his delusion.

The Celer covered in soot secures an M16 and immediately targets Tommy whilst staring at me. "Is it God? What's he saying?" he snaps, raising his chin and stretching his neck over his rifle.

With ease and neglect, Tommy spins a finger and the M16's snatched from the Celer and dropped into my hands. The Celer reaches for it, daunted but mindful about his next move.

"Now to address the man of the hour—Tommy. Welcome back to the home you've forsaken. As you attempt to finish what you started, I caution, you too be weary of the man you call father.

You were not created by love, but through an unspeakable horror. Though you do not yet know it, I empathize with the monstrosity you've become, for from a monster you're begot. May this be enough to redirect your anger and for what it's worth, I give you my blessing to satisfy whatever vengeance arises from it."

I'm shoved onto a school bus into what I fear is the unknown but get dropped off at a memory of my former self; what's old and raunchy. Except Tommy's beside me and Arnold lies on the wall ahead of me. In a garden lit by moonlight, an endless row of brilliant pink wind chimes, powerfully lit from their core, steal my interest, suspended on a high ledge above Arnold.

My heart starts to hammer. I dizzily follow Arnold's frightened gaze. Not far to the right, the cries of a woman grow increasingly desperate. She's pleading helplessly for the man plunging into her from behind her stripped body to stop. My stomach churns. Though her copious ugly tears aren't enough to screen her beauty and her swelling cries not enough to void her humanity, the man's blinded by his lust.

Tis only passion.

"You fucking slut! Who do you think you are?"

Specks of spit from the man douse her face. The woman attempts to fight back, striking the man forcibly in the gut with her knee, but because she's hopeless, it's hopeless. When she turns from him, the man tugs her by the braids like a dog on a leash and violently thrusts himself upon her, both landing on the ground. Her arms reach for a helping hand, but no one extends one. Another attempt to scream gets buried under the man's palm as he takes her from the back. Weak sobs barely escape her as I look behind me to trace the row of undergarments leading to a torn red dress.

Above it, among the many blue rose bushes and imported date-plum trees lie a massive crowd of jaguars. Hundreds stand there, staring in shock at the scene. A few try and turn their heads away, but curiosity snaps their neck back in place. Several twitch, abhorred but compose themselves long enough to see what I know—that it's me. Unlike me, they can't seem to look away, though their faces read contempt for a falsehood I know ends.

They know not what they see. What they're witnessing is an intimate moment, consensual between lovers, based on a kink. Before the curtain's pulled on an act I inspired with almost incredible fatuity, the scene ends, and I'm left looking like the culprit of what's socially improper in the eyes of truth and what's a violent and criminal act without context.

Chapter 30

I choke on stillborn words. How could I, a kite in the wind, possibly relay my innocence when even I as a misplaced bystander have seen what all else saw—an atrocity backed by grandiose evidence. I never imagined before today, until now, that I'd be seen by the world as a monster. So long as I'm here, I can't clear my name.

Who but Abeni can attest to our sex game?

I intend to escape into the otherworld for I doubt someone's bound to see me for me in this world. I'm perfectly capable of escape with Tommy's power—a battering ram fit to breach these castle walls.

"Silence speaks volumes. Silence is incriminating," Tommy says to me, his lower lip quivering superfluously.

The Celers stand still, calling for a picture of what was heard.

"Not heard. Seen," Arnold says disconsolately, rising to his feet. Arnold shuffles up next to me, places his chin on my shoulder and whispers in my ear, "He's gonna kill you. We need to go ASAP."

Tommy rises over us. The Celers blindly fire shots in his direction but the bullets freeze, then palpitate just below him. A handful of bullets that missed Tommy hit several of the books on the shelves behind him. One of the shelves gives in and collapses onto another bed of books. We dodge the falling books with those that sustained bullet wounds shooting a steady stream of teal goo into the air and belting their loudest train wreck.

The books' cries cause all men in the room to drop their guard in order to shield their ears, yet I cling steadfastly to the gold rifle entrusted to me by Tommy, summoning every ounce of willpower to resist the urge to release it and protect my own ears. Tommy's limbs contort in the air as he succumbs to an inverted spin. "Fiend!" he cries as Arnold butts his head against my back, hurriedly pushing me out of the locker. Arnold, unable to cover both ears, begins to bleed from the right, and I quickly sense my own eardrums nearing their pain threshold.

I accidentally nudge a fallen book aside as we press forward. It reacts, releasing streams of teal goo from its green skin, propelling the substance with remarkable accuracy towards us. Each droplet of the mysterious secretion appears to carry with it the uncanny ability to adhere to any surface with unparalleled strength, effectively ensnaring the gold rifle in my hands in its web of teal strands, glistening with moisture. Forced to abandon it, I grit my teeth in frustration, cursing the circumstances that robbed me of it. Yet I know, the focal point of my ire lies with the circumstance that stripped away my dignity, unveiling a facet of my being meant for veiled sanctity, not the world's probing gaze.

The cacophonous blast persists unabated. It's striking Arnold be the sensible one now after losing a hand whilst I weakly stumble in the direction I'm getting shunted. The only excuse for my sluggishness being a lack of self-worth. I feel less than that of a man. Visually stricken by what feels like the world deciding I'm something I'm not. Baba clicked 'share' on the jaguar wide web, taking my personal life for the cats to lay waste.

Arnold moves the stump from his right ear and points it towards the fire, shouting for me to snap out of it as we make it into the Lemon Room's main corridor. He forcefully clenches my tank at the chest with his left hand, glaring into me, making sure I understand. Letting go, he bolts for the exit, passing the three flaming crystal chandeliers having melted partway into the floor. It's not easy for me to keep up but I manage to do so for fear if I don't, my feet will get cemented into the ground. Pieces of the pale-yellow floor stick to the soles of my feet and singe the skin.

The biting pain wakes the athlete in me. My senses fully catch up to my speed once we're in the gray halls somewhere near the theater. Arnold stands by the grinning gargoyle materializing from a gray wall, catching his breath. I meet him at the statue. The only statue, from what I've seen, that's in these gray halls.

I now analyze the creature for the first time. Quite senseless. The same beady eyes of a bare-nosed wombat occupy its face with other, more unnerving features. Its grin overtakes half its face with a long, slim pointed nose alike a swordfish. Its horns are small and straight, peeking out of a disheveled bush atop its head. Long floppy ears alike a bloodhound's stretch down to its shoulders giving it a mild lightheartedness.

The creature's been sculpted so that intricate ripples on its long robes make it seem as though it's fighting a strong

UP STRAWBERRY VINE

wind. Its grand bat wings tear through the robes from its back, extended for flight. Only its upper torso is present, with its lower half lost in the wall. Its arms are extended horizontally at shoulder level, with palms that could wrap around my head facing outward, toward the observer. Its lengthy fingers are outstretched with fine nails that could slice open a pineapple. Its stance conveys a sense of urgency and authority, demanding the admirer freeze in place.

I remove the sparkling cat ears from my head and reach for the gargoyle's, ordaining it the new cat. It's a tad less threatening now but not a touch less farcical. In that moment, the epic theme music of a retro adventure videogame starts playing. Campy fighting sounds are weaved into the mix. "I know that sound."

I dash from the gargoyle, into a dark hall with all but a white light coming from a gaming device. The beam of light strikes the ground. Its sound gets distorted, emitting a tame buzz with small bursts of the prior theme music coming through by way of a DJ dragging the vinyl record of an animated score back and forth against the needle on their turntable. I cautiously approach it first with Arnold on my heels, getting submerged in a darkness quite nice. Such darkness reminds me of the nights I missed out on in my prison cell. The only escape into darkness was in closing my eyes or under the cover of that pink frilly apron with white polka dots. No one's around when I go to pick up the familiar gaming device, now quiet, squinting at its cracked screen and flickering light.

An icy bitterness sweeps my skin of its warmth.

"Be careful where you flash that light, lest you see shadows that belong to none," a man's voice cautions, dark and foreboding.

I shine the malfunctioning gaming device behind me, towards he who spoke. Aside Arnold is the second archer we'd lost in the blue grass. His mustard long sleeve plaid flannel and oversized lavender puffer vest have been run through the mill. He explains how he managed to catch up with us, wrestling a croc and getting rescued by a tall tweeting figure wielding a katana. Surely the same warthog who saved me. Though all he gathered at the time was that whoever rescued him didn't matter; he needed to get away.

Arnold and he had agreed the gargoyle statue would be where they'd meet should they split up, referring to it as an effigy of Totolinqua. This second archer introduces himself to me as Floki Stewter—Arnold's herald. "The false fire in the Dragon's Throat must've gone out, allowing the erehaha an easy way out." He describes erehaha as invisible, weightless creatures that bring the bite of the north with them wherever they go. They're drawn to hopelessness and despair, hence the prison's infestation.

"That fire be the only thing keeping them locked in with the prisoners," he says peeved, hovering his palm over the gaming device's dying light. "Erehaha are repulsed by fire. Everything about it. Its light, smell, and movement; no matter the size, keep erehaha at a wide berth."

"Well, they out now. So, can they cause harm?" Arnold asks, quivering slightly.

"An erehaha's shadow can but, their shadows can only be seen in rooms or corridors of pitch-black and in the direct presence of bright artificial light such as a camera's flash or a simple flashlight. Those unfortunate enough to encounter an erehaha's shadow...well, just look at Bo—Baba's personal taxidermist—alive but at the cost of his sanity."

"I thought Zorian's dad had mental problems stemming from his high exposure to inorganic mercury working in a factory below us," I recall stumped.

"That's what Baba told him. Many other Servus and Plebs work in the Extraction Plant, using mercury day in and day out to extract gold from ancient alien computer motherboards and hardware. None are mad like Bo."

"Never mind Bo," Arnold says pressed. "Magumga is still out there."

"I say we follow this hall to whoever was playing this videogame amid an animal takeover. Suspicious. Is it not?" Floki nods ahead, moving further into the hall before we can agree.

"What of my watch?" I look to Arnold frightened as we step to meet Floki's pace. "Tommy's been using it to track me."

Floki briskly turns to me and snatches my wrist, unstrapping the watch and nearly chucking it as I seize his wrist. I notify him of the watch's grander significance to me. Arnold mentions how leaving it here would do no good either way, seeing that once Tommy finds it, he'd know we discarded it specifically to lose him. Floki then suggests hiding it somewhere we could lure and entrap him.

"Hate to go back, but the prison do seem like the only viable option," Arnold admits stiffly.

As we move into the light from several spherical red paper lanterns hung on intersecting ropes above us, I recall Felix mentioning an organ in the vestry of Church Apple and suggest going there instead. Floki believes Felix likely spoke of the instrument and not of one of the fourteen organs named after each one of Neptune's moons. While more likely than not, I implore them to try Church Apple and deal with Tommy after we get a much needed power boost. The description of what Arnold and I saw happen to my herald in his hidden library makes Floki sick. Floki heeds my warning and begins pacing anxiously as he reconsiders.

Tommy did say Felix was entrusted by Baba to guard the organ, Triton. Or magumga as it's repeatedly been called. And while he no longer possesses that particular organ because Tommy stole it, and someone named Pilot was able to bamboozle him thereafter, it follows that if the Caesar—the highest, likely most respected class in this fraternity—trusted Felix, someone from a lower class would too.

Arnold agrees. Likely as relieved as me there's a side quest nulling his initial recommendation to go back to the prison straightaway. Floki hesitantly agrees but is dead set on me doing away with my watch regardless of my feelings on the matter. He returns my watch and pivots to Arnold's missing extremity in clear view, bandaged in the pages of that howling book. As the two talk over that horrific episode, I attend to an unimposing man creeping along the stone floor like a spider, frozen in place till I began moving toward him.

Nearing the man from behind, I observe small horns peeping from the top of his head. As I extend a foot toward the horned man's shoulder, he releases an eerie shriek like a military trumpet call suspended on a high note. I swivel on my heel to run the other way. His shrill wailing is held for several seconds. When I reach Arnold and Floki, the man's passed from sight beyond an extension of this hall.

Floki equips his bow and stands at the ready, fully aware and attentive to meet danger. To my left, my eyes catch the flutter of a tall hanging medieval tapestry depicting a joust without horses. Rather each knight rides atop different color variations of the snake-like Chinese dragon. Against it, an inconspicuous boy with brittle clothes partly melted to his skin is knelt trembling with an extended index finger on his lips. His body appears badly charred and the cool air from the importunate erehaha whisk chips of his skin and clothes away, disintegrating into dust as they twirl. The relaxing sounds of something in the distance clopping ahead sees Floki's arrow shift slightly to the left and shoot.

Another high energy, aggressive note emerges with the breakneck sounds of hooves against stone advancing. An ill-tempered elk appears, head forward with widely branching antlers and broad shoulders, running in graceful strides. Such hurtle does justice to highlight its aggressively muscular physique built for speed. I too prepare to engage the incoming threat by holding out the brain. The boy to our left lets out the cry of a demon and startled, the brain tumbles from my grasp. The elk fast approaching raises its head temporarily to do the same.

Arnold passes one of his arrows to Floki and he doesn't hesitate to use it. It cuts the air to meet the elk with vigor, matching its thirst for blood. I take the gaming device I'd kept on my waistband and slam it across my chest and open palm, halting its variable flickering. I strap my watch to it, get low and flick it across the stone floor into the darkness we left. Cautious not to look back, I gather the two in my open arms and tackle them onto a wall across the now silent still boy with near vacant eyes.

The elk, with an arrow lodged in its shoulder, narrowly avoids us as it dashes into the dark hall where a small beam of light now persists. Perhaps even more agitated, releasing a heavy grunt, the stressed animal employs an emergency brake, quickly turning back the way it ran.

"Should Tommy follow the tracker, he'll be welcomed by the company of an erehaha's shadow. Till then, I'd like to see if this animal is affected the same as man in the presence of their shadows," I speak to my actions atop of the two, getting shoved off as I do.

Another high pitched, demonic squeal escapes the blackened boy across from us. His head twitches temporarily like a bee's vibrating flight muscles. His eyes then widen far apart onto the sides of his head, bulging from their eye sockets and ditching their former light brown color for a coffee black. His nose caves into his face and from a sewn mouth extends an elongated muzzle with a newly formed broad, short, black and bumpy nose. All the while, long pointed antlers extend from his head, above rotating wide mule-like ears.

Forthwith, an arrow pierces his broadened neck just as tan fur began to cover his skin. Blood steadily squirts from the wound and streams down in between his broadened shoulders, seemingly stopping the transformation. Another arrow gets plunged into his forehead for good measure. The elk that missed us returns, having likely escaped the visual encounter with an erehaha's shadow despite my gimmick. It's drawn to the half human instead of us. Another species tends to its own just as it'd happened with the wolves, rats, tigers, and baboons. The elk intakes a short breath and struggles to swallow like a human on the verge of crying.

"Could it be all these freakish animal encounters are mutated men?" Arnold gulps, sickened.

"If so, there might just be some humanity left in them," Floki reckons. A few steps ahead, Floki guides us through a red door. At the foot of which is rooted one of those bulb-headed stick figurines composed of metal pipes. This one's multiple arms hang down, its legs are together, and its glass head is broken. Just as the door begins to close behind us, I notice the partial silhouette of an immense elk moping forward with a limp body pinched in its horns, carried off without any apparent weight. We hike up a moaning narrow staircase that twists around a circular steel blue bubbling pool with a delicate flow of steam pouring out.

"Tommy told us magumga's responsible for all these animals having a manic episode. But apart from their manic episode, magumga may also be a means to human transfiguration," I comment, nervously walking aside Arnold on the side with no railing, behind Floki.

"Magumga works through the people it entices to bite it. Baba Azul, as far as we know, was its first victim," Arnold notes.

"I'd say profiteer," I blurt.

"Leto was next, then Tommy, and now Pilot. All were presented with unique gifts. Mind reading and some form of control over the visual cortex that reshapes how we see the physical world," Arnold explains.

"Leto has the ability to reverse time," I share, having borne witness to it.

"Tommy appears to be telekinetic. I suppose Pilot can turn people into animals and make them go insane," Arnold concludes.

"The insane part might just be the natural aftereffect from getting turned into an animal," Floki interjects.

"Their reach and power level also differ," I add. "Zorian told me Baba, Leto, and Tommy are desert spoons. Named after a species of flowering plant with leaves that spread from the center of its apex in all directions. Their power too is meant to flow from their core in all directions till their individual limit is reached. He'd said Leto could only reverse time within arm's distance and within split seconds while Baba could reach anyone within Neptune and for an infinite amount of time. But in the library, Leto's sphere went beyond its presupposed limit."

At the height of the stairs lie scores of wooden boxes carved with anthropomorphic pigs playing medieval musical instruments. "Is there a plan?" I pester Floki. Floki proposes waiting a few hours, then heading back down to check if

Tommy's floating about aimlessly through the halls. He sits atop one of the large boxes and retrieves a black paper lettered in gold from an inside vest pocket. One of many scattered about the Honeycomb Lodge.

He rashly unfolds it, nearly tearing it and reads aloud, "Congratulations on one year and four days without offing yourself! Your perseverance has helped the Immortal Jaguars secure one part of a complex whole and brought you one step closer to proving your worth for consideration into our delightful fraternity." Floki temporarily raises his stare from the letter to give us a congratulatory clap before progressing. "For this second round of the Gauntlet, you must retrieve a feather from a mitotiqui, then make an offering to the monster above the health farm to receive directions on round three. Godspeed, Nihil!"

"Some game. Keeping me locked in prison," I speak confounded.

"Keeping *us* in prison," Arnold corrects me. "Every Nihil who arrived here the day you did had to endure the same."

"But…you knew it was a game?" I ask Arnold, puzzled and piqued at the thought he was prepared to sit in an experimental prison cell.

"This is Arnold's second go-around through the Gauntlet," Floki mentions, slightly uncanny.

"I failed the final round last time. So, I did what any brother of this fraternity would when confronted with failure. I got up and decided to do it all over again. I was chosen to go through this game because I'm special. We all are. I won't ever let failure define me."

"So, you know the rounds?"

"The Prefects change them each Gauntlet. Only they know the rounds beforehand. We find out what they entail as we progress through each with the help of our herald to guide us through." Arnold reveals, stepping across wooden boxes gaining in size till he sits on the highest, balanced by five larger ones below it. "However, being here the time that I've been, you pick up on trends, even if it's just through reading historical logs. Like the fact the rounds always center on providing an ingredient to the Immortal Jaguars' singular product—padda divinorum."

"The Gauntlet for all intents and purposes is part of a supply chain that uses Nihils as laborers to gather the resources needed to create and sell the drug padda divinorum to all other branches," Floki contributes, extending a foot to the decorative wood box ahead of him and tipping it over.

"How does a little over a year in solitude contribute to the supply chain?"

"Hard to say," Floki shrugs. "I'd have to look at the recipe for the drug and scroll through its endless list of ingredients to find which calls for such activity."

"I told Zorian I'd no interest in playing whatever game this is yet here I am over a year later," I share, feeling betrayed.

"You accepted your role as a Nihil in the Gauntlet the second you accepted the mochi leaf from Baba Azul," Arnold informs.

"I didn't know why I was being given a leaf at the time. Still don't know its significance."

"It's but tradition. The Caesar always gives a mochi leaf to those found worthy of taking on the Gauntlet. All mochi leaves vary in shape, size, and color for when a mochi tree sheds its mint green leaves each winter, all at once I might add, not one leaf is a copy of another. If you still got it, taste it," Arnold tempts.

"What's meant to happen?"

"It will aid you in letting down your defenses, making the journey into this world easier to swallow. It also prepares your body for the arrival of the Jaguar spirit, which will only come once your spirit's been broken," Arnold unfolds, staring off into space.

"To inhabit the Jaguar spirit is just a motto given to those in the act of overcoming adversity despite their weakest point. Who's to say if the mochi leaf actually yields this strength or if it's always been instinctual to those chosen for this game. I'm partially biased in that I've seen what I believe to be the Jaguar spirit through a glint of purple fire in the eyes of men who've given up all hope, only to rise like a phoenix thereafter. Of course, we all have different pain thresholds and what destroys us we'll only ever know in the moment." Floki skims the black letter in his hands, whispering to himself, "A mitotiqui eh."

"What's a mitotiqui?" I make my way to Floki to read the shimmering gold words over his shoulder.

"Death by a thousand cuts!" Arnold laughs from up high. "You dropped this by the way," he announces, holding out the blue brain in his left palm. "Don't stress ya unbridled libertine. I'll keep it safe from here on out."

"About that," I begin, disgruntled. "That wasn't the thing it was made out to look like."

"Rape." Floki's plainspoken. "Frankly, I don't know what that was about or why Baba would even put us in that state of confusion and unease. I didn't see the face of either party, but I guess I wasn't the intended audience anyhow."

"You ain't gotta explain yourself to me bud," Arnold says with a sternness in his tone. "That's with you and your god."

I tense up. "At least my god's real. Where the fuck is your god now?!" I gravitate my anger towards Floki.

"The new sheriff in town is Baba Mora," he speaks calmly, unphased by my outburst. "Although, I suppose your gripe is with Baba Azul. I suspect he'd be done packing his bags by now, over at the Wolf's Den, leaving this mess to a new order."

I don't doubt I'm lucky in finding the likely only two people in Neptune who don't feel disgust or have murder in their eyes in my presence. But I can't help but be angry at them. They know so much about this world that I'm blind to. They seem more or less unstirred. Arnold lost a fucking hand, and he seems perfectly sane now.

Should I? I wonder, pulling the mochi leaf from my Union Flag swim trunks' only pocket. A home it's made on my right butt cheek. The leaf adopts a look of seduction. I forcefully shove the pickle green leaf in my mouth and grind it with eager teeth. I swallow what tastes like cotton candy and accept the claim, this leaf will calm me. Placebo or not. "I is maikaì."

Chapter 31

With time no longer an item of concern, being that I'd lost so much already, I spent the next few weeks accomplishing a little bit of something. On the intricately carved wooden boxes with pig musicians, we'd lingered. As Arnold and I spoke of his plan for coping with life with one hand, Floki began picking at a section of the wall behind him. Within this small area, patches of light gray paint peeled away, revealing the bare beige brick underneath. The brick had gradually eroded over time with cracks meandering across its surface. An edge of the brick appeared as if the slightest touch could collapse it whole. I imagined it retrograde to its initial state of sand and fly ash.

With a mischievous smile and a tone of flirtation, Arnold suggested a true friend would help him release some steam, up until his left hand evened off to the strength and speed of his right. Likely unaware of that section of the wall's weakened state, Floki continued poking the exposed brick. Each poke was characterized by an impulsive and insistent motion, as if seeking a reaction from the inanimate brick to alleviate his boredom. He unexpectedly met minimal resistance as it completely caved in. He paused momentarily, as he tried processing the visual aftermath of the accidental breach and what lay beyond. A disturbing and unsettling cacophony of tiny bodies scraping and skittering against one another, confined in a tight space.

The rapid chorus of tiny clicks and footfalls enveloped our space. We were ambushed by scorpions with orange gold bodies and pale yellow legs as full of adrenaline to stab us as we had to get away. We managed to outrun them, catapulting ourselves off the ledge into the circular steel blue bubbling pool. As a naturally adept swimmer, I led the way blindly through the water. Prior to our jump, Floki had cried of an exit on the other side. With a fatal dose of venom on our asses, I would've attempted to run through a brick wall.

There was indeed an exit or two. The bubbles continued all the way through a linear path that remained level until reaching a sharp uphill rise. Up above, the path split in two. We rose from one of two identical pools releasing steam on the left side of the health farm. There'd been a hint of heat throughout our swim but not enough to produce steam despite its presence. We sat on the edge of the oval pool, our lower bodies enwrapped in the inexplicable steam. Flustered, Arnold revealed his quiver, which he'd strung along his back from the jump, had come loose in the water.

Floki volunteered to retrieve it. He ditched the extra weight, stripping down to his white briefs with a pattern of fan-shaped blue leaves before forward diving into the pool. While we waited, Arnold slid from his tux, leaving only his baby pink briefs with gray skulls and white and maroon gladiolus on his body. His platinum blond hair no longer resembled a skater helmet, but its matte finish shine could still be seen from up close.

A brief examination revealed that the fiery red of my sunburn had noticeably subsided. The once angry hues now

UP STRAWBERRY VINE

whispered a softer palette of relief. Perplexed, I wondered whether the alchemy of the bubbling water held an unspoken remedy, a subtle balm that seemed to cradle my skin in a soothing embrace. The impressions on my left forearm, indicative of my incessant biting, had similarly diminished.

It was a probable two minutes before Floki's hands chaotically reached for the surface. Concerned, I assisted in pulling him out. He was unable to retrieve Arnold's quiver. He stormed off towards the Dome of the Plebeian, bitterly telling us to forget about it. His words drifted off in the distance, "Not like you can use it now anyhow!"

When I peeked my head over the pool, through the bubbles and steam, a freshwater crocodile could be seen with its image wavering as if a mirage in the desert, leisurely cruising by in the deep. We later discussed the probability this crocodile was near the surface of the identical pool we didn't exit from. It must've dove where we'd just swam, missing us by who knows how short of a timespan.

Arnold neglected his bow. Henceforth, he only traveled with the blue brain. Floki still had a few arrows in his back quiver though some undoubtedly floated away underwater. His bow, he gripped tightly in his right hand, with his left hand ready to reach back and retrieve what little ammo remained. I ended up tearing my red tank top on the side, tying it in such a way it was converted into a bag. I suggested we use it to carry the organs should we find more.

It was eerily silent in the Dome of the Plebeian, but we were cautious not to be the ones to make it not so. We straddled the border between the Olympic white stone columns and tall blue grass until we arrived at a hefty solid oak door, adjacent to the Honeycomb Lodge's towering glass door. Upon pushing the door open, we approached an expansive area of rough-hewn stone where a king might hold court. More traditional of a dining hall in a gothic castle with long tables made of dark, polished wood set with fine silverware, turquoise crystal goblets, and silver gilt plates embellished with the emblem of a top hat at their center.

The one feature, not traditional of a gothic castle, was a soaring ceiling managing the harmonious balance between the imaginative and the organic. It had fractal patterns one might see in nature but through the lens of psychedelics with a kaleidoscopic swirl of hues, ranging from electric blues and purples to fiery oranges and neon greens. Amidst the dream-like display, delicate vines adorned with colorful blossoms and tropical plants with verdant tendrils cascaded down like the decorated long braids of enticing and seductive stage dancers at an electronic music festival. Some areas of the ceiling were so engrossed in hanging plants, a lush, vibrant canopy weaved through the spectrum overhead. There could be more light, but the interplay of what light was available from the few flamboyant tracery windows with intricately sculpted flowing ribs and the shadows they permitted added invaluable depth and dimension.

It was here in this chamber that another surreal bombardment of hostility had arisen. Some of the brothers had been staggering at the far end of the dining hall where a massive staircase of polished marble stretched, reflecting the cool glow of lit mint green orbs barred in the jaws of sculpted jaguar heads at each end of sheen black spiral lamp posts. One was present at both ends of every few steps. I felt their invitation to explore the upper realms of Neptune might be a ruse to forever get lost.

All brothers were badly burnt with distorted black textiles, in parts shiny, uneven, or hardened as had been with the one we'd just witness partly transform into an elk. One of elfin proportions seemed to waltz to an invisible tune, with an invisible partner atop one of the long dining room tables. Another's gait was unsteady and unpredictable with small bursts of energy in which he'd zoom forward and then stop, haphazardly swaying from side to side at each break. Floki reached for an arrow and equipped it to his bow, using three fingers to steadily pull the bow's drawstring back towards his face. The bowstring resonated with a low, taut hum just on the threshold of human hearing. Even so, this was enough to draw attention to us.

In that moment, all disoriented brothers lifted their heads to the sound. And before the sharp, twanging sound of the bow's string snapping forward could flourish, they began sprinting towards us. The arrow accelerated through the air with a high-pitched whistle, attempting a kill, but to no avail, knocking a tall centerpiece of thick steel coil jammed with blue hydrangeas and nearly black sweet potato vines. The uncoordinated brothers leapt over tables and chairs, their arms flailing erratically, leaving behind a trail of destruction and disarray. The meticulously arranged cutlery went flying across the room with crystal goblets shattering about the floor and silver gilt plates sent crashing on the walls.

We hectically exited the way we came. Thus, we were forced to scour Neptune for a haven out of sight of the many wild beasts and those on the brink of becoming ones who day by day grew to be more vicious. The bodies of fallen jaguars littered the castle grounds and blood soaked were the once gray halls underground, beyond the Lemon Room. A few brothers we'd seen lying about outside the theater had their heads crushed like a tangerine, with juice and mush becoming of a round burst, expanding outward in all directions like dispersed fireworks. I could only imagine it was a gorilla who effortlessly extracted the juice from its victims' heads by crushing, pressing, or grinding them against the gray walls.

Leonid had once mentioned that anything less than seven hundred men in Neptune would be bad luck. I can't imagine how much worse this fraternity's luck can get. This Pilot furtively moving through Neptune without any fruitful resistance has yet to discriminate in picking prey. His homicidal rampage through use of his creations is either a hefty price for the wrongs of this fraternity as a whole, an act without conscious volition, or a course apropos of nothing.

I knew I had to escape this void of decay and allowing for reflection on days of suspenseful quiet and false security, whether I'd risk so without assistance was starting to sound more compelling. In essence, the likeliness of escape lies only in the strength of my conviction. I will ram through varied obstacles and leave with my sanity intact, ignoring those who may cry out for help. Those Pilot feels just in pronouncing judgement on.

In the days we spent at the theater, we'd gathered comfortable costumes from backstage to put on, befriended three Nihils, and recounted our time in Neptune's prison. Arnold and I dressed ourselves in loose-fitting black tunics and comfy white sneakers with black laces. Floki had found an oversized, airy mint green tank top, stretchy charcoal gray trousers, and beige suede loafers his size to put on. Both Arnold and Floki decided to freeball, pitching their underwear at some mannequin heads. I, on the other hand, found a substitute for underwear with some black cotton shorts. They could also be used for pajamas if I ever found the desire to sleep again. I'd finally rid myself of David's tacky Union Flag swim trunks.

Aleko, Boris, and Culbert were found hiding amongst the many mannequins backstage. They were dressed similarly enough to ones whose wardrobe made little sense. Had they not opted to declare their presence, they would've gone unnoticed. After a few minutes of us rummaging through more clothes and props for a genuine bag that would replace my shitty construction, they made their introduction when Aleko pushed a mannequin into Floki. The other two gently stepped out from behind the mannequins providing them cover.

They'd clearly been ducking as the three were tall, emanating a powerful presence with their sturdy and athletic appearance. Aleko's brown eyes were relatively small, creating a captivating contrast to his large hairstyle. His voluminous hair was brown and curly but not nearly as curly as Boris' whose free-flowing black curls must've been prompted by a perm or curl-enhancing shampoo. His abundant tight curls framed his square face almost entirely up to his chin. His sharp facial features gave off an impression of fearlessness and the ability to slice butter.

Culbert's hair was blond and close to the scalp. His warm smile wasn't enough to distract someone from the irregular bumps and contours on his outer ears, as well as his slightly misshapen nose with a noticeable deviation from its natural alignment, possibly from a combat sport such as boxing. All three seemed to have garnered pieces of the costumes at hand to concoct their own ensemble of artistic expression. Aleko wore a white t-shirt with short sleeves that just barely covered his shoulders, layered with a slanted lavender spaghetti strap tank top. His caramel brown shorts had the grid-like pattern of a waffle cone and his white sneakers bore the chaotic illusion of blue paint splatters.

Boris' short sleeved black and white checkered shirt was open down the middle. Its pattern of squares had a slight wave to them. His holographic shorts had a crocodile skin print, and his cotton candy shoes had a nebula tie dye design. The most eye-catching piece was Culbert's hot pink sequined jacket whose numerous small, reflective discs added a touch of magic in playing with the light. The rest of his outfit lacked inspiration, consisting of a plain white t-shirt, sandy-hued shorts, beige running shoes, and hot orange calf socks.

Proceeding the initial surprise of them lurking backstage, Arnold coolly approached Boris. "What kind of shirt is that?"

"No idea." Boris studied his shirt, considering what was so special about it.

"If that's an off-brand, that's my shit." Arnold playfully guided Boris to turn so he could glance at the tag on the back of his checkered shirt. Intrigue was written over his face though the brand name was unspoken. "I'm right there with you man," he muttered, spinning Boris back around.

The ABC squad met one another the same day I arrived in Neptune. The day all Nihils arrived in Neptune. What a day it was that I missed out on, disconnected from my own and thinking I was isolated in my fish out of water experience. Arnold had chosen not to consort with the newbies that day having already been through Neptune's long and dull introduction once before. All who entered Neptune for the first time were funneled in through the front entrance, greeted by a fucking mascot of all things, by the name of 'Dapper Paws.'

Aleko described it as a walking stuffed animal, featuring a plush, black fur coat with a glossy sheen, mimicking the coat of a real jaguar. The costume's cartoonish jaguar head was fit with a mini white top hat. Its piercing yellow eyes were programmed to emit a soft, glowing illumination thanks to some embedded lights. Complete with a hidden mechanism that triggered an automated growling sound from the jaguar's mouth every time it'd raise both paws. Up until then, I believed the way I came into this castle was its main entrance.

This was no minor detail. I was purposefully kept from everyone else because of my erratic behavior on the cliff and Tommy's watchful eye over me. Every other Nihil got to enjoy their last meal together in that dining hall with wild colors and copious plants on the ceiling. Miraculously, each was served their choice of food from an infinite menu. About two hundred meals had been prepped for their arrival.

These newcomers were herded from across the world and unlike I, they came here intentionally. They were each approached at an opportune time in the day when they'd be alone. Most times, the men who'd been slated to become their herald would be who they'd meet. The men from Mercury offered these seemingly average males the chance to partake in a game of gripping adventure which if successfully completed, would grant them entrance to an exclusive brotherhood out of this world. They were lured with the angst of never getting an opportunity like this again; one whose reward was said to bottle the secret to immortal life.

One day was given to decide. Should they choose to play the game, all that was required was crushing an old, rusted copper coin engraved with the image of a mermaid on one side and strange writing, unlike any known language, on the other. These coins were provided by the heralds to potential players during their first meeting. With the coin crushed, its enchantment is activated, setting in motion a sequence of events that guide the person towards the coin's place of origin—Neptune. Anyone avoiding the act of physically destroying the coin would find that within a day the coin had vanished, back into the hands of the herald who'd offered it.

"I don't think anyone knows what makes those rusted coins work," Floki admitted in a concealed whisper. "It's true. Once you've been to Neptune, anyone who takes a coin with them to the otherworld will find that if the coin is lost or given to someone who fails to crush it within a day, the coin will always return to the one who took it from Neptune in the first place."

What united us all in being chosen, Floki revealed, was our remarkable disregard for human suffering. At this point, I'd flipped through the pages of my life and bared in mind the sad reality of my depravity. I've seen women battered, children abused, and rioters pummeling an innocent man to death, and I didn't do anything. We were chosen due to our lack of action throughout our lives when confronted by what we knew to be wrong. With year eighteen being the cutoff for when we can be approached to make a decision.

This, Floki explained, is due to the jaguars' belief we can't be shaped to the extent we need to be for their use as adults for once we've reached adulthood our worldview, personality, goals, values, and motivations are typically set in stone. The jaguars still have the opportunity to dig their claws into us, to help in defining our authentic selves while we're still kites in the wind, easily guided any which way the wind is stronger. In our adolescence, we've less autonomy than we realize due to our inexperience in life's failures and successes.

How the Immortal Jaguars know of our inaction in the face of injustice is through a relic of Mercury. The brothers of this class have various responsibilities. Along with guiding those who accept the proposal to play in the Gauntlet, a part of their recruiting duties is to identify candidates by capturing their essence. We are given one last chance to back out from the Gauntlet after accepting the first proposal, which comes when the Caesar himself personally offers each candidate a mochi leaf as a final bid.

By then, the Caesar himself has seen each candidate's profile which consists of a synopsis on where that individual is presently in their life and a photograph. This photograph doesn't necessarily have to capture the entire subject. Just enough to distinguish their face as in a passport photo. More importantly, the photograph reveals that person's nature to do good when no one is watching or encouraging them to.

The photograph is instantly developed from a supernatural camera. This, the aforementioned relic. A multi-colored aura will appear behind the subject with the predominant colors typically consisting of either lilac or burgundy. If the subject has no lilac in their aura, they are a perfect match for the Immortal Jaguars regardless of what other colors comprise the aura. If the subject has over a quarter of lilac in their aura, they're not a match. Lilac represents our goodwill while burgundy could be anything from evil to a lack of emotion, cleanliness, or vitality. Someone whose aura is exclusively burgundy is typically associated with being a sociopath.

When Culbert expressed his desire to see his photograph, Floki explicitly stated such a thing is strictly forbidden and punishable by death. Specifically, getting flayed alive. Whoever wrote into this fraternity's laws the extreme punishment for something so inconsequential must be shrouded in burgundy. If the Immortal Jaguars primarily seek the imperfect, the untruth of me being a rapist shouldn't come as much of a shock to them.

While Floki agrees the lot of Nihils here are the scum of the earth, the Gauntlet is meant to absolve us of our sins, and we're meant to leave better men than we arrived. Then again, not everyone survives the Gauntlet or is fortunate enough to leave Neptune alive. Floki confesses, it makes it easier when Nihils die in one of the four rounds knowing they weren't the gentlest of souls.

The prospect of death is not one unveiled until the Gauntlet is already in progression. At which point, a Nihil has already relinquished their right to back out. A devious trickery not done on a whim. It's necessitated to meet the manning requirements set in place by the Censor class. Impressively, the Immortal Jaguars have approximately five hundred thousand within their ranks throughout the otherworld. With the Gauntlet taking place once about every one thousand years and about two hundred participants each go-around, I don't see how their population has grown to be so large and managed to maintain its numbers. The math doesn't add up.

It also begs the question, how is this Arnold's second run through the Gauntlet? Arnold dismisses my question, claiming it's not as complex an answer as I may think it is, but it's an answer I'll have to discover on my own. Or with our new friends if I so choose.

As everyone got better acquainted, I walked the stage and peeked out the burgundy stage curtains. There was a gorilla striding gracefully at the theater's front entrance with a remarkable blend of power and finesse. Its coarse, silver-tipped fur glistened under the soft glow of fire at the tip of the thin black candlesticks that stood in the tall golden candelabras' many nozzles. Each powerful muscle moved with purpose as it confidently advanced on its knuckles towards the back row of red velvet padded seats. A muted thud could be heard as each knuckle pressed into the soft earth. I warned the group of its presence, but Floki strongly advised against approaching the sole beast with deep regard for its unpredictable nature. Arnold joined me to see what I was seeing. He gulped, then found a quiet corner to relax with deep breathing exercises.

Aleko pulled out a deck of cards, suggesting we quietly play a game to pass the time. He taught us how to play Castle, where the objective is to be the first player to empty their hand by playing cards onto a central tableau, matching the previously played card in rank or suit. Aleko won the first round, the second, the third, and so forth. It was a fast-paced game so each round only lasted about ten minutes as those of us who weren't familiar with the game quickly got the gist of it. I'd gotten up between rounds to check if the gorilla was still making its rounds.

To make the game more interesting, Aleko ultimately bowed out and set the prize. The winner of the final round would decide the teams of two for the next game of Spades. With Aleko taking himself out of the game, Floki won. He strategically partnered himself with Aleko and stuck me with Culbert. Boris got placed with Arnold. Though, with Arnold uninterested in the game, Boris retired from playing cards and joined him in some meditation. It was in these duos which we'd stay when we unanimously decided it'd be wise to patrol the area and secure this hideout. It was a whole day before the gorilla dipped.

Patrols became a good way to gather weapons and scope out any significant threats. It became apparent from my first patrol with Culbert that there was no longer any order to this fraternity. Not due to perpetual assaults, but rather due to the apparent abandonment of this place, devoid of leadership. The only beings we'd encounter and hide from were the diverse animals and strange burnt men on the brink of becoming ones. We were both confident we weren't ready to pick a fight with either. Fortunately, such a scenario never materialized. After our second patrol, it seemed as though the majority of animals and burnt men had been summoned to their creator, leaving only a handful to wander the deserted grounds, lost and forsaken.

Between what all of us had collected, we had a discarded grenade without its pin pulled, a few short blades, a golden rifle without ammo, and a light throwing axe. Arnold and Boris had reported my watch was still where we'd left it, strapped to the lit gaming device but Tommy was nowhere to be found. It was too risky to retrieve it with a few elk still roaming nearby. Nevertheless, I appreciated the gesture as it hadn't yet crossed my mind to go back.

Days later, Floki and Aleko found Tommy's olive green greatcoat and Sir Isaac Newton wig laid outside David's locker and brought it back to the theater. They reasoned from Arnold and I's recollection of that day, the Celers were able to capture him after we'd run. Culbert, on the other hand, put forth the idea Tommy escaped. "What's to say he didn't slip from his greatcoat? A Celer could've easily been gripping onto the back of it and lost his grip in a subsequent fight. And Tommy could've lost his wig as a Celer reached out for anything to detain him and snatched it." This was certainly a possibility but to quell my nerves, I placed my faith in the first.

On my eighth patrol with Culbert, I'd asked him about his experience in Neptune's prison. He was uninterested in this line of questioning. Instead, he offered his theories on the brothers of this fraternity turning into animals as a result of something in the air and that perhaps this whole situation was one of the Gauntlet rounds conjured up by the Prefects to test our ability to thrive in the fog of war. He discarded the second theory after I revealed what Arnold and Floki had told me about the rounds always centering on providing an ingredient for the makeup of the drug padda divinorum. Culbert found it funny so much of this fraternity's focus is in producing this one drug. It couldn't be what gives them the Immortal part of their name as all it did for me was make me hallucinate. We grew still, anticipating a beast neighboring the edges of the dome. Our watch became silent once more.

Atop the Wolf's Den, we'd laid on our bellies, our bodies pressed against the rough surface of the concrete rooftop. By then, we'd manage to keep our breaths slow and deliberate, synchronized like a well-rehearsed symphony, anytime we'd sense the subtlest disturbance nearby. The vast expanse of tall blue grass below was a sanctuary for whatever dangers lurked within. Our eyes, sharpened from each patrol, scanned the sea of grass below for the faintest hint of movement.

During our fourth patrol, which extended over what must have been several days within the confines of the dome, we discovered that nightfall never descends upon Neptune. In spite of time slipping like sand through fingers, the sun remained oddly fixed in the exact same position beyond the glass enclosure. Consequently, I realized, the faint beam of light that streamed into my cell through the small window, coinciding with the wind that would blow it open, could not truly be attributed to the sun. Nevertheless, I couldn't shake the strong sense that someone, perhaps an angel, was overseeing me, casting a semblance of daylight to preserve my sanity as I was able to track the passage of time through their simple act. Confirmed by the black letter Floki picked up, giving us our congratulations on one year and four days.

As our nerves tingling with anticipation became less severe, we melted back into casual conversation. Culbert revealed exposure to the drug was a prerequisite to entering Neptune. Before the ever-flowing greenery that nearly swallowed the castle whole, lay a vast courtyard where giant, exquisite jaguar idols of shimmering black stone dug their way from beneath the earth; their ferocious faces frozen in time. Their sleek bodies adorned with intricate patterns of a bygone era gave breath to legends and lore, and their piercing stone eyes imbued the courtyard with an air of the violence to come.

From all walks of life, hundreds gathered around the courtyard. There were lush gardens with vibrant blooms at the borders, their colors a stark contrast to the weathered stone of the castle, briefly seen through winds shifting vines and the rampant crowns of trees swaying up high. Fragrant blossoms filled the air with a sweet aroma, and the sound of chirping birds added a melody to the scene, making it feel like a hidden oasis. This fresh fragrance, however, was a thin layer vaguely masking the stench of something putrid. "You could see it in the faces of most, something was off. But, for whatever reason, we remained ignorant," Culbert said in hushed tones, lost in concentration, with his eyes scouring the tall blue grass below.

"While some admired the jaguar statues, others lounged on stone benches, savoring the peaceful ambiance. Laughter and animated conversations filled the air as we visitors marveled at Neptune's facade, a tangible link to a rich and storied past, with anticipation for the great adventure on which we were sold." I lost interest in this patrol and became engulfed in Culbert's retelling, shifting my body to face the blue skies beyond the sheen of the glass dome.

The dozen or so men who'd led the blind on the long hike up to Neptune were unremarkable and soft spoken, often passing word like a game of telephone. They wore tanks and shorts, a light, airy shade of cream, cool grays, or earthy greens, with beige boots, seamlessly blending with the semi-bleak foliage. Most of the vibrant leaves on the way up had fallen, leaving trees with barren branches that stretched toward a gray, overcast sky. The boundary where the last vestiges of bleakness intermingled with the burgeoning greenery surrounding Neptune was at first sight of the castle itself, still a ways away.

The guides slyly retreated within moments of their arrival as all newcomers awaited direction. It was some time that'd passed before things spiraled. An ominous shift occurred as the boys bathed in the fragile beams of sunlight that shone through breaks in the cloud cover. From the skies above, a surreal and nightmarish transformation unfolded. Suddenly, a massive, billowing cloud of vivid purple smoke descended upon the courtyard with an unsettling swiftness. It spiraled and twirled. An otherworldly tempest of color and chaos. Gasps of surprise and fear filled the air as the cloud enveloped the previously serene space.

Those unfortunate enough to be caught in the initial wave of the purple fog found themselves choking and gasping for breath. The sour, unfamiliar scent invaded their lungs, causing coughs and wheezes. Panic spread like wildfire, and boys stumbled, disoriented and blinded by the thick smoke. Amid the chaos, some individuals succumbed to the mysterious substance, collapsing to the ground, spasming violently. Their faces bore expressions of shock and helplessness. It was as if the very air had turned against them, rendering them helpless victims of an enigmatic threat.

Through the disorienting haze of the purple cloud, something even more sinister became apparent. Emerging from the depths of the smoke were multiple white drone quadcopters, their rotors whirring ominously as they hovered in the air. These silent, mechanical intruders seemed to be the source of the malevolent purple fog. Each quadcopter was equipped with a payload of the strange substance, and from their aerial vantage point, they methodically sprayed it over the courtyard below. Their presence added an eerie and surreal element to the unfolding nightmare as their bright white exteriors contrasted starkly with the chaos and confusion on the ground. As the purple fog thickened and the drones continued their relentless aerial assault, it became increasingly clear that the situation had taken a dire turn.

The panic and fear that once rippled through the courtyard turned to ire and reared its ugly head upon those who could still breathe, struggling to find safety and shelter from the suffocating haze. In the blink of an eye, the once idyllic courtyard had transformed into a nightmarish scene. A battleground between the enigmatic purple fog, the terrified lost souls within, and those whose inner demons were turned inside out. The drone quadcopters, like malevolent specters in the sky, finished their swift, silent assault. Despite their retreat, followed by the steady exit of the purple fog, the courtyard remained shrouded in uncertainty and dread as horrific wails could be heard throughout.

It was a bloodbath, fractionally less obscured now. It would only be moments before those who weren't already partaking in the senseless violence would join the masses. A sense of profound dread hung heavy in Culbert's heart. There came a fleeting moment of surreal quiet before danger exploded upon him with a sudden and ferocious intensity.

He'd briskly turned to face his first attacker, emerging from the haze like a malevolent phantom. The crazed boy, fueled by pure madness, leapt over Culbert, knocking him onto the ground. He attempted to gauge Culbert's eyes out with his thumbs, but Culbert gripped the boy's wrists, pulling them apart. The attacker then gripped onto Culbert's long blond hair, using its length against him by twirling it tight around his fists to repeatedly slam Culbert's head on the ground. It was clear whatever had made its way inside him had shattered his sanity.

His attacker's eyes glowed with a haunting, otherworldly luminescence. It was as Culbert's head was being slammed on the ground that he saw his attacker's face was no longer human. Its skin seemed to ripple and writhe as if it were a liquid. He'd thought if he pretended to be dead, this ethereal presence bearing down upon him with its malevolent gaze would vanish. It did momentarily but for the fact that another attacker bit into the distorted waters of the first attacker's face. Their heads became one, as the second attacker's face was swallowed whole by the first's. Two bodies extended from it. It crawled on all eights towards a frantic and desperate Culbert, inching backwards as fast as he could on his hands and feet.

By then, the full scope of the bloodbath was out for all to see, no longer restricted to sound alone. Culbert was pulled to his feet by a stranger he'd later befriend and know to be Boris. Unaware at the time that he'd succumb to padda divinorum's effects, he'd seen Boris as an angel with iridescent wings that unfurled like a magnificent tapestry of white light. Together, they beat their fists into the creature and twisted and stomped on its limbs till the sound of bones cracking was pronounced. The thing's watery face began to run red till its movement completely stopped and its liquid head was soaked up by the ground.

Culbert saw many boys strewn about the courtyard, paralyzed in all but their eyes which held a mischievous twinkle as they followed the slaughter fest, suggesting something gleeful danced in their depths. They fought valiantly for a time. But, as another attacker fell, Culbert turned to commend Boris' skill in combat only to meet Boris' hand as it gripped onto his neck. Choking the life out of him, Boris' vengeful gaze matched those of the others. This symbol of grace and protection had been twisted into something malevolent.

As Boris' grip tightened, Culbert felt the suffocating pressure. His airway constricting and hands failing to pull Boris' hand off him. Boris' wings unfurled with a dreadful rustle, and with a powerful and unnatural force, he began to ascend, taking Culbert with him. As the world around him shrank away, the twisted illusions of the nightmarish dreamscape faded into obscurity.

Next thing he knew, he was lying on the courtyard aside Boris, their bodies drenched in a blood rain. As his groggy eyes adjusted to the light, he stood up first. Initially, a jolt of fear shot through him, and his heart raced as he recoiled in surprise, recognizing the face of his strangler. Treading on caution, he noticed Boris lacked wings, and kicked him awake, reasoning the bloodied boy was no threat.

Ahead of Neptune's magnificent entryway, a long line of bruised survivors knelt in the presence of a blue-bearded man in a pristine white top hat and long wine purple robe with a shoulder cape. The man walked down the line carrying a hefty red spiral notebook in his open hands. With a frolicsome spirit, he picked leaves from his notebook and offered them to each knelt survivor whose heads then rose to meet the man's milk-white eyes. They extended their tongues out as though they were ready to receive the body of Christ in Holy Communion. Instead, each received a distinct leaf on their tongues.

Culbert felt compelled to follow Boris' lead as Boris joined the end of the line and knelt, awaiting the gift of a leaf. Culbert knelt, dazed, and looked upon the great dark wood doors with a pointed arch, softened by a delicate layer of seafoam green moss. The doors' handles and hinges were equally impressive. Made of glistening brass, they were shaped like stylized fish with crooked human faces and long tails that curled around as if in perpetual motion.

When the man, revealed to be none other than Baba Azul, reared his head over Culbert, he spoke without moving his lips. His words Culbert heard in his head, and he responded by nodding, taking the leaf in his mouth and leisurely chewing. Baba had asked him something along the lines of, "Now that you've had a taste of the inevitable brutality to come, will you accept this bid to play in the Gauntlet?"

"So, it wasn't trickery after all. You knew the prospect of death was high before ever stepping foot in Neptune," I said, my voice sharper and body tense, facing Culbert. Culbert acknowledged this was so and I confronted him, irritated that Floki acted as though that was not the case. That instead, the fraternity hid their welcome approach to death pending acceptance of the final bid. It was a half-truth. Culbert expounded upon many of them not even remembering the extent of that ordeal within hours of entering Neptune with those that did chalking it up to hallucinations from the smoke.

When asked if the bruises were not real enough, I was told they were gone. Upon entering Neptune, you transition from the outside world into a subterranean sanctuary with a dimly lit passageway, leading to a great waterfall. It descends gracefully from a lofty, moss-covered rock formation that seems to defy gravity; its source shrouded in a gentle mist that adds an ethereal quality to the scene. The water itself is a steel blue, almost artificial in its intensity, shimmering with a serene dove-gray hue as it tumbles effortlessly down a series of tiered bubbling pools and rocky outcrops.

Surrounding the waterfall, there're lush greenery thrives with vibrant ferns, delicate orchids, and other exotic flora. As you walk through the delicate mist at its base, you feel a gentle, rejuvenating energy suffuse your being. Wounds, whether physical or emotional, seem to mend and fade away, leaving you with a profound sense of renewal and well-being. The air within this hall is infused with a delicate, herbal scent, reminiscent of ancient healing rituals. Kept for an hour at the foot of the waterfall, while Baba Azul spoke of activities planned for the winter festival of Samhain, Culbert and all others were restored with their tranquil state of mind likely triggered by the mochi leaf they were given outside and reenergized by the mist of the waterfall inside.

Just beyond the waterfall awaited some levity in the introduction of Dapper Paws. Moments like so would become surreal for within these castle walls lingers an ever-present palpable darkness. Walls from which secrets and sorrows seem to seep into every nook and cranny, foreboding truth come to light. I wasn't privy to this heavy shroud then. How I wasn't is quite absurd in retrospect. I should've known better the minute that ominous scent, thick with toxicity, reached my senses on that tiny island.

Culbert wouldn't know what'd happened to the dead left in the courtyard till he'd met Aleko in the dining hall for their last meal. Aleko, who'd claim a seat beside Boris and Culbert, claimed to have seen what lay beyond the lush gardens at the borders of the courtyard, having walked through them moments before the purple fog descended. A cold sweat formed on Aleko's trembling skin as he saw a horror that defied all reason in a place so stunning. Rotting corpses, too many to count. They assumed this is where the dead were hauled. The truth of the prevailing stench outside being decaying flesh evoked in me feelings of disgust and anger.

"Are we so desensitized to evil that their gruesome deaths and callous disposal of their bodies mean nothing?!"

"We wouldn't be here if we were good men, would we? We made it through the door because we all have an uncanny affinity for bad choices, consistently gravitating toward the darker paths in life. Here I am hoping this fraternity will steer us on the right track," Culbert said, his voice wavering, tinged with a desperate attempt at optimism.

His herald was good to him, letting him know why he was chosen of all men prior to Floki detailing the Immortal Jaguars' approach to pinpointing candidates with a snapshot.

None from the ABC squad have seen their heralds since escaping prison but Culbert hopes to sometime soon, owing his motivation to the expert skill of his herald to inspire others. He ignited a fire within him, reminding him that excellence is attainable through perseverance and unwavering effort, showing sincere care for his success. They had talked through the difficulties in moving forward, with his herald gently guiding him through the labyrinth of what'd just happened, helping to unravel the tangled thread of Culbert's complex emotions like a seasoned therapist.

The mochi leaf undoubtedly helped ease his elevated cortisol levels. Prior to chewing the cotton candy depressant, his heightened feelings of tension and anxiety had reached a record highpoint. Still, of all the things to come out traumatized by in the courtyard bloodbath, for Culbert it was his long hair getting powerfully yanked by his first attacker and then becoming a cruel tether to the strange being. The first thing Culbert asked his herald when they were reunited at the dining hall, the first time since meeting in the otherworld, was for access to hair clippers and a warm shower.

His herald provided him reassurance that such requests would be of no concern. However, before proceeding further, it was imperative for him to select a place for repose upon clearing his plate, signifying his ultimate slumber within the castle walls. This decision, akin to the presentation of a sumptuous tiramisu with a dollop of lightly sweetened whipped cream, garnished with shavings of cocoa powder and paired with a limoncello, would symbolize his final indulgence. These basic needs, essential for survival in the otherworld, were not subject to worry or reliance in Neptune.

Chapter 32

Culbert discerned a subtle disturbance in the atmosphere, an intangible whisper that beckoned his attention. As our gaze converged, an enigmatic congregation of golden particles materialized, delicately suspended above one of the Olympic white stone columns, akin to ethereal confetti celebrating an unseen spectacle. Simultaneously, sounds that could not be shrugged off as wind captivated us—an amalgamation of deep and resonant tones coupled with speed, pervading with a clandestine dialogue. One voice resonated with a profound depth, a timbre that reverberated with an authoritative weight, evoking a sense of unwavering command. The other voice was rough and raspy emanating from a throat you'd think had been weathered by time or cigarettes.

We'd thought the Wolf's Den was empty, taking the word of Floki and Aleko who'd explored it yesterday and said they'd found nothing of value inside. Sensibly, we opted to descend the way we ascended, navigating through the understated gray bricks adorning the periphery of the cottage. As we did, I gazed upward, mesmerized by the swirling golden flakes. A clicking, rasping sound echoed from the same direction. "K-k-keh-rrrru." It sent a shiver down my spine, yet no visible threat lurked in sight.

Upon reaching the base, Culbert, equipped with the light throwing axe discovered by Floki days prior, deftly shattered one of the Wolf's Den's windows. The subsequent silence that enveloped the interior hinted at the presence of concealed secrets, leaving an unspoken apprehension lingering in the air from either side of the shattered window. Nevertheless, we overcame the hesitation on our end with a final nod of assurance pushing us to climb on through for the chance help or answers may be found.

Culbert, with a puzzled expression, remarked about the unusual sight of closed windows, as we'd been accustomed to them being left open throughout our patrols. A detail we both neglected upon arriving at the dome. With curiosity propelling us forward, the white lace curtains delicately rubbed against us. We skillfully avoided knocking over the turquoise metal pails housing vibrant cactus plants on the windowsill. All it took was a gentle push for the pots to sway, allowing passage without a clatter.

Inside, we stepped onto a rough burlap coffee sack, squeezing from it coffee beans whose distinct aroma hit us before the sound of their gentle patter, reminiscent of a miniature rain shower, made its splash about the wood floor. "Have you come to finish me off?" croaked a deep and ailing voice, hailing from Baba's office.

Following the haunting trail of groans, we entered the office where the atmosphere was charged with unexpected tension. Culbert pointed out the imposing expressions of the mounted animal heads which I'd surprisingly missed before. Even the sight of the usually serene giraffe in the wild bore an angry countenance, as if poised to pounce, challenging my preconceptions about their typical demeanor and ability to craft a mean expression.

Our attention was drawn to the ailing groans once more emanating from a man sitting on the floor in a torn wine purple robe draped elegantly over his body, its regal hue echoing the richness of aged Merlot. The tears in his shoulder cape suggested the remnants of a daring escapade through thorny thickets. Against the side of the sleek white desk with a transparent top, he rested, his face noticeably swollen, purple and scratched by the likely struggle against an attack. His suffering was palpable as he clutched the side of his stomach, keeping inside his body whatever organs could fall from such a deep gash.

I met his true eyes for the first time, a deep brown with little warmth left to discover. Had his beard not been blue, I wouldn't know the man to be Baba himself. Having never seen the old man's hair, a classic side part with the white strands neatly combed to the left, I was captivated by its grace and complete lack of gray hues or silver. Culbert knelt in front of Baba and drew the axe to his throat as Baba's deep groans dissipated. "Who was just here?" he asked brusquely.

Just then Boris and Arnold entered the office with a purposeful stride through the arched passageway. Culbert's eyes widened in surprise, caught off guard by their abrupt appearance, considering their designated duty was patrolling the three churches below.

"Ah, another one of yous wanting me dead. Kindly grant me the tranquility of solitude in my final moments, and I promise not to disturb the peace or what little remains round these parts," Baba responded dully. Arnold notified Baba peace was out of the question as we needed answers. "This may after all be our last chance to get them," I expressed, nodding in agreement with the intimidation tactic Culbert was using.

"We wish to know of magumga's whereabouts," Arnold professed, hoping that in finding the organ we may stomp out the origin of chaos.

Baba, with a resigned demeanor, uttered, "I can't help," lifting one arm and tugging on his robe, gracefully revealing beneath it an intricate array of metallic bands, one clung tenaciously to each limb. Their chromatic oscillation, transitioning from fuchsia to powder blue, was an all too familiar sight. With measured articulation, he elucidated that these bands were a confining constraint, impeding the unfettered utilization of his power. However, he noted, while they prevent a desert spoon from using their power, they may also be used by the powerless. The bands negate the effects of a desert spoon's power if that power's imposed on the wearer.

He further elaborated that the Celers were given the pro-gravy vambraces and greaves to have a fighting chance at taking out Tommy whose control over gravity ceases to function when employed against a Celer by virtue of adorning the bands. Boris questioned Baba about how he came to possess the bands. Baba revealed it was Leto who'd manage to force them upon him with the full backing of his fellow Celers to tie him down.

"Leto's always been untrusting of others but not untrustworthy. His demonstrated reliability, commitment to our principles, and track record of responsibility within this brotherhood is what led me to place magumga under his watch. He did bite it after being told it would kill him. He clearly caught onto the lie, yielding to its cerebral allure, unable to resist the urge to take a bite. What a complete letdown," Baba said disappointed, questioning the initial trust he had placed on Leto. "Still, something I should've foreseen. Magumga was only meant to leave my sight for a few weeks due to a pressing obligation elsewhere. I opted for a pragmatic solution, thinking I'd ensure its security with Leto while I attended to the unforeseen circumstance of a colossal feline infiltrating our premises."

"The mitotiqui," Arnold murmured softly.

"You couldn't just lock it away somewhere?" Boris inquired discreetly, a cautious expression playing upon his face.

"Certainty not. These organs, coveted by malevolent entities, require vigilant oversight. Locking them away just wouldn't suffice; a daily check is imperative to safeguard against the persistent threat they attract even if their purpose remains enigmatic to most," Baba responded affirmatively, his bruised visage revealing an undertone of anguish.

"Given that you're cooperating, I suppose there's no need for me to keep this at your throat," Culbert uttered, gradually withdrawing and standing back against a wall, caught between the intimidating gazelle head mount and the formidable hippo, both sporting furrowed, scowling countenances of aggression.

"After many years extracting gold from the computing systems in the Extraction Plant, we began crafting different materials from the color-shifting metals typically discarded of. It was Leto who found their use in preventing his power when wandering about places he had no business in as a

Celer. With sufficient time and analysis, he found if enough of the metallic material was gathered, contacting his skin, his power would be rendered inactive." Baba rested his head against the desk to face the high ceiling. A gradual dimming of light in his eyes accompanied his words, conveying a sense of weariness and diminishing vitality.

"With the background of a blacksmith in the civilian world, he also found that its functionality depended on its orientation in relation to the body with the composition of four bands he'd crafted above the wrists and ankles working best. When he came to me with this discovery, donning what I presumed to be ostentatious jewelry, I was already weary as I was unable to read him. I let my anger cloud my reason and ordered him to dispose of it. After magumga was stolen from Felix by Tommy, and Tommy threatened our brotherhood, this material suddenly became more than just pretty colors. It became a strategy to resist that gravity-controlling maniac. It's why Leto and I dubbed the fashioned vambraces and greaves 'pro-gravy' as a nod to our affinity for gravity, particularly considering Tommy's effortless ability to manipulate and deactivate it. Every Celer was compelled to don the bands in order to overcome our brother turned adversary."

Tommy has different motives from Leto for betraying the fraternity. Leto's came after he discovered Baba had been poisoning him. Baba pointed out of the office, ordering Boris to fetch a black loaf of bread on a mint green coffee table. Boris obliged having brought the peculiar loaf, robust and compact with its hue impossibly dark, defying the conventional spectrum of typical burnt bread tones.

In hushed tones, Baba said, "Consuming Pan de Monio shall diminish a desert spoon's power by decreasing their sphere of influence. Leto, resenting the teeth-staining effect, resorted to nibbling it with inward-turned lips to discreetly swallow it, though his lips still bore the marks. I, in passing, advised him that partaking would enhance his focus amid numerous projects—a fabrication, of course. And something I knew he struggled with. David, though not the intended audience, was outside my office at the time, overheard my fictitious tale and, desiring to enhance his focus, gave the bread a try. To my surprise, he developed a fondness for it, consistently requesting I bake more."

"That's Koata's herald, isn't it," Arnold uttered straightforwardly.

"Yes. It's who we saw get blown up by Tommy. It offers me no solace knowing the immense gravitational force that boy can exert on a person. And Leto, his ability to reverse the books falling upon us and getting David back to one piece, while not entirely adhering to anatomical precision, must mean he stopped eating the *Pan de Monio*," I spoke, making an effort to articulate the name of the bread correctly.

All four of us realized why Baba was telling us this. This bread could not only help us with weakening Tommy but also Pilot who's the primary suspect in what's causing the turning of jaguars. Baba further mentioned, although he couldn't pinpoint the current whereabouts of magumga, the most recent known location he'd gathered from reading Pilot's mind was within the Lemon Room, specifically inside his locker 718. Arnold suggested we might benefit from releasing Baba from the bands. Baba declared that idea's futility, asserting that only a specific transponder held the electronic components to liberate him from these chains and anyhow, they wouldn't accompany him into the hereafter.

While Boris did bring up the idea of employing the same bands to restrain Tommy and Pilot from using their powers, the practicality proved daunting. Additionally, the acquisition of these bands remained a mystery, with Baba offering minimal insight, deferring the details to be obtained from a Celer and distancing himself from the responsibility. All he'd previously mentioned was Leto had crafted the prototype from the strange metals composing whatever computers lie in the Extraction Plant.

Baba appeared to have exhausted his words, each breath becoming heavier and more infrequent. Urgency prevailing, I proposed an immediate departure, recognizing the pressing nature of time. While my inclination was to delve into unanswered questions, particularly regarding Baba's animosity towards me, the possibility of magumga's relocation loomed large, prompting a decisive choice to act swiftly before it vanished from Pilot's locker.

Nevertheless, my proposal went unheard by the majority. Culbert was the sole voice strongly concurring, while the others treated my words with dismissive indifference. "You're just going to lay here and die? I thought all jaguars were immortal. Isn't that what was promised? The whole point of us being here?" Boris questioned Baba with a touch of annoyance. With a voice filled with poignant ache, Baba responded, "The key to immortality unfolds before you, nestled within the embrace of death. To attain it, you must confront your paralyzing fear of death, surmounting it through the sacrifice of your corporeal form, refusing to heed to the fragility of mortal existence. Ascend beyond the fleeting breath of life, traversing into realms where immortality takes its strides. Find redemption in the kingdom of I, where even the most wicked heart discovers solace." Baba's eyes never strayed from the ceiling through his highfalutin rant.

Culbert remarked thoughtfully to himself, suggesting that according to Baba's response, the key to immortality might simply align with the teachings about the afterlife in various religions. Arnold then chimed, "Immortality is woven into the art and wars we leave behind." If either of those conclusions are the secret to immortality, immortality is the world's worst-kept secret. I harbor a slight sympathy for those enticed here by the allure of a reward promising them immortal life. One they'd likely assumed would not come by the sword or via the exceedingly rare and nearly unattainable fame they could achieve through an artistic endeavor.

Frustrated, I urged the room to expedite our exit once more, a sentiment seconded by Culbert. In that moment, an imperceptible presence traversed through me, the sensation absent but visually discernable. A tall tan figure emerged into the office, sporting chin-length, sun-kissed curls and the sides of what I could see was a caramel blond beard. His attire was suitable for a man of considerable build, donning a loose-fitting, cotton shirt in a soothing shade of forest green with vertical white stripes, well-fitted khaki trousers and leather loafers.

I only caught his large profile from the back as he spoke, his voice resonating with a reflective, thoughtful tone and a distinctive, throaty quality. "I'll tag along," Ramze affirmed.

Chapter 33

Culbert and I found ourselves alone in the Caesar's office. The uncanny transmission had ended, and the anger etched on the facial expressions of all animal head mounts dissipated, as if we collectively emerged from a dream where all was not right. We were both taken aback by the unexpected revelation we'd seamlessly transitioned into the past. And yet, for me, the comforting and heartwarming sight of my friend eclipsed this momentary daze. It was the assurance that Ramze, with his unmistakable presence—albeit I only saw him from behind—was safe and sound.

I proceeded to recount to Culbert the instance of when Baba first replayed a memory of my girlfriend and me at a wedding reception. In this recollection, open to everyone but those donning color-shifting bands, the lights casting a brilliant pink glow upon our bodies were, in reality, a vivid shade of blue. I suppose that's one method to distinguish when Baba's showing us the past. If one is a subject in the memory he's replaying or is familiar with the location being presented, they may be able to discern the fine changes in his transmissions.

We'd just seen Baba dying and now he was gone with only a small pool of blood where he'd lied. The Pan de Monio brought in by Boris was also gone. We agreed we heard two distinct voices with one being Baba's before he was able to play the transmission and deter us from finding him. Therefore, someone removed the bands from him and managed to transport his body to wherever he wanted his ultimate resting place to be, allowing him to pass away in quietude.

Yet not without revealing one last memory. The motive behind sharing that memory remains elusive; was it merely to dissuade us from disturbing him as we approached his office, or does a deeper purpose lie within? How long ago did Arnold, Boris, and Ramze converging in this exact spot take place?

Culbert surmised that Baba's final wish was for us to enter Pilot's locker, where he had directed Arnold and Boris—possibly leading them on a fruitless quest. The likelihood of it being a trap cast a strong shadow of doubt over whether we should follow in their steps. It struck me that Arnold and Boris had been absent for a few days, not entirely unusual but peculiar that they wouldn't at least stop by the theater and wait for us to report their findings after having conversed with the ailing ex-leader of this fraternity. Furthermore, this location had been inspected just yesterday by Aleko and Floki, yet it seems their patrol had been less than thorough, evident in their oversight of this pool of blood in Baba's office.

We couldn't jump to conclusions. One of them may have had the same thought I did about being pressed for time. Given the significant risk it could be a trap or the likelihood magumga had already been obtained by Arnold, Boris, and Ramze, or moved elsewhere, we opted to head back to the theater and establish communication with Aleko and Floki.

Regrettably, the theater remained deserted, and after enduring what felt like an excruciating three-day wait, we recognized the need to take action. Equipping myself with a short blade from the amassed gear, meant for defense, and Culbert continuing to opt for his lightweight throwing axe, we embarked towards our sole lead—locker 718.

During what I estimate to be the three days we spent anxiously awaiting the arrival of the others in and around the theater, a time that left me feeling somewhat futile, I managed to establish a higher level of trust with Culbert. He finally opened up about his prison experience, a revelation that kept eluding me every time I'd previously asked. Culbert even requested switching patrol buddies at one point because I wouldn't stop badgering him about it.

The narratives of the others had already unfolded over the many card games we'd indulge in to alleviate the passage of time. All were in agreement my account took the cake for most disturbed. Although it was never a competition. At the end of the day, we were all betrayed by one of the jaguars leading us astray.

Arnold was confined in a pistachio ice cream tiled bathroom with him having to endure the perpetual aroma of heavily-scented cleaning products, causing him a never-ending headache. At least for the 369 days until our release. His whimsical entrance into his prison cell came in squeezing through a bathroom mirror, a metal surface from the outside, stepping over the bathroom sink and onto its countertop. Devoid of any reflective properties, it served merely as an aesthetic illusion before the locking mechanism transformed it into something to be regarded with fear, aptly establishing his new residence.

Then there was Boris, his cell resembling an old timey suburban living room, adorned with bamboo furniture, seating occupied by tough olive cushions, linoleum flooring, and gray drapes concealing murals of what the outside might've looked like from a white picket fenced home in the suburbs, instead of windows. He came upon his entrapment by naively stepping through an oil painting of dogs playing poker. Lucky for him, his prison cell featured a vintage boxy television set, offering him a monochromatic glimpse into the prison cells of twelve others. He never discovered how to work the volume with the only constant sound emanating from the television set being a tame buzzing like the gentle hum of distant bees on a warm summer's day.

Boris described both entertaining and haunting scenes from flipping channels, including a prisoner frozen at a corner of their cell through the unbroken continuum of days, only knowing the television wasn't malfunctioning by checking the other channels and noticing the eerie prisoner's strange propensity to tilt his head ever so slightly towards the hidden camera, almost as if he knew someone was there on the other side watching.

Another prisoner he'd stalked chose an unfortunate exit mere days before we were to be released, demonstrating ingenuity through his use of a bulb and a lamp shade in an uncommon and unsettling manner. There was one he'd said looked like an academic who'd painfully removed his fingernails with workshop tools found in the outdated garage housing a budget two-door muscle car dominating most of the cell's space. The guy's nails never grew back, and Boris often observed him trying to soothe the pain he'd brought upon himself by placing the whole of his fingers in his mouth, reminiscent of a toddler without a pacifier.

The amusing scenes Boris spoke about included an inmate engaging in impromptu talent shows, mastering the art of juggling with the limited objects at his disposal, learning to backflip through self-instruction, and achieving a split after months of funny strained faces and persistent effort. Another had a record player but no records to play, a wooden bunk bed with iconic monster movie posters on the walls and different sports memorabilia displayed on a wood dresser, including an autographed baseball mitt. That inmate found paint in his cell's closet, deciding to transform the room into a vibrant masterpiece which Boris discerned through the dynamic interplay of tones.

He gleefully splashed paint everywhere in random bursts of uninhibited creativity. When he got tired of aimlessly painting the walls, he painted his body. Overcome with enthusiasm he'd often be found jumping on the top bunk bed, leaving lively traces of color in his wake. The richness of the composition transcended the limitations of the screen, evoking a sense of vividness the monochromatic display simply couldn't capture in full.

Over the months, as the chaos unfolded, the seemingly chaotic splatters gradually morphed into an intentional creation. The boy turned the walls, floor, and ceiling into an exquisite canvas, transforming the room into a breathtaking depiction of Hong Kong's skyline from different perspectives.

I only wish the jaguars had given me paint as a substitute for my cellmate—a perfectly preserved corpse.

In unlocking my guarded past within the confinements of our conversation at the theater, Culbert found a parallel narrative buried within his own history. We shared a somber melody of missed opportunities to do good and how at some point in the otherworld, we each played a silent witness to injustice. After I recounted the haunting echoes of nameless battered women in Lagos, Nigeria, each whimper a testament to my own perceived powerlessness, Culbert felt enough of a kinship with me to be able to speak to his time in prison.

Culbert served as a catalyst for my healing simply by listening. The weight of their suffering pressed upon me like never before, releasing this silent burden I'd carried throughout the years. After a few fruitful days of surfing with my father along the coastline of southwestern Nigeria, we'd returned to our hotel in the city center of Lagos.

January 10, 2003.

The walls in our room were adorned with two intricately woven tapestries, featuring vibrant hues of indigo, ochre, and emerald green. One depicted a dancer with a snake over her shoulders and the other had a tribal elder, lion and tortoise sitting together, roasting apples, bananas, peaches and pineapples over a bonfire. There were a few hand-carved dark wood masks with elongated faces, slanted eyes, and robust lips over our twin beds, adorned with plush throw pillows and blankets of burnt orange and deep red.

ALBERTO BONILLA

Out on the balcony, the air was alive with the aroma of spicy street food. Notes of cumin, coriander, and chili mingled with the tang of saltwater from the nearby ocean. The city skyline was composed of uninspired tall, blocky gray buildings and a riot of colorful tin-roofed houses below them. As my father slept soundly, I quietly stole away to the balcony, craving the crisp night air and the chance to vicariously revel in the hustle and bustle of the nocturnal cityscape one last time before our flight at dawn.

In the dimly lit alleyway below us, shadows danced with malice and desperation prowled like a hungry beast. My satiated belly, courtesy of the hearty tomato stew from dinner, settled contentedly on the balcony floor. My face slowly pressed against the cold steel railings as I found myself unwittingly thrust into the sinister theater of human cruelty.

It was a moonless night, when the air began to carry more than its earlier scents of comfort. The air grew thick with decay and despair, when the first chilling cries shattered the silence. Women, their voices a symphony of anguish, pleaded for mercy like wilting flowers under a scorching sun, their voices frail, as they became unwitting pawns in a vicious game of power and dominance.

The perpetrators, partly shrouded in darkness, wore a mix of military garb, thigh-high olive or beige robes, and what a criminal might don to execute a holdup. Clad in weathered camouflage uniforms, some of their faces were obscured by ominous black ski masks, turbans, or hijab with even less adorning Kevlar vests and helmets. All were armed with gleaming black firearms and knives that looked to have been dipped in oil, their presence casting an eerie, slick silhouette under the faint illumination of streetlamps.

This foreboding group, driven by a twisted sense of entitlement, inflicted their wrath upon the defenseless. They managed to exert control through violence, aiming their weapons at the women, forcing them to strip with their blows raining down upon those who were defiant or tried to run. The women's bodies were no match for the brutality unleashed upon them.

This marked the second time I'd ever laid eyes upon the female body like so. Both times were tainted by sadness. This was the first time I'd seen so many at once. Within one minute, their naked bodies bore the physical scars of their torment, and with the only true scream coming from that first encounter, taken by surprise, their voices turned to whimpers. And they remained whimpers throughout the duration of the assault. Spirits broken and voices silenced by fear.

As a child, no older than eight, I lay frozen on the balcony. My heart pounded in my chest, a dagger to my soul, with each hip thrust of a man with their pants at their ankles, on top of a woman. Yet I remained rooted to that spot, paralyzed by uncertainty, thinking that in my silence, I'd helped perpetuate a cycle of violence against women. I did nothing to help them.

Within two minutes, the women's bodies lay inert, reminiscent of discarded puppets, as they were violated. Within three minutes, the masked men had swiftly executed their agenda, shrouding the women's faces with black sacks before transporting them to an unknown destination around a street corner. The distant rumble of engines signaled their departure, leaving behind a tense silence that engulfed the desolate alleyway within five minutes from when I'd walked out onto the balcony, as if the events had never transpired.

Despite his perturbation, Culbert sought to provide solace by rationalizing that realistically, there were a few viable courses of action available in that circumstance beyond seeking assistance from an adult, emphasizing the challenge of responding to criminal behavior in a foreign country and being so young that I was physically incapable of interfering without suffering a beating or getting killed for trying. It was at this moment Culbert invited me to sit with him at the edge of the stage. Looking into the darkened theater with somber rows of red velvet padded seats, desolate and untouched, he reflected upon round one of the Gauntlet.

Culbert's cell mirrored an office setting with its entrance disguised as an empty bookshelf from the inside. Polished chrome accents adorned the desk and light fixtures, echoing the sleek design prevalent in mid-century modern aesthetics. The wallpaper showcased geometric patterns inspired by scientific diagrams and imminent dreams of space exploration. His only form of entertainment, apart from a few standard office supplies, was a yellow retro-inspired rotary phone resting on the desk.

Culbert fell into the habit of persistently turning the rotary dial, each rotation a stark reminder of his solitude, until one fortuitous combination successfully connected him to a static-laden droid voice. The chilling voice, void of warmth, posed the odd question, "Are there cockroaches in heaven?" before abruptly ending the call. Despite his attempts to redial, the exact number eluded him, slipping away into the recesses of his memory.

Culbert would doodle every now and again on the wallpaper with his highlighters and office pens till one day he blankly picked up the office scissors and allowed the cold metal to glide through the wallpaper, revealing a haunting sight beneath. The concrete wall he'd unveiled bore unsettling marks, as if desperate fingers had clawed relentlessly, etching a silent plea for escape into the unforgiving stone. Amidst the myriad scratches, the phrase "I EXIST" stood out in thick, crimson letters, as though they were forcefully splattered by a hand drenched in blood. Perhaps prompted by a sense of desperation and fading clarity. He knew his cell had been revamped and assumed this was not the first time it'd been polished up with a new skin.

He'd looked to his clenched hand, gripping the closed scissors, and noticed his knuckles turn a bluish hue from the intensity of his tight grasp. With an almost robotic precision, he directed them towards his forearm, cutting vertically from his wrist up. Upon the first sight of blood, he promptly utilized multiple sheets of loose-leaf paper to envelop the wound, employing cheap adhesive tape methodically to secure the paper and staunch the bleeding.

Culbert shed his hot pink sequined jacket as he told me this, unveiling the formidable wound of dried blood, with no signs of scarring. Similar to mine in size except his marked his left forearm. "I wasn't trying to die. I needed to confirm

I was alive," he said with a solemn tone, slipping his jacket back on over his shoulders. He hesitated to divulge this to the others, apprehensive about the potential ridicule he might receive. His concerns that sharing it might label him as vulnerable or lacking in mental fortitude are not unfounded as one can never be too careful around strangers.

He bore the weight of this lesson. A poor farmer's boy from Kentucky, he'd struggled to make friends in school. His parents encouraged him to participate in his church's after school program, a school club or athletic team to enhance his social skills and broaden his interactions. So, he joined both his high school's wrestling and basketball teams, perfectly meshing with the latter due to his towering stature. However, wrestling presented a greater challenge as he found himself consistently matched against opponents in the heaviest weight class with skills surpassing his own, requiring him to exert extra effort in training than he needed to for basketball.

Participation in sports failed to foster connections for him; instead, he faced relentless bullying due to his height, awkward demeanor, and academic struggles. Despite hopeful glimpses of friendship, such as an invitation to a basketball team sleepover, his trust was shattered when it devolved into a night full of merciless torment. The team had coerced him into chugging a tub of lard, teasing him with three of the boys holding him down and another holding a large kitchen knife up to his neck. When he couldn't stomach another sip of the rancid lard, thick with a nauseating greasiness and a putrid odor comparable to a neglected sewer, the boys brandished a pistol, threateningly swinging it over his head before brutally pummeling him to the ground. Their cruel taunts and laughter echoed in the air as he lay there, battered and helpless, enduring the pain inflicted upon him with no other choice.

They eventually stopped when he vomited and coughed up blood, choosing to abandon him outside the house where the supposed sleepover was to occur. Though in truth, there was never any such gathering planned. Instead, all the boys returned home including the sleepover host, leaving him broken and alone on the ground. But not before issuing a menacing warning. With a cruel gesture, he lifted Culbert's scraped chin from the concrete using the tip of his steel toe boot. "You better not be outside my house come morning boy, or else you know dang well what's fixin' to happen." As Culbert glanced up, he caught sight of a boot hurtling towards himself, and instinctively flinched, bracing himself for the inevitable impact and the ensuing onslaught of pain.

Culbert drifted into unconsciousness for several hours, awakening to find a few of his teeth on the ground and his new pajamas, purchased by his mother with what little money they had for the nonexistent sleepover, eager to think he was finally making some friends, soiled and torn by his own vomit and blood. Choosing to bear his pain in solitude, he trudged miles back to his home, nursing both physical and emotional wounds with a blank expression, feeling rather hopeless and empty inside. He lost consciousness unwittingly while making his way, near a cornfield on the side of the road, battling to maintain awareness amidst his injuries.

ALBERTO BONILLA

It was nothing short of a miracle that he managed to make it back home. Stripping down to his underwear, he discarded his clothes in a nearby trash bin before stepping into his house and walking straight into the shower. The sting of the lukewarm water against his open wounds caused him to wince, yet in all the discomfort, he found himself curiously chuckling lightly. With a sense of resilience, he confided in me, "I knew the feeling would pass. When I'm upset, I remind myself that it's okay to feel sad. It's a sign that I'm alive, that I'm human. And what a marvelous thing it is to be human." His words were accompanied by a warm smile, showcasing a complete row of white teeth, with the fresh additions being but a year old, replacing the ones he'd lost that night. A Christmas gift attributable to his father's diligent labor.

The day following his assault, reluctant to burden his family or school authorities with his struggles, he attributed his physical injuries to the rigors of wrestling practice. He sought solace in the simple companionship of his younger sister, Scout, and the loyal presence of Sally, a cow on the family farm boasting a delightful quirk in its spotted coat. Amidst the traditional black and white patterning, Sally had a cluster of heart-shaped spots nestled above its gentle eyes. Finding sanctuary in the familiar beats of farm life, he took pride in his contributions to the household, cherishing the respite it offered from the trials and tribulations of high school.

He was ultimately cut from the basketball team due to his persistent lapses and severe lack of focus during practices. Despite his improvement in wrestling and him becoming increasingly confident in his capacity to takedown more than half the guys in school, he remained a passive bystander to the torment inflicted by other students upon those who were physically vulnerable or easily targeted for superficial reasons. A regret that he now ponders, questioning its very existence. Had he intervened, he might not have ended up here. Time has yet to tell whether that regret is unfounded.

"It's admirable to see your positive outlook on life, though I must admit, I can't see myself possessing that same strength to navigate through such challenges. I find myself drawn to revenge as a means to cope," I said, my brow furrowed in earnestness and eyes locked on his with unwavering sincerity.

"In truth, I've never met a genuinely good person. They're always half good," Culbert said, seemingly resigned to that reality.

"People are not purely good. The brain's too complex to be black and white," I responded with a half-smile, rubbing the back of my neck. Our legs swung over the edge of the stage like pendulums in a clock tower as we thought of more than telling stories to occupy our time.

To uplift our spirits, we devoted the ensuing hours to the art of wrestling, with Culbert assuming the role of my mentor in this novel undertaking. I'd always been interested in trying out wrestling but hadn't due to my fear of injury, taking me away from my passion for surfing. As the theater silence enveloped us, I shed my inhibitions along with my attire, leaving only the essence of vulnerability and determination. I carefully set aside my black tunic and white sneakers, not wanting to get caught in the long fabric, opting instead for freedom of movement in my black cotton shorts. On the glossy theater stage, we unfurled a black stunt mat easily spotted among the many props. A canvas that would serve in all our athletic exploits.

Culbert shed his distinctive hot pink sequined jacket, white tee, and beige running shoes, leaving on but his sand-colored shorts and hot orange calf socks. I studied his physique with wandering eyes, a testament to dedication and discipline. With sinewy muscles rippling beneath taut skin, I grew envious of his visually evident athleticism. Each contour of his chiseled frame speaks of hours spent honing his craft as a wrestler, with defined shoulders broad enough to bear the weight of the world, chest and arms sculpted to perfection, and thick legs, strong and agile, providing a sturdy foundation upon which they stand, ready to face any opponent and lock them in firmly on the wrestling mat.

Together we embarked on a journey of discovery, with Culbert learning patience and I some fundamental high school wrestling techniques—hooks, ties, and single leg takedowns—each maneuver evoking a cascade of adrenaline and exertion. Beginning each match with a handshake—the gentlemen thing to do. Intermittent breaks offered still moments of reflection amidst the hallowed theater, where I pondered the complexities of my existence in this new world while Culbert embraced the physicality of his surroundings, weaving through rows of empty seats with purposeful strides, using the theater seats to conduct elevated pushups, and performing box jumps onto varying platforms on the stage.

As our sessions neared their conclusion, a fleeting collision with my elbow and Culbert's chin left him unscathed but brought us into a precarious entanglement on the mat. We tumbled over each other once before I found myself immobilized beneath him. With his hands clasped firmly around my wrists, held over my head, our eyes locked in a silent exchange within the seclusion of the theater. A strong tension hung in the air, punctuated only by the rhythmic cadence of our hard breathing. Culbert's large chest rose and fell measuredly with each breath. With the faint sheen of sweat glistening upon it emphasizing the definition of the deep line in between his chest.

Breaking the stillness, I ventured a hesitant inquiry, uncertain of his intentions. "What're you doing?" Culbert's gaze briefly flickered to my lips before releasing my wrists, a gesture laden with unspoken emotion. As he wiped away the sweat from his brow, he nestled softly upon me, like a whispered sigh upon the breeze, resting his head against my chest. It was a silent acknowledgement of our shared vulnerability. In this intimate moment, shared only by those who've endured the prison game, like chosen pilgrims thrust blindly into the flames, yet emerging unscathed, we are united as one.

Without saying a word, I could feel his apprehension about his own ability to continue living lost in this convoluted game with another three rounds remaining. Gently stroking his head against my chest, I sought to project a sense of fortitude and assurance for what lay ahead. In a state of susceptibility, I invoked the only source of emotion and strength that had been unwavering throughout my youth, hoping to offer Culbert some semblance of comfort. "Jesus is the king of kings and the lord of lords, and at his name, every knee shall bow," I whispered with inner conviction, though outwardly my words betrayed a hint of unease and hesitation.

"You still trust in its words?" Culbert inquired, his expression a mix of astonishment and curiosity, evident in the raise of his eyebrows and the slight parting of his lips as he looked up at me, his eyes aglow with wonder.

"I have faith they're true," I spoke with conviction, reassuring myself firmly this time.

"You know, I've long identified as a Christian, yet my engagement with the Bible has been superficial, never bothering to read it, limited to hearing its teachings delivered passionately from the pulpit, and regurgitating memorized verses I thought sounded profound," he reflected, his mind consumed in contemplation with eyes no longer staring back up at me. "Reflecting on the tumultuous events of the past year and however many weeks, I guess all the fantastical things we've experienced cede credibility to outrageous concepts."

Culbert enveloped me in a tight embrace around my waist before effortlessly pulling me up with a single hand and speaking with newfound determination, "May the holy cross be our guiding light. May the dragon never be our overlord." Had I just acted as a vessel for divine intervention, breathing new life into a believer's faith?

As I came to my feet, experiencing a sense of fulfillment with a subtle smile of satisfaction, I observed Tommy's olive green greatcoat and white powdered wig adorning one of the mannequins behind Culbert. As I approached it, memories flooded back to the day Aleko and Floki brought it here. It struck me that it must've been placed on the mannequin during our last patrol, as it hadn't been there before. Culbert acknowledged the observation but failed to see its relevance.

I admitted its positioning wasn't necessarily the thing that sparked my interest. It did, however, make me take note of its presence now. "Baba once told me Tommy forgot something back in his cell and he was bound to return sooner or later for it. Tommy later confirmed he returned to Neptune to rescue me, mistaking me for his father, and to retrieve this Sir Isaac Newton wig. But why? What's so special about a wig of all things?"

"Ask the divas of pop," Culbert responded in jest. I firmly grasped the wig off the mannequin's head and delved into its white strands, reminiscent of the sturdy, gelled hairpieces worn by judges and barristers in England. Curled at the crown, with horizontal curls on the sides and back. Just as I suspected, I encountered an obstruction within. With a forceful tug, I extracted an object. One Arnold had described once before but whose peculiar presence now struck me in real time. It was a transparent, jelly-like material molded into the shape of a human heart. Suspended within it, a miniature weathered wood barrel adorned with brass rings and a refined metallic compass rose shimmering with a turquoise hue for a lid.

"He wasn't lying when he said only a jaguar from Mercury could've taken it because only they knew of its whereabouts.

Tommy wasn't fearful of a thief amongst his class. He himself is the thief whom he falsely diverted attention from, crying wolf," I murmured quietly to myself while pacing the stage.

As I held it, I sensed a subtle pull, as if it were magnetically guiding me towards a destination. I explained to Culbert this was one of the classes' organs and his curiosity piqued. He asked its purpose, and I revealed what Arnold had told me. That it was designed to lead its possessor to their deepest desires. I encouraged him to try it, and though hesitant at first, he relented.

As he accepted it, he impulsively took a step forward, extending his hands out with the heart between them toward me. After a moment, inquisitively examining the compass rose, he took another step and handed it back to me, advising me I handle it with care. And, if I were to hold it upright, the north cardinal point would spin in one direction, lighting up a deep blue.

He was right. I wondered, what it is that I desire most in this moment that this organ from Mercury is leading me to? Despina, they'd called it. That question was less relevant now. We've devoted ourselves to patrolling these castle grounds and now, it is not only my desires that hold sway. I have this freshly discovered camaraderie and responsibility to Culbert and the other lost boys who are here just like me. Not knowing if tomorrow will come.

We make our way to the weapon stockpile and come to a mutual agreement. We can't remain passive targets, waiting for the others to show. For all we know, they could be somewhere out there in trouble. Dressed once more, with a short blade in hand and Culbert's light throwing axe in his, we knew it was time to move out.

These past few weeks patrolling yielded no significant breakthroughs or resolutions. Conversely, they offered fragments of a larger puzzle, leaving numerous gaps to be filled. In any event, through it all, I accomplished a little bit of something—I forged a friendship.